INDIGO NIGHTS

A TRIED & TRUE NOVEL
BOOK THREE

CHARLI RAHE

TRIED AND TRUE PUBLISHING

Copyright © 2014 by Charli Rahe

All rights reserved.

No part of this book may be reproduced in any form or by any electronic or mechanical means, including information storage and retrieval systems, without written permission from the author, except for the use of brief quotations in a book review.

Second ebook edition July 2023

Second paperback edition July 2023

Second hardcover edition July 2023

Cover Art by Miblart
Chapter Art by Etheric Designs
Editing by Dana Mohn

ISBN (ebook) 978-1-958055-15-1

ISBN (paperback) 978-1-958055-14-4

ISBN (hardcover) 978-1-958055-16-8

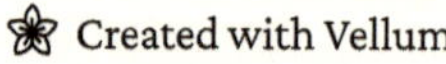 Created with Vellum

For my sisters, who model characters and work signings with me.
For my fellow indie authors, who collaborate and inspire myself and others.
Finally, for my children and my husband — I love you.

Note from the Author

Scarlett's fantastical story follows a woman's journey through her magical heritage in which she encounters several dark scenarios. It is not intended for readers under 18 years of age and includes adult content.

While I'd prefer you to experience it as you go, your mental health matters. Please refer to www.charlirahe.com for a detailed list of possible triggers.

PROLOGUE

Pearl's face was ashen as she carried the bundle from the birthing room. Lark rushed past her without a second look at the white terry cloth towel. Wren could hear Sparrow's sobs coming from the room Sea had gone into when her water broke at dinner.

Everyone had come out for a rare, greater family dinner. They sat huddled together on the couches that lined the outer room, waiting for news. Hawk took one look at Pearl's face and ran after Lark. Wren twisted her skirts in her hands until her mother cleared her throat, drawing attention to her.

"Sea and her son did not survive the birthing," she announced, and Ridge leapt to his feet to check on Sparrow, who was undoubtedly crying on Hawk's shoulder.

The Dagrs had passed on just after Yuletide leaving Sparrow with a wedding to plan in only a few months and now her sister had perished. Wren swiped the tears at the loss of her friend and her child.

Pearl stepped to where she sat alone since the men had gone into the birthing room and nodded with her coppery curls to the exit. Wren floated in a daze of numbness that allowed only the barest recognition of her sniffling.

"Take him. Go to the Tio palace until I retrieve you. Show no one, tell no one. Put your cloak on before you go."

Wren's arms were full of the white wrapped bundle and drifted from the room without a second thought. A staffer brought her cloak as she entered the portal room. She allowed them to clasp it around her throat before she walked into the blinding white light.

The Tio palace was silent. Sea's labor had gone quickly, but it had been well after nightfall when the boy was birthed. Wren continued her slow, seemingly aimless walk to the bedroom she stayed in when visiting her uncle's family.

She pressed her palm to the energy plate, so a dim light allowed her to maneuver around the room. She did not know what to do with the tiny corpse of a newborn baby. Wren crossed to the chaise in the small sitting room to set him down and looked into the bundle for the first time.

Narrow blue eyes of a newborn peered back at her, and Wren frowned. She'd never seen a dead body, much less one of a baby, but he appeared to be watching her.

She took her finger and ran the back of it over a warm cheek and he opened his mouth like a baby bird trying to root. Wren's eyes widened. The boy was alive.

Her mother's milk had long since gone dry after Steel's birth. She had no way to feed him.

"You poor little soul. Such a hard life already and I fear it will only grow harder. Your mother was a terrific woman," Wren's tears welled in her eyes as she scooped the boy up and held him to her bosom, "I cannot feed you, but I can offer you comfort and warmth until my mother retrieves us."

Wren understood now why her mother had brought the boy directly to her, but not why she felt the need to hide the boy's birth. She laid down beside the baby on the four-poster bed after removing her dress.

"I read that skin to skin is very important. I do not think Sea would mind." Wren gave the babe a weak smile and placed him gently on her chest. "You look just like your father; you could be him in miniature. It is uncanny. You are in luck. That likely means you will be extremely good looking. I hope you also inherit his loyalty and cleverness."

She took a deep breath that shuddered out when another cry threatened, "You smell wonderful. Just like Steel did."

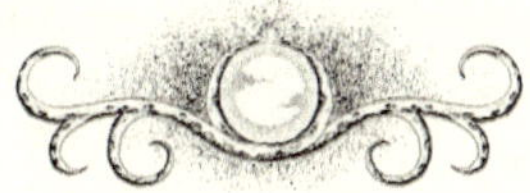

"... I hope for your sake you did not inherit her gift."

Lark's deep voice pulled Wren from her slumber. She opened her swollen eyes from all her crying and found Lark's head resting on her shoulder, looking down at his son. He raised his red-rimmed eyes to her, and Wren's nose burned again.

"I am so sorry, Lark. Take him," she offered.

"Thank you, Wren. His first few minutes of life were hellish, but thanks to you, the rest has been peaceful. He is asleep. I do not wish to wake him. You would have made an exemplary mother," he said, his voice cracking.

"What happened?" she asked, changing the subject, and blinking at tears.

"Your mother says there were so many women in the birthing room, she could not be sure. Sea's birthing was difficult, but typical. She gave a prophecy just before the pushing began. Then... she grew very sick. Your mother believes they drugged her, meaning to kill her and our son. He is strong. I can tell already. Not so easily dispatched," Lark told her and ran his hand over his son's black, silky hair.

"Why would they kill her over a prophecy?" Wren asked in a whisper, as if the walls had ears.

"I am not sure. Pearl has not told me yet. They took Sea's body and Pearl told me you took him here. I did not understand it at first," Lark smiled sadly at his son, "But I do now. She told them all he did not survive to protect him."

"I will help you, Lark. I know you want justice for Sea but ease your mind. He will not grow up without a mother. He will have two very attentive aunts in me and Sparrow."

"Sparrow is marrying Vetr this summer. I do not want her knowing about my boy yet. She is... not well. I will take you up on your offer of help. Other than his own mother, I could not imagine another loving him with the warmth that you embody." He swallowed. "A widower at nineteen. They will have their eligible daughters waiting outside my bedroom before we can give her ashes to the Mother."

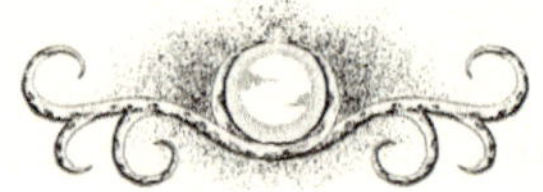

"You are avoiding me."

Wren jumped with a squeak when Alder's guttural voice came from the darkness of her bedroom. She hit the energy plate and found him lounging on her chaise.

"How did you get into my bedroom? What are you doing here? How did you even know which one was my bedroom?" she took a deep breath, collecting herself. "Never mind. You must leave. I temporarily lost my mind over Yuletide, but the fact remains, they betrothed you to a powerful family's daughter. It would be my reputation's suicide if I were to keep seeing you," Wren said, walking into her closet.

"I am sorry about Sea and her son. How is Lark? That is who you were with, yes?" Alder asked.

Wren scoffed. "If you only knew how ludicrous your jealousy was. Lark is not doing well. He was — *is* — madly in love with Sea. Has been since the moment they set eyes on one another. Sparrow is even worse, from what I hear."

"I understand how much that would hurt to be apart from the woman you have given your heart to," Alder's voice came from directly behind her.

Wren finished dressing and turned around to face him. "Why are you making this so much harder? Do have any idea what their family would do to mine if they knew? I cannot risk it. Especially since Hawk has yet to find a single girl he likes half as much as Sparrow. That Cordillera Blomi is always lingering, but Hawk only likes her aesthetic resemblance to Sparrow. My life is a disaster. Any disgrace I suffer could affect Hawk's chance at finding a suitable wife."

"I will get out of my betrothal. Then you will marry me?" Alder asked, coming closer.

Wren knew the impossibility of that happening. "Why not?" she asked with a shrug but felt the thrill of the mere thought of waking up next to Alder everyday shot from her heart to her toes and to her mind, which it must have then fried.

Alder picked her up effortlessly and Wren tried to summon up a defense against his rare flash of pearly whites. It was futile.

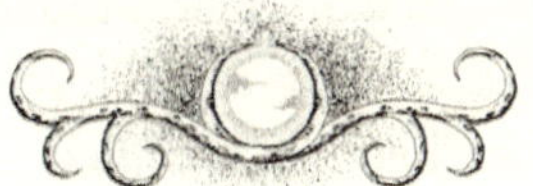

Between helping care for Lark's son, helping Sparrow plan the rest of her wedding, and being sympathetic to Hawk, Wren's spring was over before it began and it was Midsummer.

Being in the Vetr castle, having to be in the wedding party with Delta and Alder both, Wren was hating herself more and more. As a second son, Lark was not required to come, so she had come alone. It had been a monumentally poor decision, but she couldn't make Hawk watch Sparrow marry.

"Little Bird," Alder called, beckoning her down the hall.

Wren steeled herself and went after him, checking first so no one had seen them. Alder was sloppy, but his reputation wasn't at stake if others found out.

Wren shut the door behind her and held her hand out, stopping him from kissing her. They were in a china closet, so someone would likely not disturb them for some time.

"No more of this. No more clandestine meetings, no more showing up in my bed on the weekends," Wren said firmly. "You are still betrothed. It has been months. Almost four months, to be exact."

"Delta's pregnant," Alder said and Wren clasped her hand to her chest to stop the pain that threatened to explode her fragile heart.

His eyes widened. "No! Not mine, Wren. It is complicated. I have never been with Delta. She is as warm as the ice capped Frostfell Mountains outside this castle. They plan to send her away to have the child before it is noticeable. Then we can broach the subject of our annulment."

Wren squeezed her eyes shut. "I am pregnant. Almost four months."

Alder ran his hand over his chiseled jaw and pointed a finger back at his chest.

Wren nodded. "I have only ever been with you, Alder," she whispered.

When he took his hand from his mouth, he was smiling. Wren ducked her head and fought against the most idiotic grin of her own.

"Do not smile. It is a bastard. Alder, I must tell you something else. It is about why I stopped coming to the pond," she began and Alder lifted her into the air, so her feet dangled as he wrapped his arms around her.

"I do not care. Wren, I am never happier than when I am with you," he said roughly, and she felt his calling flood into her. "A son. Gods be good, let them see how much I love this woman and free me of my contract to Delta," he murmured to himself.

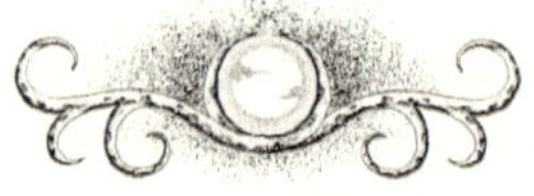

Wren's stomach roiled as she sat in her bedroom, waiting for Alder to return. Alder good, messenger bad. Sparrow squeezed her hand tight, and Hawk paced the room.

"Not smart, Wren. Not smart at all," Hawk said, shaking his head.

Silver had threaded its way into his inky hair as it had their father's. Sparrow narrowed her eyes at him.

"I doubt it was planned. These things happen," she said guiltily, and Wren looked at her.

"You are pregnant?" Wren asked.

Sparrow dropped her head and nodded. "We found out the day before yesterday. We have only told his parents. They are hoping for a boy, but I have this inkling that it is a girl." She looked at Hawk from the corner of her eye, and he was swallowing convulsively. "I am sorry," she whispered.

"Why apologize? Married women sleep with their husbands. It is the way of things. Excuse me," Hawk said stiffly before he left the room.

Sparrow burst into tears and Wren stroked her hair, handing her a kerchief she'd kept on her just in case.

Both girls jumped when the door crashed open and Alder stormed into the room. He picked Wren up off the chaise and clutched her so tightly she couldn't draw breath.

"I love you, Little Bird. They cannot force me to love that woman. Marry me anyway. Marry me now — this instant. Come, before they send their guards to take me back."

Alder was pulling her from the bedroom before she could utter a word. Hawk waited, dumbfounded, in the hall.

"Where are you taking her?" Hawk ground out.

"To marry. As I told my uncle, kill me to stop me," Alder rumbled.

Pearl and Flint stood on the opposite end of the hall. "Wren, we received a messenger!" her father shouted.

"We will be back," Hawk shouted back.

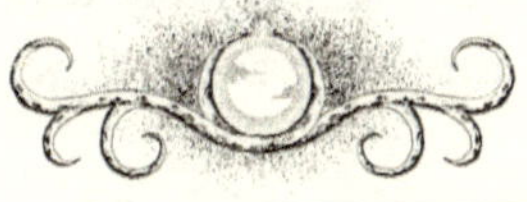

The judge looked skeptically at their old-world clothing. They hadn't picked up more clothing to change. They had gotten their marriage certificate the day before and found that they had to wait a full day before they would legally wed them.

Hawk thought they were crazy, but after Alder pawned all the gold he had on his person to get American currency, he'd bought her a ring. Hawk grudgingly pawned his own gold belt buckle with the blazing sun of the Sumar emblazoned on it so Wren could buy a brushed platinum ring.

"... I now pronounce you man and wife," the judge proclaimed, and Alder kissed Wren deeply.

They stayed to sign the license with Hawk as witness and left the courthouse to go back to the hotel. None of them had spent so much time outside of Tidings before, so Hawk went for a stroll instead of sharing the room with the newlyweds.

"Too short by far," Wren said, squeezing Alder's hand as they reached the portal door.

"I grew desperate. Little Bird, I am sorry. I am afraid for your life. Without you, mine is hardly a life, but if they hurt you or our son... I do not have a friend like you are to Lark to help me. I would rather be with you in the heavens."

"Do not say such things, love. I am your legal wife and I carry your heir. It is more than enough for me. I love you, Alder," she said thickly.

Alder withdrew from her and smiled. It wasn't often she said those words.

"And I you, Wren," he whispered, and kissed her one last time before going through the portal.

His silhouette hung in her eyes as Hawk pressed his hand to her back. "If the Vars find out about your child, they might really aim to harm you."

Steel. Wren had forgotten to tell Alder about Steel. Could she uproot the little boy's life? Tell him his father is not really his father, but his grandfather? His sister he affectionately called "Wen", was truly his mother? To tell him his brother was legitimate, but he had been born out of wedlock?

No. He had a full life as a second son. One day, when he was older, she would confess everything to him.

"I know," Wren said softly.

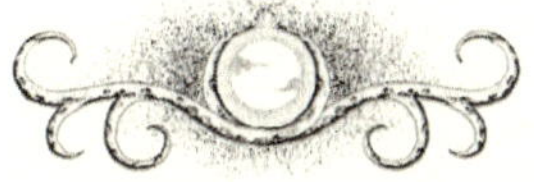

"Everyone will think the son I carry is yours," Wren hissed when Lark showed to take her to the induction ceremony.

"Good. Then they will stop sending their daughters to my castle," Lark said, zipping the back of the only dress that fit her as pregnant as she was.

Wren looked down at herself and groaned. "I cannot see my feet. This might be the biggest baby ever born."

"As big as my son," Lark said with a twinkle in his grey eyes.

Wren sighed and looked back at the wild-haired boy sleeping in her bed. "He is so quiet, never cries, hardly smiles. He is so smart — it makes me feel as though I am dim-witted."

Lark caught her chin and brought it back to him, "Thank you."

"Stop that. I know Sea would have done it for me if the situations were reversed. You do not have to thank me." Wren was practically wringing her hands. "You are sure you want to take me?"

Wren had to leave the university. She'd been in seclusion at the Tio palace all fall and half of winter. She was due any day and was dreading her next step, mostly because Alder's wedding to Delta was at the end of the month. Her only consolation was that Delta wouldn't be there that night.

"I will not even ask why you know how to do women's hair," Wren said wryly as Lark attempted to give her dark waves curls.

"Sea was a grumpy pregnant woman. I often helped her get ready."

Wren caught his hand and gave it a sympathetic squeeze. "Thank you, Lark. Without Sparrow and Hawk with... whoever it is this week, you are my only friend. I do not know what I would do without you."

Lark smiled with his full lips, "You have Robin too."

Wren laughed. "Coyote and Brass keep her busy. I hardly see her."

"Not so busy that she did not have time for Regn to knock her up again," Lark said wryly.

"You must be joking! He is incorrigible. I am so glad Hawk ended things with Cordillera, if we could say it was a thing. Those Regn are trouble, if their father is any indication."

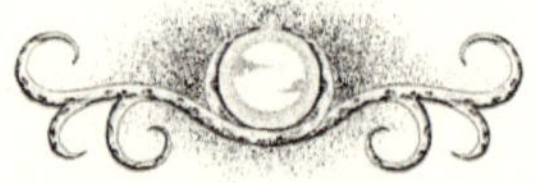

"I do not care. Let them be angry. I refuse to stand by and let another man care for my wife while my son and heir is being born." Alder growled as he carried Wren back to the birthing suite at the Sumar palace.

Lark's face etched with worry. It was only nine and a half months since he lost Sea while she birthed. Wren wriggled her fingers for his hand as he walked beside them. Lark was the only other man in Tidings other than the other Vars as big as Alder. He slid his hand into hers and she squeezed.

"I will be fine. I will not let the Vars get rid of me so easily," she joked, and Alder grunted.

"You will be around for decades to come, if only to rub it in Canis's face that his nephew won the heart of a Tio woman while he failed," Alder smiled.

Everyone knew Pearl had shot down Canis flat when he tried to court her. Orion and Flint had been her top contenders, though Flint won her early on.

"By the Mother!" Wren groaned and Alder picked up the pace.

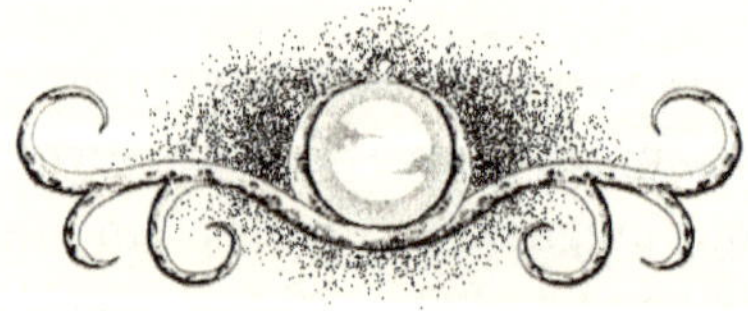

"They all but threatened your life. I must go. I do not know when I can return."

Alder whispered to Lark and Hawk as he crushed the messenger's scroll in his fist. Pearl had left them after the boy was born so they could have some privacy. She had brought Steel in, who was laying in the bed beside Wren and the newborn boy.

"Mother says he is my nephew, but I want him to be my brother," Steel yammered.

"He is your brother, Steel. You can call him such," Wren said, swallowing against the lump in her throat.

Steel beamed, "Can I give him his name until his Ausa Vatni?"

"Of course, little man," Alder said, ruffling his head of dark blonde hair.

Wren's heart skipped a beat. "Alder, I have to tell you something."

Alder bent down and kissed her forehead. "I must go. Tell me next time. I cannot visit for a short while."

After the wedding. Delta would have the child soon, and they will expect him to fill her womb. Wren blinked at tears and nodded.

"Next time then," she agreed.

Alder brushed the cheek of his newborn son and gave Steel's ear a playful tug before he left the room. He held the doorframe and in front of Hawk and Lark; he paused.

"I love you, Wren. As hard as it is, that will never change."

She nodded, unable to find her voice, and he disappeared into the hall.

"Do not cry, Wen," Steel said, resting his head on her shoulder as she struggled with her tears.

"My dutiful little, Steel. There is nothing in life you will ever fail at, bar stopping my tears," she said, kissing his little cheek.

CHAPTER I

THIS TOO SHALL PASS

Numbly, I'd walked to my room after waking in my mother's empty bedroom. We removed all of her earthly possessions aside from paperwork on the Aves. I carried it all back to my room and was happy not to run into anyone in the halls.

I set it down on the octagonal side table in my sitting room before going into the bathroom and turning on the shower as I peeled off my sea foam gown from the night before. I pulled on a fluffy terry-cloth robe I used on my worst days and walked to Indigo's room.

From the angle of where the door was, I could see into the bedroom where the carved headboard rested against the wall. It took me a moment to realize what I was seeing before I closed the door with the utmost care. Indigo, with her sky-blue satin sheet pooled around her hips as she nakedly straddled an equally naked Quick, whose hands he filled with my sister's breasts. I blushed. The look on his face as he looked up at her... if I was in a better mood, I would have had to fan myself.

Apparently, their wild night had extended into the morning, *er*, afternoon. Good for her. If there was any justice in the world, she would have her cake and eat it, too. If Indigo didn't get attached to Quick, then she would have fun with the rakish Regn brother.

Ash had come to our mother's room, surprising Jett and I both, and I'd lost it in front of him. Crying about a man to my betrothed was a new low for me.

"Ash, you shouldn't be comforting me. I have to tell you something," I said between sobs, weakly trying to pull myself away from him.

Ash held me resolutely. "Listen to me for a moment, my love. Do you still want children? Can you stand beside me while I strive for greatness? Whatever it is, I will marry you, Scarlett. Unless you are certain you do not want to marry me. If you promise to stand by me in the future, I will stand by you now."

I wiped at my face with a kerchief. The man was charismatic, I'd give him that.

"It's bad, Ash. Very bad. Unforgivable bad. You won't want to marry me."

Ash had gotten to his feet then, and I'd fully expected him to leave. "You let the orphan boy bed you," he said coolly, and I swallowed hard.

"Yes," I squeaked out, and he hung his head.

I started crying again, sucking in loud drags of air.

"Worse?" he asked stiffly.

"Yes," I squeaked.

"You carry his child?" Ash asked, and I nodded.

"Yes," I whispered, crying near hysterics.

"Now you know for certain you are fertile. Once you start to show, you will go stay with the Valkyries in Valla until the baby is born. If it is a girl, we can raise her together. If it is a boy... I am afraid I could not allow it to remain with us. Your grandmother would be amenable to raising it, or you could give it to the Valkyries and let someone else adopt it if his father did not want him," Ash said without inflection and turned around. His face was hard. "You are not the first woman to commit indiscretions, Scarlett. Though I am very disappointed in you."

I hung my head and blew my nose. What was he saying? Ash sat down next to me but didn't touch me.

"Get dressed, Scarlett. You have an engagement party to attend."

I raised my head to him. "Why?" I asked, referring to a variety of thoughts.

"Because I want you and I shall have you. Even our adopted daughter will be a Tio, our biological sons will be Straumrs. That has not changed. You have much strength in you Scarlett, I want that strength beside me. Yes?" Ash's celadon eyes locked on mine, daring me to reject his more than generous offer.

"Yes," I said weakly, and he got to his feet and kissed the top of my head.

"I have a dress I chose for you to wear tonight. I will have it sent here with the beauticians," Ash left, closing the door behind him.

I wanted my mother.

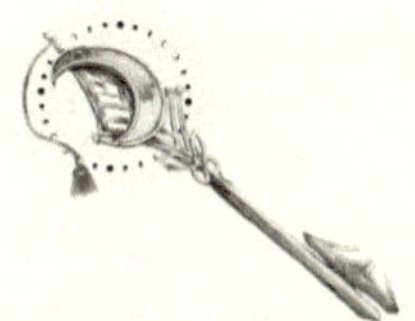

By the time I was out of the shower, I heard giggling and deep male laughter coming from Indigo's room and barely made it out of the bathroom before I heard Indi's door open and the water turn back on. I crawled back into bed and stuffed my fingers into my ears.

Pearl woke me with lunch. I sat up sheepishly as I wiped at my face. I'd been crying in my sleep and my face felt puffy and swollen.

Her wide mouth, like my mother's, curled up in a matronly smile. "Darling. How are you feeling?"

"I've been better," I admitted. "Forget what I said last night. I spoke with Ash today and we sorted things out."

"Come eat, darling," she whispered as we walked over to the sitting room.

I tied my satin champagne robe around me and sat on the chaise to a delicious smelling chicken, avocado, and bacon salad. I had no appetite, but I forced myself to eat for my grandmother's sake.

"If all is well with Ash, why do you cry?" she asked as I ate.

"I gambled with my heart and lost," I said with an honesty not even I had expected.

"Love makes fools of us all,"

Last night, I'd attacked my lover and *his* lover, then strangled them… fool was not the word that came to mind. Murderer. Psychopath. Those were better words. To top it all off, I had Slate's emotions still in my head. A constant flow of anger, frustration, hurt, and misery to add to my own, but I'd be gods cursed if I kissed him ever again. I'd rather live with his added feelings than touch him. I'd learn to ignore him and that would have to work.

She bent down next to the table where I'd set my mother's paper-work and lifted an envelope off the floor. She knit her brows as she held it up. ALDER was scribbled across the front in my mother's handwriting.

"That's my mother's. I saw that in her things my first day at Valla University."

I reached for it, but Pearl's long-nailed fingers gripped it.

"I shall make sure Alder receives it. I know he would want to know what your mother had to say. You have enough to worry about, darling." Her coppery curls brushed her silk clad shoulders as she leaned to give my knee a reassuring squeeze.

When Pearl left, Tawny came in, and she must have heard something about what happened because she looked empathetic. I told her the dastardly truth; Slate because he showed me the wing where he said we would live if we married and I spent the night with him. He proposed, and I was going to break the marriage contract between Ash and me until I caught him with Mirage. To add insult to injury, Brass delved deep to see if he'd injured me while trying to prevent me from doing Mirage and Slate serious harm, only to discover one reckless night with Slate had left me with child. Jett told me it only took a few days for Guardians to detect it with their calling when I protested the impossibility. As soon as the egg latched, he'd said.

Her wide hazel eyes brimmed with tears.

"That fiddlesticker. I'm so sorry, Scar. To think, I tried to push you two together. My mom really likes him, and she doesn't like anyone," Tawny said as we laid in my bed under the blankets.

"I don't want to talk about it. It hurts too much," I choked out.

"With everything... I can't imagine making it through the day. There is nothing I want more than to hide away and become a hermit. I keep telling myself, get through this minute and then the next, but what for? I'll still have this pain, this loss. Tomorrow I will wake and do it all over again. Not only him, either. All of it."

I missed my mom.

They threw my internal lockbox open, all the tumultuous emotions spilling free, and they were suffocating. Every breath was a chore. Slate had stolen the key to the hastily stocked box, and I was in agony.

Tawny chewed her lip and looked at me. "You love him, don't you?" she asked softly, and I laughed in a gust of exhaled air.

"Rub salt in the wound, why don't you?"

She furrowed her brow and offered me another smile.

I dabbed my red nose with the kerchief, then met her eyes with the lump in my throat growing again. "Tawny, I've been falling in love with him since the moment I met him. I feel so stupid."

Sobs raked my body as Tawny embraced me.

CHAPTER 2
JETT

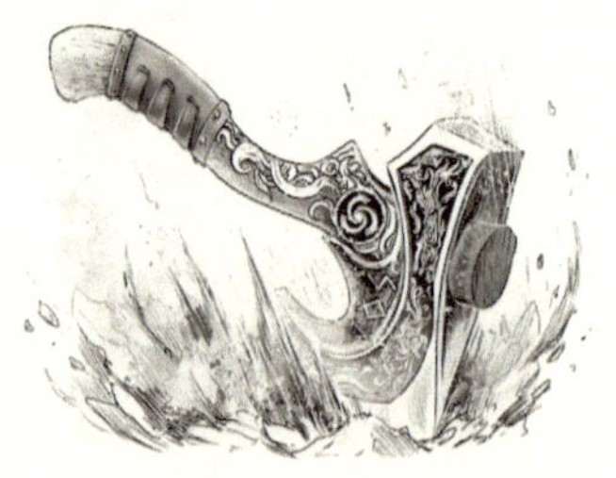

The doorknob turned as Jett stood in front of Slate's door and he barely had time to dodge it as it swung open to crash into the wall. Tawny stormed in, fire spitting from her eyes as they locked on Slate, and he lifted his head as she approached.

It didn't look good.

He got to his feet when Tawny cocked her little fist back and punched Slate in the face. Jett leapt to her and dragged her away from Slate when she pummeled his chest. Jett tried very hard not to think about how the feisty little woman smelled like Yuletide sugar cookies.

Slate shifted his jaw but was otherwise stony-faced as his grey eyes followed Tawny.

"Easy, Tawny," Jett told the petite pistol that was struggling against him.

"You're a bastard!" Tawny said with furious tears in her eyes.

"I know," Slate rumbled, "Let her go, Jett. If she wants to hit me, let her. It changes nothing."

He sat back down, and Tawny stopped struggling, but her impressive chest was still heaving as her formidable dagger stare pinned Slate.

Tawny took a step forward, pointing her finger at Slate. "You have no idea what you've done. She was in love with you, you stupid cache hole!"

Jett didn't think Slate could look more rigid, but he was wrong. Slate's face went as hard as the marble tiles that lined the floors.

"I knew it! She told Ash. She told him everything." Tawny shouted at him.

Jett spun her around. "Whoa. What?"

Tawny stepped back so both men could see her. "Yeah. She said she'd slept with Slate and that she..." she clamped her mouth shut.

Jett waved his hand dismissively. "I know she's pregnant. What did Ash say?"

Pregnant. By the Mother, what a mess. He'd broken the news to Slate, and he'd been in a stupor since.

Tawny put her little fists on her hips. "He said he didn't care. He wants her anyway. A girl would be raised as his own, but a son would have to be sent here or Scarlett could give him up to the Valkyries, which she would never do. He said that once she shows, she'll have leave the University until the baby is born," Tawny turned back to Slate, "You've ruined her life. You know that, don't you? She'll never let herself love anyone again. I hope it was worth it."

Tawny slammed the door as she left, and Jett stumbled disbelievingly to the nearest chair and plopped down. Scarlett was going to marry Ash. Tawny confirmed it.

Slate rose to his feet and turned around to the face the tufted black leather couch. Jett saw his muscles bunch and hopped to his feet as Slate overturned the couch punch it into splinters before turning on the coffee table.

Jett hadn't seen this side of Slate in years and knew it was time to leave or become part of the mayhem. He'd have to warn Gypsum not to interrupt.

Jett backed out of the room as Slate destroyed it and locked it with his calling so no one would accidentally walk into the destruction, thinking there was a fight.

Gypsum's door was the next one down and he opened it as he walked into the room. It was similarly decorated as Slate's, but in brown leather.

"Gyps? You in here, Chief?" Jett called out as he strode into the room.

He leaned into the arched entranceway to the bedroom, and he started.

"Hi, Jett." Ama giggled as she lifted her head from her bent over position.

Gypsum cursed as he grabbed the blankets from beside them and tossed them over the back of Ama. Shale's head lifted from where she laid beneath Ama and smirked. Jett had done that very position enough times to know what was at work.

Jett turned around and cleared his throat. "I wanted to warn you not to disturb, Slate."

"Oh yeah, I hadn't heard. Cool, thanks," Gypsum said breathlessly and Shale snickered.

Jett started to leave. "Right, okay. See you at the party later."

"Wait, what? I thought she was marrying Slate?" Gypsum said between panting breaths.

"Who?" Ama asked.

"Long story. Ash is back on, Slate is off," Jett said.

"Scarlett," Shale said, sounding exasperated.

"Oh, my!" Ama said, "It explains so much. What about Brass?"

"Right. I'll leave you to it then. Ladies. Chief." Jett got out of there fast.

CHAPTER

THREE

The Straumr palace looked remodeled during the height of gothic style and Dahlia had liked it so much, she hadn't bothered updating it. Not that any of the other palaces had been updated. Aside from the indoor plumbing, the Sumar palace probably hadn't been restored since the Byzantine empire. Dahlia and Diamond guided me to my new rooms.

Diamond hooked her arm through mine as we walked the maze of halls. I knew where we were going through. I may have had my own room, but I shared a bathroom with Ash.

Diamond walked into the room and spread her caramel arms as she spun. "Tell me you love it," she said with sparkling celadon eyes.

The walls were as light as Ash's gorgeous green eyes. My furnishings were all done in matte whites and creams with matching floral bedding. An intricately carved bed crown with panels of cream fabric flowed from over the plush bed. I had a cream upholstered bench at the end of the bed and a sitting area with cream and green upholstered couches complete with pillows that matched my bedspread. A white writing desk was against the wall shared with the bathroom, and a white dresser with an enormous mirror that matched with my bed crown was next to double doors that led to a balcony.

I threw back the balcony doors and saw delicate white furniture on a semicircle balcony that was temporarily enclosed for winter. The cushions matched my bedspread as well, and the white table that was the centerpiece for the little room went with the rest of the furnishings perfectly. I'd want for nothing; I even got my seasons back. Valla would give me my taste of fall, with snow in the winters, flowers in the spring and tropical sun in the summer.

I went back into the room and closed the French doors behind me. The room was lit by a single white chandelier that hung above the sitting area.

"It's better than I could have hoped," I admitted, and Diamond beamed at me.

"I feel like we are already sisters."

I missed my mother.

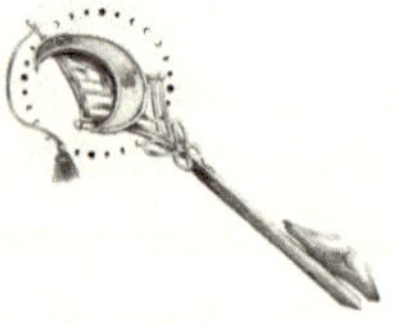

The Straumr informal dining room housed a long mahogany table with golden candelabras that lit the wood paneled room along with a multitiered gold chandelier. The marble fireplace was lit when I came into the room with Diamond, our heeled feet muffled by the maroon gothic carpet.

The men at the table rose as we entered, and I realized how different this was going to be.

Moon Straumr, Prime and Overseer of Valla University, sat at the head of the table, with River on his right and Crag on his left. Basil sat at the foot of the table with Dahlia on his right and Ash on his left. River's wife and teenage children sat beside him, and Fox sat next to Crag, who stood as I passed him to give me a kiss on the cheek. I sat next to Ash with Diamond to my right. Several empty seats separated Diamond from Fox, as did Dahlia from the youngest of River's brood.

Ash gave me a chaste kiss before pulling out my seat. It was the first time he'd kissed me since the Ragnarök. Everything inside me twisted as I put on a brave face at dinner.

"Good evening, Scarlett." Moon greeted me and sat down once Diamond and I were seated.

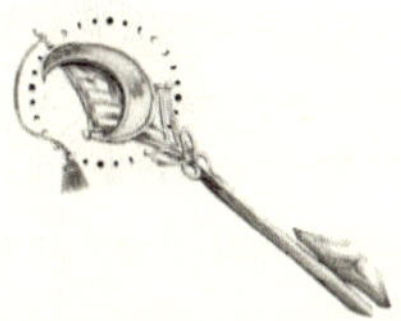

Ash gracefully led me around the dance floor as the guests clapped. I smiled my brightest smile; Ash had never been more charming. My purple gem colored dress swung behind me; it was a beautiful color. Ash had chosen well. The day had been a crash course in what life would be like once we married.

Ash was a micromanager and had overseen Dahlia. The purple and silver decor had been vibrant and rich, making the entire ballroom smell like the purple blooms that poured over the towering vases.

I faced the baroque style ceiling as Ash dipped me, and the crowd clapped. We straightened and kissed to more applause. Ash led me by the waist through the room with a smile plastered on my face so tightly it hurt.

I'd avoided Tawny and Jett since they arrived. They knew the whole truth and I couldn't look them in the eye. Not yet. Indigo had shown up with Quick, which had been the highest point of my evening.

Once Ash and I exited the dance floor, the other couples flooded it as the band started again. There were well over a hundred people in the Straumr ballroom. All the greater families were there with their spouses. Crimson had even shown up, which I didn't mind in the slightest. I'd even made a point of greeting her and her mother, Magnolia. She shied away, but she'd come around. I had no right to throw stones. I was welcoming them all back into the fold. All except Jonquil, that tramp was unworthy of even my scandalous fold.

I knit my brow when I saw Gypsum looking more like Jett than himself with an arm around Ama and Shale on her other side. I hadn't seen the pair last night and I thought I knew then where they had been.

There was a great deal of mingling and small talk with people I barely knew, and the only thing I wanted to do was curl up in my new bed.

I patted Ash's arm, and he watched me as I walked over to where Pearl, Alder, Hawk, and Sparrow mingled with Reed Tio and Fern Rot. I played with the neckline of my dress. It cut across my arms, so I had to wear a corset which tightly forced my breasts up to my throat, or that's what it felt like. It looked amazing, but for comfort it was a three out of ten.

Alder saw me coming and angled towards me, lifting his arm up so I would stand next to him. I draped my arm around my father's waist and faced the others.

"You look beautiful, Scarlett." Sparrow told me as she pushed her long, dark tresses over her shoulder.

"Thank you. Are you all having a good time?" I asked.

"We are. How about you, Scarlett?" Hawk asked. His dark, intelligent eyes probed, and I offered a smile.

"Good," I said without preamble. "The Straumrs have a separate room from Ash's made up for me. I'm going to have my things brought over once we return from our getaway."

Hawk knit his straight brows as he looked at me. "Can I ask why the sudden rush?"

"It's not really a rush. Ash had been courting me for a year, and we've been engaged for two months. I don't see the point in waiting to move when it is inevitable." I could feel my father's eyes on the top of my head.

"I don't see the point in moving now when you have a year left of Valla U and you spend so much time there as it is." Sparrow noted.

"Exactly. You guys won't even know I'm gone," I added and watched Quick pull Indigo out onto the dance floor.

"Did you set them up?" Alder bent down to ask me.

I had a reason to smile. It was the happiest I'd seen Indigo in a while. "Yes. It's not serious, but Indigo needs to get out more," I said, plucking a goblet of water from a server passing by.

Alder grunted. "She looks happy."

I smiled as I watched them. Quick was literally sweeping Indigo off her feet. Jett and Amethyst were dancing, as were Steel and Tawny and Sterling and Diamond. I should have been out there too, but I wasn't in a dancing mood. I looked around for Ash to make sure he wasn't searching for me and made eye contact with him from where he stood next to Sage.

Sage had not spoken to our father since he moved out of the Var castle when my mother died. I couldn't blame him; our father had disinherited him and gave the keys to the castle to Jett. It must have irked Sage to no end that Jett was so blissfully happy. There Jett was dancing with one of his stunningly gorgeous wives, who might be pregnant with yet another heir, the heir to Ostara and the Var castle.

"Take a few days to think about it. Indigo is getting to know you and I am sure your father wishes to know you better as well, darling," Pearl trumped me with a guilt card.

"I'll think about it," I told them, sipping from my glass.

"Come. I want to dance with the daughter I shall lose sooner rather than later." Alder rumbled, and led me out onto the dance floor.

Alder admitted he had had dancing lessons as a young man while we glided across the gleaming dance floor. M giant father towered over me. It was a good feeling. Like — I was finally safe. All my secrets were out in the open, well, to almost everyone, and I had been feeling anything *but* safe.

Jackal's tall form approached us with a puckish grin. "May I dance with my niece on this momentous occasion?" he asked with a courtly bow to Alder, who smiled back at his brother.

"Be my guest. I have another daughter around," he quipped.

Alder being playful? I didn't think I'd ever seen that before. I watched him as he approached Quick and Indigo. Alder was an intimidating man, but Quick held his own nicely as he shook Alder's hand and offered Indigo a parting smile before exiting the dance floor. Jackal took my hand and led me around to the soft music.

"You look positively miserable," Jackal said. I thought I was hiding it well since no one else had commented. "Do not worry. I am well versed at pretending and know how to spot an amateur. What bothers such a young beauty? Is our strapping young Ash not rising to expectations?"

"He surpasses all expectations," I told him blankly. The surrounding faces were a blur as he moved.

"I bet he does. He would do nothing less," Jackal said as he looked down at me, "What is it then, Miss Scarlett? If not the Guardian Golden boy, then who?"

I sighed, "I'm exhausted, that's all. One year down, one year left. I don't feel like I've made much progress at all."

"On the contrary, you have inserted yourself nicely into our world. Here you are, after a single year, marrying the most eligible bachelor and well on your way to becoming a Guardian. I have it on good authority from Crag that your fighting skills are elite. Such a shame that your language skills are lackluster," he teased.

Jackal had put things into a different perspective and my mood boosted a bit, despite Slate's miserably angry knot of emotions in my head. I started when a hand came to my shoulder and Jackal stopped dancing.

"May I?" Brass asked, and Jackal held my hand out to him.

Brass looked dapper in a black and bronze embroidered waistcoat. His hair was getting longer, the bronze and ebony beads now fell behind his back. His deep amber pools regarded me as we danced, and I did my best to avert my eyes. He reminded me too much of Slate. Way too much.

"I did not think you would look so well," Brass admitted, and I scoffed.

"Bronze put enough makeup on me to make a cosplayer blush." I looked at him from the corner of my eyes and his lips were curled in a warm smile. "You don't know what that is. A costumer."

"Ah. Regardless, you look stunning, Scarlett," he paused, "I am sorry for tackling you —"

"Oh. Please, don't. I never want to discuss last night. I am sorry if I scared you. To be honest, I scared myself. I did not know I was capable of all that." I cleared my throat, trying to force the growing lump down. "Is everyone... in one piece?"

Not okay. I didn't care if they weren't okay, but alive would be good.

I didn't want to go to Karkinos. The prison on the back of a giant crab could stay far, far away from me.

"They are," he said as we danced, "Scarlett, she came to him as you." My heart twisted and I must have made a face because he sighed. "I thought you should know."

I nodded and swallowed. "He has an extraordinary nose. If he had been thinking, he would have known it wasn't me. She wouldn't have my scent; she wouldn't have felt like me. Maybe there would be similarities, I don't know, but there would have been obvious differences." A tear fell, and I ducked my head to wipe it away.

"I did not mean to upset you. You are right. I am not defending him, just giving you the facts."

He pulled me in close, and I sighed.

My mind had not turned off for an instant all day. The only reasonable conclusion I'd come to after seeing the surprise on Slate's face was that Mirage AKA Anthias had come to him as me. I didn't know how she knew that would work, but it did. It could have been that she thought I was his type, and he would buy it easily enough. Slate's joyous behavior outside Hopper's shop as he swung me around in broad daylight stuck out in my mind.

After I'd been short with her, she might've had it out for me. She wouldn't have my mannerisms. I doubted we kissed the same, tasted the same... and I stopped that line of thinking right there or my heart would implode.

Brass squeezed my hand. "I hate to do this tonight, but Scarlett, do not marry Ash. I implore you to wait and not make any hasty decisions. Many men would raise another man's child. Hawk is a prime example," he paused as if nervous and I knit my brows at him, "I am —"

"May I have a moment?" Alder asked from behind Brass.

I wiped at a tear and smiled. "Of course."

I linked my arm through Alder's as he led me off the dance floor. I had felt Brass's emotions, he never hid them from me. He had a sweet spot for me. I'd never know the depth of his emotions. I was Ash's.

Alder led me through the halls like he knew them, and I supposed he had. The greater families had lived in their homes for generations.

"Which way is your new room?" Alder rumbled, surprising me.

"This way." I led him down the now familiar hall to my new room.

I swung open the door and gestured for him to enter. "Here it is," I said, hitting the energy plate, so the chandelier came on.

Alder was out of place in the floral room. He looked around and appeared satisfied as he sat down beside me on the pink and cream floral bedspread.

"I do not want to preach, so I will tell you what I know from personal experience," he started as he played with a ring on his finger.

"Okay." I said, pulling my heels up to rest on the mattress frame.

"I married out of obligation and for the safety of my... Jett. Wren was not what my father and uncle wanted for me, and Orion had more influence. They wanted me to have a Vetr bride. I wanted your mother," his guttural tone was forlorn. He rarely talked about my mom.

"There is not a day that goes by that I do not regret my decision. I was relieved when she married Lark as much as it hurt because I had husbandly duties to attend to and it was not Delta's fault we were together. Delta and I never could fall in love. Her only loves are power and ambition and I care for neither," Alder explained and my mouth fell open.

Alder's full lips quirked. "Wren was not in love with him, but between you and me, I knew she had a crush on him when she was younger. All the young girls did. He was a very young widower and greater families were sending their daughters to him by the score. I always knew Lark loved your mother, as a sister at first, but it was blossoming into something else. They were compatible. She was in love with me, he was in love with his deceased wife, so they made a bargain to wed. I had agreed with your mother for her to marry him, I should not have had a say since I was living with Delta by then, but your mother..." He paused, "She loved me more than I deserved, stood by me when she should not have. I do not want to see you marry because it will be safe. Marry for love, Scarlett. A love so bright and hot it would as soon sear your heart as it would melt it."

My breath caught. My mother had said something similar, and I wondered if they said those words to one another. I felt like I was peering in on their younger days, that my mother was briefly alive and with us — as if she would enter the room and support everything my father was saying.

Alder took my hand and turned it palm side up. A ring. His ring. It was platinum with a brushed stone finish and could probably fit around two of my fingers.

"I don't understand," I whispered.

"You let Indigo have all your mom's old jewelry and first pick of her things. You kept some clothes and a handful of pictures, but I want you to have this. It is the ring your mother gave me."

I raised my eyes to his narrow powder blue eyes, blinking at tears and searching for words.

His eyes were watery as he looked away. "I miss your mother every day, Scarlett. Our love seared as often as it melted."

I let out a shuddering breath, trying to still my wobbling chin. My clumsy fingers slid his ring around my stone pendant necklace that now held Slate's emerald ring as well. Alder embraced me before I looked up and I let my tears fall.

"I'm pregnant with Slate's baby," I sobbed out, and he didn't loosen his hold for a moment.

"Slate is an honorable young man, Scarlett. He is very much like his father. Do you care for him?" Alder asked, rubbing my back. His other hand slid into his waistcoat, and he pulled out an envelope that had seen better days. ALDER was scribbled across it.

"I did. You knew Slate's father? Ash —"

"Did or do, daughter?" he asked, holding me away so he could read my face.

"Do... for now. Did you read it?" I asked, gesturing to the envelope.

Alder's full lips pressed together as he looked at the envelope, which shook slightly in his big hands, "Your mother... this letter answered questions I had. Questions she never wanted to answer. She wrote the letter to me, but I think you should read it. I will tell your siblings soon enough, but it is most beneficial to you, I believe."

He handed me the envelope with my mother's writing across the front and I ran my fingers over his name, imagining her writing it.

"Strangely, reading it made me feel better and yet, worse. Better because for a time, I believed she fell out of love with me, and I could not find her to ask her why. When I saw her again at the masquerade... I knew I never wanted to lose her again. I have never been happier than when she was with me... it is the only time I have been happy in recent memory."

I sniffled. "Why worse?" I asked, afraid to read the last words I would ever see in my mother's handwriting.

She would have nothing else new to tell me outside of what the envelope held, and I wasn't sure I could read it. I didn't want to. I wanted to hold on to it forever, letting my mother keep one more secret to reveal in the future as if she was still alive.

"Worse, because I have made Jett an heir, and it has been too long."

I glanced up at my father's eyes and he offered me a small smile.

The door to the hall opened as Alder turned his head.

It all happened so fast.

Alder spun me around, so his massive frame covered mine and I heard him grunt.

"Dad?" I asked, panic gripping my stomach.

His powder blue eyes lowered to mine; his face strained, "Tell Jett I am proud of the man he is. I love you all." Veins popped from his tan skin.

"Dad?" I said in a high squeak and heard footsteps come closer.

His hands moved to either side of me and he pushed off the bed, lifting me with him. "Run!" he blocked me with his body.

That was when I saw the daggers in his back. Three black handled daggers stuck out from his back and a little red circle bloomed on his jerkin. Two masked men in all black blocked the doorway and Alder called.

A hand gripped me from behind, and I shifted when a collar slammed around my throat. A cry was rising to my throat when a knife sunk to the hilt in my stomach.

For a moment, I didn't feel the pain. I looked down at the blade in disbelief as Alder whirled around to watch me fall backwards onto the bed and saw the third unseen masked man behind me.

I waited for the shock to set in, but it didn't come. My body bounced on the bed, jostling the blade buried in my belly and pain set fire to the blood in my veins. I couldn't move to roll off the bed. There was only the pain and the fear. Death lurked in the darkening of my sight and the last of my will to fight for life seeped from me into a yawning abyss that promised peace.

Alder roared and charged the man, only to have a fourth knife thrown in the center of his chest. He staggered back and fell next to me as the bed shook. I fumbled for his fingers and gripped them tightly as tears poured down my cheeks. He turned his head and looked at me with so much love; I cried harder through the impending darkness.

It wasn't my time. If Alder and I died, we'd leave Indigo. Jett stood a fighting chance with his growing family, but Sparrow would never recover either. I had to fight while I still had an ounce of it left in my body.

I wrapped my fingers around the blade in my belly, trying to pull it free. I could hear the men closing in.

Alder's powder blue eyes glazed over and he saw through me.

"Wren," he whispered, and my father's chest fell for the last time.

"Hurry. Pick her up," one of them men said in a cultured tone and the man behind me shoved of fabric in my mouth.

"We should leave her. They will find her and heal her."

Another black clad man stood above me and pulled my ankles, so I fell off the bed. Pain shot through me as I winced, jostling the knife in my stomach. The man sneered down at me and put a booted foot on my stomach as he tore the knife from my body. My vision blackened, but I didn't pass out.

Oh, how desperately I welcomed the darkness.

"Quiet. I am the lead Knight on this. Do as I say," snapped the first man.

The man put his hand over my wound, and I felt warmth flood me. He held back his head and laughed cruelly. "That is not your betrothed's child, is it?" he mocked, and I gritted my teeth.

He looked at the other two men. "This simply will not do," he said to them, and slammed the knife into my stomach again.

I cried out against the gag and tried to hit him with my fists and kicked, to no avail. The other two men grabbed my limbs as the man slammed the knife once, twice, three times more into my stomach. I blacked out from the pain, from the sickening sound of my dress and flesh tearing, and from the sound the blade made as they pulled it from my body.

"Enough. He will kill you if she dies." I heard, as if in a dream.

"Heal the khoraz," the first man spat, "That gives me an idea."

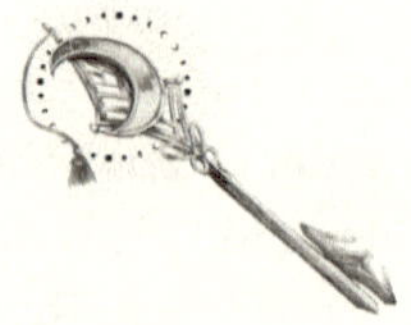

Someone was beating on the door, and I woke up being thrown over someone's shoulder. My hands and ankles were bound, still I fought and tried to scream against the gag. Alder's body was still on my pink and cream bedspread, and I couldn't stop screaming.

"SCARLETT!"

My heart lurched. Brass.

... Help! They've stabbed Alder! They stabbed my stomach, Brass!...

A blast sounded from behind me, and I was being carried out through the balcony. Another blast showered the room with debris and Brass broke into the room, spotting me.

My breath caught as the man carrying me threw my body over the balcony. I was weightless. I free fell from the balcony wide eyed through the winter air with the fluffy snowflakes until calling slowed my descent and another man caught me in a tumble of my heavy skirts.

They tossed me over another shoulder, and a nix torque snapped around my neck again. It had been off to heal me.

A fight was going on upstairs and I was terrified for Brass, but I couldn't see a thing with my hair tangled around my face.

... Tell Jett my father is proud of him, and he loves Indi. Do nothing stupid like dying for me, Brass Regn...

A man flew over the balcony, flapping his arms like a bird until the other two men called, slowing his descent. Two of the men started running through the woods and another ran in a different direction, out of sight. I spotted Brass pulling himself up to the balcony as they tossed me over the front of a horse.

I tried to think quickly.

... They healed me. I don't know what that means, but if they wanted me dead, they would have left me. I'll know you'll find me. Please be careful, I won't lose faith in you...

The horses galloped away when a second man, then a third,

came into sight. I saw another man leap over the balcony and start running towards us and I gave a strangled laugh from where they'd thrown me over the horse. Jett was trying to catch us on foot.

"SCARLETT!" I could barely hear his bellow as he fell to his knees.

I swallowed hard and put my mind to surviving. The man I rode with placed a hand on my back and called.

I drifted off to sleep.

... I love you, Regn...

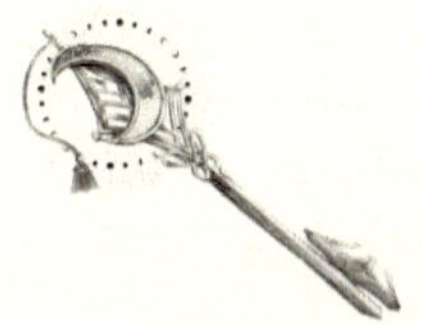

Cold water splashed over my face, and I startled awake. While I was trying to make sense of where I was or what was going on, a man pinched my nose and forced my mouth open before pouring a sweet, tangy liquid down my throat. He shut my mouth with a hand, holding my jaw closed until I swallowed.

After a lot of grunting and struggling, he released me. I coughed and gagged, but nothing came up.

Somehow, these men got me back to Thrimilci because it was sweltering. It was the two bearded men, not the clean shaven one who stabbed me. It wasn't much of a reassurance, but at least these men didn't seem inclined to hurt me.

"What do you want from me?" I asked, wiping my mouth on my shoulder.

They'd torn the stomach of my bloodstained dress. They'd healed me, but I also knew that I wasn't whole. Something was off, and I couldn't let myself think about it or I'd be a bawling mess — worse than I was already.

"Nothing. We have a contract; we mean to fulfill it. Nothing personal." The bearded man turned to me and flashed me a smile and my stomach dropped.

Stygians. He was the same man who tore open my dress on my birthday.

"Fulfill it how?" I asked.

"You know, I said you were to battle that monster, the bies, topless," he shook his head, "Should have listened, girl."

He strode over to me, and the other man turned around. "Do not damage her. We need to go; I do not want to be around her when the rousen kicks in."

Bearded man number two hopped onto his horse and kicked it into a canter.

The other man picked me up effortlessly and tossed me over his horse again before swinging himself up. My mind was frenzied. Every time I tried to touch on a subject, my mind recoiled from the anguish.

Father, no. Mother, no. Slate, no. Baby, no, no, no. Brass, maybe. Survive.

I could think later. Now, I needed to survive.

I'd fight until I failed.

We came to a water's edge with nothing else around and the men dismounted. The first bearded man pulled me off his mount and I fell to my knees. The rousen was working, and I was gritting my teeth against it. It was still dark, without a hint of dawn. Maybe the others would come back to Thrimilci and find me in a few hours. It took around three to get there from the palace, so they would need to track me. It could take a full day.

Bearded man two stalked towards me with a dagger and I tried to retreat, but bearded man one held my shoulders and chuckled. "Be a good girl. We do not want to cut off anything vital."

I swallowed and wondered if I could get that knife away from him. Then what? I didn't know. Perhaps cut my bonds? I'd have to find the right moment; I'd lull them in complacency, then attack.

Good plan.

"This is where we part," the second bearded man said as he brought his knife to my neckline.

I sucked in a breath. "Why didn't you just let me die with my father?"

That was not what the rousen wanted me to say, but I forced it out.

Bearded man one chuckled, "That was not to kill you, girl, but your bastard."

I crumpled, not caring that the knife was there. They let me fall and nudged me with a boot as I covered my eyes as I lamented. They grabbed my hem and heard the tearing and felt tugging. I looked down to find the men slicing off my dress. I tried to roll over and scramble away, but one of them sat astride me and started on my bodice. The red clay was gritty against my bare skin and they tugged up to my feet, still bound.

They were making a point of leering and had washed up my face. I did not know why they'd bother; it made no sense. Then they cut the bonds on my ankles and watched me for a moment, hands still gripping my bonds around my wrists.

I didn't want to run. Want flooded me. They smiled and looked at one another before frog marching me into the cool water.

The two men held me inside a bubble of their making as we floated deeper into the dark water. Their hold on me grew tighter as the more the rousen kicked in.

I didn't see where they took me until I was facing it. A coral castle, much smaller than the palace I'd gone to with Steel, reached up from the bottom of the ocean. It wasn't as vibrant as the king's palace, but maybe that was because it was night.

The men guided me around the castle and down to a hidden cove. As we approached, my mind finally grasped through the rousen stupor that they really were passing me off. I was a payment. I wondered if I was ever the goal or if it had been my father and my presence was simply an opportunity.

A Merfolk man waited on the other side of the archway, and I recognized him right away. Non're, the Merfolk prince, with his sunny blonde hair that fell to his waist and light blue skin. His overly large pupils almost swallowed his bright green irises when we came through the wall of water, and he rested his eyes devoid of sclera on me. The gills under his jaw to the sides of his face flared as he sucked in a breath.

"Payment, courtesy of the Stygians," bearded man two said and Non're smiled. "Will she do?"

Non're took a step forward, shifting the kelp and pearl skirt he wore and raised his hand to my face. I nuzzled it, making a needful sound in my throat, and he smiled.

"Goodbye, Guardians. I find her acceptable," he said, but his eyes told me differently. I was much more than he hoped for.

"I do not have to warn you not to take off the nix torque. We are unpredictable on rousen."

Non're's face darkened. "We do not harm our gifts, we cherish them." His eyes slid back to me and then slid lower as he raked my nude body.

"They hurt themselves. Try not to damage her too badly. She is from a greater family; they will look for her."

With no further preamble, Non're and I were alone in the coral hallway.

"Come to me, pet," Non're said in a purr, holding out his toned arms.

I launched myself at him, and he chuckled as I tried to kiss him. "Not yet, my pet. Scarlett, correct?"

I nodded, incapable of speech.

His body was cool — all Merfolk were. They coveted human warmth; it was rare one ventured down to them and they almost never saw coveted women amongst the Merfolk.

"I knew you would be back. I cannot tell you how glad I am that it is you." he pressed his cool hand to my back and led me deeper into the coral castle. "In case you were wondering, that was not an unsavory transaction. We found one of their people in our territory. We captured him and in exchange for the trespasser we demanded a willing woman." He smiled, flashing human like teeth, "So here you are. Do not worry, we have no intention of damaging you."

My hand ran down his chest as he spoke and it was having physical responses in him, but he was being dutiful while leading me to wherever we were going.

"Here. We would not want you losing interest."

He produced a purple vial and handed it to me. I drank it without a single thought, much less a second, and he smiled.

He turned me down another hall and knocked on a clam shell door before entering. The room was empty save a large circular bed and a nightstand. The lights dangled from the center like little starfish, keeping the room partially darkened. Non're took my hand and led me to the bed. He turned around, and I groped at will. He breathed heavily as my hands ran over him and he spun back.

"Not yet, pet," he said through clenched teeth.

He wrapped a thick silver chain around my waist and connected it to a hoop on the torque at my neck by another chain. He gazed down at me, hard as a rock, and sighed raggedly as he walked away, leaving the room and me in it. I tried to follow him out when I heard the door lock.

I stopped and stared at the door. The rousen was in full effect. Waves of pleasure radiated just beneath my skin. My breasts were aching to be touched. My skin was feeling burned, as if my nerves had come alive and danced under flames. The bearded men must have given me a small dose, but Non're's had been a full vial.

"Good eve, Guardian." A deep voice behind me sounded, and I spun around.

Dion're, the Merfolk king, was blonde with a long matching beard. He had a powerful build, like the rest of the Merfolk, only covered by on a skirt of sapphires and pearls. His skin was more peach than a human's and his eyes that drank me in were as blue as the sapphires on his skirt.

He strode deeper into the bedroom and stood before me.

"You." He breathed and his eyes slid down my body again.

When he raised his head, he was smiling, enraptured by his good fortune.

Rage tore through my mind that wasn't mine. Panic was close behind it, but it all paled to my lust.

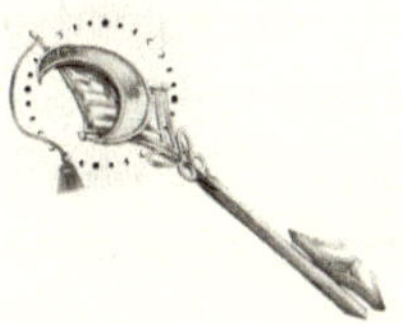

Non're stood over me, ready and waiting. I scooted to the end of the bed and reached for him. He slapped my hand away.

"Come, now. I will not wait a moment longer."

Non're gripped my hand and led me from the room. His blonde hair fanned behind him as he rushed me down the hall until we reached yet another room.

He opened the clamshell door and tossed me onto the bed. It became apparent why we needed the unfamiliar room. Ropes hung from the wall and something Sear're said came into my mind. "Non're would have you bound to his bed in the time it takes a goldfish to forget."

How right Sear're had been.

Non're turned me over and looped the rope over my neck and tied it around my arms, forcing my elbows closer together. He ran it down my legs and pushed them apart with his knee. He tied my ankles to my thighs and took a step back. The ropes were tight and dug into my skin the more I moved, which was hard because the rousen made me want to squirm. I heard Non're's skirt hit the floor.

Non're blindfolded me face down in his bed, tying my thighs to my calves and binding my arms behind my back. Later, I would realize Non're had envisioned what he would do to me for months and once, given the opportunity. He was livid I'd turned him down for the first time. He wanted me to feel pain with my pleasure. I knew nothing about ropes, and Non're could tie the ropes rapidly in a variety of vulnerable positions.

That would be how I'd described my time with Non're; painfully vulnerable. I would ever after crave a little pain with my pleasure. As he had trained me to.

I could feel Slate in my mind within the lost murkiness of the rousen. He was murderous and so far away. Even further away than he was before. I didn't think it was a good sign, but what did I know of signs? I was drinking rousen every time they offered it. My body only had one wish, and that was to be pleasured. I wasn't seeing things straight. I saw them as objects of pleasure — exactly as they saw me.

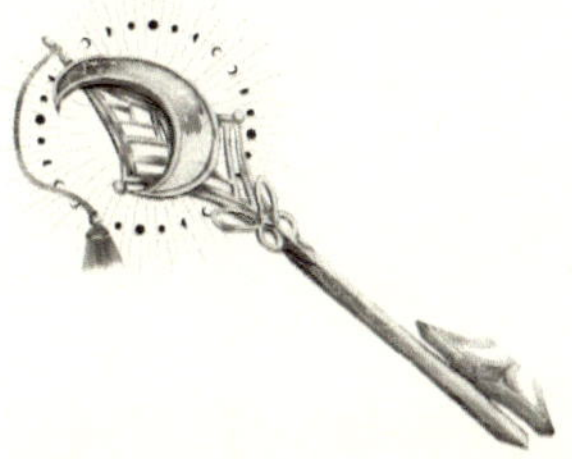

"You are welcome to her, Larn'ra." Non're sounded irritated.

"This is the Guardian who told the others I was a traitor, yes?" she asked, and I felt her fingers trail down my thighs. The blindfold didn't permit the slightest peek to confirm her presence.

"Yes. Scarlett. The future wife of the Prime's nephew," he said with a smile in his voice.

Larn'ra laughed. "You must be happy." I heard Larn'ra's skirt hit the sand and another thunk, which must have been her top before her cool fingers slid against me.

They were purposely speaking in English, knowing I would understand and remember it all if I ever came down off the rousen.

"Do not worry. There is a first time for everything. I will teach you. Are you eager, girl?" Larn'ra asked.

I nodded emphatically and Non're chuckled.

I no longer remembered why the other voice in my head was so angry.

CHAPTER 4
JETT

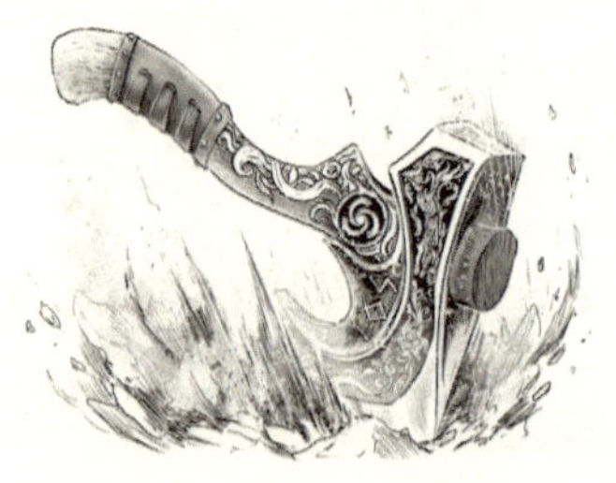

Their ragtag rescue team sat on the raft Steel steered on the River Sol. No one wanted to sit, but they couldn't very well have five men who weighed over two hundred pounds apiece stalking about the raft. Jett sat behind Steel at the tiller against the low wooden wall. Brass and Quick sat across from Gypsum and Slate. The scorching sun beat down on them from the cloudless sky as they passed the red desert landscape.

Jett had not wanted Slate to come, but he was the only one who could track Scarlett.

Three hours ago, Slate had come storming into the shop they had set up camp in. He pulled aside Jett and Brass, who were readying for another round of searching for Scarlett. He told Jett and Brass that the bond was active, and Scarlett was far away. They jumped through portals until they determined she was in Thrimilci.

It was their home island, the land of perpetual summer, and they had all been in Valla where they abducted her. The father he'd known, murdered. All right under their noses.

Jett had run after the retreating horses until he'd broken his ankle and fell. It was winter in Valla, the only island of the five to have traditional seasons, and they had needed to track them down as soon as possible. With all the snow falling, the tracks were light, if visible at all.

Brass and Jett had gone after they stole horses from the Straumr's stables while Quick went back into the palace to inform the people gathered for Scarlett and Ash's engagement party of what happened. They murdered the Var heir of Ostara in a bedchamber of the Prime's estate.

They'd searched every room, under every bed, and found no sign of how the men could have gotten in with no one noticing.

It had been hours before anyone remembered Slate and Scarlett's bond. Gypsum had asked if anyone had told Slate and Brass had left that instant. Brass had been bleeding profusely from a gut wound when Jett sailed over the side of the balcony. Quick had called, slowing his descent. Quick had healed Brass, and Brass had jumped over the balcony after Jett.

They hadn't been thinking clearly. Seeing Alder dead on the pink floral bed had done things to his emotions... Jett shook his head to clear it.

Time for that later. Scarlett first.

The only girls they'd allowed were Shale and Ama, who sat on the other end of the boat. Shale and Ama were Shadow Breakers — trained assassins. Tawny, Indigo, and the Jett's wives had wanted to come, but the men had braced their ground. They had enough to worry about without putting another one of their women in jeopardy.

Shale and Ama were there because no matter how many times they'd told them no, the girls had ignored them and came anyway. It was a good thing, too, now that Jett thought about it. Scarlett would hate all the men. Better to have the women for when they got her out so they could take care of her in a way they couldn't.

Jett hung his head in his hands. Brass said they stabbed her in the stomach. Slate said she was not in extreme pain, but occasionally there was a little streak of it. Mostly she was climaxing, he had said in a growl. That she was in some sort of suspended sexual stimulation. He had changed pants twice and had now begun dropping trou whenever he felt one of her sensations coming on until they had spent him. By Jett's calculation, it had happened almost every twenty minutes until

Slate sat gritting his teeth as his chest rose and fell heavily. There was no way to make Slate feel better. Knowing everything Scarlett was going through would have killed Jett.

Steel's face had grown dark then and with all the other facts, they knew she was with the Merfolk, but how? The why of it was even more damning.

Slate shouldn't have come; they'd waste more time trying to restrain him from committing genocide than taking care of Scarlett.

Jett massaged his forehead. Ash and Slate had gotten in one another's faces from the moment Slate set foot in the base they'd created. Ash wanted Slate gone. Slate asked who would make him leave. Hawk refocused him and asked Slate to work on establishing a bond with Scarlett, to let her know Slate was concerned — *anything*.

The bond had come out because of it, but only their family knew.

While they were sprinting to get ready, they received the message that clinched it. Sear're, the Merfolk king's advisor, had sent them a messenger. The attackers delivered Scarlett to them for safekeeping. Sear're would wait for the rescuers where she was being kept. It was the morning of the fourth day when Slate had felt the bond and an hour after that; the message had come.

Three nights of hell.

Jett knew none of them had been so miserable in their lives. None of them had wanted to go home and give up at night and rest comfortably in their beds while she was out there. It admitted that they wouldn't find her soon.

Sparrow had been beside herself. Tawny had surprised them all by being the rock her mother could lean on and had resolutely decided that Scarlett would come back alive, no matter what. She said there was no way Scarlett would let herself die, not with the loss of Alder and Wren so fresh. Brass agreed and said Scarlett relayed as much when she was being taken away. Scarlett had been alert before they carried her off. She'd told Brass she wouldn't lose faith that he'd find them. She had said things before that when she must have thought they were going to kill her, but Jett couldn't think about that now.

After Slate's initial explosion, he seemed determined to find her. If someone would die, it would be him. She would hate him for the rest of her long life, he'd said. He'd make sure of it.

The family had gathered in the informal dining hall when the Merfolk had sent the message. Merfolk meant rousen. Rousen meant drugged. Drugged meant Scarlett would not be herself when she returned. Rousen infused the pleasure center of the mind and shut down the reason and behavioral control.

She'd have one goal in mind — pleasure. She wouldn't want to eat, sleep, she wouldn't feel pain like she was supposed to. Three nights on rousen. Jett's wildest imagination couldn't fathom what had happened to Scarlett while she had been under the Merfolk's care.

"If she had been with me, it never would have happened." Slate had told the others around the light wood carved table. The warm lantern light in the Moroccan styled palace glimmering on the silver and gold carving that covered the tabletop.

The blue morning glory vine stretched up to the high domed ceiling had curved white beams trimmed in gold. It started out dark blue at the walls and faded to white at the peak of the dome, with white birds painted in the segments between the beams. Subtle mosaic patterns in teals and blues stretched along the white walls.

"Don't blame yourself. What is best for Scarlett? That is the focus. No point in dancing around the subject. Scarlett will be addicted to the rousen when she comes back. We won't know how bad it altered her mind until she can break through the fog and the other parts of her mind begin to work again. Until then, someone must get her to eat and drink." Hawk's dark, intelligent eyes bespoke of the sorrow he felt despite his pragmatic tone. "She will have to be weaned off the rousen."

They had all gathered for a vote. Do they hand Scarlett over to Ash to do what Scarlett needed, or do they find someone else? Jett had been firmly against Ash, as had most of them. The vote had taken a turn when Tawny spoke.

"Right. Someone she trusts and likes who she won't hate herself for having been with. I vote for Brass." Tawny's wide hazel eyes shone bright against her fair heart-shaped face; her wide mouth pressed firmly together. "They're friends. He is a trained fighter, so he can protect her, and he can read her mind, so he'll know when she is resurfacing. When Scarlett was in mourning after Wren's death, Brass was the only one whom she could communicate with." Suddenly, she didn't seem so confident when she added, "She chose Brass, if you catch my drift."

Brass had been in the room pacing behind the seats with Quick. He had lifted his head in disbelief, amber eyes wide. He hadn't volunteered for the job; they hadn't even asked if he wanted the job. Everyone knew Scarlett had had a sweet night with the middle Regn brother and come back for more — one last night. Slate had been looking for her all night before he had given up and gone to headquarters, where he ran into his team sans Brass. He put two and two together quickly enough and charged into Brass's bedroom.

He had no right to disrupt them. Scarlett would've been dating Brass if Slate hadn't brawled with Brass while Scarlett stared on in mortification.

"Me, too." Indigo had seconded, and Quick had snapped his head to Brass.

Jett had noticed that when Quick showed up in the mornings over the last few days, he'd arrived with Indigo. Her hair was in a braid that bared the M.O. of a night spent with 'Quick' Silver Regn. Jett was glad she had comfort, but he would have preferred a more reputable man. None of Jett's friends would have been good enough for his sisters.

"If that is what you decide, I do not have a problem with it." Brass swallowed, not commenting on Tawny's statement.

"Slate. He's trained Scarlett, she's taken orders from him, and she dislikes him, so, it stands to reason, she would fight harder to break free from the rousen to get away from him," Gypsum said matter of fact.

He had a point. "I say Slate," Jett said, not meeting Tawny's glare.

"Slate." Sparrow had agreed, and Hawk supported her.

"Brass, if we are not involving Ash." Amethyst crossed her arms at Jett's side. Her dark, dreamy eyed glare spoke volumes.

Scarlett would not be happy about all the secrets that had come out in her absence.

Steel's green turquoise eyes had regarded Slate. "She will hate you."

Slate's silver narrow eyes were cool as ice had met Steel's. "I know."

"I cannot do that to you, brother. I choose Brass," Steel sighed as Tawny laced her fingers through his.

The tension was thick. Brass and Quick had stopped pacing and stood waiting for Cherry and Pearl to place their votes. Pearl's emerald cat eyes took in both men before she spoke.

"Slate, darling. I know you care dearly for our Scarlett. She will not be herself; she will not have the ability to filter what she says. If she has been angry with you, she is likely to say hurtful things. Are you prepared for that? For the nix torque she will probably have to wear, to keep her locked away until she can begin thinking for herself again? We cannot risk her getting out and losing her," Pearl said, knitting her delicate brows on her tanned face.

Slate's hard face turned ever stonier. "I owe her that much," he said.

"And you won't be seeing other women?" Tawny snapped, tossing her long, dark waves over her shoulder. "Doubtful. It would disgust Scarlett." She shook her head. "If you could have stopped yourself, then she never would have been at the Straumr palace to begin with!"

Tawny's fair cheeks were flushed, and she had risen to her feet. She had guts. Jett gave her that.

"I'm going to have a fridge brought to the wing and make sure it's stocked with food." Tawny stood behind the chair. "I don't need to be a mind reader to see that you've all made your decision. Brass, thank you. I know Scarlett will appreciate the gesture. For what it's worth, I think she should be with you." She turned fiery hazel eyes on Slate, who was clenching his jaw again, letting Jett know just what Scarlett was going through then. "If I so much as think you're with another woman, or you're not doing right by Scarlett — I don't know how, but I will find a way to hurt you."

Tawny stormed from the room with a new purpose in mind. Indigo got to her feet and went after her, Quick hot on her heels. There was silence for a moment until Sparrow cleared her throat. Her dark eyes were bloodshot and long, dark hair was limp around her olive face.

"Tawny and Scarlett are closer than sisters. She doesn't mean it so harshly," Sparrow said in a soothing tone.

Slate rose to his full six and a half feet, as tall and broad as Jett himself. "I will do nothing unnecessary to or for Scarlett. I do not want to do it, I must. No one here knows better than I the aftereffects of rousen," he rumbled.

Jett, Steel, and Gypsum had gotten to their feet to depart.

Gypsum wore his hair like Slate and Brass. His thick sable hair fell halfway down his back with dozens of braids with copper beads threaded through it. He had the same lean, toned body as Hawk, with straight brows and a dimpled smile that was winning girls' hearts all over Tidings.

"She is sleeping." Slate rumbled from his spot on the raft, breaking Jett out of his memories.

Jett let out a gusty breath. That had to be a good sign. Better that than anything else.

Jett ran his hands over his close cropped dark blonde hair. They'd brought a few supplies they weren't sure if they'd need. Clothes they didn't think she'd willingly put it on, plus other items to care for her physically that healing wouldn't help.

Ama's honey blonde curls glowed under the sun. Her round, dark eyes were closed, and rosebud mouth pursed as she rested her shoulder on her petite lover. Shale's legs crossed in front of her, her sheet of glossy black hair spilled past her shoulders as she looked back the way they came with her dark up-tilted eyes. There was a time where Jett had been sure Shale had a crush on Scarlett. The tightly muscled woman had spent more than a few days hanging around Slate when Jett was positive she had little to no interest in men.

The breeze ruffled Steel's dirty blonde hair. "Not much further," he announced, and every person on the raft stiffened. "Slate, I need your guarantee you won't kill anyone. We don't know the whole story and even if they are guilty, we'll take them to Valla's Guardians."

Slate's silver eyes opened and lifted to Steel's, but it was Jett who answered, "As long as she is safe and in good health... and no one is with her." Jett's square jaw tensed.

Sear're had to know they would come immediately and separate her from... whomever. Jett's hands balled into fists.

"I agree to Jett's terms." Slate met Jett's turquoise eyes in acknowledgement and Jett nodded.

Jett wanted to go through wherever she was being held and find every person, then fry them all: anyone who may have been with Scarlett, or who had seen her vulnerable.

Jett's insides twisted.

"Ama and Shale can stay here with Quick," Brass said, his amber eyes resting on Slate.

Things had been tense since the voting. Slate may have been stoic during the process, but Jett knew Slate would rather be dead than let Brass see to Scarlett's needs until she was better. Quick nodded instead of arguing. Someone would need to stay with the women, and they couldn't risk bringing more temptation into the Merfolk's dwelling.

They changed into fitted shorts. Slate climbed to his feet, the muscles in his body bunched as he faced out towards the ocean. They were close. Jett saw a figure standing near the river and slowly got to his feet. It was Sear're.

Dusky blue skin covered his powerful form that only hidden by a kelp skirt. He had long black hair peppered with silver streaks. The Merfolk advisor was a humanoid on dry land, but a shark hybrid in the water.

The others on the raft rose to their feet and faced the Merfolk man as Steel steered them to the silty riverbank. Slate was the first to hop off, followed by Jett. Sear're's eyes were wary as he took in the group who would save Scarlett. There were no pleasant greetings. Once Steel hopped off the raft and left Quick and the girls, he made his way over to Sear're.

"Steel," Sear're said.

"Sear're. What happened? Is she safe?" Steel asked, tan brow furrowing.

Sear're nodded. "Scarlett is safe and unharmed, mostly. She has not been eating, as far as I can tell. I swear to you, Steel, I was told she was here and sent for you straight away. Scarlett is a good woman and I owe her a debt; I would never have let Non're have her."

Slate turned around and walked away. Non're, the Merfolk prince, had a penchant for binding and tying his women and none too gently. It was common knowledge among the Merfolk and the Thrimilci people who lived along the rivers. Jett squeezed his eyes shut, trying to control the conflagration of his anger.

"How did she come to be here?" Steel asked in a lower timbre.

"One of the border wardens caught a trespasser and took him to Non're. The man said he belonged to a guild and that they would purchase his freedom. Non're agreed and his price was a willing woman. Four nights ago, two men came with Scarlett. Non're asked her if she came of her own free will and she nodded." He held up his hand when Steel protested, the gills to the sides of his jaw flaring as he sucked in air. "No need to tell me they had drugged already her, but you understand why my hands are tied. Non're is my prince, and he abided by our laws."

"What guild?" Brass asked.

Sear're shook his head. "I do not know. I should warn you; I do not know what state her mind will be in. No human I know of has indigested so much rousen in such a short time. I apologize profusely. Come, I will take you to her." Sear're turned around and headed towards the water.

When the clear water was waist deep, Sear're shifted. His bottom half turned into a shark tail and a fin grew from his back. Three rows of sharp teeth flashed in a wide mouth. The men called air bubbles in front of their mouths and noses so they could breathe underwater.

Not long after they dove under, Jett spotted a coral fortress. Sear're led them around the side of the small formation to a hidden cove and crossed through, shifting in the process. Steel, Slate, Brass, Gypsum, and Jett came through the arched entranceway. A wall of water separated the sand floor before it was dry.

"This way. We should hurry. I do not know how long she will be out, but it will be easier to transport her while she sleeps. There is a store of rousen to wean her off over the next few days. I do not know how long it will take or how many days after she will need it to prevent damage to her mind," Sear're said soberly as they wound through the coral halls, past clamshell doors and urchin shaped sconces.

"Thank you, Sear're," Steel said.

Brass's thick dark brows pulled down above his amber eyes.

"What is it, Brass?" Jett asked.

"You do not want to know." He answered in a smooth, deep voice with an edge like a razor.

Sear're looked over his shoulder. "There are still other Merfolk here. I am hoping we do not run into any of them." Gypsum waited with Sear're.

A low growl rumbled from deep in Slate's chest.

"This place reeks of lust," Slate growled.

Brass grunted in agreement and Sear're opened a door on his left and stepped aside to wait in the hall. Jett filed in with Slate and Brass.

Scarlett laid on her side in a large circular bed with ivory satin sheets. A starfish chandelier draped with pearls hung from the ceiling was illuminating the room just enough to see.

Scarlett's caramel waves spilled over the pillow. Her brows were smooth, as if she was having sweet dreams. Her long lashes fanned across her high tan cheekbones and her full lips pursed as she slept, her upper lip a little fuller than the top. She could have been anywhere and looked like she was at complete peace. Jett's anxiety seeped from his body.

Steel walked to the side table where a metal case held dozens of purple filled vials. He shut it, locked it, and tucked it under his arm. Jett walked to Scarlett's side, where Slate stood gazing down at her. Brass hung back, knowing impeding either Jett or Slate would've been a bad idea.

Jett cursed when he got closer. The satin sheet was under her arm and Jett saw at her wrist and elbows were red rope burns, at the corners of her mouth, red streaks marred where a gag had been tightly wound, and around her neck was another rope burn beneath a nix torque. Someone attached a chain link leash to the pewter nix torque and connected it to a loop at the head of the bed.

Slate didn't hesitate. He pulled the nix torque off and passed it to Brass, who had stepped forth to collect it. Slate laid his hands on her and pulled them back as if burned.

"What is it?" Jett asked, voice thick with concern.

Slate put his hands to Scarlett's hand again and the red abrasions faded away to flawless skin.

"The pregnancy is no more. She is barren," Brass whispered.

Jett had to feel for himself. He put his hand to Scarlett at the same time as Steel. They both called. Slate and Brass were right. It was why women didn't come to the Merfolk, despite their allure. Their fluids were toxic and could cause you to lose a child. In small doses, no actual harm was done, but there was no such thing as a small dose of Merfolk once on rousen. Female Merfolk were just as toxic to men. Scarlett was exposed without protection, and her reproductive organs were fried. Sometimes men would go sterile for a time and their body would eventually right itself. That would be the most hopeful case with Scarlett.

Arguing at the door made Jett turn around. Slate scooped Scarlett into his arms, wrapping the ivory satin around her. Brass walked out into the hall and Jett stopped in the doorway. The Merfolk prince was in the hall talking with Gypsum and Sear're. Jett had never seen Gypsum look so angry.

Jett stopped in the doorway, preventing Slate from seeing him. Steel side stepped around him and approached Non're.

"My niece. You knew she was my niece, yet you kept her? Why, Non're? Have I not always been fair to your people? Given leniency when I could? She is barren," Steel said in a rasp, his voice thick with anger and frustration.

Non're pursed his lips. "She said she wanted to stay. It was accept her or let the men who brought her keep her. Really, I did you a favor."

Brass growled through clenched teeth. "A favor?"

Non're smirked. "Larn'ra seemed to think they exchanged many favors. Your lack of gratitude does not offend me."

Sear're stepped in front of the Merfolk prince. "You should leave now, Non're. The girl is betrothed. What will he say when he finds out she cannot bear his children?"

Jett's heart hammered in his chest. He coiled his muscles and prepared to strike. He could feel the rage rolling off Slate behind him and he was certain if he wasn't holding Scarlett, he would have attacked Non're. Just when the tension was boiling over, Non're smirked and moved on.

Sear're turned to them. "You should leave. You have everything you need?"

"Yes," Steel said with blotches of red in his cheeks.

The men moved down the hall. Brass took up the rear as they marched towards the cove. Scarlett hadn't moved a muscle from where she was curled up against Slate, looking frailer than he'd ever seen her, and yet something was different about her he couldn't quite put his finger on.

Non're turned a corner in front of them and they walked past as he opened the door at the end of the short hall. He tossed his blonde hair, leaving the door open as he walked further in and gave the passing men a good view of what was going on inside.

Brass sucked in sharply as Slate growled. It was a room full of Merfolk engaged in a variety of acts. A bed was at the center of the room as a sort of focal point. Jett knew Non're had showed them on purpose to let them know what Scarlett had been involved in. Jett prayed to the gods that her resting had meant that she hadn't entered the room.

Jett cursed and kept walking, knowing Slate wouldn't waste time there with Scarlett on the premises. Once Scarlett was better... well, that'd be a different story. Jett would come with Slate and level it.

Gypsum went through the water first with Steel, Jett, and Slate wrapped Scarlett's limp body as best they could so she would remain covered. Sear're placed a dusky blue hand on Slate's shoulder and looked at him with sympathetic eyes.

"Slate, if I had any idea they had your woman, I would have carried her back myself. I am truly sorry. Our king is as well. I hope she comes through unscathed. Let me know if there is any more I can do," he said.

Slate's silver eyes appraised Sear're over Scarlett's body. "You helped me escape Larn'ra. You would give no woman to Non're — mine or not. It is your prince that owes us a great debt. I plan to collect when my mate is well." He held Sear're gaze for another moment and he nodded.

Jett swam beside Slate as the two men went to the surface and back towards the raft.

At least that had been the plan.

They had not replaced the nix torque around Scarlett's throat and when she hit the water; she woke. Jett's air bubble had popped when her normally turquoise almond eyes swung his way. Her pupils were overly large, like the Merfolk, so no color existed beyond the sclera.

Slate struggled with her as she groped for him, and Jett swam to help him. That was when she looked at him. She no longer had a way to breathe and released Slate to blow past Jett and sail towards Steel and Gypsum. Jett went straight up to the surface. Scarlett was stronger than anyone he'd ever met in calling. She might accidentally kill one of them.

Jett broke to the surface and gasped for air. Slate popped up next to him and then dove back down, chasing after a rapidly disappearing Scarlett. Brass was on her heels when Steel dropped the case of vials and swam to the floor to retrieve them. Gypsum was just getting to the shore when Scarlett caught him.

All Jett saw was Gypsum go down and Scarlett roll on top of him before Brass reached them. Then Scarlett disappeared with Brass, leaving Gypsum half laying in the crystal-clear water. Jett pushed faster to get to shore. He expected to see Quick, Ama, and Shale rush to help, but Gypsum's lower half was still in the water.

Steel made it to shore first, and Jett could feel the air impact of power like a thunderclap through the waves.

Freya's burly boar!

Jett made it to the shore right before Slate to find Steel on his knees next to Gypsum, who was lying on his stomach. Quick, Shale, and Ama stood frozen a few feet away from Scarlett. Each one of their faces contorted, but not with pain. Ama let out a high moan just before it sucked Jett into Scarlett's vortex. Jett dropped beside Steel.

Pleasure — like a dozen women sucking and stroking all over his body.

Scarlett sat astride Brass; his hands angled up as if frozen mid reach with the nix torque at his side as if she'd knocked it away. Shale let out a curse and Gypsum groaned where he laid face down in the sand. Jett's breaths were quickening. He had to get that nix torque on her before something extremely awkward happened.

"Fuck," Quick gritted.

Steel's tan face was beet red, and he looked to be holding his breath. Jett's breath rushed from his lungs as he fell limply to the sand, feeling utterly disgusting.

Slate came up behind Jett, panting. Water splashed over Jett's back, where Slate sloshed from the shore.

"TORCH!" He roared, and Scarlett whirled around, rising off Brass in the same fluid movement.

The air heated, and she released her constant swirling pleasure. Brass stumbled to his feet, picking up the nix torque and snapped it around Scarlett's neck from behind.

Jett cursed as Brass staggered to remain upright. He'd received the brunt of Scarlett's... affection, as well as her calling. She had stripped him of his shorts, which were laying in tatters at her feet. Jett cursed again. Steel was on his knees, panting and coughing. Jett saw Gypsum sitting in the sand, looking shaken as the others came out of the water after washing themselves and making a great deal of noise.

Slate squared off with Scarlett, and Jett stared, dumbfounded. If he wasn't certain that the woman he was looking at, he would not have believed it was her. She was dripping with a predatory sexuality, ivory satin sheet wet and clinging to her body from a knot Jett had tied around her throat like a toga, was his sister. It was in her very gaze, in the way she held herself. The being before him was not his sister.

"Come. Now," Slate commanded — to Jett's surprise, Scarlett obeyed.

She sauntered over, swaying the few curves she still had after days without eating, until she stood in front of Slate, licking her lips and fell to her knees in front of him. Slate ran his hand over her head and Jett's mouth fell open as he watched her close her eyes and moan as she leaned into his hand.

When Cordillera had weened Slate off rousen, she'd taken to calling him her pet. Jett thought he understood why.

Jett heard Quick choke as if suppressing a gasp as he walked past to check on Gypsum with Steel. Ama and Shale trudged up on his other side and went straight to the raft, stripping off their clothes as they went.

Those two had no modesty.

"Jett." Slate rumbled from his side.

Jett turned his head towards him, unable to pull his eyes away from his sister, who was acting like a well-trained dog.

"Give us a moment," Slate rumbled, and Jett cursed as he trudged over to the raft to make sure Brass was relatively unharmed.

He heard Steel, Quick, and Gypsum walking behind him and slowed so they could walk together and watched Slate picking Scarlett up and bringing her back into the ocean. Jett was glad the raft was a suitable distance away from the water.

"Hey, Chief, you alright?" Jett asked, trying to keep things light.

Gypsum lifted his head, looking dazed and ashamed. "Yeah. Brass... saved me. She didn't even recognize me." His eyes fell again, and Jett thought he understood.

"It's not your fault. It's not her fault either. Her mind isn't processing those kinds of things," Jett said.

"Truth. It was just a little kiss." Quick teased.

Jett's stomach turned.

Gypsum's face reddened. "I think I got more than a kiss," he muttered, and Steel met Jett's eyes.

"You know, I bet Ama would wipe the slate clean if given half a chance." Jett joked.

Gypsum raised his eyes to the raft where Ama was in her bra and panties, changing her clothes.

His lips quirked a little and Jett felt a little better at having cheered up the youngest in their group.

Brass had pants on and was tugging on his boots when Jett and the others reached for the raft. "Everyone okay?" he asked gruffly.

"Some better than others." Quick joked, and Brass shot him a look of annoyance through his strands of damp hair.

Gypsum moved to stand beside Brass. "Hey, thanks a lot. She would have done to me what she did to you if you hadn't tackled her off."

Brass clapped a hand on Gypsum's shoulder without looking at him. "She is not thinking. She would never have forgiven herself. I do not know if she will forgive herself as it is."

Jett walked over to his clothes and changed, not wanting to know what Slate was doing with his baby sister out in the ocean. He knew what it would come down to and if they were very lucky, it would be the only time it happened on the trip back.

"What happened?" Steel asked no one in particular.

"Scarlett woke up while we were coming to shore. She cut through our calling and got away," Jett explained.

"She tackled Gypsum and planted a wet one before Brass sent her sprawling," Quick said, "The three of us started for her and she called so much air." Quick shook his head. "She must keep the nix torque on. If she had been out to kill us instead of... we would all be dead. As it is, I do not think Indigo is going to be very understanding." He was trying to joke, but Steel was frantically scrubbing his boxer briefs as if he could erase the memory with the stain.

Jett thought he should clean himself, too.

"Brass, you cool?" Jett asked, and Brass gave one curt nod.

Quick walked over to his brother in his boxer briefs, the jagged Celtic tattoos that covered the left half of his body exposed on his olive skin and slapped a hand to his back. "Ah, nothing she has not done to him before," he teased. "I can see now why he wanted to keep her to himself."

It was too soon.

Brass lifted his head, and Quick took an involuntary step back. Jett couldn't see the look Brass gave Quick, but he knew Brass was dealing with a lot. Quick had made a good point, if not Slate, then Brass. They should have thought of what they would do if she tried to break free.

Brass pulled a dry shirt over his head. "I was carrying the nix torque; I should have put it on her before we left the fortress. Barring that, I should have put it on her while distracted with Gypsum."

"Gods, she ripped your underwear off in a heartbeat. I have seen nothing like it," Ama said, pulling on clean pants. "Her calling is so powerful. It is going to be hard to look at her the same way now that I know what she can do without even touching me." Ama giggled.

Jett was trying very hard not to look at Ama's breasts as they bounced while she shimmied into her pants. Shale's body was just as hard as he'd expected. The petite girl was toned all over — not masculine, but not soft, either.

Brass shot Ama a look, and she turned away. "Oh my," she breathed, and Jett turned around before he could stop himself.

Slate and Scarlett were up to their shoulders in the ocean with her arms were wrapped around his neck, pressing herself tight to him as she kissed him deeply, the water rippling around them from their movements. Jett didn't need to see under the water to know what they were doing.

"Now is a good time to eat lunch," Steel said, pulling food he'd packed and passing it out.

Quick laughed. "Yeah, this is not awkward at all."

Ama giggled, making Gypsum smile, his cheeks dimpling. Jett shook his head. They were all slap happy. Too many stressful nights with little to no sleep, and now it was over. Her calling had gotten them all, but it could have been worse. Scarlett was as good as they could have hoped, and she was coming home with them. There were still a lot of big issues, but they could wait.

Scarlett would have to face Ash. She would have to be told about the baby and the impossibility of having any more, and worse, the death of their father.

Jett sighed and Brass sat down next to him.

"She is strong. We will her help find something for her to live for and she will prevail," he said, taking a bite out of a sandwich.

"What did she do to you, Brass? Is Slate going to come up here and try to kill you?" Jett asked, eating a sandwich of his own.

Brass swallowed before answering. "He wanted to kill me back at the palace. Still does. I did not touch her any more than necessary. Your sister is powerful," Brass said soberly, "We were lucky."

Jett had no doubt.

Slate climbed into the raft carrying a sleeping Scarlett with the wet sheet draped over her body and handed her over to Ama and Shale. Slate walked to his pack, unspeaking, and changed. Red scratches marred his back, and Jett closed his eyes and counted to ten. It was going to be a long few days.

"What happened on shore, Brass?" Slate rumbled suddenly and the raft grew unnaturally silent.

"Whoa. We agreed the shore never happened," Quick interjected.

"I think you know." Brass retorted, and Slate stilled his movements.

"Emotions are running high. No one has done anything unnecessary," Steel said in a reassuring tone.

Slate turned around, silver eyes flashing. "Did you enjoy it? You wanted her to fuck you again. To see to her needs until she recovered."

Jett got to his feet and walked between where Brass sat and Slate. "Don't ask questions you don't want to hear the answers to. Let it go. Take care of my baby sister, you bastard. It's the last chance you have at redeeming yourself," Jett whispered, locking his eyes on Slate.

Slate needed to hurt something. He could see it in his brother's eyes. Anything would do.

"I told her she should not be with Ash, that the reason she was still a maiden was because she felt no passion for him. I asked her about you that night. She told me it was because she could not trust you with so much of her heart. So, yes. You want to hear it from my mouth? I accepted what she offered *gladly*, and I safeguard the trust she put in me." Brass got to his feet. "I took her in the alley, in the bath, in my bed, and in the prep room *twice* and that was only the first day. I would have never let her go if she was not so afraid to feel. When she came back to my rooms the day she returned from the Jorogumo, I never wanted her to leave. She was going to leave Ash and stay with me. She didn't because she was afraid of hurting you."

Jett held his breath as Brass pushed up against his shoulder.

"I would have given her whatever she wished the night of your competition, but your bond was active, and I would never do that to you. You just made love to the woman I love while I sat idly by — so sit down and quit belly aching about the past," Brass ground out through gritted teeth.

The silence was deafening. Brass was Slate's beta. He didn't think anyone would debate that. Where Slate led, Brass followed. Brass always questioned Slate, but he never got on his bad side.

Jett was regretting his decision to come between them. Slate's eyes shone silver with rage and Brass's eyes were molten. Neither was backing down.

Jett patted them on the shoulder and cleared his throat. "If you two fight and cause the raft to overturn, you won't have to worry about one another because the rest of us will kill you both."

"You wake her again and I'll have to fight Scarlett to keep Ama from leaving me," Shale barked. "I cannot even call half of what she used; how can I compete with that?" Her dry humor made Ama giggle.

Brass shook himself out of it and sat down, returning to his sandwich, and Slate slunk down next to Gypsum, who handed him an orange. Jett walked over to where Shale was drying Scarlett's hair, since she wore the pair of grey sweats and a white NEIU t-shirt Tawny had given him.

Comfort clothes, she'd said. Something familiar from her college days.

They incinerated the satin sheet and Jett took Scarlett from them, much to their dismay, and Slate looked like he wanted to take her back. Jett would like to see them try. While she was passed out, he would hold her as much as possible.

"If you do not eat, I will leave you. Then how will you get your pleasure?" Slate threatened for the millionth time.

I quirked an eyebrow and slid my hand down my stomach and lower until he growled and yanked my hand away.

"I will tie your hands as well."

Another threat.

I ate his stupid food as fast as I could so we could get to the pleasure part.

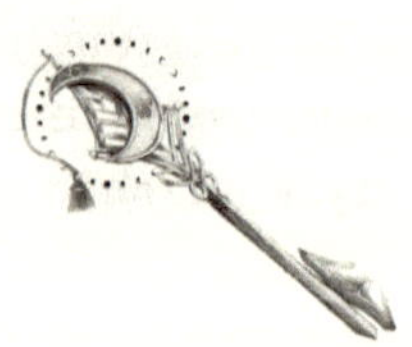

"When you do that, the showers take twice as long." Slate growled as I pulled him into my mouth.

His hands tried to work shampoo into my hair, but I had no desire for such frivolities as cleaning. I just wanted him.

Slate told me all kinds of terrible things. My father was dead. I already knew that. We'd lost our baby. I knew that. I was barren. That was new, but not surprising. Ash thought I was still missing. That was new, too. I needed to get better faster because we had to address things with Ash and put my father to rest. I didn't want to do any of that.

My day comprised waking up to Slate and making love to him for hours on end until he made me eat and sleep again. He claimed I hadn't slept or eaten in days and had made myself weak. Then he would threaten me, so I ate, and I slept. Then I woke, and we made love and repeated the process over again.

I saw no one else.

They had fastened my leash to a loop at the side of the bed with a great deal of slack. I didn't know whose bed it was. Not one I'd ever seen before. Beams of sunlight speared through the spacious room from the windows. The massive bed had a white down comforter and billowing sheer white panels swathed around it in a canopy. Piles of pillows ran along the white upholstered headboard. The walls were a pale green with a white chaise and a long-distressed dresser, which had my mother's pictures shoved into the mirror frame. Light pink peonies in vases adorned the nightstands.

There was an attached bathroom, so I never saw the rest of the house, but the bathroom was like the one at the Sumar palace. They built dozens of shower heads right into the tiffany blue tiles. The waterfall separated the shower from the rest of the bathroom was activated by an energy plate when you used calling, which I wasn't allowed to do. Two white ornate mirrors hung above the ivory sinks in front of the huge ivory clawed foot tub that fit both Slate and me easily. Bright pink floral accents decorated the bathroom, giving it a feminine touch.

"It is all for you, Torch," Slate said one day while he dried my hair.

I did not know what he meant.

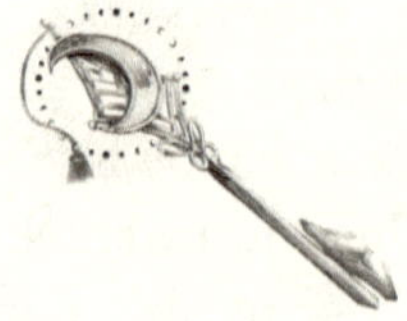

"Three days, Torch. Time to wean you off. Your eyes are returning to normal, and I want to take the gods' cursed leash off you. Let me know when it hurts," Slate said as he sat on the chaise in nothing but his black boxer briefs.

Slate crossed his powerfully sculpted legs at the ankle. A silky midnight happy trail led beneath his boxers from his navel. Corded bronze muscles formed a 'V' below his hips that drove me wild, his stomach was sculpted by countless ridges of muscle and two perfect dark pink nipples that peaked on each sculpted pectoral. His powerful jaw was set as he went over some papers, his full soft lips pressed together pensively as he read. Silver eyes scanned from beneath thick, long midnight lashes.

His dark mane spilled over his shoulders. Little braids were scattered through his wavy locks with silver Celtic etched beads and white carved fetishes threaded through them. He had a solar cross, a jumis, a sun, and a starburst. I had the same starburst threaded into my braid along with an ivory pearl, a jade canine, and a turquoise tree of life.

I scowled at Slate. It had been hours since he last gave me the rousen. My doses were smaller and less frequent than my first day in the mystery room. I could also recognize things again. Not well, but it was a start.

Every time I looked at Slate, something nagged at me. We kept the bond activated at all times, so he knew how I was feeling. That was another one of his rules. We did nothing unless I initiated it, and even then, I had to push, practically beg, before he gave over.

He rubbed absently over the high cheekbone of his hard planed face and my need for him grew. He kept telling me to fight it until the last possible moment and then we could give in, but we had to keep trying. The sooner the better.

The problem was, whenever I had a moment of clarity, the pain was overwhelming, and I would lose myself in Slate. In the touch of his silken skin, the taste of it, his spicy clove scent that intoxicated me when the unique smell of our sex together blended with it. I wanted Slate every way I could have him and he had let me. I'd encouraged him to do the same, though he was reluctant.

"Stop staring, Torch," Slate rumbled, and I made a face at him, and I saw his lips curl.

The smiling was new. He didn't smile at all at first, but the more I followed his rules, the happier he became.

I could make him happy — it had been a revelation. I wanted to make him happy anyway he desired. I woke up wanting to please him, waiting for him to ask me to do something so he would reward me.

I was wearing my champagne robe. One of his rules, at least one article of clothing unless we were making love, then we could remove them. He was happier when I covered up. I tied it loosely around my waist and slipped out of the soft white blankets to walk over to him.

He watched me, cocking a midnight brow. I flashed him my very best smile, and I felt his surprise through the bond. He had seen nothing yet. I had this urge to express myself that I hadn't felt capable of doing before.

I ran my fingers down the top of his foot as he watched me, trailing up his leg to his thigh and over the corded muscle at his hips. I bent forward and pressed a kiss to each muscle before raising my head back to him. His perfect nipples hardened from my touches. His bronze skin prickled. I swung my leg over his hips and sat astride him, bending my head to look at the papers he held — updates on the Shadow Breakers.

Something nagged at me, and I felt something other than frustration or lust. Jealousy? Anger? Yes. Both. Gods, hurt too.

I tried to raise my walls again and Slate grabbed my hand.

"What was that, Torch? What were you thinking about?" he asked, searching my gaze.

Yes, I wanted to speak.

"You and all your lovers," I said, and he clamped his mouth shut.

It was the first time I'd spoken in almost a week. I had wanted to say something better, something that would get me rewarded, instead it looked like I'd upset him.

"Torch, I am sorry about Anthias. I have no excuse. I should have known she was not you," Slate spilled out.

His hands rested lightly on my thighs and more emotions surfaced. I didn't like a single one of them.

I made a face and swung my leg back over so I could walk. I ran my fingers through my hair. Slate and Anthias, by the Mother. Thinking about that hurt like a searing knife being stabbed into my heart and at that point I was a pro at what knife wounds felt like.

Slate was on his feet behind me. "Speak."

The new confusing pain was making it hard to focus when combined with my arousal. I crawled back into our bed and Slate slid under the blankets with me.

"Scream at me, hit me with your fists. Do something Scarlett, damn you. Do not say that, then go to sleep," he said.

He turned me around roughly, so we were face to face. "You broke my heart," I said, not understanding the words or why I'd said them.

I knew what they meant, but not if that was really how I felt.

Slate's eyes flitted between mine, and suddenly I was feeling panic through the bond. "I cannot let you go. I want you better, but I want you to be mine. Both things are not possible."

I bent forward and slanted my mouth to his. Slate sighed and wrapped his arms around me. He started pulling off my robe, and I raised my brows. That was new. He never took charge unless we were already engaged in our acts.

"Forgive me, Scarlett. I want you. I need you," Slate breathed as he tore his shorts off and rolled me onto my back.

He stared down at me, memorizing my face and the way I looked at that moment. "Say something. Anything. You can tell me not to, Torch," he said breathlessly, but we both knew he didn't want me to say stop and I didn't want to.

I was ruining the day and I had to fix it. I raised my hands to Slate's face, cupping it, and gazed dreamily into his eyes. "Make love to me, Slate."

I felt his heart lurch and mine did with it. Slate lowered himself between my bent legs, his chest pressed to mine as our mouths met. A thrill shivered through me I hadn't felt with the Merfolk, even with their cooler bodies. It was excitement beyond my carnal desires. It was antic-ipation.

My skin thrummed wherever Slate's skin touched. His body's senses overwhelmed mine so there was only him. Slate's mouth was demand-ing. I tilted my head back as his tongue found mine. Our bodies moved together in the soft sheets in a torrent of unchecked emotions. There was a sense of savoring the experience. His hair fell over his shoulder in a midnight sheet, cocooning me in glossy waves, brushing my cheek. Soft moans drew from my throat in a purr that never failed to make Slate lose his restraint.

His muscled body moved over mine in slow sensual moves as my hands glided over his silk over steel skin. The intensity was pulling forth memories like a vacuum to the forefront. Things I hadn't wanted to face.

Gods, so much anguish.

"Open your eyes," Slate breathed, and I forced my eyes open. He sucked in a deep breath. "Do you need me to stop?"

I shook my head, and he kissed the salty tears away. I pulled his mouth to mine and kissed him fiercely, needing the contact with him. Slate moved faster, deep inside me, and my body responded. Like a lodestone, my body was keenly aware of the delicious friction of him, drawn to where he slid himself.

"Say my name, Torch," Slate rumbled roughly, and I opened my eyes, looking up at him through lowered lids.

My lips were parted. "Slate," I moaned, and his neck corded with strained muscles.

My insides clenched snugly around him as he shuddered into me. Aftershocks ran through my body, and I turned my face to where his head rested on my shoulder. I stroked his hair away from his face, kiss-ing, peppering his forehead, his nose, his cheeks with soft slow pecks of my lips. He watched me with heavy silver eyes, and I could tell some-thing was wrong.

I ran the tips of my fingers down his back and rested my palm on the hard curve of his impeccable backside, keeping him inside me. I rubbed my nose against his and kissed his lips chastely before I spoke. It would be easy to make him happy again.

"I love you, Slate. Forever and always. Yours, mine — for all time," I whispered, and kissed his lips again.

He didn't kiss back. Slate pushed himself up onto his elbows and hung his head. I pushed his mane away from his bronze chiseled face and he kissed the inside of my wrist.

"You should not say those things, Torch. Perhaps you could have forgiven me with time, but I no longer believe it. Not after that," Slate rumbled and exhaled a rasping breath. "I think your family should be able to see you now. You promise to play nice?" Slate swung his silver eyes up to mine.

"I could never hate you; I love you. Can't I stay here with you?" I asked, and Slate's lips curled in a mocking smile.

"You *will* hate me and have every right to. Try to remember it was not awful the entire time."

I wrapped my legs around his waist, locking my ankles, and ran my hands through his hair. "You're wrong. I don't find this loathsome at all. Nothing about you could be." I ran my fingers over his lips as he puckered them. "I love your lips, and your silver eyes that are sometimes grey like a winter storm and sometimes silver like the still waters of a reflecting pool. The feel of your hair as it slinks over my stomach and over my thighs."

Slate laughed, his stomach muscles flexing against mine. "Gods. Any other time, Torch."

I continued, undeterred, "The way your body moves, muscles flexing, when we move together." I ran my hands down his chest to the corded 'V' at his hips. "Whatever these are, and we mustn't forget these." I smiled coyly at him as I moved my hips and his silver eyes danced.

"But if I had to pick what I loved most, it would be this." I rocked my hips back and slid my palms down his backside, squeezing tightly, pulling my tongue between my teeth teasingly.

Slate chuckled, "Oh, that is all?"

"No, but it would be obnoxious to find a book of human anatomy and read every body part off," I said playfully, and he kissed my lips.

"How do I love thee? Let me count the ways. I love thee to the depth and breadth and height. My soul can reach, when feeling out of sight. For the ends of being and ideal Grace. I love thee to the level of every day's. Most quiet need, by sun and candlelight. I love thee freely, as men strive for Right; I love thee purely, as they turn from Praise. I love with a passion put to use. In my old griefs, and with my childhood's faith. I love thee with a love I seemed to lose With my lost saints — I love thee with the breath, Smiles, tears, of all my life! — and, if God choose, I shall but love thee better after death."

Slate held me tight as he rolled us over, so I laid on top of him. "You are killing me, Torch."

"Then best we die together because I'd be lost without you," I breathed as I kissed him.

He stiffened beneath me. "No. Never say that. You will live on and find a greater happiness, much greater than anything I could dream to give you," he rumbled, brows knit. "Likely with a man you already know. One you already love."

"Shh. Love now, lecture later. I'm starving. I want you one more time before lunch," I said, lowering my mouth to his throat.

"If you are still doing well after lunch, I will bring up some of your family," Slate growled as his skin prickled at my swirling tongue.

"If you must," I said, running my teeth along his throat.

"I must," he rumbled.

Pearl sat with Hawk and Sparrow across from me. I wore a pair of my favorite sweats I hadn't worn in ages and a t-shirt from college. White marbled tiles spanned the floor of the light dusky blue room. A soft looking beige couch and oversized chair occupied the front room, throw pillows in varying shades of cream scattered across them. The sheer curtains blew across the floor on a light breeze. A rectangular, light wood table sat before it on a modern white and beige rug.

It was a full apartment, complete with a small kitchen. We headed into the dining room. There was just enough room for a circular table that sat six, the wood the same color as the coffee table. The chairs were the same dusky blue as the living room with a white hutch. One of my mother's paintings hung on the wall across from the collection of Moroccan lanterns that hung in white and blue above the round pedestal table.

They had each hugged me warily. Slate sat next to me with his hand on my knee, giving it a squeeze to occasionally to remind me of our deal. I play nice, show the family I was in good health, and we wouldn't have to wear clothes all night. My choice as to what we would do. Now that I was no longer wearing my leash, and two new rooms had become available to me, I knew what I wanted to do.

So many flat surfaces, so many options.

We'd activated the bond, the EH rune on the inside of our lower lips, so he would know when I was being too tempted. I was feeling sick, like my brain was sluggish and didn't want to process words and thoughts. It wasn't the same as what the rousen did. Then I still had energy. It was a lethargic feeling, like my body was too heavy to move.

Sparrow had gone through bouts of crying with Hawk's arm around her shoulders. I'd never seen Sparrow so weak; I didn't fault her. She'd lost her best friend, her best friend's husband, and nearly lost one of their daughters. Sparrow must've felt fried. Hawk and Pearl hadn't been looking very well either when they arrived, but when they saw me, and I smiled, everyone's moods lifted.

"How have things been?" Hawk asked, and Slate responded.

"Very well. Tomorrow she will be more herself, though she will probably have to be confined once she must take the rousen, but she is already showing considerable restraint." Slate squeezed my leg, and I smiled over at him as I pulled my hair up into a sloppy bun with the hair tie they'd brought me.

Sparrow's eyes had widened when she saw my ring hand. Slate had slipped his emerald engagement ring off my ring finger to put in place of Ash's, which was around my neck, sharing a necklace with my stone pendant and my father's wedding band. The oblong emerald sat on a silver setting with diamond antique styled arches around it and I absolutely loved it.

"The goal is to get you to one dose at night, darling, so you can function during the day. Your second year at Valla University starts in only a week," Pearl told me.

I ran my hand along the beige fabric of the couch. It was so soft. "A week? How long was I with the Merfolk?"

"Three nights," Hawk said softly, as if I would explode at any moment, but my energy was quickly draining.

Somewhere inside me I was upset, hurt even that it had taken my family so long to find me. "I've been in this apartment for four days?" I asked, looking at Slate.

Slate nodded. He was head to toe black, but not a single weapon I could discern. I knew it was because they didn't know what I would do if I got my hands on a weapon.

"Yes, darling. Ash has been worried. Do you think you are well enough to speak with him? It is better we reveal you are safe than to let them continue to search for you. Your brother, Silver, and Brass have been going on expeditions to keep up the ruse, but it is not right," Pearl explained.

"That should be fine." I looked to Slate, whose jaw clenched but nodded.

"He would have to come here. Perhaps Jett, or one of you, could stay with them," Slate rumbled in a tight voice.

"Scarlett, your father's funeral will be in two days. We didn't want to do it without you," Hawk said in a thick voice.

My hand clenched around the ring on my necklace, and emotions started pouring forth. "He didn't want me to marry Ash," I said numbly, and everyone got still. "He said his love for my mother burned bright and scorched as often as it melted, and he wanted a love like that for me. His body blocked me when the assassins came." Tears fell down my face and Slate pulled me close to him. "He told me he loved me and Indi, that he was proud of the man Jett has become."

Sparrow choked on a sob as Hawk's Adam's apple bobbed as he swallowed hard. "He pushed me behind him. We didn't see the third man. He snapped the torque around my throat, and I screamed, but one man threw a knife." My hands flew to my stomach. "Alder was telling me to run... when he turned to the third man, they hit his heart with the dagger, and we both fell onto the bed. He whispered my mother's name," I choked.

Too much!

My brain was screaming for a reprieve.

"What happened next?" Hawk asked, gently coaxing me to let it out.

"One man grabbed my ankles, yanking me off the bed and pulled his knife out of my stomach. I think he meant to heal me, but then he found the spark of life." Slate's arms tightened around me as if he could protect me from the memory.

Sparrow's hand flew to her mouth. Hawk looked at Slate, and Pearl's lips pursed.

"The man laughed. He knew somehow it wasn't Ash's, and he said he wouldn't let it live." I swallowed convulsively, "He kept stabbing until I blacked out. The next thing I remember was Brass breaking down the door, then they threw me off the balcony to a man waiting below."

Pearl wiped a tear from her cheek with a graceful, long-nailed finger. I didn't remember curling into Slate's lap, but I buried my face in his neck as he stroked my hair, murmured soothingly, but I could feel the rage emanating from him. After my days spent with Slate when my mother died, none of them felt the need to ask whose child it was, which I found some comfort in.

I wept against Slate. "I don't want to feel this anymore."

"I do not want you to feel this way, Scarlett. I would take your pain and bring into myself if I could," he said, kissing the top of my head.

I heard the click of the door shutting and Slate produced the rousen vial. "Three more visitors. You do not have to answer questions if you do not want to," he promised, and I nodded.

"All three at once."

Slate agreed and disentangled himself from my arms. He gave me a kerchief before he went to the door.

CHAPTER 6
JETT

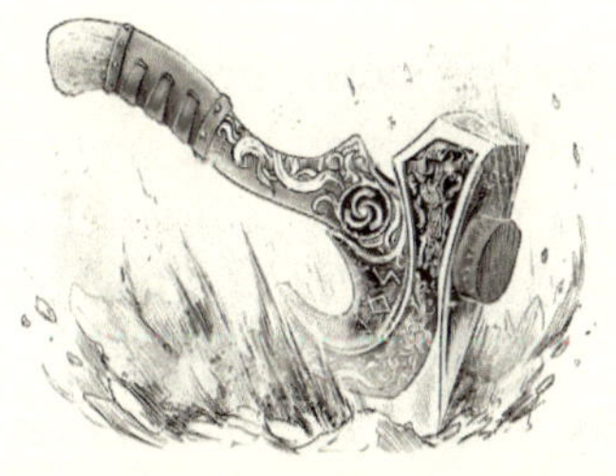

Scarlett had been back for four days, and he hadn't seen her yet. He had walked past their wing and heard her. He'd met with Slate and the others to get updates, but it wasn't the same as seeing her with his own eyes.

She had remained asleep on the trip back until they started the walk up to the palace. Jett hadn't felt her looking at him until she'd shifted. Slate had felt her wake and grabbed her from Jett's arms before she could do anything she'd regret. Then Slate and Scarlett had walked at the back of the line. They'd gone in a side door so no one would see what she was doing to Slate, and he'd left them to take her up to the wing that Slate had set up for her.

Tawny was pacing while Indigo twisted a lock of her corn silk hair in her slender fingers. His sister was a beautiful woman, slim and tan with warm blue eyes and a pretty pink pout. She had a beauty mark below her right eye that only added to her looks. Her beauty was timeless. She met Jett's eyes and gave a small smile.

Quick was at breakfast again, which wouldn't have been a big deal with everything going on, then all still pretending to be searching for

Scarlett. The truth was, Quick had been all but living with Indigo. Jett knew the need for comfort. The times they lived in made you feel like life was too short and you should grab for every happiness you could, but couldn't she grab someone else's happiness?

At least Quick hadn't been his usual smug self. In fact, Jett thought him substantially subdued. Gypsum had sought comfort in the arms of Shale and Ama. Diamond might finally have been out of the picture.

Tawny growled in frustration. The little spitfire had been bringing up the food for them herself everyday so she could get updates from Slate directly, and probably tore him a new one at every encounter.

The locks clicked as the tumblers moved and the door opened. Slate appeared in the doorway and closed the door behind him. Jett knew their time was next. They hadn't wanted to overwhelm Scarlett, so they were coming in groups of three. Gypsum had reluctantly agreed to wait until she was ready to see people since it was so close for her time to take the rousen.

"Only twenty minutes. Her mind is shutting down because she needs the rousen. She has only had it once today; Scarlett is doing very well," Slate rumbled and filled them in on everything Scarlett had already told Sparrow, Hawk, and Pearl so they wouldn't repeat her questions and put her through it again.

Jett clenched his teeth in anger, and dry washed his face. Scarlett was an empath; she'd pick up what he was feeling in a heartbeat. She might even feel it from there. The best thing to do was try to keep a brave face so she could get better faster.

"While I am certain she remembers what has gone on between us, she is choosing to ignore it. It has gone the opposite way than what we expected," Slate admitted.

Indigo furrowed her delicate brows. "I don't understand. We thought she hated you, so instead she's acting like she loves you?"

"She is. Though past events resurface, she fights them," he confessed, and turned around. "Come, there is not much time left."

They followed Slate into the little love nest Slate had created and found Scarlett sitting on a plush beige couch with her legs folded beside her. She looked almost like herself, her eyes showing a sliver of turquoise. There was still that indefinable sensual quality to her, even sitting there in sweats and a t-shirt with her caramel hair piled on top of her head.

The whites of her eyes were bloodshot from crying, and she tensed when they walked in. Her fingers curling in the hem of her shirt as if restraining herself from doing something with them. Slate came around the couch to sit next to her and she leaned against him when he put his hand in her lap.

Tawny pinched her lips together but said nothing. "Do you mind if we give you a hug?" she asked.

Scarlett looked to Slate, and he nodded, so she nodded. Tawny, Indigo, and Jett gave Scarlett hugs that didn't last nearly as long as they should have. Jett had to pull Indigo away, who kept sobbing and bring her to the couch across from Scarlett and Slate.

"You're looking well. How's he treating you?" Tawny asked first and Jett internally rolled his eyes.

"Do not ask questions you do not want a blunt answer to," Slate rumbled.

Scarlett looked at Slate again. It reminded Jett of when she kneeled before him on the shore. She did nothing he didn't want, or at least she tried not to.

Scarlett took his hand and clasped it between both of hers. "He's been amazing, Tawny," she shrugged her shoulders.

Tawny snorted and tried to mask it with a cough. "That's good, Scar. Is there anything else you need? Slate says you won't be up here much longer."

Jett had noticed she wasn't wearing her leash and found that profoundly comforting. He didn't think he could sit across from them while Scarlett kept giving Slate those looks if she had a leash on as well.

"A dress or two to choose from. I have to see more people tomorrow and as much as I like my sweats, I don't think Ash would like them."

She said it so casually Jett thought he'd misheard her, but from the way Slate was glowering at the coffee table, she'd said what he thought.

"So, you remember Ash, but have no problem being here with Slate?" Jett asked, carefully trying not to upset her.

Jett noticed the ring on her hand and closed his eyes until his temper cooled. Scarlett cocked her head as she furrowed her brows.

"Ash will never marry me now. It's as good as over."

Slate's frustration was palpable.

"Enough, Torch," Slate murmured, sounding defeated.

Slate hadn't known the extent until that moment, Jett realized. What a way to find out. She'd been right about Ash though, how breezily she'd said it had flummoxed Jett.

"I'm sorry. That must disgust you," Scarlett said, tucking her narrow braid into the bun on her head.

"By the Mother. No, you could never disgust me. It hurts me you speak so casually about these things. I know you cannot help it, but it bothers others," Slate said, gesturing to Jett, Indigo, and Tawny.

"I'm sorry." Scarlett cupped his jaw and planted a kiss on his lips before turning back to them.

Tawny cleared her throat. "I'll bring a few dresses and your makeup and stuff so you can get ready before Ash comes. Don't you let him devalue you, Scar. Any guy would be lucky to have you, breeder or not, you're fiddlesticking amazing."

"You could always adopt. Don't get hung up on the baby... thing," Indigo said, and Scarlett looked at Slate.

"It's so funny. I imagined your baby would punch its way out of my body with a blade concealed in its chubby fist. It probably would have had unruly dark waves and silver steel eyes." Scarlett looked at Slate's face and tucked a lock of his hair behind his ear.

Slate's face had gone stone hard. It must have been the first time she'd mentioned what happened with anything but anger. It proved too much for Slate. He patted Scarlett's hand and rose to his feet.

"Give me a moment. She promised to be good," Slate said as he walked out into the hall.

Tawny took his spot, and Scarlett curled her fingers into the hem of her shirt again. "For someone who didn't want children, I think it hurts him to talk about your loss, Scar. Maybe, if you can help it, try not to mention it?" Tawny urged, and Jett nearly spluttered.

"I will try. He is magnificent, isn't he? I don't want to leave this apartment. Everything hurts too much. I don't enjoy thinking about it, but he makes me. It makes him happier when I try, so I do." She shrugged.

Jett leaned forward. "Do you remember anything about Slate before the Merfolk, baby sis?"

Scarlett frowned. "I remember everything. Why wouldn't I? I remember that when I was afraid of getting close, he slept with Lera that very next morning. That the first time we were together, he left with Lera again. He came to my birthday with a girl who looked just like me and they were all over one another. I have seen him with Amber, Lera, and a few others, which I believe he lets me see intentionally. That he chased me for a year before I finally gave in because he'd proposed, when he'd convinced me to marry him, he was kissing Anthias. Why? Is that what you meant?"

Jett started. "When you say Slate slept with Lera..."

"When mom died, and I was staying in his room, he said as long as we shared a bed he wouldn't be with anyone else even though we had never been intimate at that point. I left that night after he fell asleep and the next morning, when I went to Shadow Breaker headquarters, I walked in on Slate and Lera together. That's how I became an elemental. Gods, how betrayed I'd felt. I don't know what I would've done without Brass."

"Brass," Tawny repeated and Indigo and her shot Jett death glares.

Scarlett smiled salaciously at the mention of the Regn. "Brass." She inhaled deeply. "He and Slate are so similar, yet so different. He tastes like cinnamon and his... I would very much like to see Brass." Her voice had a throaty quality that made Jett uncomfortable with the flare of her sleepy eyes.

Tawny's eyes slid past Jett and narrowed.

"If I could take it all back, I would, Torch. How does that all make you feel now?" Slate asked, and Jett held his breath.

It didn't seem like a good time for honesty.

"I already told you," Scarlett said, exasperated, "You broke my heart. If I can help it, I never want to experience that with anyone else ever again. One heart break is enough for a lifetime." She sighed, "Not even with Brass, though I think he was going to tell me something profound the night of my engagement party, until Alder interrupted him. I love him too. I told him when I thought I was going to die. That makes me *your* sister," she said, looking at Jett as she laughed at her own joke.

Jett was growing concerned about how disconnected she seemed. Her posture was growing laxer as she leaned against the couch, as if the simple act of breathing was exhausting her. Jett thought a subject change was in order.

"The girls say hello. They are excited about when things get back to normal and you can start leaving this place."

She scoffed, "They must not know I molested my rescuers with my calling. I am sorry, Indi. I am certainly sorry to you too, Tawny. I can barely look at you, Jett, without remembering what I did." She glanced at Slate, who was trying to signal her to shut her trap. "Where am I?" she asked lazily, and Tawny furrowed her brows at Slate.

"I did not want her getting out. I thought if she did not know where she was, she would be less likely to leave," Slate said from behind the couch.

He hadn't moved. The impact of Scarlett's words floored him. Tawny had been right. Once Scarlett left the room and she was better, she wouldn't even have Slate to comfort her.

"You're in the Sumar palace. One of the higher floors for families," Jett told her, and she looked thoughtful.

"I thought this place was for me. It's how I would have decorated my first apartment if I'd had a fantastic job. Well done, Slate," Scarlett told Slate with a megawatt grin, and Slate walked over to her.

That's all it took, and Scarlett had knocked down Slate's walls again. Jett wasn't sure who he felt worse for once this was over.

Tawny got to her feet and gave Scarlett a hug that she limply returned. "Is there anything special you want for dinner tonight? I can have them send up extra dessert."

Indigo and Jett rose and hugged Scarlett as she ran the pad of her finger over her upper lip. She glanced slyly at Slate in a way that made Indigo blush.

"Chocolate pudding. Slate promised if I didn't grope anyone, we could do anything I wanted." She turned to look up at him. "I want to rub pudding —"

Slate clamped a hand over her mouth, and Jett thanked the gods. He did not want to know where that sentence was going. Slate gave Scarlett a playful glare.

"Play nice, Torch."

Scarlett's eyes glittered above his big bronze hand, and she nodded.

Tawny smoothed her dress. "Right. Pudding, clothes, makeup. Got it. I love you, Scarlett. If you feel up to it, I'd like to come back with Gypsum tomorrow."

Scarlett looked to Slate. "Depends on how things go with Ash," Slate said in a tight voice, and Tawny nodded in understanding.

Twice, Tawny had not argued or said something biting when Jett was sure she would. They said their goodbyes and left the room. It locked behind them.

Tawny and Indigo immediately started crying. It had been too much for them to see Scarlett so detached. Jett draped an arm around each girl, surprised Tawny let him.

"Slate is taking good care of her. She's taking things very well. In no time, she'll be well, and we'll put all this behind us," Jett soothed.

"She acts like his dog. I hate it. That Stepford wife is not my best friend." Tawny pushed away from Jett and paced. "What was she apologizing for?"

"Take it easy Tawny. We're all doing the best we can. It doesn't matter. Ask Steel if it really bugs you, but trust me when I say you won't feel better for knowing. Brass is coming tomorrow; he'll read her mind and try to pick up the details on her kidnappers. Then we'll all have something to work towards. This is Slate's part. She looks a lot better than when we brought her in, trust me," Jett said, and she stormed off in a huff.

Indigo looked up at Jett, tears streaking her tan cheeks. "I don't care what she did to Silver. I tried rousen once, and I'd never do it again. What if Ash tells everyone?"

Jett clenched his jaw. "He will. He's spiteful. We'll try to do damage control and keep the worst of it from getting to Scarlett. You're doing great little sis, you know that, don't you? You're… taking care of yourself?" Jett asked hesitantly as her lips quirked into a smile.

"If you're referring to Silver, he's being good to me, but don't worry about me. Silver knows it isn't serious."

Jett nodded and was feeling bad for Quick.

CHAPTER

SEVEN

Seeing Jett, Indigo, and Tawny caused an upheaval of my emotions. Slate sat next to me in silence on the couch, the purple vial rolling between his hands. I wanted it and hated that I wanted it. I didn't know why I was being so nice to Slate. His proximity was making my stomach twist and I couldn't stand his thigh touching mine.

I stood to go to the bathroom, and he stood with me. I scowled at him. "Your little prisoner will be right back."

I rolled my eyes and stormed into the bathroom. I closed the door. My temper heated by the second. He shouldn't have been touching me. Gods, the things we'd been doing! The things I'd been saying!

Brass. It should be Brass. Not Slate. Gods! I'd told Brass I loved him! I confessed it to the others, had had no filter — I couldn't stop things from pouring from my mouth like verbal diarrhea.

When I came out of the bathroom, I walked to the couch across from him as he watched me with silver eyes.

"Hating me yet, Torch?" Slate asked without looking up.

76

I made a disgusted face and wished I had a hoodie on. "Take this thing off me. I won't run off, but I won't stay in here with you a second longer than necessary," I said brusquely, and he slapped the vial on the table.

"You keep it on while you take the rousen. Hold off as long as you can, but do it before you lose the function of your limbs. I can wait here with you or wait in another room. You cannot get out; I have the key," Slate said, lifting his grey stormy eyes to mine. "Your precious Brass will be here tomorrow to save you from me."

"Don't do me any favors. This is a business arrangement. I need a warm body; you don't care what body you use. Win-win." I picked up the vial from the table and popped off the cap before swallowing it all in a gulp.

The sweet liquid coursed down my throat and I got to my feet to head back into the bathroom. Slate didn't ask, and he didn't follow.

I locked the door behind me.

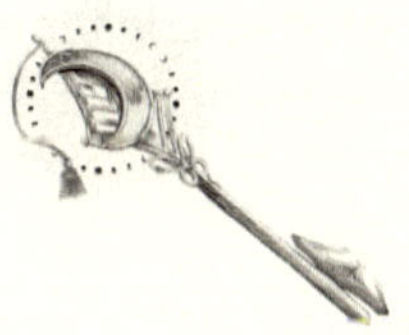

Twenty minutes later, I was singing a very different tune. I came out of my shower and saw my too huge pupils. I had haphazardly dried my hair, then slathered on lotion that made my skin satiny soft before exiting the bathroom with my champagne robe on.

I searched the living room, dining room, and finally, the bedroom for Slate. His eyes were closed on the white chaise where he laid on his back, his long muscular legs crossed in front of him. I could sense the knot of emotions in my head that were Slate's, and knew he was upset. I'd have to fix it.

I slid into his lap, and he opened his eyes. Two cool silver eyes peered out from beneath his long dark lashes to regard me.

"Come to bed," I purred, letting my robe fall open just a peek.

"Fight it, Torch. I will not make it easy on you. This is not playtime.

You are here to get better so you can move on with your life. Like you said, it is a business arrangement," Slate said coldly, and I slunk forward, pressing my breasts to his chest.

"You don't mean that. I feel you here." I pressed my hand to his chest. "It is much more than business, no matter what you say."

The clock was ticking, and I could feel my mind focusing in on one thing only. If Slate resisted, I might try to force myself on him like I'd done to others. I unclasped my stone pendant necklace and slid off my father's ring. The stone brushed platinum caught the sunlight coming through the windows.

"Stop, Scarlett. Do not start reading my emotions. They are more complicated than that," Slate admonished.

I picked his hand up by his wrist and gave him my very best smile as I slid my father's ring onto his finger. Slate stiffened, but I gripped him.

"Take it off. No more games," Slate said with an edge in his voice.

I pulled the hand up to my lips and kissed the ring on his finger. "My love for you sears as often as it melts. I think he meant for me to give it to you. I'd say my blood oath to you right now if you wished it."

I slanted my mouth over his and felt a thrill when he returned the kiss.

I'd won.

My ability to use sentences didn't return until well after dinner, when the rousen had been in my system for a good three hours. Turned out I didn't need sentences to lick chocolate pudding off Slate's body. I took note for future interactions. After my tongue bath, we decided on a proper bath, and climbed into the big ivory tub filled with lavender scented bubbles.

Our interludes were changing. We didn't need to discuss it, but things had taken a turn for the slower and sensual rather than the quick and fevered. There was a kind of reassuring complacency that I knew would be dangerous. That didn't stop us from falling into it, though.

I straddled Slate's lap as I undid his dozens of narrow braids, removing the beads and fetishes. The water sloshing over his partially submerged chest as he stroked my skin unfettered. I lowered my eyes to his and gave him a pert smile as he tugged on my pink nipple. He couldn't stop touching me.

I removed the last bead and leaned forward to run my fingers through his wavy mane from scalp to ends. He leaned his head back and let me have at it.

"I want to wash your hair. Maybe I'll give you a shampoo mohawk," I teased throatily, and he arched an eyebrow at me with a curl of his lips.

"Do I look like a man who does shampoo mohawks?" he asked, sliding his hand over my hips to cup my backside.

"How do you know if you never tried?" I gave him my very best smile and picked up the shampoo to begin my work. "Why haven't you given me any other carvings?" I asked distractedly, as I worked the shampoo through his hair.

"You received a fetish for your birthday. Your braid is complete," he said grumpily, and I laughed.

"Dunk your head. You have my promise that I won't drown you," I told him, and he sunk under the surface, sliding me further away in the tub and back. "You're jealous Solder gave me the turquoise tree," I said matter of fact.

"Jealous," he scoffed, wiping his face with an enormous hand.

His long lashes were even darker with the water drops on them. Rivers of water poured along the ridges of his muscles in a way that made me sigh.

"You know, I can feel what you feel," Slate teased, and I put my hands on my hips.

I gave a coquettish smile.

Slate pulled me closer in his lap as he nuzzled my breast, making me giggle.

"Enough of that. Let me finish washing you," I told him, pulling his face away with my fingers gripping his hair.

"Gods, Scarlett," Slate embraced me tightly, and I rested my head on the crook of his corded neck. "If you want to still do the blood oaths tomorrow, before you need to take the rousen..." Slate trailed off.

I took his ring hand from my body and kissed it, lacing my hand through his. "I love you, Slate. Forever and always. Mine, yours, the world's, for all time," I promised.

"I am yours," Slate murmured against my chest.

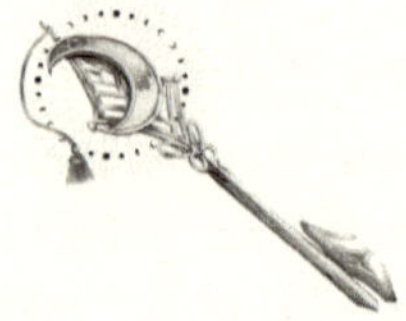

I wore a flowing teal chiffon dress with a sweetheart neckline and capped sleeves. My hair fell in waves to my waist, and I even applied some makeup before Slate's growling made me put down my brush and turn to him with a wry grin.

"You do not need all that. Are you looking to impress him, Torch?" Slate asked from where he stood with his arms crossed over his broad chest in the doorway to the bathroom.

I'd taken his ring off and switched it with Ash's. Since then, Slate had been looming over me like a dark storm cloud. I was being vain, and I knew it, but if Ash was going to turn me down today, I wanted to at least look like I had it together.

I crossed the bathroom and slid my arms around his waist. "Someone is pouting," I chided.

"Someone is going above and beyond to entice her betrothed back to her." Slate looked down his straight, masculine nose at me.

"I've spent a year with him already. I may not love him, but I knew he would take care of me. Perhaps not now, but that is what he is coming here for, isn't it?"

"How easily your heart changes," Slate murmured, disentangling himself from my arms and I sighed.

Slate waited in the dining room with Jett when Pearl came in with Ash. The caramel skinned man was slightly shorter than Slate and leaner muscled, but by no means small. His brown hair was cropped close to his head like Jett's and his winged brows were masculine and dark above celadon green eyes. He smiled at me with sensual lips when he stepped into the dusky blue living room and saw me sitting on the beige couch.

He strode purposefully across the room and picked me up, swinging me around and making me smile. Slate's anger flared through the bond at my brief delight. I had promised to be good. My urges were not as intense, and it was before the lag of not having taken the rousen kicked in. I was more myself than at any other point during the day.

"May we have some privacy, Pearl, please?" Ash asked without looking at her.

Pearl's emerald cat eyes accessed us and smiled. "Of course, Ash. Remember, she is not herself yet," she said before joining the men in the dining room.

The door opened to reveal Slate and Jett sitting side by side at the round table, their heads lifting when Pearl came through and spotted us embracing. Ash placed a finger under my chin and turned my head back to him. I couldn't focus, though, my bond with Slate burning inside my mind with his fury.

"They have filled us in on what happened. Scarlett, I am sorry about Alder," Ash said sympathetically as he ran the pads of his fingers along my jaw.

"Thank you. We should sit. There's a lot more you don't know," I told him and led him to the beige couch. "I'll tell you from the beginning."

I gave Ash the abridged version. The Stygian Knights captured me. I left out Dion're, Non're with his rope room, and Larn'ra. I told him the Merfolk saved me from the Knights.

"There's another thing." I told him nervously and took his hand and placed it on my stomach. "Delve," I said, and he knit his brows.

He was silent during my story, his face hard. I felt the warmth of his calling flood through me and the muscle in his jaw leapt.

"You are barren," Ash said flatly. His fingers slid from under mine. He got to his feet and started pacing.

"I am," I admitted.

"You slept with the Merfolk. You were on rousen? Are you still on it?" he asked, looking down his nose at me.

I shifted uncomfortably in my seat. "I take it at least twice a day, depending how bad things get."

"Who sees to your... needs?" Ash asked, then glared at the dining-room door. "It is the orphan, yes?"

Ash stalked to me and yanked me up to my feet. "Does he use your body like the Merfolk did? Like a kerchief to blow their waste?" His eyes darted between mine and hurt flickered through them, "Consider the marriage contract void. I could never marry a khoraz."

My chest constricted. *Khoraz.* The Tidings word for a person who desired the tribes. Ash's former lover had attacked me months before and carved the word into my skin. An inguz rune with a hidden Shadow Breaker tracker was tattooed over it.

Ash's cruel words were like knives slicing away the remains of what I'd hoped my life would one day be. In one night, I'd lost everything when those men captured me.

His hands dug into my biceps where he held me. "Ash, I'm sorry. There was no way I could have predicted any of this. I care about you," I said in a strain.

He sneered with his sensual lips, and then it became a smile. With my empath abilities, I could feel the mask of his emotions. Betrayal gave way to vengeance, but that underlying hurt couldn't be hidden.

"I cannot marry you, Scarlett. You will never have children. What you have done will become gossip. Perhaps we need not end on a sour note. You are still a beautiful woman," Ash said as his celadon eyes scanned mine.

It was like someone pulled a trigger in my mind. He was letting off something I found irresistible, more so than my other visitors. My eyes slid lower, and my lips parted as I licked them. His eyes glittered as he gripped the back of my head roughly with a wicked smile.

His lips crushed over mine and I moaned against his mouth. I still had the nix torque on. Slate wouldn't remove it until after today. He promised it was the last day I would have to wear it all day. I wound my arms around Ash's neck and his hand picked me up under my backside as he laid me down on the beige couch.

The dining-room door crashed open, and Ash lifted his head as I kissed along his throat, my hands eagerly roaming over his body.

"Torch, get up. Now," Slate said low and dangerous.

I balled my hands into fists and squeezed my eyes shut.

My chest heaved as Ash righted himself, leaving me laying on the couch with my dress pushed up around my thighs. I opened my eyes and found Ash looking down at me. Jett stood in the dining room door-way. Pearl was nowhere to be seen.

Slate was furious. I could feel it. Ash made a point of adjusting himself and smirked. He bent down over me.

"We can explore other avenues of this relationship whenever you wish, Scarlett," Ash said, and placed another kiss on my lips.

He turned to Slate and Jett and walked by, but turned his head when they were side by side.

"Does it bother you she only comes willingly to you now? When it was her choice, it was me." Ash looked back at me. "But not even he can keep you, Scarlett. You will never be happy with nothing." Slate bared his teeth in a growl and Ash sniffed as he left the room.

Pearl hurried out of the dining room and to my side, helping me get upright and smoothing my dress over. "Are you alright, darling? Did he hurt you?"

"Only my feelings. I feel like an emotional punching bag," I told her, and she wrapped her arms around me.

"Give it time. None of this will matter in a short while," she soothed, her floral, musky scent wafted around me. "Gossip has a short shelf life."

"It's over. No more wedding. Ash will no doubt have his family send out a release today and he'll have another woman on his arm by the induction ceremony," I said dryly, and shook my head.

"You don't sound very upset," Jett said carefully and sat on the armrest across from me.

"I expected it. No one from a greater family wants to marry a woman who can't have children."

I leaned against the armrest and ran a hand through my hair. It was too easy. Ash wouldn't let it go. He wasn't built that way. Dealing with the retribution would be the harder part.

A knock sounded on the door, and my gut twisted. I couldn't take any more of Ash. The rousen was causing a lag and my emotions were surfacing in painful ways that made me almost desperate for it.

Slate hadn't moved. Jett set his jaw and went to the door. Pearl rose beside me and crossed the room with Jett.

"It's Brass," Jett announced, and my heart skipped.

Slate's jaw flexed, and I tried to temper my emotions.

"I shall be going. Slate thinks tomorrow will be the best day yet, darling. I am looking forward to seeing you at breakfast." Pearl gave me a warm smile that reminded me of my mother, and I felt an ache in my heart that would never mend.

Pearl and Jett left. I gave Jett me a tight hug, and I inhaled my brother's woodsy, amber scent that blended with sunshine. My brother's scent didn't make me lose my cool. Why had Ash?

Brass filled the doorway. He was a few inches shorter than Slate, but just as broad and muscular. His skin was a shade darker, a dark honey that went beautifully with his dreamy amber eyes. His dark hair was pulled back in dozens of braids with bronze and ebony beads that fell just past his shoulders. Plump defined lips curled into a smile when those amber eyes met mine.

I got to my feet and flashed my best smile before I crossed the room. I stopped just before I reached him. Touching him might prove to be too much for me.

... I'm sorry for what I did to you on the shore...

Brass's cheeks reddened. It was the first of many apologies I'd have to make before it was over.

"Water under the bridge," Brass said, and he took another step forward.

I scanned his eyes and chewed my lower lip.

"You did not know what you were doing. We are good, Scarlett."

I let out an exhale and smiled. Curse my fickle emotions. I was blinking at him through tears.

... I don't know what I would've done if you hadn't shown up. If they had taken me and no one knew what happened. You gave me hope that someone would start searching for me right away...

I took a shuddering breath and swallowed against the lump in my throat. Brass closed the last step between us and wrapped his arms. I cried hard against him; my fingers dug into the back of his black linen shirt. I tried to ignore my body's response to his but it was difficult.

"I heard your thoughts and ran upstairs, trying every door. I am sorry it took me so long," he murmured into my hair.

I breathed him in. Cinnamon, spring rain, and man. There was that scent Ash had that swirled around him, but muted. Still, I could feel the slow stoke of the fire in me that had never quite died anymore.

... I shouldn't have said what I said. I thought I was going to die and being gone without you knowing...

"I understand," he whispered, muffled by my hair.

My breaths were deep, and I was losing control. I buried my nose in the crook of his neck and pressed my lips to his dark honey skin. His jaw rasped against my cheekbone, and I kissed higher, no longer hiding what I was doing in our embrace. I needed Brass. He took a step back, prying himself free with great effort.

... I'm sorry. If I rip your clothes off, Slate will murder us both...

Brass turned his head, acknowledging Slate for the first time who had sat down on the couch, his legs crossed in front of him while he watched us. The knot of raw emotions in my head let me know just how pleased he was with our silent communications and kisses.

"Please, come sit," I told Brass and led him over to the couch across from Slate and patted the cushion next to me.

Slate's emotions flared with frustration, and I could only imagine what Brass heard from him.

I made pleasantries with Brass, not wanting to talk about anything that had to do with me. I asked about Quick and Indigo and confirmed what I'd suspected about Gypsum, Ama, and Shale.

Quick was Brass's younger brother, a notorious playboy in Tidings. The man was cockier than anyone I'd ever met and had good reason to be. He was darkly handsome with olive skin, dark eyes that always seemed to twinkle with mischief and was built like his brother, though a little leaner. You knew just by looking at him that all that energy translated into the bedroom.

I wasn't sure how I felt about Gypsum. I wanted him to find a good partner and not get caught up in the craziness that happened when you were the heir to a palace or island like Gypsum.

"I hate to interrupt your gossiping, but I am not sure how much longer you have." Slate's eyes had been cool while his anger built.

"I haven't seen Brass since they captured me, not really anyway."

"Do you remember who captured you, Scarlett? Any description would help," Brass said, ignoring us both.

I knit my brows together and ran my thumb along Ash's ring. I took it off — I didn't know why I still had it on. Flipping over Brass's hand, I placed Ash's ring into his palm. My fingers trailed around his palm until I stilled them.

"Take it, please. I don't care what you do with it. I never want to see it again," Brass nodded, and I ran a hand through my hair, trying to fortify myself. "It was the Stygians. Two bearded men and a fair skinned, clean-shaven man. I couldn't see much else. The one was the same man from the night of my birthday. He taunted me, telling me I should have fought topless like he'd said."

Slate interrupted me, "What is this?"

Brass looked at me. "When we were tied to the chairs after they captured us, this Stygian did not like how Scarlett spoke to him, so he sliced her dress down the front and told her to fight to the death exposed. Scarlett rotated the dress, so the exposed part was at her back. Clever." Brass tried to lighten my mood, and I offered him a small smile.

"Why was I not told?" Slate growled.

"Because it was not important. You are sure it was him? What else happened? They did not..." Brass trailed off.

"No. No humans, *um*. I'm sure it was him. Beyond a doubt. I don't know where the third man went. He had left us at the Straumr palace. The other bearded man was less offensive. They put me to sleep and when they woke me, they forced me to drink rousen. They brought me to the waterline and cut off my clothes while I was bound and dragged me into the water. Non're was waiting for us at the fortress cove."

I swallowed hard. Emotions rose with images of Non're, and his rope room and my stomach twisted.

"Do you want some water, Torch?" Slate asked, rising to his feet.

I nodded, swallowing again.

Brass was looking away. I didn't want anyone knowing what went on in that fortress, but I felt the need to explain.

"Non're asked me to stay two nights with him before and I turned him down. Obviously, he was insulted. I'd ousted Larn'ra's role in the Merfolk traitors. The men knew who I was, but not my relationship to Non're."

Slate handed me a glass of water and I thanked him for it, taking large gulps to quench my dry throat.

"Non're accepted me as payment... Do you need me to keep going?" I asked, looking between the two of them.

Brass looked at Slate and patted my hand before withdrawing it again. "It may help to talk about it. We will pass no judgement, Scarlett," Brass gave me a warm smile.

"Non're led me to a room, and I should have known something big was going on because I was throwing myself at him and he kept turning me down. He leashed me and left me in the room. That was when Dion're entered from a side door."

Slate shot to his feet, startling me. "Dion're? The Merfolk King? He took you? He knew who you were?" Slate's hands curled as if he was imaging strangling the king.

"Sit down, Slate," Brass said in his smooth, deep voice. Brass got very stiff, and Slate looked at him.

I knew Brass had picked up images in my mind. "If I tell you..."

"No, of course I do not care. Gods, Torch. How many times do I have to say it?" Slate growled.

"Perhaps it is how you say it?" Brass offered and Slate shot him a look.

My jaw set. "I already told you! They had me drugged and blindfolded!" I threw my glass at Slate, and he caught it out of the air and, since I finished my water, I didn't even have the satisfaction of spraying him.

Brass placed his hand on my knee, and I sucked in a breath, trying to control how badly I wanted him to keep inching higher. "He isn't condemning you. He is not very good at expressing himself. Are you, captain?" Brass looked at Slate, who grunted.

"I need air," Slate said and crossed the room to slam the door behind him.

I stared after him. He'd left me. He hadn't left me other than to shout out into the hall since we'd arrived. I'd even forced my way into the bathroom with him occasionally.

Brass rubbed his brow with his fingers. "Scarlett. Maybe you will tell someone one day. If you do not, know that I know already. You can always talk to me about what happened with Non're and Larn'ra. The Merfolk princess took Slate. Did you know that?"

"Sear're mentioned that on Steel's first visit there, he lost track of Slate and Larn'ra had him for almost a day," I told Brass.

"Yes. Slate was too young, and Larn'ra was inexperienced with rousen. She gave him too much. Rousen had a stranglehold over Slate for months afterwards. It took him weeks to get to where you are now, and you probably had twice as much as he had. By all rights, the both of you should be dead. You would not eat and only slept if you passed out from over exertion. Cordillera was Slate's trainer. She took him in and cared for him like he does for you. Except Lera's interpretation of caring for someone is profoundly different."

Brass sighed and took his hand from my knee to run it through his thick hair. "Lera also trained Steel and Jett. Lera thought Slate was getting attached to her. I am sure he was. Lera was a woman he was sleeping with regularly for the first time in his life. She let him catch her with Jett."

I made a face. "Lera slept with my brother?"

Brass nodded, "Something may have happened with Steel as well, but Lera has always been one to stack the odds. Slate was heartbroken and furious. Jett and Slate got into a fight and since then Slate has not gotten involved with a woman. Not seriously. My point is, Slate understands better than anyone else what you have gone through. His was not as... intense, but he has been there."

Intense.

I scoffed internally. When I thought about it, I grew disgusted with myself. If Dion're had kept me, I would have been safe. He had thought Larn'ra would take care to make sure Non're wouldn't hurt me, but he'd been wrong. It was Larn'ra who had been out to teach me a lesson.

EIGHT

The time passed with painstaking slowness until Slate came back. Brass ignored how I ran my hands along his arms and thighs as we spoke, unable to keep them to myself. Slate left a vial of rousen on the dining room table for me and by the time Brass had to leave, I was having a hard time walking, so he'd had to hand me the vial.

"There is something else."

He pulled out an envelope from inside his jerkin. Blood stained the corner. Across the front, ALDER scratched across the crumpled front. My heart sunk.

"Thanks," I said numbly.

"I can put it away. Whenever you work up the nerve to read it, I can tell you where to find it."

I nodded, and Brass took the envelope from me. I couldn't process whatever my mother had to say in that letter to my father. Both of whom were dead.

Brass disappeared further into the wing before returning a few minutes later. "I guarantee you will not accidentally stumble upon it."

He bent down to kiss the top of my head, and I searched his eyes as he withdrew.

"You could stay," I told him, popping the cork from the vial.

Brass froze, "You do not know how tempting that is, Scarlett."

He promptly left, flashing me a rueful smile, and locking the door from the outside.

It was a good thing too, because a half hour after I took the rousen I was climbing the walls trying to get out. I tried the door half a hundred times, screaming in frustration. It only kept getting worse. Without release and constant touching, my skin was feeling like someone had set it on fire. I stripped off my dress and pulled on my robe and prowled around the room, hissing in futility.

Slate was punishing me for kissing Ash. Not that I blamed him, but this was his job. All he had to do was show up! I had no qualms about doing the work.

I sat on the couch and glared at the door.

It wasn't Slate who entered the room four hours after he left. When the deadbolt clicked, I shot to my feet, preparing to tear his clothes off with my teeth if he tried to restrain me. I was past the point of being able to speak. All I had was body language.

A shadow much taller and broader than Slate's filled the room, and I came to a standstill across from it. He was charcoal grey, with long pointed ears that would have been in the place of human ears with three sets of horns curling from its head. The barghests short snout pulled back in a canine smile, revealing teeth as long as my fingers. Horns adorned his head, and it had black hair that hung down. It was easily seven feet tall. The barghest man rippled with sleek, bunched muscles ready to attack as it locked the door behind itself.

It had pants on and nothing else.

I knew about this game. I turned my back to it and glanced over my shoulder. The barghest hybrid's nostrils flared as it lifted its snout into the air. I opened my robe and slid it past my shoulders. Its eyes flared as it watched, his clawed hands moved down to its pants and the much too large bulge straining against it. I turned back and let the satin robe billow as it slid to the floor.

I didn't look back as I took off running. It pounced on me just before the dining room doors and clamped its teeth on my neck as it kicked my ankles apart. It pinned me under its body to the floor before he gave me a little slack. I tilted my hips to him. He growled as he pushed into me, making me moan.

The barghest had visited me a few times before. They were often brief interactions, too short. We'd never took it to that level.

His teeth never let up. It wasn't lovemaking; it was a claiming. He was hard, reducing me to mindless mush.

He slid his clawed hand between my legs, and I clenched around him. He roared as he poured into me.

"*Mine,*" he growled.

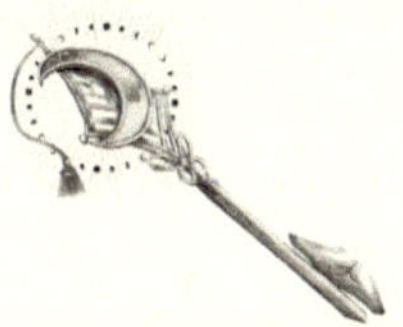

Slate woke me with breakfast in bed the next morning and there wasn't a muscle in me that wasn't sore. "Where did you go last night?" I accused, pulling the comforter to my chest.

Slate arched a brow. "Do you care, Torch?"

"Of course I care," I snapped.

A smile curled my lips. I was feeling good, more like me than I had in ages. Slate seemed to recognize it, too.

"Do you want me to remove the torque? You can leave it off until you take it tonight. Brass said you waited as long as you could. Good job," Slate said, laying on his side fully dressed beside me as he picked up the fork on his tray.

"Did you see a woman?" I asked and hated how it'd sounded.

Slate's lips curled mockingly as he chewed a piece of his omelet. "What do you think?"

"I think I want a straight yes or no from you or you can leave," I huffed, crossing my arms.

Slate reached up and unsnapped my nix torque, and I sighed in relief. Gods, it was good to get that thing off.

"I was not intimate with a woman when I went out, Scarlett. Happy?" Slate teased and I nodded.

"Don't worry. Tonight is the last night... weren't we supposed to have breakfast with the family?" I asked, frowning.

"Yes, but I let you sleep in. You are well again, Scarlett. Free to leave. I recommend locking yourself in your room or this one, if you wish, when you take the rousen. That is it," he rumbled.

His hand touched my hand, and I felt the warmth of his healing melt into me. My soreness faded.

That was it?

"I'm better?" I asked, looking down at my tray.

Fear and anxiety beat in my stomach.

"Do you not feel better?" Slate asked distractedly, and I nodded.

"I suppose," I muttered.

"What is wrong, Torch? Do you wish to stay?" Slate asked, lifting glittering silver eyes to mine.

With me.

"No, it's fine. Maybe I'm still feeling the effects of the rousen. Is that why you didn't stay with me all night?" I asked, trying to sound nonchalant.

"Effects from the rousen? I did not stay because you did not need me."

I made a face as I pushed my food around my plate. I set it aside and pulled the plush throw blanket from the chaise with my calling and wrapped it around myself.

"Forget it. Thanks for everything," I murmured as I walked from the bedroom.

I went into the closet and pulled out a taupe, strapless chiffon dress and a pair of gold flats. The sooner I got out of the room, the sooner I could work out my emotions. I didn't like how I was feeling. How *Slate* was making me feel.

"Come eat," Slate said from behind me.

His energy crackled around me; he had a draw to him like no one I'd ever met. I didn't turn around while holding my clothes.

"I'm not hungry. I can get something from the kitchens later," I muttered to the back wall of the closet.

I felt Slate so close his breaths puffed at the hair on my head. "What is your plan for when you need to take the rousen?" he asked.

"I'll fight the urges," I told the wall.

"You can come see me. I promise not to touch another woman until you are through, Torch," Slate breathed and my skin prickled.

"I'll activate the bond if I need you. Is that okay?" I asked.

"That will work. Scarlett?" he asked.

I sucked in a steadying breath and turned around. "Yes?" I asked weakly, and he gave me a salacious grin.

"Are you still having urges?" he asked again.

"If I was?" I breathed.

"Then I suppose I could help you," Slate rumbled.

Slate and I had been greeting one another in the mornings with sex every day. Maybe that was why I was feeling so off kilter. My body still needed it. I dropped my dress and shoes and reached to his belt, pulling his shirt from his pants, then pulled it over his head, making his hair fall around his hard muscled shoulders.

He watched me intensely. "Do you need me, Scarlett?"

"Yes." I breathed, and I let the blanket fall to my feet.

Slate's eyes slid over my body and back up to my face. "Good girl, Torch."

He scooped me up by my thighs and I wrapped my legs around his waist as we kissed deeply, passionately, and the feeling of something ending hung heavy in the air.

WE MADE love like two people spending their last day on earth together. I wanted to be with him in every way possible, in every room. He obliged me vigorously and we laid on the living room floor in one another's arms. He called his pants into the room and the down comforter from the bed.

We cocooned ourselves in the big blanket and he pulled something out of his pocket and unwrapped it.

"A gift," he said, and he made a new braid in my hair.

He pinched the two silver beads between his fingers around my braid, and I noticed they were the same ones he wore. I rolled onto my side so our stomachs touched and ran my fingers down his side.

"I didn't get you anything," I said, feeling disappointed that they had trapped me in the apartment so I couldn't get him a gift.

He held up his ring hand to display the band I gave him and his lips curled. "You did."

My cheeks heated, and I nestled against his chest.

"One day at a time. One hour, one minute. That is how you make it through. Soon it will be a week, then a month. Before you know it, a year will pass, and you will feel better."

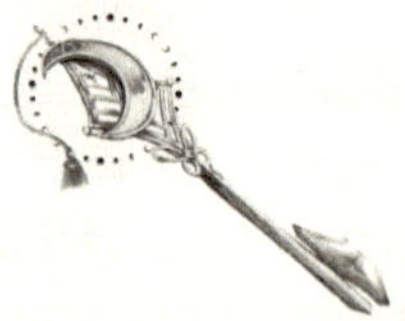

We left all our unsaid words in the apartment when we went to lunch. They held meals in the informal dining room when there were less than seventeen people. We were usually in a packed house. I told Slate to go ahead so I could get ready, and he reluctantly left the apartment.

I put on the dress and shoes I'd dropped in the closet and took a little extra time on my hair and makeup since it was the first time I'd been out and about since my engagement party, ten days earlier. The induction ceremony for Valla University's first-year students was in a few days, and I had no intention of missing it since people would count on it.

If they were going to gossip about me, it would have to be to my face.

Tomorrow was Alder's funeral. We'd see all the greater families and the ambassadors from the islands. I'd always hung back in Ash's shadow, but now I'd be on my own. Especially if Indigo and Quick went as a couple, which they seemed to be, according to Brass, who was at a loss to explain Quick's sudden interest in Indigo.

The apartment was on one of the higher floors, so I had to walk down six floors through the Sumar palace. The warm breeze blew over my skin. I leaned on the windowsill, letting the sun warm my face. They erected the Sumar palace on the side of a cliff. Hundreds of white pueblo-styled houses stacked along the side of the cliff in a slope, each one with a royal blue roof, some with gardens that were call assisted since vegetation tended not to flourish in Thrimilci. The town heart was at the base of the cliff where the portal gate was.

I didn't get crushes on boys like other girls did. When a boy had asked me out on my very first date, it had been a group date when I was fifteen. I had had my first kiss, and it was terrible. The only boy I'd been attracted to before Tidings was Chris, my prom date. I'd given up on boys.

I had appalling taste in men. It wasn't some big secret; Tawny knew it best just how badly it was. That's how I knew I had to stay away from Slate. I'd been attracted to him from the moment I saw him on a visceral level. Ash had found me mere moments before I'd seen Slate, and I'd been thankful for the distraction. Ash was gorgeous and charming, but I didn't see in him what I saw in Slate. It grew each time I was alone with Slate — which he had gone through great lengths to ensure.

Brass was the only man that made sense in my life, and I'd ruined things between us by shacking up with Slate. I was in the process of accepting the consequences of those actions.

Then Ash and I had broken up the day my mother died; the first thing I did was go crawling to Slate. I'd slept in his bed, let him take care of me, and then after he'd slept with Lera, I went to Brass. It was the story of my life. Then there was the pregnancy. I'd thought about it hundreds of times. After I caught Ash with Crimson in Mabon, I'd crawled back to Brass. Slate was a fluke. I was so swept away by his proposal and the wing he'd remodeled for us; I'd given myself to him without a second thought.

My mother would not have condoned the way I was living my life.

She'd hate that I was relying on men to build me up, when she'd done everything on her own. She was stronger than I was. I'd always known that. It was time to put men aside and work on myself, to stop letting men decide who I was or where I was going with my life.

I would start by finding the Stygians who killed my father and wipe them out from the face of the earth, but not before I found out who hired them and if they were the ones who killed my mother. It was something I'd been thinking about but hadn't uttered aloud. There was this nagging feeling like I was missing something bigger, but the bottom line was this, the Stygian Knights wanted Slate dead, they killed my father, had sold my body for the royal Merfolk's pleasure, and might connect to my mother's death. They had it coming.

I knew exactly where I would need to start, too. I'd need to get trained by the Shadow Breakers and get the connections they had. Like Styg, the black-market dealer I had tracked to the Shadow Breakers for the first time. I had no delusions that I could get Slate and the others on his team to help me, but Styg wouldn't give two sugarfoots about me. I needed something he wanted to be privy to his secrets.

I walked into the informal dining room with purpose. It was like someone stopped the record. Pearl sat at the head of the table with Steel on her left and Hawk on her right. Sparrow searched for Hawk's hand, with Gypsum and Indigo beside them. Tawny sat beside Steel with Jett between the girls. Slate sat next to Amethyst on the end and his silver eyes followed me as I glided into the room.

My usual routine would be to hug and kiss everyone around the table before sitting, so I did. My heart twisted when Gypsum cringed away. I put it on my mental agenda to apologize profusely for molesting my cousin after I gave him some time.

I sat in the carved cream upholstered chair next to Indigo and flashed everyone my very best smile. Jett's eyes widened, and Steel blushed. I needed to work on less provocative and sunnier and brighter.

"Good afternoon. I'm sorry I didn't make it to breakfast, but I'll try to make it to dinner," I said as I took dishes from the beautifully carved table.

The blue morning glory still clung to the wall from the first morning we'd arrived, reminding me of my mother and adding a floral scent to the room. The others stared at me, and I tried to ignore it. Something had changed in me. I moved differently, more fluid and alluring than purposeful. I'd always been clumsy, but I didn't think I would be anymore. The rousen had changed the very makeup of my mind, and that eternal fire inside me that never quite went out was present. That fire concerned me the most. It affected my will — that wouldn't do.

"What are your plans for today?" Tawny asked with a wide mouth smile.

"I was hoping to get some fresh air. Maybe do a little shopping. I want to train tomorrow, um, but today I thought I'd take it easy. I don't want to go too far from... home," I said, dropping my eyes to my grilled lemon chicken and avocado salad.

"Should you be leaving the palace yet?" Jett asked, trying not to sound too concerned about unleashing his sex crazed sister out into the public.

He looked at Slate, and I felt a pull of irritation. "Yes, Jett. If I didn't think I could handle it, I wouldn't jeopardize others. Tawny. Indi, would you two like to join me? I was thinking we could go to Valla to shop."

And look for a certain black-market dealer.

I'd purposefully made sure Slate and I wouldn't have the bond. Besides, if things were going to go back to normal, I couldn't go around with his emotions in my head — quoting poetry to him and telling him I love him.

I cringed.

Gods, even remembering it hurt. I'd overindulged in Slate that morning, and I hoped it would work like food. Too much of a good thing was bad, could make you sick. Ash had been right about one thing. Slate would dump me on my fanny pack as soon as a bigger, better deal came along, and I had to put as much distance between us as possible.

Last night had clinched it. He'd asked me to say the blood oath with him, the Guardian equivalent of vows, and he'd never shown up. If that wasn't cold feet, I didn't know what was.

Not that I would have.

I'd offered while on rousen and, I mean, *okay*, I gave him my father's ring, but I was also on drugs. Lots of drugs. Slate couldn't be faithful and after Ash, I didn't want to deal with any of that.

"Just asking, baby sis. Are you bringing any guards?" Jett asked, and I tried very hard not to be irritated.

"I don't think anyone cares about me anymore. I'm all but forgotten," I said dryly, and stabbed a grape tomato with my fork.

Hawk cleared his throat. "Scar, there was a messenger today —"

I gestured with my hand, dropping my fork. I'd been expecting it.

"It's bad, isn't it? It was too easy yesterday." I giggled hysterically and shut my mouth tight when my family looked worried.

"Sorry," Indigo whispered as she handed me the scroll.

Notice of Annulment

We have granted Ash Straumr an annulment from the marriage contract between Scarlett Tio and himself because of the revelation of several infidelities perpetrated by Miss Tio.

The most recent being the manhunt after the murder of her father, Alder Var heir to Ostara, that resulted in finding Ms. Tio with the Merfolk.

Consequently, she is unable to bear children.

Notice Of Engagement

Quartzite Natt and Ash Straumr have signed their marriage contract.

We will announce a betrothal ball at a later date.

All Hail The Happy Couple!

I unrolled the vellum and read it. I stared at the paper until the words no longer made sense. They made it sound like I had collaborated with his murderers, and my time with the Merfolk had been some sort of vacation.

I didn't even mean to do it. My calling sprung up and lit the heavy vellum up like flash paper, so not even the ash remained. Someone yelped, and I mumbled an apology.

Annulment and engagement in the same message — at least they didn't waste paper. Ash believed in going big or going home. I should have seen it coming. Quartz was a surprise. Part of me felt bad for Crimson. She must've felt passed over yet again.

CHAPTER

NINE

After lunch, I cornered Gypsum and apologized profusely. My hands wrung of their own volition. He forgave me and gave me an incredibly awkward shoulder punch before leaving. Indigo and Tawny met me in the portal room at the Sumar palace. Its blue faux starry light reflected all around the room like a cloudless night.

My twin looked stunning in a cotton candy pink chiffon dress, and Tawny was gorgeous in deep purple. We walked through the huge mirrored double doors with spokes radiating from a gold center circle, with white ovals around each spoke. The portal door in the palace looked like a blazing sun.

A fifteen-foot-high mosaic arch was the town's portal gate, done in whites and blues, spiraling ironwork below it radiating from a blazing sun and below that an iron patch work door. The blazing sun was the sigil of the Sumars and it was everywhere.

Behind us, the white palace sat atop the cliff with its sky reaching turrets and pointed gold and metallic blue domes. The rivers Mani and

Sol ran behind it to a waterfall that my ancestors had built a huge balcony over so we could look down into its watery depths.

We walked the shiny roads made up of white stones compressed into a flat surface that shimmered from the hot perpetual summer sun. Shops lined the market street. White plaster buildings with gold embossed signs and blue mosaic patterns that stretched as far as I could see.

"Where did you want to shop?" Tawny asked, looping her arm through mine.

I took Indigo's arm with my other one as we walked. "Nowhere in particular. Something for tomorrow. Then maybe we can head to Valla and see Bronze, Katydid, and Cricket? I could really use a change," I said.

"You won't color your hair, will you?" Indigo asked, looking scandalized.

I shrugged, "Maybe."

I wouldn't, but it was worth the look on Indigo and Tawny's faces.

Quality girl time was exactly what I'd needed. I'd spent so much time with Slate, the bottomless well of virility and testosterone. Some estrogen in my system was just the ticket. I found a suitable dress for Alder's funeral and a thank you gift for Slate before we left for Valla.

Sculptured tree branches framed the freestanding stone portal gate. A statue of a woman twisted up, hands extended to form branches that crested the top and were covered in freshly fallen snow. They designed the center of Valla in a star formation. There were only three gates to leave the city. Six roads split and led to the gates, Urd, Verdandi, and Skuld: past, present, and future. Urd gate led to the Straumr palace, Verdandi to beyond the city, and Skuld led to the Tio palace. Urd and Skuld both had paths that led past the farmlands and up to Valla U. The store fronts along the cobbled roads reminded me of a quaint European town, though the town was hardly quaint.

I knew from personal experience Tidings was a surprising mix of old world and modern. Away from the guarded portal gate was a bustling town with vendors selling their wares along the roads.

The salon was off the road that led to Urd. We clasped on our cloaks since it was midwinter in Valla.

The busty brunette welcomed us with a big smile. Business was slow with the snow, so they took us right away. Good thing too, since I needed a serious update.

The blonde, Katydid, had a big crush on Brass. She got all doe eyed whenever he was around. Her twin sister Cricket ran the salon and was all business, all the time. She always had beautifully quaffed big, blonde hair and a serious expression.

"Come on in," Bronze welcomed us, swaying her curvy hips as she led us back to our chairs. She stood behind me with her hands on her hips, looking at me through the mirror. "So, what can I do for you today?"

"The works and a haircut. I was thinking a fringe like Katydid."

Bronze pursed her lips.

"Oh my gods, you're kidding!" Tawny said, but she was grinning.

Indigo bit her lower lip. "Change is good. You'll look great with any cut." She offered a smile and Bronze sighed.

"I can tell you are going to do it at home if I do not do it for you. I think I get the look you are going for. Something a little more edgy?" Bronze asked.

I nodded, "Yes. Edgier." I knew Bronze would get it.

Tawny and Indigo did whatever I was doing, minus the cut. We were deep conditioned, our bodies scrubbed, hairs zapped away, nails painted, and hair styled. All the while getting a double dose of gossip.

"So..." I started grinning moronically at Indigo.

Tawny grinned at me and looked over at Indigo. "Is Quick as good as I think he is?" Tawny teased, and Indigo turned tomato red.

It was a safe question since Katydid was into Brass, and both Bronze and Cricket were married. Katydid even laughed at our teasing.

"He's a lot sweeter than he lets on," she said demurely, and Tawny rolled her eyes.

"Who cares? I want to know the juicy details," Tawny said, and I couldn't hold back a laugh.

It felt amazing to laugh and feel normal. The bright orange and white ultra-modern salon had ornate mirrors and molding. The whole place was very trendy, which made me believe one of them must've been pretty good on the internet or visited outside of Tidings.

Indigo fought against a smirk. "He is... what you'd expect."

We all started laughing, and Tawny beamed. "I knew it! You lucky duck. Quick is sex on two feet. I can say that, I'm happily married."

"It's not like that. I mean, it is, but we're just friends. Besides, it's over. Things got weird," Indigo said, and Tawny glanced at me.

I could feel Indigo's emotions. Most were in direct conflict with others. She cared about Quick, that was obvious. It was more than a casual fling, but there was something else, like she cared about someone else more. That was impossible. In the year I'd known her, I'd only ever seen her with Quick and they looked happy. *Couple* happy.

"At least you know if you're ever feeling lonely, Quick would be more than happy to perk you up," Tawny told her with a waggle of her brows.

Indigo gave her a small smile, but something about it made me think it wasn't an option with Quick and Indigo.

"What about you? Slate's kind of scary, but he's good looking. If he doesn't look right at you, then he's scary again." Indigo blushed at her own words, and Tawny guffawed.

My spike of jealousy that anyone else noticed Slate irritated me to no end. "A lady never tells."

Tawny snorted, "Well, Steel —"

"No!" Indigo and I shouted, and Tawny laughed hysterically at our twin expressions.

We could all do girl talk, but we would not be talking about our uncle's sex life. Tawny leaned towards me in her chair, and I knew the real questions were coming since the salon was empty, aside from us and the trio of hairdressers.

"How are you doing, really? I'm worried about you. I know you kind of need Slate right now, but the morning you hated him. If you guys are all buddy-buddy — cool — but I'd hate to see you hurt again. I worry you're not dealing with things; you're just pushing them away and eventually it's going to be too much."

She was right, but if I dealt with the jumble of things I was feeling I didn't know where that would leave me. There were so many things I couldn't touch upon. I was ashamed that the thing in the forefront of my mind was Slate and Anthias. I'd been trying to pretend it hadn't happened. It only worked when we were together and that couldn't be healthy. I didn't even know what we were anymore. Dealing with the public humiliation Ash had dealt me had me at a loss. I didn't know where to begin. The cruel words he'd said... I wished I hadn't been on rousen, I would have snapped back, and I certainly wouldn't have let him kiss me after that. The memory of it enraged me.

Finally, the death of my parents and the forced abortion.

When I tried to get a handle on those things, it felt like my soul was screaming for mercy. The things that happened with the Merfolk were easy to ignore. Slate had erased what had happened with them with his own body. They were out of sight, and out of mind. It was like it happened to someone else, not me.

Then there was Brass.

I did not know what I was doing with my life anymore. It shouldn't have been possible to care about two men at once. Specially those two.

With my hair straightened, my nails painted OPI Honk If You Love OPI Purple Nail Lacquer, and a new deep burgundy lipstick, I felt like a new woman. Tawny and Indigo had commented on how it made my features less soft. I liked that.

We walked back to the portal gate, and I caught more than a few eyes, which made me glow. The bad thing was, I needed *not* to be drawing attention. The lust rolling off some men was doing deplorable things to my willpower. With my fingers curled into my dress, Indigo and Tawny quickly led me back to the palace where I could breathe easy again.

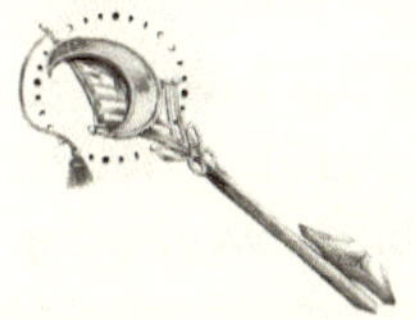

Dinner was ready and the three of us hurried to the informal dining hall, where we found everyone taking their seats. They followed me with their eyes, and I was feeling like a sideshow in a circus.

"Your hair looks lovely, darling." Pearl kissed my cheek when I greeted her before I took my seat.

"Thank you."

"I almost didn't recognize you." Sparrow blinked her dark, tilted eyes at me.

"I barely recognize myself," I said, taking my seat and grinning at them.

Slate's silver eyes glittered at me. It was the longest we'd been apart since he'd carried me into the apartment and the rousen was almost completely out of my system so late at night. I was pushing it close. The lag was in full effect, and I was getting hostile. It happened right before I took my next dose without fail.

"We're going to leave the palace after breakfast and go to the Var castle for Alder's funeral," Hawk announced, and the conversation stopped at the table.

We ate the rest of the meal in a somber silence.

When I got up from my seat feeling heavy and thick headed, Slate got up with me and we bid the rest of the family goodnight. He didn't ask before he snaked his arm around my waist, and I didn't comment.

"I wanted to get a few things from my room, if that's all right," I said, looking up at him.

He raised his black brows and looked down at me. "It is your wing as well. You do not need my permission."

"I was asking if it was all right to go there now, not if I could bring my things to the apartment, wing... whatever," I snapped and faced straight ahead.

Slate chuckled, and the insides of my ears burned with anger. "Activate the bond, Torch."

Rather than argue, I did as I was told. I bit my lip so hard it drew blood, and he did the same, so his emotions knotted in my mind.

Gods. There was a bittersweet sting that was currently being soothed, presumably by my presence and proximity.

He missed me. The knowledge made me uncomfortable.

He led me upstairs to the girls' floor, where poor Indigo was alone. I opened the arched wood carved door and gestured for Slate to make himself comfortable on the royal blue and gold upholstered love seat and matching chaise lounge in the seating area. There was an octagonal table and end table around the seats resting atop a large blue and beige fringed rug. Through a gaping archway was the bed. It displayed an intricate woodwork on the enormous canopy bed, its bedspread matching the gold and royal blue of the couches.

"I'll just be a minute," I said as I walked into the closet.

I'd be upstairs for the rest of the week, so it made sense to have a few dresses and shoes brought up, not to mention some bras and panties. I gnawed my lip as I perused my array of silky, lacy articles and felt Slate's eyes. When I lifted my head, he stood in the doorway watching me with an all too amused look on his chiseled face.

I scowled, trying to fight off a blush, and he entered the closet that became ten times smaller with all his Slateness in it. He took the clothes from my hands and called them into the next room, then he pushed through my panties with a big index finger. I fisted my hands on my hips.

"Please keep your paws out of my underwear drawer, thank you. If you think you can dress me up in whatever you want, you're mistaken."

Slate's full lips curled. "I think you will. You put something on me," he purred, except Slate didn't purr. It was more of a low, sexy growl.

My cheeks flushed, and I turned back to my drawer. The pudding. It was the only thing I had made him put on — the cache hole.

He shifted behind me and pushed my hair over my shoulder before bending his lips down to kiss along my neck. His breath tickled the hairs at my nape. My whole body tingled, and I wasn't even on the rousen yet.

"I think these are necessary, Torch," he breathed.

His finger looped around a scandalous lacy black thong, and it pulled out a small box with it caught in the elastic. My heart twisted when its content fell on the floor. I froze and felt Slate's inquisitive emotions. He stepped back and picked up the tiny silver silhouette of a mother holding a baby charm that I was going to put on my silver torque I'd received after completing the Wild Hunt. It was a reminder of what was important in my life. I never had the chance.

My heart thudded in my chest as he rubbed the tiny charm with his thumb. He put it back in the box and stuck it in the drawer, closing it before he turned back towards me. He pulled me into his arms and, with the tumult of emotions I'd been feeling unleashed.

I pushed at him. "Stop it. I don't need your comfort. I only knew for a day. Don't read more into it."

I stormed into the sitting room and picked up my clothing from the chaise. Slate followed me out and knew he wouldn't bite his tongue.

"You want to lie to yourself, Scarlett, go on ahead. I can feel you. You are heartsick and overwhelmed. You wanted that bairn — our bairn. No one would fault you for it. It was not smart, but nothing about you and I is smart," Slate barked at me and my anger melded with his.

"I —" I started.

He held up his hand. "Watch what you say now, Scarlett Tio. You are on thin ice. If you tell me you did not want my bairn, I will leave you here and now," Slate growled, and I snapped my mouth shut.

I didn't think he'd ever used my full name. He rarely used my first. I was only thinking about myself, my pain, what happened to me, but it happened to him, too. I licked my lips and picked up my shoes.

"I know you didn't want children, but you would've made a great dad," I murmured and started towards the door, hoping to leave the conversation in the room.

Slate moved preternaturally fast. He caught me before I even opened the door and spun me around. Silver eyes so full of pain, sorrow, and much more saw to my heart when they locked on mine.

"Gods, Torch. It is bitter or sweet with you — no in between. I did not want children, but I wanted you to have my child." I gasped, and he slanted his mouth over mine. "If you were not so weak right now, I would take you on this floor. We must get you upstairs. Do you have everything?"

I nodded numbly; he was right. I was weak and heavy, and his words had scattered my wits in a million different directions.

Slate carried my things as we walked up the flights of stone stairs to our, um, the apartment/wing. I hung the things up in the closet and changed out of my dress, putting on a bubble gum pink baby doll nightie and went into the bathroom to get ready for bed.

TEN

Slate was in the shower. His form blurred in the cascade of water that separated the section, and I sighed as I drank the vial of rousen, then put on my nix torque. I didn't know if he wanted me to join him, but things were still too weird for me to go bursting in on him in the shower like it was my right. I didn't know if I had any rights or if I should want any. Really, the second I could walk out of that place, I should have found a substitute for him that hadn't caused me so much heartbreak.

If I could start falling asleep before the rousen kicked in, even if that meant an eight o'clock bedtime, then I was free to leave Slate for good.

The big white canopied bed beckoned, and I climbed in with a little time to spare before the rousen flared through my system. It usually took about twenty minutes and then it was at its most intense from the hour and a half mark for about two hours. Then I'd come down. During that high time, though, I was unpredictable and could become violent if I didn't meet my needs.

It was my first time spending the night with Slate without the rousen already pumping through my system. No excuse for why I would lie next to him, other than it being by choice. I didn't like that thought at all.

Slate slipped into bed not long after I had and tucked me to him. My body fit against his like we were two pieces of the same puzzle. His arm curled around me to nestle his hand between my breasts. He pressed a kiss to my neck, and I felt a thrill shoot through me.

Slate always had that scent I'd picked up on Ash and was muted in Brass, but not in my brother or Gypsum when I'd hugged them. Slate's was like a foghorn in my ear blaring, beckoning to temptation. I turned my head and lifted my hand to his nape to pull his face down for a kiss. It was soft and warm, doing more things to my heart than it did to my loins, and I settled back against him.

He slipped his leg between mine as he held me tight. "Did you take the vial?" he murmured against my hair.

"A few minutes ago," I told him, and I felt his emotions stir in my mind, "Goodnight, Slate." I closed my eyes, letting his emotions wash over me.

"Scarlett."

"Hmm?"

He pressed his lips to my ear. "No child could have a better mother than you. One day you will take in a child that needs your love, as your mother did for me, and you will share all the love you have to give."

I held my breath, willing the lump in my throat to sink and the tears fell as he held me. He called, and I drifted into my dreams.

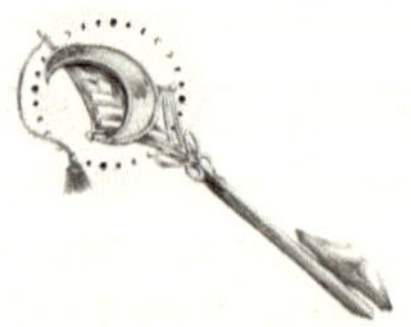

Hours later I awoke burning and in need. Slate woke when I did from our bond and we made a slow, passionate kind of love that one felt

echoes of years later when you tried to replicate it. All other love making would pale in comparison.

We fell back to sleep a few hours afterwards, only to wake up early and pick up where we left off. He laid on top of me with his elbows resting on the bed as we discussed how long I'd had to be on the rousen. Two weeks more, four maximum. I wasn't sure how I felt about that prognosis.

"Oh!" I exclaimed and Slate lifted his face from where he teased my chest with his tongue.

"Torch, you gave me a start," he laughed, muscles along his abdomen flexing against me.

"Sorry. I just remembered something. Close your eyes," I told him, grinning like a complete loon.

His lips curled, and I stared at him for a moment with his sexily tousled wavy mane, his beads, and fetishes in the bathroom after his shower last night so I could run my fingers through it. I smiled and called my purse from yesterday, flying into the room. I took out my gift for Slate and set the purse on the floor next to the bed.

"Okay," I told him and handed him the small, wrapped box.

He cocked an eyebrow and smiled. Slate sat up, undaunted by his glorious nudity or mine and unwrapped the little box.

"It's nothing big, but when I was shopping yesterday, I saw it and thought of you."

His eyes slid to mine and suddenly I felt like shifting. I sat up, so my body wasn't completely on display, and rested my cheek on his arm.

He stared down at the open box and I chewed the inside of my cheek. "I, *um*, stole your other jade piece, so I wanted to replace it."

While we were licking our wounds, the creature we had been hunting ambushed Slate and me and nearly killed me. When I'd come to, Slate passed out. I'd taken his only jade fetish, a canine carving the size of a copper skoll, and it was my first fetish. He'd never asked for it back, or even commented that I'd taken it.

Slate plucked the jade rune from the box and slid his silver eyes to mine, expressionless. I would've killed for the bond. I'd never gotten a man I was seeing... sleeping with... *dating* a gift that wasn't a weapon and was feeling uneasy.

"You got me something the other day. I only wanted to balance things back out. If you don't like it, I can return it for something else," I said, pulling my cheek from his skin and pulling my knees up.

"Easy, Rabbit. Do not scamper off. I am merely... surprised. Do you know what it means?" he asked in a deep rumble.

"No," I lied.

I'd planned on lying. Who bought runes when they didn't know what they meant? What if it meant grandma, cow, or ballet?

His eyes narrowed, but he looked down at it again, and his retort died. "I suppose it will do since someone stole mine from me," he teased, and I nearly choked on my laugh of relief.

Slate bent his neck towards me, and I leaned forward to kiss him. The entire morning had felt so natural, yet the rousen was still there.

"It means love," Slate whispered against my lips and a wave of heat rolled over me.

The little inverted key shaped rune was so unassuming, but I couldn't help myself. I'd had to buy it when Indigo and Tawny weren't looking, because explaining what I was doing wouldn't have been easy. Mostly because I had no fiddlesticking idea what I was doing.

"We should get ready. We have a long day ahead of us," I breathed, and he withdrew, pursing his lips.

"I do not think I like you getting better, Torch."

I laughed, "Why's that?"

"This is the first time you have turned me down since this started. I do not like it at all." He pulled my thighs as he pounced on top of me, and I let out a squeal as I giggled.

"I shouldn't be laughing. I should be mourning," I said, sobering from beneath Slate.

"What do you think Alder would prefer?" Slate asked, and I blinked up at him.

I took Slate's hand in mine and ran my fingers along my father's ring that Slate had taken to always wearing. I looked up at Slate and wrapped my hands in his hair, pulling his mouth down to mine.

CHAPTER II

JETT

Breakfast had been an unfortunate event. Indigo had been doing shockingly well when Quick was around. Quick didn't stay that night. He left one morning, jaw clenched and pissed. Jett had asked what was up, but Quick waved a dismissive hand.

"Tio women should not be allowed to find their own men. Your sisters play with men's minds," Quick had cursed and stormed past.

"What —" Jett had stopped.

He didn't want to know. His sisters didn't play with men's minds, not intentionally, it just sort of worked out that way. Frankly, Indigo surprised Jett by letting Quick around her so much to begin with. They'd hung out in the same group before and had never said two words to each other. Then Scarlett officially introduced them, and they'd been inseparable for two weeks. Now it was apparently over and Quick was the one feeling shafted. Jett just shook his head and went to breakfast.

It was the day of Alder's funeral. Scarlett and Slate were still pretending they weren't basically living together like a married couple, complete with wedding rings.

Honestly, what the fuck?

Jett noticed Alder's ring the second Slate had shown up. Scarlett had been wearing the emerald ring where Ash's engagement ring was.

Jett never paid particular attention to what his adopted brother wore. It was usually black, black, and blacker just like himself. Slate showed up at breakfast with a jade fetish in his dark hair. Upon closer inspection, since Slate sat next to Scarlett, which had never happened before, it was a gods be damned love rune. So much for Tawny's theory that she'd hate him, Slate didn't buy it for himself.

It was a slippery slope. Scar didn't seem to be dealing with things. She kept pushing things away with a, "I'll deal with it later" mentality was going to catch up fast. Like when she ran into one of Slate's many lovers he had scattered across the five islands or, gods forbid, she ran into Anthias who lived on Thrimilci.

That was when the shit would hit the fan.

Scarlett had changed, but one thing was the same. She was wary of Slate. Slate knew it too, Jett could tell by the way he seemed to tiptoe around her, afraid to push too far or say too much. She'd snapped at him a few times and he took it. Slate would never take that kind of talk from anyone, and Jett had picked his jaw up off the floor and walked away.

At least she'd stopped deferring to him for every single thing. Jett still caught her glancing up at him with this *need* for his support. Jett didn't think she knew she was doing it. He supposed Slate let her think she was winning some by letting it go when she back talked since really she was doing exactly what he wanted. Jett wondered if he should say something, but let it go. They both looked happy enough and after everything that had been going on a little happiness, even if it only lasted a short while, was better than none.

Pearl and Hawk had their hands full with Sparrow. The poor woman was not doing well with Alder and Wren's deaths so close together. No one was, but she was the worst. Since she was a council member, they needed her. She couldn't get lost in her grief. Her votes tipped the balance in their favor nine times out of ten.

Gypsum still had two late night visitors. Diamond seemed to be completely out of the picture, which was a good thing. Chief was getting a crash course in Tidings rebounds — no holds barred.

Steel and Tawny were just as good as ever. Those two could make a grown man sick with their insanely happy marriage. Not a bad word to say about one another, and all the P.D.A... Jett wasn't one to shy away from public displays of affection, but those two were lovey-dovey, not touchy feely. It was a miracle she wasn't already carrying his chubby cherub.

They had come through the Var castle portal from the Sumar palace. Having never been before, even under the circumstances, Jett was curious. Tall, narrow windows and gold chandeliers hung every few feet greeted them. It trimmed everything in gold, the entire cream-colored room bathed in light. A staff member in a sheer, silken pale green caftan met them at the door and led them deeper into the Var castle over the marbled floors and through the pastel and cream rooms all trimmed in gold that reminded Jett of the Ostara's town heart.

They walked to where the others gathered just outside the castle, the warm breeze beating against them. Var's castle sat atop a rock pillar at least a hundred stories into the air above a circular lake. Long white stone bridges met the pillar and connected the castle to the lands of Ostara with their arching forms and metallic globes that lined the rails. The sky was bright, and puffs of pure white clouds trailed by at a leisurely pace, as if Alder's death meant nothing to them. The day was much too beautiful a day. It should have been dark and stormy, lightning should have crashed around them, threatening their mission to release their father's ashes, but it didn't, and it wasn't. It was so beautiful and nice in the land of perpetual spring that a cloak wasn't necessary.

It surprised Jett when the Vars demanded Alder's ashes be released in Ostara. They'd fallen out after Alder left Delta and moved into the Sumar palace. He had to deal with his father's family to decide who would release Alder's ashes. It had turned into an argument.

Their grandfather, Cygnus, stood with their grandmother, her thin frame looked to be blown over the edge at any moment. They had seen her a few times before, but she had never been so rail thin. Her large dark eyes were puffy under her high arched eyebrows. Dressed in black as we were, she looked completely washed out with her porcelain skin and dark hair pulled high into a bun on her head. Ruby Geol could've been a ballerina years before, now she looked tired and worn. Cygnus didn't seem to notice. His square jaw clenched so wrinkles formed from his pressed lips to his chin. His skeptical blue eyes weighing Jett, his green sleeveless ambassador's robe being tossed about being the wind, the gold threads of the tree of life glinting on his back.

Canis had probably been the same sandy blonde as his twin brother, Cygnus, before his hair had gone white. His hair was so short it stood straight up on his round head. He wasn't as good looking, his jaw hinted at a jowl, and his dark blue eyes were hooded, his sparse upper lip barely moved as he interjected into Jett's conversation with Cygnus. A black leather jerkin covered Canis's barrel chest. His look was almost militant, but he was an ambassador to the eel hybrid tribe, the Anguillan. You could almost see them swimming about in the waters far below where their cove lay at the base of the stone pillar.

"Alder had four children. Four people will not fit on the steps," Canis spoke in a way that rushed out in a harsh breath without moving his upper lip.

Jett ran his hand over his face for the hundredth time. "So, let the girls do it. It is a happy medium. He raised Indigo, and Scarlett was getting to know him. Same as if Sage and I did it, but it will mean more to them," he pushed.

Crag Straumr, his ebony skinned partner, and Indigo sandwiched Jackal's lean frame. Jackal looked like he hadn't slept in days. His normally stylish blonde hair clung limply to his head, his round blue eyes almost as vacant as Indigo's. He was always ready with a joke, with a hug, smoothing out Crag's rough edges. The son of the Prime, and Amethyst's oldest brother, stood stoically, the sun reflecting off his shaved head, his black brow drawn down over his intense dark eyes. Out of all the Straumrs, he looked the most like his father.

His youngest brother, Fox, was there with his new wife, Novaculite. Their wedding was while they locked Scarlett down with Slate. Pearl and Amethyst had gone as representatives from their family. Fox was Amethyst's brother and his evil wife, Quartz's twin. Technically, she was Alder's niece. The brunette stood next to her sister, Quartzite or Quartz for short, who looked like her opposite with her light blonde hair. One similarity was that the sisters had wide almond eyes.

Ash had his arm slung around her waist possessively, which made Jett want to roll his eyes so hard he might dislodge his retina. The twins' brother Sterling stood next to his mother. He had always looked boyish to Jett with his carefree brown hair combed to the side, his almost violet eyes under his dark straight eyebrows and shy grin. Diamond had laced her fingers through his as they stood side by side. Her chestnut hair falling over her caramel skin. You could never forget that she was Ash's sister with those identical light green eyes.

Sterling's mother had those same eyes, with Nova's dark hair, hers in short curls so they curled to her jaw, and Quartz's fair heart-shaped face. Her eyes had the same cool gaze that her sister Delta's did, like their mother, Cassiopeia. Peak Haust, the patriarch of the Haust family, was the council's smart aleck. He ran his hair through his crop of unruly, inky curls. Eyes, almost lime green, scanning the group gathered before draping an arm over his much shorter wife. He was tall and broad like their father had been and while their father appeared cold, he was warm — a false warmth that was more of a lure.

The odd couple at the gathering of people were Orion Vetr and Cassiopeia Natt, who didn't look to have arrived with one another. Tawny's real father's parents stood on opposite ends of the lip of the pillar as if they had drawn an invisible line across it. Orion stood on their side with Tawny and Steel, his white hair combed to the side, his down-turned mouth curled up as he gazed at Tawny. She had given old man Vetr a second chance at his legacy being his only son's child. She had taken her father's last name, which wasn't typical in Tidings, and became heir to the Vetr castle.

Cassiopeia cast cool eyed glances at her husband from where she spoke to Delta and Sage. Her shoulder-length blonde hair curled impeccably like an old movie star, her wide blue eyes had a permanently lowered lids as if nothing was very impressive. She was an icy beauty, her thin lips pursed as Sage said something low, leaning towards his mother so they did not overhear him. Delta's round, light blue eyes flickered to mine, glittering with amusement. Pouty lips were painted red, making her soft, fair skin look angelic. Someone so icy shouldn't look angelic.

Sage raised an eyebrow as he straightened, a smirk playing on his pouty lips. He was his mother's son in looks, the same round eyes and soft looking fair skin. His combed back hair was a warmer blonde than his mother's pale blonde.

"The girls are in too fragile a state to handle such an important deed," Cygnus said.

Jett ran a hand over his close-cropped blonde hair, a move Jackal noted, and moved Indigo over to where Jett stood.

Amethyst's dark almond eyes were red rimmed, but her wide mouth smiled as she looked up to Jett. Cherry stood with her arm linked in Amethyst's. Amethyst's willowy frame had the beginnings of a baby bump now that she was in her second trimester. Cherry's fair skin and dark hair with her naturally red lips made her look like a pinup Snow White, or she would have if she didn't seem so sad. Freya's burly boar. It irked Jett that his wives were unhappy.

River Straumr stood with his wife and kids beside Moon Straumr. The stoic Prime hadn't been the same since his wife died and had only reopened the university when Amethyst had gotten old enough to attend a few years back. The middle Straumr brother had Amethyst's mocha coloring and dark eyes. Jett knew lots of the female tyros had crushes on the married battle trainer, but it was Fox who gave late night private lessons.

"I will do it. Alder is dead for the Mother's sake. This is ridiculous," Jackal snapped.

Jett left his spot with the others, considering matters settled, and strode towards his family, his thick dark blonde eyebrows drawn down so a line creased between them. He stopped before Scarlett, who stood so close to Slate the big man's arm was behind her. Her new blunt cut bangs and straight hair would take some getting used to. She was less soft looking that way, sultrier, and Jett didn't think that was accidental. Slate didn't seem to care either way, but his newly gained lover seemed to be going through a dark phase with her deep red lips and dark purple polish. Even her dress was something he hadn't expected from her, black lace mock neck with long sleeves with a thin strapped fitted dress underneath. She wore a little fascinator with a blusher veil to offer a little cover for her face.

Her big, almond eyes were red rimmed and watery, her symmetrical nose red tipped from wiping. Jett realized Slate's hand was on her back, and she was leaning on him right there in front of everyone, rings on and everything. Now was not the time to lecture, though. Sage and Ash were watching them. Scarlett and Slate seemed oblivious to it, but he knew better.

"I can't believe I share a last name with those people. The only one who is worth a damn is Jackal, and they treat him like a joke because he won't reproduce. Unbelievable. We settled on Jackal releasing father's ashes. They said it wasn't right for me to do it because of Sage, but Sage doesn't seem interested in the least bit." He turned his head back across the invisible line where Sage must have told Quartz a joke since she was laughing with an opened mouth smile.

Jett stewed. Scarlett turned her head and her eyes lit with her elemental fire like red-hot coals. Slate's arm pulled her tighter to him.

"Easy, Torch," he rumbled, and Scarlett turned her head to him, and her fire blinked out.

Jackal looked back towards their side of the family, and they knew it was time.

Their family converged with the Vars in front of the stairs, and Jett took Indigo from under Jackal's arm. Scarlett moved to stand beside Jett, a muscled arm around each of them. Scarlett leaned into him so her ear rested partially on his chest, and she could grab Indigo's hand behind his back. Jett kissed Scarlett's head, and he smiled at her spiced vanilla apple scent. He turned to kiss Indigo's corn silk hair and squeezed her tighter when he felt her body shake from crying. Indigo smelled as sweet as she was, like honey and freesia.

The pyre portion was always the hardest part of the Guardian funeral. Jett was thankful it was over. Sage sidled up beside Slate on Scarlett's other side, almost close enough to touch, and Slate stiffened. Arrogance radiated from Sage. Jackal climbed the stairway to the sky to spread his ashes as he chanted.

"Lo, there do I see my father. Lo, there do I see my mother. My sisters and my brothers. Lo, There do I see my people. Back to the beginning. Lo, there do they call to me and ask me to take my place in the halls where the brave may live forever."

Alder's ashes extended out in a simple golden bowl. What the wind didn't take, Jackal called into a swirling vortex up and into the sky in front of him. A lump choked Jett's throat as his chest tightened. Indigo was sobbing into his chest and Scarlett had laced her fingers with Slate's as tears ran beneath her veil over her cheeks.

Jett heard Sage's honeyed voice murmuring to Slate, and a low growl responded to whatever Sage had said. The others filed into the castle and Scarlett shifted to face Sage, heat radiating off her body.

"Speak that way to him again and I will incinerate you so completely, your mother will not have a pinch of ashes to weep over," she hissed, and Jett's eyes widened.

Sage snicker made Jett's skin crawl. "The two of you belong together. The khoraz of a whore and the man known for fucking every unhappily married woman in Tidings. We would have to build a grandstand to seat your combined lovers."

Scarlett let go of Jett and moved to stand in front of Slate, her body loose and voluptuary. She tapped a finger to her lips in mock consideration. "Slate, I had not realized you fucked his mother," she said with a too sweet smile for Sage.

Sage's jaw tensed and Slate's muscles bunched. "Think again," he growled, low and dangerous.

"You are a stupid little bitch, and everyone knows Non're, and a score of Merfolk fucked you six ways to Sunday, khoraz," he spat.

"Sage."

Ash stood near the entrance to the castle looking back at us and he flashed Scarlett a look that would have made a woman of the night blush, but Scarlett merely took it.

Scarlett stood facing the blue sky, the wind ripping at her hair. Slate moved to stand behind her and she let him put his arms around her. She'd gone from the most naïve, inexperienced woman their age to people accusing her of being a khoraz and not the malicious way girls did to one another, but in a serious way. It wasn't right.

Jett led Indigo away. She was still crying so had missed the harshly whispered clash. Amethyst and Cherry waited for him by the door, and they walked in somberly with the setting sun at their backs.

He turned around to make sure Scarlett and Slate would be okay on their own and Scarlett had wrapped her hands in the big man's hair, pulling his mouth down to hers. They looked alone in the world out on that ledge, and Jett felt a chill down his spine. Theirs wasn't a love meant for a lifetime. It burned too bright and scorched until there was nothing left.

TWELVE

I loosened my fingers from Slate's waves and brought my heels back to the stone. "I'm sorry for saying something so nasty," I said as I ran my fingers along his full bottom lip that looked primed for a nibble.

"For the record, I never bedded his mother," Slate joked, and I gave him a dry smile.

I wanted to feel anything but the suffocating depression that descended upon me from the moment we arrived in Ostara. I wasn't even upset to see Ash and Quartz together; it was the looks everyone was giving me. *Us.* Slate had a reputation of his own that preceded him, but I could ignore that for the moment. He may have been a debauchee, but he was *my* debauchee. No one was going to make smart remarks without feeling my wrath.

When Sage had turned to him and asked how he liked the barren, sloppy seconds of a Straumr, I'd almost gone full elemental. I added Sage to the list that included Jonquil and the Stygians, of people I wanted dead. It was more than his pitiless words. He had picked on me when I dated Ash, who used to put an end to it with a look. It was our father's funeral. He should have shown the proper respect and shut the fiddlestick up. gods, I had dropped an 'F' bomb at my father's funeral, cementing my place in hell.

Slate pulled me to his hard chest and held me there. The crimson setting sky reflected off the surrounding lake. It was a paradise and Jett would rule it one day. There had been more people than I had expected at Alder's funeral. Where had those friends been when he'd lost my mother?

Non're's exploits were common knowledge among the Merfolk. I hadn't known others knew it as well. Of course, he was so much older than he looked and had been doing it for decades. Word would've made it off Thrimilci, perhaps in warning or enticement. Sage's words had cut me to the quick.

"Does it bother you now that everyone knows about me and the Merfolk? You're being seen with me? People will scramble to conclusions." I pressed my palms to his back as I rested my cheek on his chest, breathing in his heady scent.

"Why do you care what anyone else thinks of you, Torch? Do you know who you are?" Slate said, holding me away from his body, making me feel cold.

"You're not just anyone," I admitted and pursed my lips to the side as I thought on it. "I don't think I know who I am anymore."

"That is not what I meant. You are Scarlett Tio, daughter of Wren Tio and Alder Var. She was the last female Tio, and he was the heir to Ostara. You come from the Sumar bloodline of rulers. The purest Guardian blood runs through your veins. You and Indigo are the first elementals in hundreds of years, and you are stronger at calling than anyone I have ever met," Slate said firmly, leveling his eyes to mine.

"You make me sound so much cooler than I am," I mumbled, and he tilted my chin up with a finger.

"You are an amazing woman, Scarlett. Any other woman that has gone through what you have would have barricaded herself in a dark room and not come out, but here you are. You are vibrant and full of life." Slate slanted his mouth over mine. "Did you mean to be protective or were you saying what needed saying?" he asked against my lips.

I pulled my lips between my teeth. It was the time for blunt honesty.

"You will probably rue the day you ever tried to seduce me in the ladies room. I don't enjoy being out in public with you because I don't like other people looking at you, especially women. I'm insanely jealous of every woman who's ever laid eyes on you, much less touched you. When people are unpleasant to you, it makes me boil inside because I'm the only one allowed to hate you. If I could keep you hidden and force you to stay so, I would have all your attention and words and smiles... I know how psychotic this all sounds."

I probably could have left out the whole caging him up bit, but at least I didn't actually say cage even though that's what I had envisioned. At least I didn't say love, that had to count for something. Bottom line, I wanted to pluck the eyes out of every woman who'd seen him naked and remove any appendages that may have touched him... that had to be normal, didn't it? I wasn't sure. To admit that I was in over my head would've been redundant. I'd been in over my head since the moment I set foot in Tidings, and I'd only sunk deeper with every step since.

Slate's eyes flared with silver that reflected the crimson sky behind us. Heat rolled off him and if I said go, he'd strip me down and take me right there. As it was, he lifted the skirt of my dress and pulled out my seax. Its black handle had a woman carved into it and etched in gold. Its black hand-stitched scabbard had gold embossed wings and gold buckles strapped to my thigh where I almost always wore it. Slate had bought it for me my second day there and I should have known then that where we were now was inevitable. He never intended to let me get away.

Slate took the wickedly sharp blade from me and ran it across his palm, causing the blood to well red and bright and handed it back. His eyes were so fiercely intense I took the knife without question. My heart made it impossible to hear with all the blood and adrenaline pumping. His chest was heaving, and I knew if I could see my face it would mirror his. My lips parted as I dragged the sharp blade across my soft palm. I'd gotten a few callouses in the past year from handling my blades, and I was proud of them. I slid my seax back into its sheath and lifted my eyes to Slate's.

My mind drifted me far away on a cloud where none of my worldly responsibilities or worries could touch me. All that existed was Slate and I and the moment. Nothing mattered before and nothing would matter after, only that we were together. He clasped my bleeding hand to his.

"You are mine and I am yours," he murmured.

"I pledge myself to you," I whispered.

"My name is not my own, it is borrowed from my ancestors. I must return it unstained. My honor is not my own, it is on loan from my descendants, I must give it to them unbroken. Our blood is not our own, it is a gift to generations yet unborn, we should carry it with responsibility."

We said it in unison without being prompted. We felt what didn't need to be said. They were the Guardian marriage vows, a blood oath, completely unbreakable, and I felt it sink into my skin as my body and soul accepted the promise for eternity.

I gasped, my eyes widening. What did we just do?

Brass.

Slate's eyes held a note of triumph. He angled his body towards mine possessively, letting me know without words that I was his. He'd staked his claim. *Mine*, his eyes said.

"We should go inside," I breathed, and his lips curled.

"Do not scamper, Rabbit. I will chase you and I will catch you. Then, I will make you sorry," he purred, and a thrill shot through me. "Come now."

"This is wrong on so many levels."

I still went with him as Slate led me up pale, cream marble steps veined with gold until we found an empty hall. I did not know where we were in the Var castle, but I knew what we were looking for — a bedroom.

Slate opened a door at random on what had to be the third floor, and a safe bet we'd finally find a bedroom. We'd tried a few other doors, which ended up being staff quarters, and had to apologize a few times with me giggling the entire time. Slate was practically growling with frustration. The front of his pants strained past capacity.

We peered into a sitting room done in pale pinks and cream with a simple white coffee table. A little further in was a big white and pink bed and a naked man. Slate slapped a hand over my mouth before I could gasp and pulled me back out of the room. Slate dragged me a few paces away to stand in front of a large window that spanned the end of the hall. A single cream-colored chair sat before it.

Slate was smiling knowingly down at me as I scowled up at him.

"You knew!" I accused, and he nodded, still smiling, and trying to hold me, but I pushed his hands away. "They can get into so much trouble, I should know!"

"Everyone knows Sterling and Indigo are having an affair. They have been for years," Slate explained.

My mouth fell open. It was so unlike Indigo. Sterling was a betrothed man, to Diamond, whom we were friends with no less!

"But she was with Quick the other night…" I protested.

Slate sucked in a breath like he was trying to explain as simply as possible for my befuddled mind to comprehend. "As far as I know, Quick is the only other man she has been with. I believe her and Sterling were on the outs because Diamond will attend Valla University with them so they can no longer be together. Sterling and Diamond plan to wed next Yuletide."

A lot was making sense. Sterling and Indigo were always together. She'd been seeing Quick since the masquerade when Sterling and Diamond were together. Slate said a man because Indigo had also been with Rikke, a Wemic cat hybrid scout.

"How do you know all this?" I asked, bewildered.

His lips quirked. "I make a point of knowing all those around you very well, Torch. She is careful now; she was not when she was younger. Men talk, not Sterling, but men who know," Slate said, and I sighed.

I turned towards the window, and he moved behind me to wrap his arms around me, his hair brushing my shoulder as he put his cheek on my head.

"You don't talk about me, do you?" I asked charily.

"Usually with Jett about the latest catastrophe you have gotten yourself into," he teased, and I elbowed him in the stomach.

"I suppose the memory of Sterling's face buried between my naked sister's legs is imprinted on your unerring memory now."

Slate chuckled and ran his palm over my stomach. Slate was a prophet. His mind held generations of prophecies passed from his mother to him and he would pass them on, or he would've to his children. It was an inherited talent like my empath abilities, and he could remember every detail of his life.

A sprawling view of the waters beyond Ostara stretched from the window. My geography knowledge of Tidings left much to be desired. I had no clue which of the islands was closest. I could only see the fading sunlight glistening on smooth waters until it reached the horizon. If I could sit there all day, I would have. I felt at peace, tranquil even. Such rotten people shouldn't be allowed to live in raw beauty.

Water started to bubble and froth in the distance; I wouldn't have noticed it if I wasn't in one of the highest floors of the castle. Slate moved with me closer and pressed my hand against the window. Water shot up like geysers into the clear sky and dark jagged pillars rose into the air, slowly at first and then in a rush spraying water. I realized they weren't pillars, but towers.

Frozen, I watched as the burnt umber colored flat land surfaced, the dark jagged towers extending from first crookedly, then righting itself. The towers didn't appear to be very high, only a few stories, and were connected by a single level that touched all the wicked towers that ripped through the sky like claws seeking to grip the sun.

"Are you seeing this?" I whispered and Slate grunted.

One massive claw, its underside the color of khaki, swung forth from the water only to crash back like a tidal wave. Karkinos. It had to be. There couldn't be two giant crabs with prisons on their backs, and if that wasn't a prison, then you could slap my fanny pack and call me Sally.

As quickly as it surfaced, it sank so peaks of the towers were above the water, and then nothing. The waters grew still, and it was as if it never happened.

We stood there for another moment in shocked silence, and I turned around in Slate's arms to face him. His face had gone stony, his silver eyes narrowed.

"Does that normally happen?"

"No. Come. We will talk about it later. Your family will wonder where you are," Slate said, and we started back down the stairs.

We followed a staff member to a large sitting area. Light blue couches with white wood carved backs were arranged around the coffee tables full of appetizers. The artistically painted ceiling of the sitting room was rounded with arched windows at the top of the walls, the pastel green walls trimmed in carved gold. I took a seat next to Pearl and Sparrow. Across from us sat Tawny, Steel, and Orion. Pearl's emerald eyes regarded Orion dubiously, Sparrow downright glared.

He offered a small smile as he sat shifting his sleeveless crimson councilor's robe with white trim and a white auseklis embroidered on the back. After he had greeted us all, he leaned towards me over the coffee table.

"Miss Tio, I am sorry for your loss," he said in a croaky tone. He may have been handsome once, but grief had left its mark on him.

"Thank you," I replied.

For my mother's funeral, I was completely despondent. I did not know what was going on or what the right thing was to say. I didn't see any of Tawny in old man Vetr. Her dark hair and wide mouth she got from Sparrow. I wondered if her real father's eyes were wide and hazel like hers, with her fair skin.

"Tawny was informing me of your situation. I must say, the Straumrs could have been more tactful. If you should wish to spend some time out of the public eye, Elivagar is as secluded as it gets. You could bring a guest with you if you wish," Orion offered and his eyes slid to where Slate stood with Jett.

Elivagar would be secluded. The land of perpetual winter was all snow, all the time. Gorgeous, but cold, and it was where my mother died.

"Classes will start again in a few days and I'm sure I'll be able to lose myself in my work, but thank you for your kind offer." I gave him a wan smile.

"Generous of you, Orion." Pearl said. Her coppery hair spilled forward as she picked up her own goblet pursing her lips, her high cheekbones becoming even more prominent.

Orion's eyes glittered at Pearl's attention. Was that a spark?

"No darling? I do miss the old days," he said, leaning back. Darling being my grandmother's pet name for everyone.

She laughed, and the warmth in it startled me. "Ancient days, Orion."

Making pleasantries with the Haust, Var, and Natts was too difficult for me. I wanted to leave, but didn't want to seem insensitive to my father's memory. Sage kept glancing over to me and my insides burned with anger.

Karkinos appearing out of nowhere had stunned me. From what I knew, it was not supposed to come that close to land. Was the giant crab getting senile or sick? Could it have gotten lost?

My body was getting heavy and my thoughts slowed. My usual amiable attitude was becoming volatile. Using a bathroom break as an excuse to leave the room full of fake smiles and networking Guardians, I made my way into the neighboring hall. Indigo and Sterling had come back, and he had walked to Diamond as if he hadn't just been with Indigo at all. He didn't even look guilty. It wasn't their first rodeo, though Indigo did cast a few glances their way, looking like a kicked puppy.

"How unfortunate."

I pivoted to the voice, and Canis detached from the shadows.

"What is?" I knew it was a trap the moment I opened my big mouth.

His arms were clasped behind his back, his barrel chest held proudly. He was as tall as my father had been. Canis towered over me as he moved closer.

"Less than ten days ago, you had a future. Now you have a reputation. I do not need to inform you; you are not the first Tio woman to be so." He spoke in quick breaths, his chest squeezing his words out.

"I have a different future. Things change we adapt, or we die. It is the natural order of things and I am adaptable. Are you?" I didn't mean for it to come out as a threat. He had pissed me off and that time of day was bad for messing with me.

Canis's blue eyes bored into me and I didn't flinch. I was sick to death of being pushed around by bossy greater families.

"Ash tells me you were carrying a bastard. That was unfortunate. It is a good thing Ash got away when he did."

My eye twitched. "It's fortunate my grandmother married Flint. It's unfortunate you couldn't lure anyone into marrying *you*. I'm sure Cassiopeia makes a great mistress. Not having an heir of your own, though, is unfortunate — a fate we'll share. Good night to you, ambassador."

I was an empath. I felt what others felt if their walls weren't up, and everyone slipped occasionally. Cassiopeia hid it well, but as sure as the day was long, Orion's wife had been or was still having an affair with Canis. If he wanted to bully a naïve little girl, he missed her by two weeks.

Canis's face darkened, and he grabbed my wrist in his enormous fist. His hands were rough and dry and made my wrist look like a baby's. That was the man who went against my father when he wanted to marry my mother. I would not fear him no matter how much bigger he was than me.

"A smarter girl would still her wagging tongue before she bit it," he said, low and harsh.

"I've been accused of many things lately, but being smart has not been one of them," I retorted dryly, and I felt the electricity behind me.

"Ambassador Canis, thank you for helping Scarlett. I can manage," Slate said from behind me.

Canis's hooded blue eyes never left mine. I wondered if he had a talent. Could he read thoughts like Brass? If he could, he'd know I hated his guts and was looking for any excuse to singe him into a pile of dust to be swept out with the trash.

His hand loosened around my wrist, and I felt the circulation come back. I resisted the urge to shake out my hand in Canis's presence. His gaze slid over my head, and I felt Slate's body heat just behind mine. Slate pulled me behind him and Canis's hand fell.

The two men could see eye to eye. Tension hummed in the air. I wasn't afraid before, but I was now that Slate was in the middle of things. If I tried to pull him away he'd be angrier with me. I had to stand back, let it play out, and hope it didn't get too messy.

Canis took in Slate, weighing and measuring. "Enjoy it while it lasts, son. Life is short." Canis skirted us and walked away.

I finally rubbed my wrist. "I can't tell if he insulted me or threatened you or both."

Slate turned around and I took a step back. His silver eyes were hard and incensed. The muscles in his shoulders bunched and his chin canted so his hair fell over his shoulders.

"He was right. Your mouth will get you in trouble. You should have kept his secrets and not advertise that you know of his clandestine meetings with Vetr's wife. What do you think a man like that would do to a person who knew something that could damage his honor?" Slate growled.

I closed my eyes and sighed. He was right, of course. The stress of the situation sapped the bit of strength I'd had left. I needed to have dinner and drink my rousen.

"You don't seem to have a problem with my mouth any other time," I teased, and I saw the corners of his lips quirk, but he was truly upset with me.

"You do not understand what it does to your family and me whenever you get into these perilous situations. You bounce back faster than anyone has a right to, but one day, you will not because you will have pushed your luck too far."

"Careful. You're sounding like you care about more than my body," I said as I slid my hands over his waist.

His eyes narrowed, "You cannot use sex to hide your grief, Torch. It will catch up with you. Mourn. I am not going anywhere." Slate's tone had changed, his eyes softened and part of me felt better for it, but the other part of me grew agitated with his honesty.

I took my hands back and set my jaw. "I'm going to say goodbye. Then, I'm going home." I started towards the sitting room.

"Do not forget to put on the nix torque," he called after me and I stopped.

"You're not coming home with me?"

My tone made me cringe. Slate gave a lopsided grin and swaggered to me.

"I will be home shortly. I need to inform the others of Karkinos coming so close to shore," Slate said, cupping my face.

My face was a thunderhead. "You mean inform Lera." Slate's smile fell. "Brass told me about you two and my brother. She did for you what you've done for me." Irritation brewed in me.

"That was not Brass's story to tell," Slate said softly.

"Maybe you should have been more specific about what he could and couldn't say to me. Besides, he was only trying to help," I defended Brass.

Slate didn't exactly volunteer information and I would take anything anyone told me at this point and try to fit it to the man I knew.

"I bet he was. Do you still want him, Torch? Feel that twinge when he comes around because you were falling in love with him?" Slate's eyes burned into me.

He went from zero to a hundred in a blink. There was unbridled jealousy in his eyes and a lethal danger lurking just below. I blushed and tried to look away, but he held my face steadfast.

"I won't apologize for giving myself to Brass," I said sternly, meeting his gaze.

"Did you take him into you on the shore?" Slate's teeth gritted, and his tone took on a brutal edge. He'd been imagining the worst.

"Whoever thought to put that sheet around me was clever. I would've..."

"He was ready for you?" Slate ground out.

"It's not his fault and unless you hold me accountable for everything I've done under rousen, that one time doesn't make me accountable either. I won't apologize for it, but I am sorry it bothers you."

"Go say goodbye. I am walking you to the portal gate." Slate let go of my face and walked past me without waiting.

I followed him, but only because I had to since my family was that way.

I said goodbye to everyone and headed home with Slate. I walked one step ahead of him the entire way, even though I knew he could catch up with me at any point if he chose. He went through the portal with me, as if I'd try to go anywhere else.

The blue twinkling lights cast an ambient glow over Slate's hard features. "Are you good to make it upstairs?"

I crossed my arms facing him and blew at my new fringe that kept sticking to my fascinator's veil. "I'll be fine. Run back to your lover," I snapped, "It's what you're good at."

Slate drew his brow down. "When I get back, I am going to fill that cheeky mouth until you cannot so much as moan," he growled.

I scoffed, "So, you're bringing back dinner? Great, that will save me a trip to the kitchens."

Slate moved too fast for a man and way too fast for a man of his size. I hardly blinked before he'd growled and gripped my head by the hair at my nape. Slate crushed his lips over mine, triggering the bond in the process. When he tried to pull away, I caught his bottom lip and bit down hard so it would trigger his as well. He pressed his forehead to mine and gave me a wicked grin.

"I always knew this girl was in you, Torch."

"Take care not to sleep with anyone while you're out. I'll be able to feel it... again."

He growled in frustration, his mood changing in an instant. "Go eat your food and take your gods be damned rousen."

I pressed my lips into a firm line and waited for him to leave first. When he realized what I was doing, he threw back his head and laughed so the hard planes of his face creased, and he smiled a rare smile with his full soft lips and flashed straight white teeth. His eyes met mine, glittering, and he knew the effect that rare smile had on me.

"Just go already," I muttered, and he flashed me a mocking smile before the bright light of the portal door engulfed him.

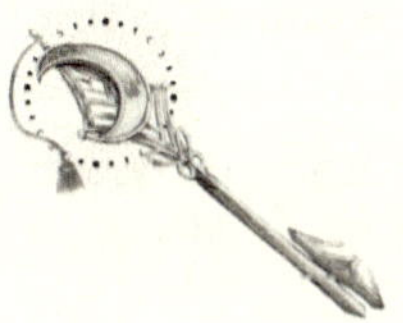

After dinner, I readied for bed and took my vial of rousen. Each day would be less than the day before. Slate still wasn't back and my outrage was palpable. He should've been there with me, not with her. That's when I locked him out. At that point, I didn't care that it was immature. I was mad and if he got in, I would be too deep in the rousen to properly argue with him. *If* he came back. Mustn't think like that.

Twenty minutes after I'd barricaded the front door with the couches, Slate tried the doorknob and it came up against the couch. I felt no small part of satisfaction despite wanting to open the door myself so bad I had to ball my fists at my sides. When he tried again a few minutes later and I took a step forward, groaning with the need to be touched.

Slate's amusement was taunting through the bond. I narrowed my eyes at the double doors and spun on my heel, going back into the bedroom and praying I fell asleep before I started climbing the walls.

Slowly, Slate's amusement faded to irritation. I'd like to think I made it an hour or so, but I lost track of time and it felt like several hours. The coral slip I had on felt like heaven over my burning skin, and the walk to the door was torturous.

Since I had the nix torque on, I had to manually move the heavy couches away from the door and all my muscles were strained with my ache and the effort. I almost cried out in relief when I pushed the second couch aside.

I faced the door and threw them both open wide. Slate sat on the tiled floor across from the door with his legs crossed in front of him, his head tilted back to rest on the wall, silver eyes glinted with primitive lust. Our bond made him feel just how intense my need was.

My chest was heaving, making my breasts rub against the slinky fabric. My peaks went as hard as pearls. I launched myself at him, and he caught me effortlessly as I licked up his exposed throat. He stood, carrying me with my legs wrapped around his waist until he called the doors shut behind us.

Slate yanked me away from his body and spun me around, putting my front to the door and grabbed a fistful of my hair, pinning me in place as I panted. "You are a jealous creature."

I was beyond speaking. I could only moan in response as I pushed my hips out, seeking friction. He gave it to me. I hadn't even known he'd pushed his pants over his hips before he was inside me, making my insides pulse.

"You are going to have to trust me," he growled as he moved.

We'd see about that.

CHAPTER
THIRTEEN

"You do not have to do this competition this month. Take some time off. I can speak to Lera for you," Brass said as he sat on the bench beside me as I readied.

He always faced the other way in the preparation room when I dressed. It seemed pointless, but I appreciated the sentimentality and there was always that smoldering fire inside me now. Being undressed in front of Brass was hard enough without adding his eyes to me. I wasn't sure how far I could push my control yet.

"It's not for nine more days. I'm healthy, Brass. Please don't treat me like an invalid or some wounded animal."

I missed the Shadow Breakers' headquarters. The smell of leather and cool metal. It had a provocative element to it that made me feel at home. The ultra-modern prep room had black metal cubbies and gray marble tiles with white skein and black marble benches. A section for massages after particularly trying training days and a wall-to-wall shower section that had retractable frosted shower partitioned that Breakers rarely used since they lacked modesty. I'd have to stay away from it if I was going to play nice, as Slate put it.

My first time competing in the Crash Course would be the first Friday of January. The Crash Course was an elaborate obstacle course A simulated earthquake, complete with falling boulders, a lava pit with floating rocks on its surface, wooden rafts that rested on crashing waves. That was just the right half. Tall trees stood in the center of the room looking like a small woods dividing the room. The left half had a battle ring and the Guillotine full of wickedly sharp blades.

Brass's amber eyes leveled at me over his shoulder. "I know you can, Scar. It is the patron's room I am concerned about, or Vegas, as you like to call it. Can you handle being alone with someone at night?"

I hadn't thought of that. Brass slid to face me on the bench once I was dressed if that's what you wanted to call it. My competition wear left little to the imagination. I wore a cropped black leather halter vest and matching boy shorts. Shiny gold buttons accented the pieces, two on each hip and two between the low neckline that exposed an impressive amount of cleavage.

"I won't know unless I try," I lied, and Brass scooted on the bench closer to me.

That muted scent was a little stronger, and it pulled on something in my stomach that made my control weaken. I bit down on the inside of my cheek to fight it. It was Brass, my *friend*.

"There is no need to push and lose control. Scarlett, you can hardly stand to sit next to me," Brass said softly, and I gave him a rueful grin.

"Well, hopefully my patron isn't as handsome as you and it will be easier," I joked.

"I am serious."

He raised his fingers to my cheek and let it trace the steep ascent of my bone into my hair. I leaned into his hand until his palm cupped my cheek. My back arched to him as my eyes slid shut and I pulled a harsh breath between parted lips.

"See what I mean?" he said in a rough voice.

I stood balling my fists and shoved them under my arms to keep from trying to touch him. I couldn't be that close. Not yet. Slate was easier. He wanted me to touch him, and it wasn't inappropriate when I did. If I started running my fingers through Brass's hair like I wanted, that'd be more than inappropriate.

"I know, Brass. I'll wait and see what I'm like the day before. If I haven't progressed enough, I'll bow out and royally piss off Cordillera in the process. You're right. I wouldn't feel good about myself if I got to Vegas and couldn't control it with nowhere to go for an hour and a half," I conceded, and he gave me a warm smile.

"Slate is still with Lera, so we will get started now. He should be down by the time we run the course a couple of times," Brass said, heading to the metal double doors.

I seethed. Lera had all but banned Slate from my training. I didn't see the problem, she and Chafer were doing the dirty. She didn't need Slate anymore. He was mine.

Brass led me through the shiny, flawless metal doors and into the combat ring. A ten-foot stone wall lined the arena. A wrought-iron balcony railing lined the top to prevent people from falling in along one side. On the other side were the two-way mirrored suites for patrons and Cordillera's Grand Mistress's suite, where she entertained the crème de la crème of patrons.

There was another team of Breakers training out there and when I walked out in my skimpy outfit lust hit me like a ton of bricks. I held my breath, standing totally still as my control faltered. Brass came into my line of sight and my lips parted.

"Go away," I ground out.

His eyes widened a fraction and he nodded before moving behind me. I breathed deep, waited until everyone got their chance to drink in the new girl and let out a shuddering breath.

"Okay. I'm okay. Let's do this," I said roughly, and Brass moved beside me, rubbing his lips together.

"I think it may be chemical. When someone finds you sexually attractive, they release pheromones and I think the rousen increased your pleasure center so you are sensitive to it," Brass said thoughtfully, reassuring me.

I walked forward. "That makes some sense," I said stubbornly as I approached the maze of blades.

At the end of the combat ring, I felt Slate rear up in my mind. It was the mental equivalent of a snarl. *Play nice, Torch.*

Brass stepped up next to me. He'd move up to the side of the course to use calling in case I fell or drag me out of danger if need be.

"I am almost certain that is what it is."

I shifted uncomfortably with him next to me. "It's a scent. I guess that's pheromones but still... there's a flaw in your hypothesis."

Brass chuckled, making me turn to him, knitting my brows. His amber eyes glittered and his defined plump lips pulled into a smile.

"Is it because you pick it up so strongly from me?"

I broke our gaze and looked out towards the Guillotine blushing.

"Scarlett, is it that hard to believe that I still want you?" Brass said in his smooth, deep voice.

My head whipped back to him with a gaping expression. "Whenever you've kissed me, you said it's because I needed it. I thought that was because Lera needed to be reassured I wasn't after Slate or she wouldn't train me. The night I came to you... you turned me down."

Brass stared back at me, dark hair brushing his dark honey cheek that I longed to tuck behind his ear. "I also told you I did it because I wanted to. I took you that second night without a word uttered between us. My hot pink present in thigh highs."

My breath quickened and eyes widened as I looked out towards the course. "By the Mother, Brass. I had no idea... maybe a small one, but I dismissed it." I sucked in a deep breath. "You told Slate. That's why he grilled me about you?"

Brass's smile was impish. "We have never been attracted to the same woman before. I do not think he likes the competition. I did not tell you to make you uncomfortable, Scarlett. Only to explain why you feel the way you do — it is not all you."

"Uncomfortable does not quite cover it. Pride aside, I can't be trusted to be alone with you, Brass. Please don't repeat it." I heaved a breath, trying not to take in any of his spicy cinnamon scent.

"Your honesty is a redeeming quality. I promise to do my best not to tempt you," he teased, and I gave him a dry smile. "Hop to it. You have an audience."

Brass nodded up to Cordillera's suite and there were Slate and Lera sitting side by side watching the Breakers train. Cordillera was middle-aged, though she didn't look a day over thirty. Her red lips matched her nails, her dark chin length wavy hair was the same dark brown as her eyes. She was the same size as Shale, tiny but toned, with a soft swell of bosom she usually had on display. One of her thick, high arched brows quirked at us both looking up at them. I communicated the most aggravated emotions I could summon through the bond and watched as Slate's full lips quirked. *Right back at ya,* the bond reflected.

I rolled my eyes. Brass made his way over to the sidelines to "coach" which was code for shout-unpleasantries-until-you-fail.

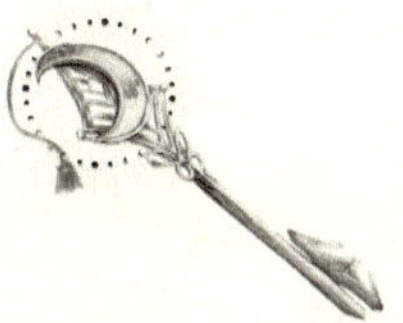

I hadn't needed to restart the Crash Course in months, and I was happy that I didn't lose any of my skills. In fact, I was more flexible than I'd ever been for, ahem, unknown reasons. Brass had me go through twice until I was pouring sweat and feeling utterly fantastic, but exhausted. It was the training I'd been hoping for. I was ready for my competition and was going to win.

I was still beaming when I jogged around from the dock at the end of the course and met Brass, whose broad warm grin matched my own when I forgot myself. Brass did too when he reached down to give me a congratulatory hug, sweeping me into his muscled dark honey arms. My legs wrapped around him of their own volition, and I sucked in a sharp breath.

"Oh! Put me down," I hissed.

"Kind of hard to do with your ankles locked," Brass said evenly.

I let go of him completely and slid down his body to the ground, flat on my fanny pack and hung my head, willing him to take a few steps back. Slate was roaring with anger in my mind, and I didn't blame him. That had been way too close.

"Walk away," I said hoarsely. I balled my hands into fists so I wouldn't try to grab his pant leg.

Relief washed over me when he obliged and fell onto my back with my eyes closed, just breathing. I could do it. I was in control, not the rousen or, if Brass was right, a bunch of crazy chemicals in my brain.

While I was dusting myself off, I felt someone approaching, brimming with an indiscriminate lust. A man who appreciated women's bodies in all their shapes and ages coming right for me. I stiffened and raised my head. It was Hopper, the owner of the weapons shop in Thrimilci and Anthias's older brother. A wave of heat went through me, taking the edge off my unraveling control.

Hopper was average height for a Guardian, which was tall for everywhere else in the world, at six feet. He was burly and heavily muscled, with dark blue tattoos the same color as his eyes around his arms and a long blonde ponytail down his back.

"Looking good out there, sweetheart," Hopper said gruffly, and I smirked.

I'd told him my name, and he never used it. Hopper was a true pervert and had perfected his leer, which I was privileged to in that moment.

"How's it going, Hopper? Did you check out my run? Getting pretty quick," I said, smoothing my fringe.

"Nice haircut. Yeah, I suppose you stand a chance," he said wryly, and I felt Slate coming nearer with the bond.

"So, what's up? I've got to go change and get some more training in today. I've been out of commission."

Hopper laughed. "Everyone in Tidings knows you have been out of commission. I thought I would warn you, maybe you could do me a solid when you got the chance in return."

I pulled my sweat slicked hair over my shoulder and cocked my brow. "I'll bite. Warn me of what?"

"The beast you are making two backs with got into it with Lera last night."

My insides heated. "Yeah? And?" I cocked my hip and went for nonchalance.

"And I got to tell you, sweetheart. You are wasting your time with that one. I got to give it to you, though. I have been around them since it all started, and he always comes back. Even when there is someone else in the picture for her. Think about it. You meet some greater or lesser family super son who wants to court you and can offer the things all your uppity types crave, like a khoraz for rousen. You think that guy stands a chance now that Slate has weaned you off the purple passion?" He cocked an eyebrow. "Let us pretend you give this other guy a chance. What do you think it will be like running into Slate again on the street? You think that attachment goes away? Every time you see him, your body will respond like an involuntary muscle. It is not just you, it is like that for all recovering rousen addicts. No offense. Cordillera tried to break Slate of it by bedding another man, did not quite work out. When he moves on, he will not care either. You will care, but it will not matter."

"That seems pessimistic," I said in defense, and he chuckled.

"Realistic, sweetheart. You are a good girl. Get out before you get in too deep."

"Why are you telling me all this?" I asked, with a bag of rocks sinking in my stomach.

"They went in fighting; they came out like two peas in a pod," he said, and I thought I saw sympathy flash through his eyes.

I nodded. "Wasn't Chafer with them?" My palms felt cold, like all the blood was rushing to my legs, telling me to get the hell out of there.

"Chafer is out on a mission." He gave a reluctant smile.

"Thanks. I'll take it under advisement."

"I did what I came to." He shrugged his bulky shoulders.

"Can I ask you something? Has Styg been around?" I asked flat out.

I needed the black-market goods dealer's help. I didn't know anyone else who had ties to the Stygians that would be even remotely willing to speak with me, and it would be a remote with Styg after I cut off his hand the last time we saw each other.

"He comes and goes. I would stay away from him if I were you. He will know you are on rousen and that would be a very bad day for you... or good I suppose, depending on what you are into," he said, flashing me a leer.

I wrinkled my nose. "Not in this lifetime. Thanks, Hopper."

Hopper's dark blue eyes glittered. "After you knocked my sister unconscious, I would say you owe me two, but knowing her, she deserved it. Thank you for not killing her."

"Thank Brass for that or I might have." My smile had too many teeth to it to be friendly and Hopper snorted before walking away.

Hopper had voiced the worries that had sprung up in my mind since I started forming coherent thoughts. I knew Slate was terrible for me. He'd shown me that repeatedly by betraying my trust and by making executive decisions about me without consulting me. I kept telling myself that he was always there, though. Whenever I needed to be pulled back from the abyss, he healed and cared for me.

Right?

Just who oversaw my poor decision making while I was half drugged, being seduced by some sinfully savage sex god and let me swear a blood oath of marriage to him? I would have done anything he asked. He only needed to open his mouth. I was starting to understand, with horrendous clarity, the dynamic between Slate and Cordillera.

"Torch."

I was staring into my cubby feeling like a world class idiot in my snug black pants tucked into black supple leather boots and a chocolate brown ribbed, long sleeve shirt. The stone pendant necklace nestled into my shirt and squeezed my silver torque at my wrist and the emerald ring. I strapped my seax to my thigh. I had a knife belt with a golden Daymark buckle around my waist and daggers tucked into both my boots; my usual weapons collection.

My wrist blades sat on the bench beside me. They had solid gold lace work over the black bracer so it would deflect. Three blades angled away from the outside of the bracer as the blade shot out, giving me three added blades on the sides of them. Slate had given them to me when I was inducted into Valla University. Things had certainly changed a lot since.

I lifted my blank gaze to Slate. I hadn't showered and was still feeling sticky, but we had more training to do and wearing the little leather outfit was too much for my fragile will. The more clothes, the better.

"What did she say about Karkinos?" I asked without inflection.

The jade love rune hung below his right ear and would easily hide in his wavy midnight mane. He was also wearing my father's ring on a different finger. I decided not to mention it until I was sure I didn't need him anymore. I would try to make fewer waves. It would be harder when I was weak from the rousen and cantankerous, but I would make more effort.

Slate was head to toe black, like all the Shadow Breakers. His silver predatory eyes took me in and I turned away, buckling my wrist blades on.

"We are going to send out a team on reconnaissance and set someone local up on each of the islands to keep their ear to the ground. No one has ever broken into or out of Karkinos, but if something is wrong, we need to know. It is out of Shadow Breaker hands to handle it, but Lera wants the Prime to owe her a favor."

He walked down the aisle with his graceful swagger and leaned against the cubby next to me. He towered over me, dark and dangerous, crossing his corded bronze muscled arms over his arms. I dropped my gaze and picked up the other wrist blade.

"If anything big goes down, I want in. Don't argue. If you don't let me, I'll find out," I said, buckling the wrist blade on.

I twisted my pinky and triggered the blade with a satisfying shing, then retracted it again. I'd never tire of that; it shot a thrill through me every time.

"What is wrong, Torch?"

"Nothing. Are you going to train with us now, or are you going back upstairs?"

With Lera.

He ran his thumb along his powerful jaw as if he was thinking about it. "I do not think it would be good for us to train together."

I nodded and rose to my feet. The prep room was mostly empty, so there wasn't anyone else in our aisle.

"See you later," I said before turning towards the metal doors and heading out.

Slate grabbed my wrist and whirled me around so my face almost knocked against his chest.

"What are you doing?" I hissed. "You want your girlfriend to see us?"

Slate squeezed me tight around my hips. "I do what I want, whenever I want, with who I want, Torch." He growled.

I set my jaw. "I believe you."

"What is wrong? What did Hopper say to you, or was it Brass who got you hot and bothered?"

My cheeks heated. "I do what I want, whenever I want, with who I want." I threw his words back in his face and he snarled. "Doesn't feel very good? Welcome to my world. Did you sleep with her the other night? Or last night? Tell me the truth, so when she rubs it in my face I'll be prepared."

"What did I say about when you are in my bed?"

"We aren't in your bed, though, are we?"

"No, it is *our* bed," he stressed, and butterflies who had no concern for my laundry list of complaints about Slate beat in my stomach.

"What happened the other night then? Why did you two argue?"

He loosened his hands on me. "Does everyone have an opinion about what we do together?" He sighed, "It was what you would expect. She does not want one of her captains distracted"

I snorted derisively. "Right. That was exactly what I expected." I yanked away from Slate and shot him a look of disdain. "Do whatever you wish, with whomever you wish. I am properly ensnared. I'm not going anywhere."

"Enough! When you listen to others, you let them get into your head," Slate growled.

"I can't trust you!" I shouted over him, "You tattooed me while I was unconscious. You've paraded your lovers in front of me. You brought another woman to my birthday. You told me you didn't bring women home, but I caught you with that brunette. I bet you just took her outside on the balcony or something, so technically, your rules weren't broken. You ruined the infinitesimal chance I had to be happy with Brass. I was willing to end everything I'd planned for my life for *you*. You slept with Anthias! I'm irreparably broken; my heart has been sliced and diced in a thousand different ways from you to my parents, to the Stygians.... the move. I lost our baby!"

I took a great ragged breath.

"I may not have been happy in Chicago, but I would have been once I finished college and met a good, nice, *normal* boy; one who didn't kill people or wear blades hidden all over his body. I would have married this wonderfully ordinary man, had his children, and my mother would have been alive to see me grow old and play with her grandkids."

The dam had burst and there was no returning all my emotions back into my figurative little lock box that I had crammed full of things I couldn't deal with. I missed my mother more than anything in the world. Every day without her was a struggle within me to get out of bed in the morning. I wanted to be selfish.

When Alder was dying, I wanted to die with him. The only reason I didn't get myself killed during my time with the bearded kidnappers was because of Jett and Indigo. Tawny and Gypsum would get over it in time, so would everyone else. They had each other, but Jett and Indigo had lost so much already. I couldn't do that to them, and truth be told, Sparrow.

Anywhere else but there, my breakdown would have been okay. I needed to cry, my body demanded it. It wouldn't solve a thing, but it was a long time coming. Slate took a step forward, and I held out my hands as tears poured in torrents down my cheeks. If I was feeling charitable, I would have kissed him and deactivated the bond, but I couldn't bring myself to be touched by him.

He stared, grey eyes soft and gleaming, his hands slightly lifted as if he wanted to hold me. I couldn't allow that, not after I tore the scab off all my old wounds and rubbed salt in them. I skirted him as I hurried to my cubby and pulled my cloak out, not caring how strange I looked with the hood pulled up indoors. It'd be worse if the Shadow Breakers saw me a blubbering mess.

I'd failed completely at not making waves. I'd done the exact opposite. I kept my head down as I climbed the stone stairs from the bottom level until I reached the rumpus room also known as the Shadow Breaker's recreation room and where they took their meals.

I passed the pinball machines, the scattered round tables and Breakers eating lunch. The bartender wiped at the polished counter as I hurried by to the crack of pool balls on the other side of the room. It was a high-ceilinged loft like room with scattered rugs over the wood floor. The walls were a dark purple and to the left was a single door that led to Cordillera's office. If she opened it, I would bolt. I didn't know if I'd ever come back.

As I turned towards the hall that led outside, Ama and Shale came around the opposite stairwell that led to the higher floors lost in conversation. I ducked my head and stayed out of the hanging lamps above direct light. Once I made it into the hall, I started to run and sob and pray no one was coming in through the secret dead-end passage as I was running out.

I went through the stone wall that camouflaged the entrance and didn't look back.

FOURTEEN

When I got back to the Sumar palace, no one had expected me home so I went up to the apartment, stripped off my clothes and weapons, and had a long cry under a hot shower.

The tears kept coming. The floodgates were down and I couldn't stop. I managed a bleary-eyed conversation with one of the staff, so dinner we be brought up later, assuming I would have an appetite. I crawled into bed and let the tears fall. There was nothing else to be done. I didn't want to be held or comforted, I only wanted things to go back to the way they were. If past me met future me, I would've thought I was crazy with all my magic talk and assassins.

I felt Slate drawing closer and knew he had come home. He didn't come into the bedroom, though he knew I was there. He must have left shortly after I did, which made me wonder what he did before he came and why he bothered to at all.

I dozed off with a wad of tissue in my hand that'd I'd been using to wipe my runny nose. Slate stroked my half damp hair away from my face until I stirred.

I rolled over and looked at him. His silky waves fell over his shoulder as he leaned over me. He'd changed into a pair of low-slung drawstring pants. Light poured through the windows, so I knew I couldn't have slept for very long. I was miserable and could feel how swollen my face was from crying. Probably red, too.

"Come. I want to show you something," he said gently as he ran the pads of his fingers over my swollen lips.

I wiped my nose with the clutched tissue. "Can't I stay in bed? I'm not feeling well. I don't want to be healed, either. Some things you should feel."

"It is not far. Please."

Swinging my legs over the side of our big white bed, I pushed loose strands of my hair back into my bun high on my head. I'd pulled on my ultra-soft, knee-high socks and an old Chicago Bears t-shirt with a pair of white cotton boy shorts before climbing into bed. Someone had moved a bunch of my stuff into the apartment while we were at the funeral yesterday. It saved me the trip, but now I wasn't sure if it was a good idea. What if I moved it all right back the very next day?

I walked leadenly to Slate, who stood barefoot and shirtless, looking down at me. He slid his hand into mine. I hadn't investigated the apartment. They confined me to the bedroom for the first few days, and after that I spent some time in the living room, but otherwise I'd only just passed doors with a goal in mind.

The short hall between the bedroom and the dining room held two doors. I figured one was a guest bathroom and the other a closet, but when Slate opened the door, my breath caught.

It was a nursery with sea foam green walls and an off-white crib and dresser, complete with changing table. An off-white plush chair sat in the corner piled with stuffed animals next to a short bookcase filled with brightly colored titles. A wood carved rocking horse sat to the side. Pictures my mother had mailed to Pearl of her and I doing things while we lived in Chicago were framed on top of the dresser. There was one of us laughing while she tickled me when I was ten, another of us picnicking at the lake. The third one my mother took while I was being pushed in the swing that hung from the gigantic tree in our front yard, but what really caught my eye was the painting.

Above the crib was one painting my mother had sold right before we moved. Sparrow had tracked a bunch down after her death. I had one in my room, but that one had always been my favorite. I thought she'd held on to it for a reason, but I understood it better than ever. It was the tree of life with deep, curling roots, a blazing golden sun shone down on a cat and a deer dancing next to a pond where a mermaid leaned on sparse grass. I thought it was whimsical, and it was, but it was also home.

I raised my hand over my mouth in disbelief, dropping Slate's hand as I moved around the room. Tears stung my eyes as I tried to comprehend what he was showing me.

"You?" was all I uttered, and it came out thick and throaty before it choked off.

He gave a curt nod, and I looked around again.

"I don't understand," I strangled out as I wiped at my nose with the soggy tissue.

He stood in the doorway watching me intensely. "I started having this wing redone around your birthday. I kept away because you have a penchant for fighting with me. I had to reevaluate. Pearl allowed me to move into the wing without giving her any details and had things brought in. I felt I knew you well enough to see to things on my own and any adjustments you would make would be minor."

Through the bond, I could feel how nervous he was, but looking right at him, he was the picture of calm. He'd guessed right. I loved everything.

"You did it yourself?" I asked shakily and decided sitting down would be a good idea before I passed out.

I plopped down on the plush chair and shifted to pull a stuffed teddy bear out from under me. Anguish strangled my throat, and I put the bear behind me. I would have been taken care of; Slate had planned to be there for me after all.

"Pearl uses a decorator to order furniture and help bring in people to remodel if needed, but yes. I chose the furniture, the colors and all." Slate explained, filling the doorway.

I breathed in a deep breath. "You didn't want kids."

The corner of his mouth quirked. "I knew if I came to you with a proposal and nothing to show you, that you would shoot me down."

"But now I can't," I said, feeling tears come again.

"I do not want to give you hope, Scarlett. After a human has been with a Merfolk, and been in a similar position, things heal. It is a slow process, but as far as I know, no one has been has had as much to heal from as you. It is like the rousen, why we cannot simply counteract the potion with our healing. We are not all powerful. Some things only time can cure."

He stepped into the room, looking phenomenally out of place. Slate was darkness personified surrounded by stuffed animals and a rocking horse. He moved to my side and held out his hand with my father's ring back in its rightful place.

"You weren't wearing your ring." I didn't want to get into another fight.

Slate ran his thumb along the brushed stone surface. "Lera does not know. We will wait until Chafer returns, then it will not matter."

I scanned his face for any flicker of jealousy or unrequited love. I didn't see it and I didn't feel it through the bond. If anything, it irritated him. He didn't mention the vows we exchanged. Normally, Guardians didn't exchange blood for the marriage vows but we had. I did not know what the repercussions of that would be, but I didn't plan on finding out.

"Do you still care about her?"

There was no stopping the question from coming out. I had to know what I was dealing with. Slate held out his hand again, and I placed mine in it tentatively. He pulled me up and into his arms. His grey eyes scanned mine.

"I care, but not as a man does a woman. As a friend for another friend. I do not love Lera. Many years ago for a short time, perhaps, but that is long past."

"What about the others?" I pressed and rested my hands on his biceps.

"Amber and Lynx are the only other two I have seen regularly, and I never loved either."

"Lynx?" I asked, feeling a hot pain shoot through me at this new, unknown rival.

"The brunette," he answered, and the insides of my ears heated.

"What about Anthias? She made it seem like you two saw one another frequently."

He drew his brow down. "When did you speak to Anthias?"

"Quick and I went into Hopper's shop to replace the blades I'd lost during the Wild Hunt, and she was there talking about you."

Slate drew in a deep breath and pressed his lips into a firm line. "Did you two get into an argument?"

"Not really. She called you her lover and at the time I was... It pissed me off so when Hopper asked if I'd put in a good word for her if Cordillera recruits, I told her Lera didn't let girls you slept with into the Shadow Breakers."

I bit my bottom lip.

"I thought she chose your looks because she thought I would be attracted to you. I did not know she spoke to you about me. She sought me out that night intentionally to hurt you. Fucking Mirage." Slate cursed, loosening his arms at my waist. "She and I have been nothing more than the occasional drunken go around."

I cringed at his words, and his anger dropped in an instant. I moved past him and into the hall, heading towards the sitting room. When I had given myself to Brass that night after we'd gone to the movies, I'd done it knowing I'd be leaving a piece of myself with him. That's why I'd chosen Brass. He could be trusted and didn't have *drunken go arounds*.

Someone knocked on the door. It was the perfect opportunity to collect my thoughts and get away from Slate's cavalier attitude about his relationship with Mirage. I pulled on my robe and answered the door, unsurprised to find that there were two trays instead of one. The staff member dressed in Sumar royal blue pushed in the cart and I smiled, dismissing her before closing the door and wheeling the cart over to the table.

I'd gotten used to eating in the bedroom or the sitting room if I wasn't eating in the informal dining hall and it felt strange to eat in the dining room alone.

Slate moved into the room behind me and watched me set things out on the coffee table for us both. "Say something, Torch."

"Where are you keeping the rousen? I think I can monitor my dosage myself," I said, ignoring his comment.

He stormed back into the dining room, and I heard him open and lock something before returning with a single vial. "We do it my way. I will not risk your well-being in case the temptation is too great." He picked up my hand and slapped the vial into it. "You will drink it and when you need me, then we will talk." Slate scoffed.

"The room is beautiful. The apartment is, too. There isn't anything I would change about it," I said as I replaced the plate covers on the cart.

"Compliments from you are like pulling teeth unless you are drugged," Slate huffed, and my cheeks heated.

I was liberal with compliments when I was on the rousen, and I didn't lie. It was humiliating. I turned to him, placing my hands on my hips.

"What more you want from me? I'm here. I'm not running and I'm trying, Slate. Do you know how hard it is to forgive you when my nose is constantly being rubbed in one of your lovers' faces every time I turn around?"

"If I could take back the night of the masquerade, I would a hundred times over."

I sighed and sat down on the beige couch, pushing off my satin robe. "We can't be nice to each other for a full day. We never could. Since I met you, we argue constantly. I don't know why I thought it could be different."

Slate moved beside me and pulled my hands away from my face where I'd buried it. "Do you care about me, Scarlett? Truly care?"

I gave him a tired, rueful grin. "If you really wanted me to pay you a compliment, I can do it. What about you? Do you care about me?"

He was irritated I hadn't answered, but he let it go. "Scarlett, you make me want to live. You give me hope that someone will love me and miss me once I am gone. You are my hope that if, on the off chance, the prophecy is wrong I can make a life with you."

My mouth dropped open.

"You will not die anytime soon. Stop that talk, Slate. I won't listen to it. I..." I trailed off, biting my lip. His eyes searched mine, trying to read my emotions through the bond. "I'm in love with you. I have been falling in love with you since the moment I saw you. It scares the sugarfoot out of me because you've hurt me so badly. I knew if I ever let myself get close, you'd crush me." I laughed nervously, "If you hadn't been with Lera in the powder room that night, when you came to my bed... I would have done whatever you wanted."

"You wanted me that same night," he said, looking more like himself as his lips curled.

I rolled my eyes. "I thought you were a dream."

"I know. You wanted me then, though. I could smell it on you. You could fight me with your words, but your body, your scent, said otherwise," he purred.

I looked at him from the corner of my puffy eyes. I'd gambled on Slate before and lost big. There I was doing it again. I was all in or it would never work. My hands lifted from his and slid over his jaw, my palms rasped against his blue-black stubble as I cupped his face.

"All that I know of a certain star is, it can throw (like the angled spar). Now a dart of red. Now a dart of blue, Till my friends have said, They would fain see, too. My star that dartles the red and the blue! Then it stops like a bird; like a flower, hangs furled: They must solace themselves with the Saturn above it. What matter to me if their star is a world. Mine has opened its soul to me; therefore, I love it. I love you, Slate. Forever and always. Yours, mine, the world's, for all time."

The Brownings were some of my favorite poets. My words tended to be on the caustic side, but I could make them sweet. I slanted my swollen lips over his and he sighed, filling my nose with his heady scent of cloves and freshly fallen leaves.

"Scarlett," he breathed, "I do not want to wait until you are on the rousen. I need you now."

I made some indiscernible noise of assent, and that was that.

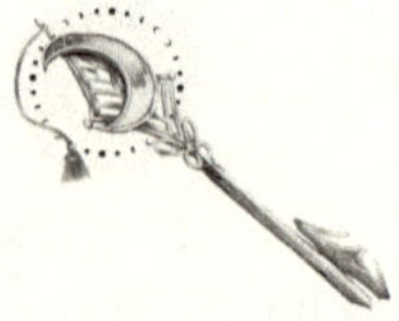

We trained at the Sumar palace. The training room was enormous. It was a conservatory the size of the stadium my high school football team played at. Many plants and trees lined the gravel track. They divided it into several sections: an obstacle course, a weightlifting area, an area that held all different weapons with mats, and a section for archery. It was all things Tidings — beauty and potentially lethal.

It'd been ages since I'd trained with the others, and they were all excited for us to join them. Slate fell easily back into training mode, bossing me around and demanding more from me than I was willing to give. Gypsum was the only one who loved the challenge. The rest of us, including Cherry and Amethyst, shot Slate more than one glare behind his back.

"If he's half as demanding in bed, no wonder you look the way you do," Cherry muttered, not having trained much with Slate since moving into the Sumar palace after marrying Jett.

I blushed down to my toes. If they only knew.

The girls joined Tawny, Indigo, Pearl, and Sparrow for lunch in Thrimilci. Something we'd never done before. They could not withhold their pestering comments about Slate. They wanted to know what was going on. It wasn't a topic I was comfortable with, but I answered as honestly as I could.

"It's still new, so I don't really want to put a name to it yet," I said cryptically, and Tawny snorted.

"You're living together. While I agree, he's taken care of you and you seem happy, it would have been impossible for you to separate how you felt from how he's cared for you. Don't get me wrong, he was the best man for the job, but he was also the worst. I hope it works out, but if it doesn't, I'll help you move out of there so fast his head will spin."

"Tawny, a little optimism would go a long way. Don't rain on her parade," Sparrow chastised. "How would you have felt if Scarlett hadn't supported you and Steel?"

Tawny's fair, heart-shaped face blushed. I might have been Tawny's only supporter in the beginning. "Point taken," Tawny sighed with a groan. "I'm sorry. You just deserve two heaping helpings of happiness, and if he hurts you again, I'll have to kill him."

I smiled at her. "Thanks."

"Scarlett, I wanted you to know that the way Ash acted after was deplorable. I know my brothers are embarrassed by his actions, as am I." Amethyst gave a small rueful smile.

"That means a lot to me coming from you, Amethyst. Thank you." I got up and hugged my sister-in-law.

Her big dark eyes grew watery, and she chuckled weakly, "Hormones. I cry all the time."

Pearl squeezed her hand. "I do not think you are the only one, darling."

The subject turned lighter after clearing the air. I'd wondered how Amethyst felt about the whole thing but had been too nervous about her response to ask. There were a few topics we didn't touch: Alder, my mother, the Merfolk, or the spark of life — a term I was far more comfortable with than *baby*.

I didn't bring up the Stygians or Karkinos. They might retaliate against my family worse than they already had. Not understanding why we'd been targeted was the most frightening aspect by far. Slate had been a target, but I understood that it was because he was so close to Cordillera and was a Shadow Breaker. Though, killing their men when fighting the bauk and then the vodyanoy were the likeliest of reasons when it came to their vendetta against me.

The day had been blissfully normal. I could have days like it for the rest of my life and die a happy woman. When I got back to the apartment, Slate had gotten in shortly before me.

"Chafer back yet?" I asked, and Slate looked over his shoulder at me with an impish grin.

"Impatient to claim me, Torch?"

I walked behind him, my silvery flowing dress floating along the floor. I wrapped around his waist and rested my cheek on his back, startling him.

"Not wanting to tempt fate, but you are in good spirits."

"I had a normal day. It was wonderful. Be my date for the ceremony." I tugged on the hem of his shirt from his pants and slid my hands against his hot skin.

I traced the ridges of his steel muscles with my fingertips and wondered if a fallen light had knocked me out at my college graduation and I was in a coma that I'd soon wake up from to find out the last year wasn't real. Slate turned in my arms and deprived me of his abs, but there was plenty more to fondle from the new angle as I slid my palms under his waistband to run over the hard curve of his delectable fanny pack.

His silver eyes glittered as he looked down at me. "I do not want to go." I knit my brows and pulled my hands from his pants, but he stilled them and wrapped his arms around me. "We both know we will argue. We could stay here, gorge ourselves on one another and find creative ways to eat our supper." Slate ran his fingers down my spine, making me shiver.

"If they're going to talk about me, I'd rather it be to my face. What if I promise not to argue? If we get angry, we'll come back and go with your plan with lots of nakedness... and chocolate. Actually, that sounds like the perfect ending to a perfect day. We could do that tonight too," I joked.

Slate made a contented sound deep in his throat and intertwined his fingers in my hair, canting my mouth towards him. "If I had been a cleverer man, we would have had this for months instead of only beginning."

"Clever how? You mean instead of trying to force your way into my bed? I never said no when you asked me to go somewhere with you as long as it wasn't to your bed."

He ran his teeth over his lower lip as he reversed me through the apartment. "If I had asked you out to sup with me, you would have said... how did you put it? Oh yes, find someone else to buy what *you're* selling. We're all full up here."

I giggled at the memory. "I said that, didn't I? You were so pushy, and you were always with other women."

"From the moment you met my team, you have been spending all your free time with them. Certain subordinates in particular. I was always there."

I failed miserably at hiding a blush.

"I see you now," I purred.

Slate growled as he lifted me and threw me backwards onto the bed.

CHAPTER 15
JETT

All the ladies had gone out for some shopping, lunch, and the inevitable gossip session. Slate and Scarlett had shown up to training. It was the first time she'd been there in months. She'd spent her time between Ash's and the Shadow Breakers since their mother's death.

It astounded Jett how much she'd changed. She'd always have soft curves, it was in her genes, but other than that she was all lean muscle. Cherry had hinted at the overwhelmingly obvious answer for that. Little food and enough sex to last a lifetime. *Thank you, Cherry.*

Brass and Quick had shown up shortly after the girls left to check in with Slate and see how things were evolving. Slate said Scarlett had finally released all the bottled emotions she'd hoarded away inside her, making her a ticking time bomb. He said she was doing better now, but yesterday had been hairy. He confided he thought she was going to run back to Chicago or to find another way to lose herself, but she'd stayed.

Progress.

"Lera wants to make sure she is ready for her competition. Personally, I do not think she is ready for a patron," Brass said, crossing his arms. "Whenever we are alone, her hands wander, though she fights it."

Slate grunted. Jett seconded that grunt. He didn't want Scarlett ever to be locked in one of those rooms with one of those jerks. They wouldn't know she was from a greater family and had more money than she could spend in three lifetimes from birth. She'd be touched and paraded around like a coveted little trophy. They'd treat her like a toy to be played with.

Granted, most Shadow Breakers enjoyed it. It was the closest thing they had to professional athletes.

"I do not mean to pry, but a couple from Hopper's team said they heard her shouting at you in the prep room. All is well on the happy home front?" Quick asked, leaning against one of the weight machines.

The corners of Slate's mouth quirked, and Jett suppressed a sigh. gods, he'd never seen Slate act like that in all his life. From all accounts, when they weren't in bed, she was yelling at him. Not that he didn't deserve it.

Slate and Scarlett had been throwing off so much heat at one another, the training grounds were downright uncomfortable. If he never had to watch Slate lick his lips as she jogged in front of him for the rest of his life, he would die a much happier man.

"She is coming around," Slate said cryptically, making Jett want to tear his hair out.

"Now what does that mean?" Jett asked, exasperated.

Gypsum, Steel, and Hawk were sparring, so they couldn't overhear what the four men were discussing. Hawk seldomly came to train with the men, but when he did, he taught them a thing or two about speed over strength. Hawk was lithe and built like a dancer, with lightning-fast reflexes that made Jett feel like a bumbling ox.

"I moved her in. I left some of her items in her old room, but the bulk of it is in our wing." Slate smirked then, and Jett rolled his eyes.

It was a smart move to not clear out her room. She needed to feel like she had options and that she wasn't trapped, or she'd dig her heels in even if it was what she wanted. Even if she was now trapped with Slate.

Brass rubbed his stubbled jaw and looked at Slate speculatively. If Jett didn't know any better, he'd say Brass was trying to cover up a frown. Slate and Brass had a plan or deal of sorts and if Scarlett ever found out, she'd give them an ear searing that'd leave them sizzling. They both knew it, and they both kept their mouths shut about it.

"Why do I feel that is not all that is making you so smug?" Brass asked.

Jett pointed to Brass. "As if we didn't notice you both wearing those rings. You have my father's wedding band on, Slate. Which could have only come from one person unless you're sucking face with Indigo."

"What?" Quick asked, drawing down his brow.

Slate held his hands up. "I did not. I swear it."

"Why would I care?" Quick asked as his face grew stony.

"I'm going to lose my shit if you guys don't stop talking about my sisters like objects," Jett cursed.

"Scarlett vowed herself," Slate boasted, and Jett's eyes widened.

"When you say vow, do you by chance mean marriage vow?" Jett asked, dumbfounded.

Slate nodded, "Blood oath sworn."

Quick let out a low whistle and Jett dry washed his face.

"Your first goal has been met," Brass said, looking reluctant. "I guess that means she cannot say the vows to anyone else."

Slate chuckled darkly, "She is mine." Slate's smile held too many teeth, but Brass only smirked.

"All is fair in love and war." Brass shrugged, "We will see how she feels when she is no longer on rousen." Slate's smile fell. "What is next?"

"We keep her safe until we can find the Stygians responsible. Plan for her to be doing her own investigation as she still does not under-stand the danger she is in. She does the opposite of everything I say," Slate said with strange admiration.

"I will try to lead her away from the truth," Brass offered.

Slate set his jaw. "Do that." Brass smiled puckishly and Slate growled. "I do not know why she is fond of you."

"Only fond? Last time we were alone, I would say she was more than fond. Because I am the opposite of you. Good with people, smiles often, and I do not seduce her. One thing I have learned with her is the simpler you keep things, the more she is drawn to you. That is a free tip, next one will cost you," Brass said.

"You are lucky we have known each other as long as we have," Slate growled.

Brass waved dismissively. "Words. You are jealous. Welcome to what we mere humans deal with." Quick and Brass laughed, Slate smiled grudgingly, and Jett thought he was losing his mind.

"Just don't let her go chasing down some Stygians and get herself killed or worse, sent as a khoraz to the Crathode or the Anguillan." Jett ran his hand over the back of his head.

These men, scratch that, sociopaths oversaw Scarlett's safety. Jett shook his head. He'd do anything to protect her, even abiding by her moving into the lair of the most dangerous man Jett knew. He doubted Scarlett knew half of what Slate was capable of.

Slate made a face at the iPod player Jett had played on a side table and Jett crossed his arms.

"You don't like it. You can leave," Jett said defensively. They always gave him crap about his music.

Gypsum thought it was awesome, so at least one other person than himself had a taste. Jett had someone new to appreciate the refurbished technology he smuggled into Tidings.

"Turn it up!" Gyps shouted, and Jett called air to push the volume button.

Quick snorted, "Myopics. Your whole family."

Jett jutted out his jaw in an arrogant smile. "I like Myopics. Simple humans, no calling, or tribes to worry about. I'll take that as a compliment." Jett turned around and started dancing as the other men laughed.

"Up all night to get lucky?" Slate pursed his lips. "Perhaps it is not such an awful song after all."

Jett stopped dancing and turned around. He called to make it skip to the next track. The other men laughed.

"For the record, I wish the three of you had sisters so you knew what torture you're putting me through." Things would've been easier if they had been hermits.

CHAPTER
SIXTEEN

Sex for breakfast. Mmm.

Slate's life philosophy must have been anything worth doing was worth doing extremely well. I was wondering if there was anything he'd tried that he didn't excel at.

Lying in a naked tangle of limbs, I had no desire to go to the induction ceremony any longer. He'd made a very convincing argument twice that morning. I ran my palm down my stomach, unable to believe how amazing I felt.

After my breakdown, I decided not to dwell on the things I couldn't change and focus on the things I could do to fix them. Stygians being foremost on my list. They had to pay for what they did to my dad, to me, and I knew they were the ones responsible for my mother. Then there was the simple matter of them having a contract out on Slate.

If I lost him too... best not to think about that.

"Ooh. What was that thought, Torch?"

I lifted my head to look down at him. We'd kind of fallen over where we finished so Slate's head was down by the foot of the bed.

"Bad thoughts. I'm trying not to think them. How much was in the vial last night? That was the latest I'd ever taken it," I said, feeling pretty fiddlesticking awesome.

I'd kick the rousen in record time.

"Come." Slate crooked a finger at me, and I arched an eyebrow.

I called. I'd sort of lifted Slate with my calling before and once I learned to do something, I didn't forget. It helped that I was extraordinarily powerful at it. Slate's eyes widened when he began to levitate only a few inches, but still. I pulled him clear of my limbs before gliding him up to me and turned him over so he hovered directly above me. I bit my lip at how his hair swung, as well as other, um, parts of him.

"Can you levitate yourself?" Slate asked, placing his hands to either side of my shoulders.

I shook my head, "No."

He cocked a brow over his dancing silver eyes. "Let us be sure."

He slid his arms around my back to lift me and my calling slipped, dumping his body on top of mine. His nose hit my forehead, and the air was forced from my lungs by his weight.

Slate rolled off me and held his nose, I rubbed my forehead and leaned to my side to inspect his nose.

"Let me see. Are you bleeding?" I asked, trying to pull his hands away.

A little trickle of blood trickled from his straight masculine nose and his full lips curled mockingly at me. "Hardheaded woman."

I ran my finger down his nose healing it and settled over the small flat spot on his bridge. "Why didn't this heal right?"

He rolled to his side propping his head up in his palm freeing his other hand to roam over my body. My skin prickled at his attention, his eyes watched my nipples harden and I watched him grow hard. I cleared my throat with a smirk.

"Jett hit it with a barbell when we were younger. It was my fault; I would not let them heal it. I wanted a reminder of what my temper could lead to," Slate said, kneading my breast.

I gaped, "He hit you with barbell? Have you guys always fought like that? You seem like best of friends now." He lowered his mouth to my hard peak, and I pushed him off. "Tell me. I barely know anything about you."

Slate's smile was arrogant and mocking, it was an old Slate smile. "Jett, Steel, Quick, and Brass are my closest confidants along with Lera. Not what you wanted to hear was it, Torch?"

"How can I not be upset? You didn't name me. You trust all of them before you would me and I'm the one here with you sharing your bed. Maybe I should go back down to my room so you can keep your secrets," I huffed.

"Idle threats, Torch. We both know you could not leave me now if you wanted to. Some things are better kept secret. You know all you need to."

Slate slid his hand down my stomach and I held it still. My face was fiery with anger, and he'd just stepped over my invisible line. Only I was allowed to joke about how I was stuck with him. He couldn't because then it felt like he was rubbing it in my face.

"Freya's burly boar! You can be such a jerk, you know that?"

I clambered over him slapping his hands away as he chuckled trying to grope me and stormed into the closet. I could feel him follow me in there and tried to shut the door on him, but he caught it by the tips of his fingers and pushed it open.

"What do you want to know? Ask away," Slate said, standing gloriously naked in front of me, making thoughts difficult.

I was undressed too and only a fraction as comfortable with it as he was, so I crossed my arms and tried to look nonchalant. "What was the fight about?"

Slate sighed. "I saw Lera and Jett in the prep room here together. The fight dragged out into the training grounds."

"Why would Jett use a barbell? You are evenly matched — seems like a low blow."

"He needed to. I was out of control."

I frowned. "Did you really not sleep with Amber after my party?"

"I did not have sex with Amber after you fought her."

"But you did other things." I dropped my arms and growled. "I hate that you bandy your words. Just be honest! Scarlett, she sucked my big fucking cock until she choked," I mocked in a deep bass.

I wanted nothing more than to get dressed and I started pulling out clothes for the day. Clasping my bra and stepping into panties as I walked almost made me trip.

"You were engaged."

I wrinkled my nose and swiped my hand through the air.

It was the international symbol for shut the fiddlestick up. I didn't want to hear excuses.

"You are a sugarfoot prophet. You said you knew Ash and I wouldn't get married, but you didn't know why. Well, why couldn't you see that this would end up happening and not slept with every woman ever?" I pulled a long white sleeve shirt over my head and smoothed my bangs down before looking for pants.

"You went to Brass for your needs. Do not tell me nothing happened with him that night. You wanted one another. Still do. You want answers, but when I give them to you, you do not want the truth. Tell me what you want to hear so I can feed it back to you." Slate turned around showing me his best side, that back side, and pulled out clothes of his own.

"Are you planning a way to get back at the Stygians?"

He stopped moving while only wearing a snug pair of black boxer briefs that barely contained him. I wondered why he even bothered with the stupid things.

"Focus, Torch. Stop looking at my big cock." He threw my words back at my face with his own brand of exaggeration — naturally. "Do you think I would let it go?"

"Where are you really from?" I asked.

His brow quirked surprised at my change in questions. "Mabon and Thrimilci both."

"Tell me something I don't know about you, Slate. Isn't there anything you've never told anyone? I want that. I want to have one of your secrets. You have all of mine." I raised my hands and let them fall with a slap against my bare thighs.

Slate dropped his pants to the floor and stalked over to me. He turned me against the wall and ripped my panties from my legs, so the tearing elastic burned against my skin. The worst part was that with Slate, I was in a permanent state of readiness, and he claimed to smell it on me. My back curved when I felt the smooth skin of his hips rub against my backside before he drove deep into me.

I cried out as he sunk to the hilt, and he growled against my ear. "I can tell you things I have told no one else, Torch. You are the best fuck I have ever had," he said as he pinned me to the wall, hands high above my head closed in a rough hand. "I have never been with a woman the way I am with you. Spending the night, waking up to you, even the way we fuck. Only with you, Torch."

I moaned in response feeling my insides coil deliciously at the words I didn't think I wanted to hear. His muscled body moved behind me, forcing me up onto my toes, as he drove deeper and harder.

"When you got here, I thought I was going to take you if you wanted it or not. You may have fought me at first, but I knew you would enjoy it in the end. I would have too, Torch. It consumed me. I walked around painfully hard trying to fuck you out of my mind."

He wrapped his fist into my hair and pulled my head back and crushed my mouth with his, kissing me possessively as his thrusts quickened. "I saw Amber because she resembled you and it satisfied a visceral part of me. I never slept with girls before you came around. Whenever I saw you kissing Ash, I did not care who she was as long as she could make me forget about you, even if it was only for a moment."

Slate's voice was rough, and pleasure built inside me as I pulsed around him. "It got so bad, whenever you touched me unwittingly, I left the palace. That afternoon you slapped me and had me carry your undergarments, I was going to make you, Torch. I had already been with Lera that morning, but it was not her I wanted — it was you. Always you. When you got into the argument with Jonquil and we were in that vacant room... Scarlett, if you had not kneed me — I would have fucked you in that classroom until the next dawn."

Slate slammed into me with powerful thrusts that lifted me off my feet. I cried out as I clenched around him, and I could feel his heart beating against my back after he filled me. He breathed harshly on the top of my head as he let my heels touch the floor.

"I hate you chose Brass over me," he ground out.

I took a deep shuddering breath now that my lungs could expand again. "That was more honesty than I bargained for," I said huskily, and I heard a breathy laugh amidst his panting.

"You are bad for my self-control, Torch. If you had only given yourself to me that first night." He laughed and stepped back sliding out of me and releasing my hands. "I would have been a less angry man."

"And I wouldn't have lasted a month with you. I'm not wired the way you are. I can't have sex and not feel. I'm a cliché. Sleep with me and you take a piece of me with you." I bent down and picked up the shreds of my panties and shook my head. "You could have just pushed them down."

"It was for effect, Torch. Do not tell me how to fuck you. Brass has a piece of you. Several pieces if he gets one each time he was inside you."

I never engaged him when he spoke about Brass. He was my one subject I wouldn't discuss. There was something there I hadn't addressed, and I knew it.

"Stop saying that word. I get the idea."

He was still hard and sweat glistened on the crease that separated his pecs. I had the most insane inclination to lick him there and shook my head like a dog. gods, I was spending too much time with him.

"Get dressed. I want to test your will today. If you fail, we will try again in a few more days. If you cannot pass it before your competition, you do not compete." Slate rumbled and my eyes widened as he walked away still wet from me and our sex before he pulled on his pants.

"Go shower. You can't tell me I can't compete, Slate. That's not up to you," I argued and went to find another pair of underwear.

"I will shower later. And it is up to me." He buckled his pants and yanked a shirt off a hanger.

I watched his muscles work as he pulled it over his head and used the back of his hand to pull his long midnight waves from under the shirt.

"You smell like sex and me, shower now. It's *not* up to you."

I used my underwear remains to wipe off his cum and incinerated the whole thing in the air. I would have to discuss a replacement word for it because I could not utter the word aloud.

Slate watched me intensely with his predatory gaze. He thought everything I did was sexual, which it wasn't.

"I enjoy smelling sweet like your —"

"Okay!" I interrupted.

'F' word was one thing, but if he said anything vulgar about my lady bits, I would fade from existence. During my meeting with Tawny, that would be the second word we found a replacement for.

Slate moved so he stood before me and held himself in a way that made me think I wouldn't like to hear his next words. "It *is* up to me,

Torch. You are my mate. You are mine. If you go into that room with the patron and anything happens, I will find out what is happening on Karkinos from the inside because I would tear whomever it was limb from limb," he said low and dangerous.

I shivered.

"Okay."

Slate stared at me a minute longer waiting, teeth grinding, to see if I'd offer any biting comments or retorts and when he was satisfied that I wouldn't, he walked away.

"You don't have to use your size to intimidate me. You could have said, 'Please my love, it would break my heart if you were intimate with another. Spare me my broken heart and wait until you are ready'."

I held the back of my wrist to my forehead for my dramatic performance and Slate spun around and stalked back over to me, making me back up against the wall.

"Do I intimidate you?"

Slate wasted no time in gripping my hair at the nape and exposing my throat, my heart rushed blood into my pulsing arteries he ran his tongue along. I felt his teeth graze my sensitive skin and sucked in a sharp breath.

"Sometimes," I whispered, and felt my legs turn into limp noodles.

"Wrong. You confuse fear with excitement. If I were to slip my hand into... ah." Slate slid his hand between my legs and my body responded. "You do not fear easily, Torch. You dislike losing control, and when you feel that thrill you always lose control. Give in to it. You will live much happier."

Slate dipped his finger into me, and I wondered where my dignity had fled to. "Is that how you live?"

"I only had to fight my urges with you, but no longer. Now I have you whenever I want you." He pulled his hand from beneath the fabric of my panties and slid his finger between his full lips, sucking hard before pulling it out with an audible pop.

Most things didn't embarrass me anymore, but that did. "Are you resorting back into your old self? Should I be worried?" I breathed, sliding along the wall to skirt him.

I didn't show him my back. When his primal side of him came out, he was unpredictable. His body pivoted to follow me, that mocking smile playing on his lips that simultaneously made me want to tear his clothes off and slap it from his arrogant face.

"Who is he that would become my follower? Who would sign himself a candidate for my affections? The way is suspicious — the result uncertain, perhaps destructive; You would have to give up all else — I alone would expect to be your God, sole and exclusive, Your novitiate would even then be long and exhausting. The whole past theory of your life, and all conformity to the surrounding lives, would have to be abandon'd; Therefore, release me now, before troubling yourself any further — Let go your hand from my shoulders. Put me down and depart on your way."

Slate's words gave me chills. I pulled my pants off the floor never letting my eyes leave his.

"You're always warning me. I think it's too late. Whatever you are, for better or worse, usually worse, I'm here," I said as I stepped into my pants and buttoned them before reversing out of the closet.

Slate followed me calling the knife belts he wore over his chest from the table and starting to buckle them under his shirt. It was disconcerting to watch them snake under his shirt. He was stalking me; I didn't know why he woke up on the crazy side of the bed this morning, but I was equal parts aroused and cautious. Did all his lovers feel this way or were they oblivious to the primitive beast that lurked within? What side of him did they see?

I called my boots and backed onto the bed so I could pull them on. Only then did Slate stop his chase. I finished readying, and we went down to breakfast with Slate still in his weird, territorial alpha mood. I hoped no one looked at him funny or at me indirectly, who knew what he'd do.

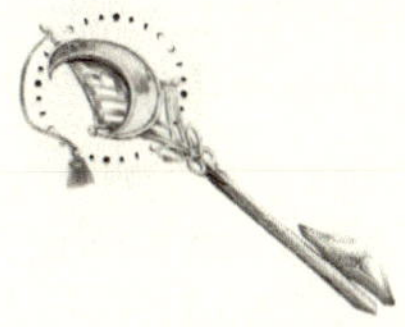

Breakfast was full of surprises; Slate had taken to sitting next to me at the palace table where he used to sit across from me. Indigo sat to my other side and would occasionally glance past at me in disbelief at the Brobdingnagian in the next seat over. Once or twice, I caught Jett looking at our rings. Fiddlesticking Slate must have told him. I had a feeling that Jett knew more about us than I did.

Pearl was slowly returning to normal as were the rest of us, and Sparrow had looked much better since our lunch date. Routine and time helped with the grief. We had to keep ourselves busy or my mind strayed to unpleasant thoughts.

"Sparrow and I have spent some time in the old Dagr palace. We're going to rehab it and get it back to working order," Hawk abruptly announced and Tawny frowned across the table from them.

"Since Sparrow is the last Dagr, we're also trying for an heir," Hawk rushed out and Tawny's mouth fell open.

"But what if you have another boy?" Tawny asked.

"It's unlikely we'll succeed, but we must at least try since there is no one to continue the line. Guardians do not have children after twenty-five or six, it's the price we pay for being longer lived. We understand the Vetrs needed a line more, and we'd much rather have you than one of the Natt twins take over," Sparrow reassured her.

"Well, can we make any sons of ours Dagrs?" Tawny offered and looked at Steel who only gave a shrug.

"It's an option we've been discussing," Sparrow gave him a small smile, and he inclined his head.

"Why now?" I asked, absently eating my omelet.

"Now we know there will be no heirs from the Dagr side," Hawk said.

"Yeah, but you've known that since Tawny took Orion's name. It's been almost a year."

"We were hoping another Dagr would resurface and be willing to take over as Dagr heir and have children. That is very unlikely now," Sparrow sighed.

"There may be more Dagrs out there? Wouldn't someone know if that were true?" Indigo queried, and I grimaced.

"You'd think they'd come out by now knowing the situation. It seems rather selfish not to help. How hard is it to pop out a few kids who are yours and need only have your name?" I chuckled darkly,

"Unless you're me, of course. Good luck continuing the female line of Tios, Indigo." I gave her a scornful smile, and she frowned.

"Do not say that, darling. You can adopt," Pearl said, and I nearly scoffed.

As if Slate would want to adopt. "The good news is, I can marry whomever I wish now. Right? There's no need to worry about family lines or anything because I can't continue them," I asked leaning forward to look at Hawk and Pearl.

"You could always marry who you wanted to, Scarlett, but it isn't as important to find a greater family companion as it was. For you, that is," Hawk finished.

"For me? Does that mean if I'd fallen for a man who needed to continue his line that it wouldn't be prudent for us to marry?"

Hawk, Sparrow, and Pearl nodded like a bunch of bobble heads.

"Well, I have absolutely no interest whatsoever in any greater families and their broods." My tone was haughty, and I almost missed the mood change. "What?"

I looked around and checked the faces that could not wall their emotions up from me. Steel and Jett being my prime suspects.

"I'm an empath. Please don't hide things from me, I'll find out and get more upset. I'm sick to death of secrets," I said, exasperated.

"Adopting could be an option," Slate said. My head nearly get turning I whipped it around so fast.

"Really?" I asked, amazed.

"Once you finish at Valla U, you could do whatever you wish."

Slate didn't meet my eyes, but I hoped he meant he would adopt a child with me. I felt a thrill that made my eyes well with tears. Even though I'd already given so much to be with Slate and forgiven if not forgotten his past actions, I was always fighting against falling deeper for him. Then he said something so hopelessly romantic, and it felt like my heart had grown too large for my chest.

I ate the rest of my breakfast thinking about names for my adopted children.

"So, what last name would my adopted children have?"

Jett laughed, "How many do you already have, Scarlett?"

I smiled ruefully, "I always imagined a few." I bit my lip, "So?"

"Tio, boys and girls, none of which would be eligible to be heirs, but could keep your name until they married and then they would take their spouse's last name and so on." Steel said, and I sighed.

No Sumar for Slate. That might've meant he had my last name? I turned to find Slate smiling arrogantly at me as if he read my mind. No, I wouldn't discuss that now and he knew it.

SEVENTEEN

When we went to Shadow Breaker headquarters, I had no idea Slate was going to make good on his promise to test me. Cordillera must have lifted the ban we didn't speak of, because Slate led our training today with Ama, Shale, and the Regn brothers. When Slate said he'd test my will, I thought that meant against him.

On the floor above the arena, a studio reached temperatures over one hundred degrees. When we reached the studio, it blasted me with the hot air. I'd done it a few times with Brass and the others, but that was when I was old Scarlett. Willpower Master Scarlett, not Broken Moral Compass Scarlett — the two looked a lot alike.

"No need to be shy. We have all seen what you bring to the table," Shale said smirking. Her long dark hair brushed her back as she pulled off her boots.

Quick, Brass, and Ama were all in on my training. Slate was there to supervise in case I lost it. Our bond was active, so he'd know how bad it was getting. I squirmed standing up with all the lust bouncing around from Shale and Ama, Quick always had a sort of muted desire like Brass, but somehow different. Like he appreciated my appearance, not that he wanted me. Brass's was less muted which I knew was because of the changes in me. Slate's was bone deep carnal pleasure — all night and day. I'd felt it from him before the rousen.

Ama, in her baby blue bra and white boy shorts, had a tight enviable body. Shale wore a black sheer bra and panties, and you could see everything. My eyes widened, but there was nowhere to look with all the mirrors and practically naked people. My sexuality was thrown into question.

Resigned, I pulled off my boots and socks. I wanted to be more flexible, I wanted to be faster, and I wanted to compete just to prove how wrong they were about so-called Myopics. My parents would be proud of the Guardian I'd become.

They were all taking time out of their lives to help me get to where I wanted to be.

"Take off your clothes, Torch," Slate purred, and it irritated me that those four words sent such a thrill through me.

It didn't help that the others chuckled, knowing how hard it was for me. "Don't take it easy on me or anything." I muttered.

Brass stood in his dark blue boxer briefs, his tall dark honey body looked velvety soft over all those hard muscles. By the Mother, I knew his skin didn't just look that soft — it was. The copper beads in his dark thick hair almost matched his skin where it met his shoulders. I found myself glad I'd already seen him naked or I might have been caught off guard.

"Focus," Slate growled.

Brass gave me a lopsided grin, and I dropped my eyes with a grimace.

Quick was just as tall as his brother with black jagged Celtic tattoos that covered his left side to his ankle. Quick was a little less body fat and lighter than Brass with just as much muscle. His dark hair was much shorter and styled like he'd walked off a movie set from the roaring twenties. His dark eyes glittered at me, and I cursed an impressive stream of profanities as I pulled my shirt over my head.

"Good looking bunch, eh?" Slate taunted, and I gritted my teeth as I shoved off my pants.

I wore a light pink bra with yellow and hot pink flowers with hot pink boy shorts because Slate had torn off the ones that matched this bra. Bastard. I kicked my pants off and felt the temperature suddenly get higher around me. I balled my hands into fists.

"It would be easier if everyone kept their eyes to themselves," I ground out.

"Whoever is in the patron room will be keeping nothing to themselves. Get used to it," Slate growled.

"Hot pink is my favorite," Brass said suggestively.

I held my breath as a wave of heat sent all my body's fluids rushing south, depriving my brain of essential blood flow.

"We will discuss what that means later," Slate growled.

I swallowed hard and saw my eyes in the mirror. My pupils were larger than usual, but not as ridiculous as they had been. It was progress. It made me look a little like a lunatic, which didn't help with my parted swollen lips and watching my stomach muscles flex with my heavy breaths. I closed my mouth and worked on taking measured breaths through my nose.

"I think *you* are making it worse," I accused Slate, and he shrugged from where he leaned against the mirror.

"Deal with it, Torch."

"By the Mother," Quick breathed, "She is throwing off serious heat. This is going to get weird fast." The girls were nodding emphatically in agreement.

I growled and blushed when it sounded much too much like a moan. "Why are we standing around? Let's do this," I said roughly and with Ama on one side of me and Quick on the other on three feet apart —the torture continued.

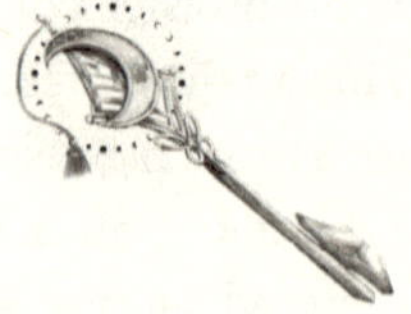

An hour and a half later, twenty-six different poses, and I was ready for a cool shower. My cool shower lasted about a minute before everyone changed into their battle gear and trudged onto the Crash Course.

"Scarlett!" Slate barked, making me jump. I trotted over to Slate's alter ego Savage Storm; he glared down at me. "Quick has been waiting for you. Move it," he ordered.

My eyes widened and I noticed his silver eyes were glittering. He was enjoying bossing me around. I narrowed my eyes at him before trotting up to Quick.

"No knives. Hand to hand," Quick said as he pulled off his shirt, "Come here."

I made a face, watching him warily. They'd tried to give me hugs after we finished our stretching and I'd shouted at everyone not to touch me. I'd stormed off in my underwear to the prep room so I could shower before anyone else got there. I looked to Slate, who nodded, and I looked up to the sky, wondering why I was letting this be done to me.

I walked over to Quick and he spun me around. His fingers laced through my hair, and he braided it deftly like the first time he had when I'd fought Jonquil for battle training.

"I don't think I like the implications of this braid, Silver Regn." He gave me a yank, so I craned my head back to look at him.

His smile was dazzling. "You have no idea." He let my hair go, tying it off. "You know what I find effective when training women?" he asked, circling me.

"No, but I'm sure you'll tell me," I snapped.

Quick was deliberately trying to tempt me. I didn't even think was focusing on me; he was probably conjuring a hundred different nasty in his dirty little mind just to be elevated to a level so near Slate's.

His lips curled. "Let us see if we can remedy that smart mouth.

Why do you think Slate chose me over the others, Scarlett? Am I just the right amount of temptation? It is indignation. It makes women crazy, their sense of fairness, rightness, but the hard truth is all is fair..."

"In love and war," I finished. "I heard that one too," I said maintaining my mouthiness.

"Oh, I am going to enjoy this," he said, almost growling as his body flexed.

Quick was prowling around the combat ring. Brass stood with Slate watching, both men stony faced. Shale and Ama were sparring off on the side, but it was halfhearted since they were also watching us. It made me wary.

Quick was too fast. I barely saw him coming before he knocked me on my back and put me in a compromising position with my legs in the air. He grinned devilishly before releasing me. I was indignant. Sugarfoot, he was right. I stood up, red faced, and dusted myself off. I swallowed back the breathless noises that wanted to spring from my lips and glowered — not at Quick, but at Slate.

"Fight it, Torch," Slate rumbled.

"Does that make you angry?" Quick smirked.

"Do not let his taunting distract you."

He was Savage Storm, jerk extraordinaire.

I heard Brass chuckle.

"What's with the braid, Quick? Need something firm to hold on to?"

His smirk deepened, and he came at me again. I blocked his hands as they shot out at me. He landed one against my chest and I felt the air gush from my lungs with a grunt. Quick hit like a sledgehammer. I curled in feigned defeat. As he approached, I rolled backwards, sprung back onto my feet, and jumped over his swinging leg.

He was low, so I swung my foot out and kicked him flush in the chest. I didn't give him a chance to react. I slid down, grabbing his arm, and pulled while wrapping my feet to either side of his neck, locking my ankles behind his head and squeezing against his throat.

Quick smiled the whole time, which I found vaguely irritating. I squeezed tighter while pulling his arm. I could tell it was working. He couldn't pull away. His face was turning red, but instead of trying to pry off my legs, he slid his hand between my legs and rubbed where the seams met on my pants. I let go with a high groan, as if something had electrocuted me.

Quick didn't let me recover for a second. He threw himself on my back while I lay on the ground and locked his arms around my throat and his legs around mine. His hips pushed up against my backside.

"Do you like it like that?" he asked, his lips brushing against my ear.

I tapped out, and he let go.

I wanted to scream; I wanted to beat the crap out of Quick's face. He was right. I wanted to say it wasn't fair, because it wasn't. I stayed there for a moment, panting with the exertion of fighting, physically as well as mentally, against the aching body part he just so casually stroked. My head hung as I tried to collect my thoughts.

I did not want to sleep with Quick. I absolutely did not. Those were not my actions, it was the rousen's. I said it over and over in my mind until I could breathe through my flaring nostrils.

"Giving up already, Torch? It was just a little tease."

I raised my head and Brass looked at Slate. My eyes were glowing coals in my face, and I struggled to put out their fire.

"Is that how you get your girls? Molesting them into submission?"

My voice was a throaty growl, and I saw Quick falter a step as I got to my feet. Good, my newfound charms worked both ways.

"Other men will touch you and if you balk at the slightest grope, you will lose. Be glad it is Quick and not an actual enemy," Brass said.

I growled internally in frustration. Et tu, Brass?

"You don't want me to lose control, Quick. Despite all your bark, you don't want me. It will take all of them to pull me off you and I don't see any nix torques around. Do you?" I threatened, and I felt unease through the bond.

Quick's grin deepened, and for a moment he looked like my friend again. "You would, would you?"

I didn't know if that would work on Quick, but it was a worth a shot. I didn't wait for him to come at me, so I attacked first. His arms were stronger than mine, faster, and his hits harder. He landed one against my cheekbone that sent me spinning. He moved in to hold me, sugar-foot, my cheek smarted. I waited until he got close and punched him below the belt. He grunted and fell to his knees. I did a classic leg lock to end it. He submitted, and I let him go.

I felt bad, so I knelt beside him. "You said to fight dirty," I said, trying to fight a smile as he held his bits. "I could rub them better," I joked, reminiscent of what he'd said during our first interaction when I head-butted his manhood.

I placed my hand over his and healed him. He grinned at me from his back.

"I am just upset that that might be as close as you get to touching my twig and berries." I rolled my eyes but couldn't stop the smile that bloomed on my face.

"Get up, Quick. Best out of five," Slate said sternly.

Quick's dark eyes slid back to me and he stood up as I took a step back. Since I knew what to expect, I was doing better. Quick submitted again when I bit his neck for getting too close, though it turned into more of a lick. I thought it surprised him more than anything. I laughed as he tapped out.

I had gotten too cocky, though. My last tap out was more embarrassing than the previous ones as Quick gripped both my arms behind me with a knee in my back while he wrapped his hand in the hair at the nape of my neck. I was on my knees in front of Slate and Brass, or I would've been if Quick hadn't pulled my head so far back I was looking at the ceiling. I let out a yelp and Quick planted a kiss a scant inch away from my lips before releasing me.

That pissed me off more than anything. Like he was showing off, he knew I was going to tackle him. His smile deepened, as if he'd expected it right before I lunged. He caught me midair and slammed me down on my back, pushing my legs apart with his own.

"What did I tell you about your indignation?" he asked, quirking an eyebrow.

He had both my arms held above my body, his hips pressed against mine. My face was on fire from the intimate position.

"Fight back. Get away. You can do it. Fight dirty, Scarlett," Quick said, huffing.

His panting was my consolation prize.

Fight dirty, he says. The rousen part of me let my anger burn to cinders.

If he wanted me triggered, he'd done it. My empath abilities cranked to the max, I reached out to Quick. I manipulated his emotions. I stopped resisting and rocked my hips against him. Quick was already inches away from my face.

Slate growled, but it was too late.

Quick's mouth slammed over mine, his tongue found my own. He let go of where his hands restrained me, and my legs wrapped around his waist. My nails dug into his shoulders as he sucked air from my mouth in a harsh breath. Quick's big hands gripped my cotton shirt and tore it open as Brass and Slate dragged us apart as we clawed back to one another.

Ama and Shale stared open-mouthed at us. Quick and I were locked on each other. We both panted with swollen lips, my shirt hung open and his shoulders bled from where I'd scratched them. Brass held him tightly as Quick struggled.

"Let him go, Torch," Slate growled.

He yanked my face towards him, breaking my contact with Quick and I refocused my attention. Slate's lust would always trump Quick's for me. I made a pitiful noise and Slate led me towards the prep room, my feet practically dragging. Slate stopped and turned me around and gave me a light slap on my cheek to snap me out of it.

I heard Ama gasp. I canted my chin just before I jabbed my fist out and punched Slate right in the eye.

"I hate you!" I hissed.

His head barely moved on top of that bull neck of his before I spun on my heel and stormed into the prep room.

I was shaking with anger. They could have at least warned me what to expect. I growled in frustration and threw a tantrum, kicking the walls childishly. I didn't care. My body was a weapon, but I thought that meant a killing machine, not one of seduction. I'd failed miserably and if Slate and Brass hadn't stopped Quick and me, we would have gone at it right there in front of everyone.

When I'd wrapped my legs around him, I'd felt him — it.

I slumped down on a bench, running my fingers in my sweaty braid. I must have looked crazed. Ama and Shale walked over. I was glad it wasn't one of the guys.

Ama pulled my hair out of my face and healed my hand that was aching from hitting that thickheaded behemoth. Shale handed me a wet towel.

"I didn't mean to manipulate him. It just sort of happened." I could tell by the way they'd been watching me before it started that they were wondering what would happen.

"Ama is not allowed to spar with Quick anymore because she likes it too much," Shale said dryly. Ama smiled prettily.

I mopped up the sweat at my neck and assessed the damage to my shirt. "Slate shouldn't have gone that far today."

"Maybe. Quick is good at training women. It is harder not knowing what you are in for, but better because you never know what your enemy will use against you," Shale said with irritating pragmatism.

"It sounds awful, but as women, sometimes the last weapon we have are our bodies. We might get screwed, but at least we will live because that asshole will be too busy getting his rocks off to know what you are planning," Ama said in a calculated tone.

I sighed. "Quick is going to want to strangle me," I said, looking for some commiseration. "My sister has already forgiven me once."

Shale shrugged, "About time Quick knew what it is like to have someone come on too strong. Come back out. Let us show those men we are made of tougher stuff."

Ama stood with her, and I followed them out holding the scraps of my shirt together. I brought out a fresh towel and called water to it. Slate and Brass warily watched me approach. Slate had already been healed, to my dismay. Quick locked on me from the corner of his eyes. I held up the towel like a white flag and Quick smiled, making me sigh with relief.

He took the towel graciously. "I did not expect that. Well done," he said.

I could feel the surprise from him, as well as some other things I cared not to acknowledge. "Look, I'm sorry," I said, chewing my lower lip.

"Which part? Ripping the skin off my shoulders or for leaving me high and dry?" Quick nearly blushed while he poked fun at our brief interlude.

I shrugged, lifting the corners of my torn shirt. "All of it."

Quick looked down at my shirt and made a little grimace before giving me a lopsided grin. "If it does not work with Slate, at least we know we can always tear one another apart for fun."

"Maybe less tongue next time?" I offered, my lips curling.

"Noted." He tried to wrap an arm around me, but I held up my hands.

"I'll blow you a kiss. Best not to touch me for a while until I cool off," I said it as a joke, but I was unfortunately serious.

Quick licked his lips and nodded. I gave another apologetic smile, gripping my shirt tighter in my balled fists. gods, I hoped Indigo never found out about it. I had ignored Slate and Brass during our interaction though they stood so close I could reach out an arm to touch either of them.

I turned to them. Twin walls of fury met me, and it was hard not to look amused. Obviously, they hadn't expected the extent of it either.

"Shale next?" I asked innocently. "She might want to make out with me, too. Shouldn't be too hard to manipulate."

I pretended to crack my knuckles while purposely dropping the scraps of my shirt. Two sets of eyes fell to my exposed chest, which was comical, because they'd just seen me in the studio in much less. There was something about being partially dressed that somehow hinted at delicious indiscretions.

Quick laughed heartily. The way Brass and Slate's eyes swung from me to Quick and back was laughable. They were not amused. I couldn't stop myself.

I ran my tongue along my lips. "Sandalwood." I sniffed the air, closing my eyes. "Patchouli and... cedar. Gods, you smell delicious."

Part was an act, part was genuine. The line was getting blurred again. Quick made a strangled sound and Brass's amber eyes darkened. If Slate hadn't closed the space between us, Brass would have.

Slate stood imposingly before me, his eyes glinting gunmetal. Dark promises of all the things he was going to do to me floated behind those thick, long-lashed eyes. None of them what I wanted to be done now. I could tell he was debating whether to yell at me in front of his team or not. I could hear Brass say something to Quick, who was completely defiant in whatever he was saying in return.

"If I had called, what then? I could've really done damage to Quick," I said, lifting my chin and crossing my arms.

Slate's hands curled into fists. "You push even the most even-tempered man, Torch, and I am far from even tempered," Slate growled low, so I wasn't sure if the others could hear. "You would fuck Quick in front of me?"

My cheeks stung at that one and I wanted to look to see if anyone heard, but Slate would've pounced. I was finally understanding why he had been so domineering that morning. He had expected me to screw up and needed to reassure himself that I was his. I was livid he'd known I'd fail, that I wasn't ready and still made me do it.

I backed up, so I was in the combat ring, and I held my arms out to trigger my wrist blades. "I don't want to have sex with Quick. Right now, I don't want anyone."

"Truth," Quick affirmed with his interrogating talent.

Slate snarled, prowling into the combat ring.

I brandished my wrist blades with a satisfying shing and crooked my finger.

Bring it on, big boy.

Sparring with Slate would give him the release he needed without sounding like a badgering boyfriend... and I wanted to kick his fanny pack for putting me through that. I tore my shirt the rest of the way, so it fit like a ragged cardigan on my shoulders.

He was fuming. He pulled a knife and threw it at my shoulder. It glanced off my blade. It wouldn't be the first time he'd drawn my blood. He was still coming at me with a growl. Two hundred plus pounds of rippling bronze muscles moving towards me with deadly grace. I crouched as if ready for his impact, but slid and dropped between his legs as he passed me.

He turned around quickly, his blade coming down between my arm and the side to pin me. I let it rip at what remained of my shirt and spun away. His eyes alight with the primordial beast that lived by the three Fs: fighting, feeding, and fiddlesticking. I threw a knife from my belt at his thigh, thighs I loved. He knocked it away and launched at me.

I kicked my leg out. It wasn't enough to stop him, but it did leverage him so when I fell back, he spun over me to land on his back. I used his momentum to pull myself over, so I straddled his trim tight hips. My blade at his throat. His eyes flashed silver, the muscle in his jaw leapt. I lowered my knife to his shirt and slowly sliced at it without breaking eye contact to reveal his hard, sculpted chest. I sliced him carefully as he hissed in a breath.

Quick cleared his throat. Slate's face transformed. The chiseled planes of Slate's face quirked when his lips curled. I bent down close.

"To be continued." I filled my words with dark promises.

I stood and helped him up. He blatantly adjusted himself, and I blushed.

"*Now* you blush?" Quick asked, his eyebrows near his hairline. "Look at him," Quick pointed to Slate.

Slate was dusting off his pants, smirking, his shirt cut open halfway down to his stomach the way mine had been, and a thin bleeding cut exposed. He smirked, his wavy hair falling over his shoulders. I knew my eyes were sparkling.

All mine.

Shale, Ama, Brass, and Quick stood there. Hopper had joined at some point and even he looked surprised.

I shrugged. "He didn't want to hurt me."

"He threw a knife at your chest, which you deflected," Shale said in disbelief.

"Shoulder," I corrected. "We've sparred before. I know all his moves."

"No, we have sparred before," Quick said, gesturing to the group he stood in. "That was... foreplay with knives."

I rolled my eyes. Slate came up behind me and kissed my neck. I raised my hand to heal him, ran my thumb down his chest to wipe away the blood. Then, I licked my thumb and his lips curled. All prior transgressions erased.

"Still here," Brass said in a dry tone.

"If I did not see it, I would not believe it." Quick was still shirtless.

"I'm better with my knives. I can't hit as hard as you guys can, but I'm faster and more flexible," I told them.

"Training is over for today," Slate said in his authoritative tone.

"I am so turned on right now," Ama said aloud.

A silent communication passed between Shale and her and they took off into the prep room.

I gaped after them. Brass's expression said it was no surprise. Hopper and Quick looked like they wanted to join them. Slate walked over to where they stood, signaling for me to follow.

"What is your team looking like these days? She has too much emotional influence over my team," Slate asked Hopper.

Brass and Quick were unfazed by his comment.

Hopper nodded. "Let me know what you want done with her, and I can work with it. Her skills with blades notwithstanding." His gaze had taken up residence below my neck.

"They can always be better," Slate said in total seriousness.

I scrunched my face; I couldn't get one compliment.

"Come. Let them talk," Brass said, and I walked alongside him.

Slate nodded, and Hopper snorted. I ignored Hopper and let the tension with Brass wash over me.

"So, that was awkward," I said, trying to break down the wall that had cropped up between us.

Brass gave me a wry smile. "He tried to swallow your face at the first invitation." he paused. "You did not see him after he stood up."

My eyes widened. Oh.

I'd felt it. My insides squirmed, and I took another step away from Brass, making his amber eyes follow me. I gave an apologetic smile.

"I wouldn't be kissing Quick if it wasn't for the rousen," I explained. "He's charming and good looking, but not my type. There's the small matter of him and Indigo, too. Which now I feel like I should tell her what happened in case she ever wants to pick that up again," I sighed and rubbed my forehead, feeling terribly guilty.

"Why are you telling me this, Scarlett?" Brass asked.

I stopped once we got inside the double doors and cocked my head. "Because I wouldn't, that's all. I'm sorry."

Brass's warm amber eyes flitted between my eyes. His plump, defined lips rubbed together. "Why else?"

Now I rubbed my lips together. "What do you mean?"

He leveled his eyes at me with a wry smile.

"I care about how you feel — how do you feel about me," I continued, "I wouldn't disrespect you by doing something with your brother," I said, feeling like I wanted to shift around.

"Why do you care?" Brass asked in his smooth, deep voice, and I swallowed.

My mouth felt dry.

"You know why. You're special to me. If you weren't one of Slate's closest friends, I would have… I mean, I *did*. Twice. Technically, like ten times." I tried to lighten where this talk was going, but it was coming out all wrong and I was growing more anxious by the minute.

"But I am."

"You are."

"So, where does that leave us?"

I searched his face. "Right here. Friends, but… I should go shower. I'm still feeling out of it," I said, turning my back to him.

Not having to look at him helped a lot. His smooth voice wrapped around me like a satin sheet, and I was not to be trusted. I'd decided that since I nearly tore the skin off Quick. Luckily, he seemed as ashamed of what happened as I was.

Slate was passing me off to another team, but I had a sneaking suspicion it had to do with Brass. There was too much competition there to have me around him. Not that Slate couldn't handle competition, but Brass and I had a history that was far too present.

I could hear giggles from Ama at the cubbies. I tried hard not to listen after going through great lengths not to see them naked, and as free as they were all with their bodies, it was quite the feat. Brass leaned against the cubby at the end of the aisle. I was wrapping my towel around myself. Of course, he knew that. Brass had a towel wrapped around his waist, a dark, happy trail led south below his belly button.

I stood up and avoided his eyes. "I only wanted to warn you about what is going on in the showers," Brass said dryly.

… I can hear it…

Ama's moaning echoed through the prep room, as well as a rhythmic slapping sound. I blushed at the sudden spike of pleasure I felt at their intimacy. Brass looked to be hiding a smile.

"Quick has joined them. It is not supposed to be allowed in the prep room, but almost no one pays attention to that rule," Brass said, and I nodded.

"We sure didn't," I said, feeling my fire suddenly flash. "I don't think I can go over there right now. You should probably leave too, Brass. No offense, but the towel isn't doing much for my restraint." I had already gone rigid from trying to not walk over to join them.

Brass gave a lopsided smile as he read my mind. "Relax, love. Close your eyes. I can guide you."

Love. I practically swooned.

"I don't think I can touch you right now," I whispered.

I could feel Brass's thrill at my statement. "I will not let you touch me that way."

I gnawed my lip and gave a curt nod. I did really want a shower, and Slate must've been feeling what I was feeling. He'd be in any minute.

We turned the corner to the showers, and at the far end, we could see everything. Quick was behind Ama and Shale stood in front of her doing gods knew what. I immediately turned around and felt the moan pull from my throat. Brass stood close beside me.

"Close your eyes," he said in that smooth voice of his.

"Stop talking, Brass. I'm a wreck. My control is slipping," I said throatily, but I closed my eyes.

He took my hand, making me gasp, and walked to my usual shower spot — the closest shower to the far wall. Brass let go of my hand.

"Good job, Scarlett. You only thought incredibly dirty thoughts every other step of the way."

Brass had to pry our fingers apart before I heard him walk away and let out of a harsh breath.

I took off my towel and hung it up, pulling out the frosted partition and turning on the shower head. Cool water poured over me and I let it soak my face. I should have been taking an ice-cold shower.

I turned around to dampen the back of my head and saw Brass in the adjacent shower. He took off his towel and my jaw dropped. I'd always been extra careful with Brass, with the knowledge that he could unwittingly read my mind. Every inch of him had a silky dusting of dark hair. The 'V' leading south... I groaned aloud and forced myself to turn before I charged over to him.

By the Mother. Who did I piss off up there to place such temptation in my path?

Before Slate, I could've marched over there and had Brass in every way my dirty mind was conjuring. Instead, I was shaking with desire for him. I couldn't betray Slate — I just couldn't. I had to be stronger than the rousen.

I looked around me on instinct, and Brass met my eyes. He'd noticed my noticing. Water poured down his sculpted body. He was purposely giving me an optimum view of him. Gods, there was so much to look at.

My breasts were tight and heavy, my hands went to them of their own volition as I sucked in a deep breath.

What was the male equivalent of a temptress? Brass's eyes dropped lower, and I felt my skin prickle. I caught his smirk just before he turned around, showing me the hard curve of his backside.

I berated myself for not immediately closing my eyes after my first eyeful of Brass. My body hurt, I was so turned on. I took one trembling step towards Brass and then another before I curled in on myself on the tile floor. I couldn't sleep with Brass with Slate in the next room, but I *could* physically.

Big hands slid around my stomach from behind and I moaned at the contact as he pulled me up. My skin was singing from listening to the performance in the stalls further down from Brass. I turned in Slate's hands as he brought me to the shower.

I hungered for him.

"I've been terrible today," I breathed.

Slate's eyes flared to life at my admission and I felt acceptance of whatever he wished to do to punish me. "Brass is across from you."

I craned my head back. "He is," I rasped.

"Were you a good girl, Torch?" he asked, and I nodded. "You saw him." I nodded again and Slate grit his teeth. "You did not touch him?"

"I didn't."

"Good girl, Torch. If I did not see your and Quick's finishing performance, I would have said today was a success."

"And since you did?"

"Since I did, I think I need to punish you most severely," he growled with a mock severity, "I want your mouth."

I licked my lips and nodded as I bent to my knees. Slate threw his head back and wrapped his hands in my hair as I pulled him into my mouth.

Slate rubbed his hands together, making his hands sudsy and washed me. I was sore all over. He'd made sure I was good and sorry for making out with Quick in front of him and seeing Brass in the buff. I was sorry four times up against the shower wall.

I listened for anyone else in the prep room and heard nothing.

I scowled at him, and he leaned down to kiss me. I pulled my head back, so he contented himself with washing me. My breasts were extra dirty — as always. We finished our shower and Slate grabbed his clothes to change near me. He watched amusedly as I pulled on my clothes in a rush.

"You're not embarrassed that we could have had an audience?" I asked him.

I didn't think I would ever let go of my preconceived notions of modesty. I would never be as free with my body as they all were, but I was getting there.

"Worried your boyfriend saw your lips wrapped around my cock?" Slate asked, balancing on the fine line of teasing and being obnoxious.

"If you are referring to Brass, then yeah — maybe I am."

Maybe I was a lot. I wanted Brass to see me not as Slate's... whatever, but his friend. I cared if it bothered him.

Slate's strong jaw clenched as he looked at me with narrow eyes. "Get over it, Torch. You are mine. I do whatever I want with you whenever I want to."

I rolled my eyes, mostly at myself and the spike of pleasure I felt, but at him too. What a Neanderthal. When I didn't deny it, I swore I could feel the smugness roll off him.

"You are mine too, Slate Tio," I teased.

Slate stopped tugging on his boot and lifted his gaze to mine, and my cheeks flushed. Sugarfoot. I wasn't ready to talk about it. I looked away and buckled on my seax.

"Are we acknowledging that now or are you scampering off, Rabbit?" he purred.

"We can take it one step at a time."

"Scamper it is," Slate said, rising to his full height and hooking his arms under mine. He lifted me so my feet dangled, and we were eye to eye with my back against the closed metal cubby door. "Say it, Torch. I need to hear it."

I rubbed my lips together. I always felt vulnerable saying it. Slate didn't have to say it back, but then I didn't want to say it. My actions should speak louder. We were together. That was enough for now.

Unless I'd made out with one of his best friends and totally eye fiddlesticked the other one.

I sighed.

"I love you, Slate. Forever and always. Yours, mine, the worlds. I'm sorry about Quick. You're right. I'm not ready, but I hope I will be. Don't give up on me," I swallowed.

I saw the moment he completely forgave me and helped me get better. There were going to be a lot of embarrassing days ahead.

EIGHTEEN

It was near dinner time when Slate and I came up to the rumpus room. I had a stash of shirts and pants in my cubby, so I had pulled on a fresh white long sleeve top and tucked it into a snug pair of taupe pants. Brass, Quick, Ama, and Shale were looking over the dinner menu when we took our seats.

Ama lifted her menu to hide her giggling, and I knit my brows. Shale was the only one who would meet my eyes, which was never a good sign. Her dark tilted eyes twinkled as she looked me up and down.

"I would not have pegged you for a screamer."

My mouth fell open, and I shifted in my seat as the others burst out into laughter. Slate's lips were pulled into a mocking smile, and I wanted to crawl under a rock.

"Who's hungry?" I said, ignoring their laughter and comments.

"I bet *you* are," Quick jibed and my face flushed all over again. "Poor Brass, we will take you out tonight and find you a woman who does not think very much."

I couldn't help the disgusted face I made as Brass gave Quick a rueful grin. "No need. I am seeing Katy tonight."

"Katydid?" I asked in a treble voice, drawing everyone's attention.

Brass flashed me a genuine smile. "Yes. I gave her a second chance."

"He means she finally wore him down and he was sick and tired of being alone. I keep telling him drunk women do not think at all. He could come out with me one of these nights and —"

"We get the idea." I interrupted Quick and got to my feet to place my order at the bar. "Know what you want?" I asked Slate.

"I do. Do you?" Slate asked, arching a brow while wrapping his arm around the back of my empty chair.

It was not the time to be asking cryptic questions with double meanings. I spun on my heel and walked to the bar to place my order; he could place his own stupid order if he wanted to eat.

I was just thanking the bartender when Slate's hands were placed to either side of me at the bar keeping me in place. He placed his order over my shoulder, his hair brushing against my cheek as he leaned and his front just grazing my back with his heat.

"Jealous of Katydid?" Slate growled in my ear.

"I have you, don't I?" I purred, meaning every word, and Slate made a noise deep in his throat.

"Good girl, Torch."

I didn't know why it irritated me they would talk about Brass's love life so vulgarly, but it had. Not that he was going out on a date. That was nice and romantic. More than I ever got unless Brass had taken me out. I may have romanticized Brass a bit, painted him the wholesome hero in my epic tragedy and I didn't like anyone coloring that view. I realized it was putting a lot of pressure on Brass that he didn't know was on him, but he had never failed me.

They filled dinner with lots of teasing that I dutifully ignored as Slate made no pretense of laughing or finding any excuse to touch me. Truth be told, it made me uncomfortable. At home was one thing with Slate, but out in the open was another, especially in the hive of the queen bee.

When Ash had been affectionate, I could accept it as a duty. Not sentimental, but there it was. With Slate, it was because we wanted to and letting others know we wanted to touch one another didn't sit well with me. It could have been because I was so used to hiding what I felt with Slate that having it out in the open tied my stomach in knots.

They were little things: a stroke of my hair, a trail down my back, his arm around the back of my chair. It would've been easier if the others didn't seem completely stupefied by it, or if Slate would recognize that the only one who seemed to take it in stride was him.

When Slate got up to go to the bar for another drink and he leaned close to my cheek, I licked my lips and turned towards him, giving him a quick kiss before dropping my eyes down to my empty plate. He lingered there for a moment and chuckled as he walked away.

Slate had always enjoyed making me uncomfortable and every time he won some minor victory, he walked around with a triumphant air that made me want to punch him in the throat. I chanced a peek, looking up through my eyelashes at the others. They stared blankly at me, and I sighed.

"We are not used to seeing him with someone. If I had to guess by your aura, you are uncomfortable in the extreme." Ama's rosebud mouth smiled at me, and I ran my teeth over my lower lip.

"I'm not big on P.D.A.. I didn't think he was, but —"

"Claiming what is mine," Slate said as he came back to the table.

The man's hearing was impeccable. I shifted in my seat.

"I'm not an object."

"Chafer came back today," Brass noted. His amber eyes met mine when I lifted them.

It was easy to forget to guard my thoughts around Brass. He didn't do it intentionally, but he always knew what I was thinking or envisioning. Brass understood me better than most since we both had a constant flow of other people in our minds, him from his mind reading, and me with my empath abilities. He had figured out how to communicate things to me by his emotions alone, and sometimes we spoke only with our feelings and minds. It was an uncommon gift. *He* was an uncommon gift.

"That he did." Quick added, "Lera has kept him busy all morning. This is the first time I have seen him all day."

I looked over my shoulder as Chafer approached the table and gave Slate a sneer worthy of the lowest life forms on the planet. Slate smiled arrogantly at the other man.

He would've been handsome if his face wasn't so sharp. Chafer had slanted dark brows over wide almond eyes, his thin mouth was always pulled back in a wicked grin that was always at someone's expense. He didn't hide it. He was brusque and didn't care one bit about anyone else's feelings. His brown hair was messily tousled, with his long seax pommel sticking up from behind his shoulder. He was a solid six feet, without a spare pinch of meat on his tightly muscled body.

Chafer flashed me that patented wicked grin with a dash of lewdness to set Slate's teeth on edge. Chafer didn't have many of them and unfortunately, since he and I got into a thrown down drag out fight, I counted myself as one of a few he respected and was as close to a friend as a man like Chafer had. The funny thing was, I kind of liked Chafer. He was a no bull sugarfoot guy and had never once viewed me with desire.

I couldn't help the lopsided grin that tugged on my lips. "Chafer. You're looking marvelous this evening."

Chafer smelled like sex and upon closer inspection, there was sweat along his nape. His grin deepened.

"You are looking properly fucked as well, Scarlett," Chafer said bluntly and Quick coughed to hide a laugh that Shale bothered not to mask.

Slate snarled, and I spoke over him. "To what do I owe the pleasure?"

"Lera wants you now," Chafer ignored the others entirely as he addressed me.

"Why?" Slate growled.

"It's fine, I'm coming," I said as I stood, giving Slate a reassuring smile.

"By all reports, not the first time you have said that today," Chafer said smugly, and I shook my head.

"I didn't miss you, Chafer."

"Good. I did not miss you either." Chafer never smiled with his lips, not a real smile. They were with his eyes, which he was doing now.

"Activate the bond," Slate growled.

"Brass will be listening, I'm sure," I said, sparing a smile for Brass, who gave a single nod.

The last time I opened the carved walnut door with the filigree knob was the morning after Slate asked me to move into his room and when I didn't stay the night. I found him post coitus with Cordillera.

I glanced over my shoulder to find Slate and Brass watching me. Brass offered a reassuring smile, which was the exact opposite of Slate's glower. Despite the eerie similarities in appearance, the two men could not be more different. I flashed Slate my very best smile.

... Thanks, Brass...

Chafer opened the door and moved aside to let me in and closed it behind me without entering. I'd never been alone with Lera before. The office held a couch and two sofa chairs that faced an ornate deep cherry wood desk and matching chair upholstered in a dark red that the petite woman sat in.

Cordillera Blomi gestured with a red nailed hand to the chairs, and I nodded, taking a seat. She'd made me her second in command recently — a delegate or a prodigy of sorts, or so she said. She didn't trust me as far as she could throw me and wanted me close.

Cordillera pushed back from her high-backed chair and crossed to sit on top of her desk before me. My red flags were all flying. What was her game and why was she radiating a level of ardor that should be reserved for a lover? The rousen was dangerously low in my system and for once I was glad.

"You need to sit in on contracts. I know you have been... incapacitated, but I see that time has passed," Lera said in her smoky voice with her dark penetrating eyes locked on mine.

I couldn't show weakness to Lera. "Absolutely," I said with a smirk.

Her red lips curled, and I wondered if that mocking smile was a Shadow Breaker attribute.

"Good."

As if she would have accepted any other answer.

"My Breakers tell me Slate has finally trained you. He was a very pliable student, he learned quickly. I imagine he must be an even better teacher to one so inexperienced as you. It gives him a lot of flexibility, as you do not have much to compare to, unless I miss my mark. You are looking well despite your extended time with the Merfolk."

Not a compliment.

"My only other experience has been with your nephew. As you know. I would never call what we did together inexperienced. He is a mind reader, after all. Slate takes care of me." I kept my tone even when what I wanted to do was tell her it was none of her business and to shut her pie hole.

She purred. "Yes, he takes excellent care of his lovers. I think it will be awhile before he returns home. I mean it as a compliment." She smiled superiorly, and it took extra effort to school my features.

"He is welcome to leave whenever he wishes. He's the one who wants me to claim him. This discussion is best to have together instead of with me." I rose, and she placed a light hand on my shoulder.

My heart started beating at a rapid pace.

"We both know you cannot handle him alone. It is not your fault. He is accustomed to certain things, in certain ways. Slate was not my first to wean off rousen." Lera shifted to sit next to me on the couch and I pivoted on the couch to face her.

"Like I said, if he's unhappy he can leave." I balled my fists to the sides of my lap and kept my eyes on her.

"Do you know why he gravitates to you? You chose him. He had you innocent and sweet. Like a ripened plum ready for him to sink his teeth into you. Now he has you, now that your innocence is gone, and you depend on him, you need him. Slate has only known want. That alone will not be enough to keep him. He likes... variety," she purred, and my hackles rose.

"Get to the point, Cordillera. Unsolicited advice on how to make love was not what you called me in here for, is it?" My voice was gravelly, and I tried not to make it too rough. I was still walking on eggshells around Lera.

Her thin red nailed hand rested on my thigh, and her dark eyes glittered at me. "I can help with him. With both of you. As I said, I have extensive experience with those of you recovering from rousen." Lera's hand slid higher on my thigh and my eyes fell to it. "It could free you to spend time with Brass. It is him you chose first. If Slate had never interfered, your father might be alive today. You would call out Brass's name in the showers, possibly carrying his child already."

My breath caught. She'd been lulling me into letting her near me and now that she was, that ardor I couldn't understand blossomed into a heat that would have made the dirtiest debauchee proud.

How?

"It is not the first time I have shared a woman with Slate," she said as she cupped my face.

I was holding my breath and at her caress it came out in a moan as her fingers slid into my hair. Her hand moved higher on my thigh, and I gasped when I felt her call. I never used calling with Brass or Slate, but I had always used it with Ash. Ash had used his calling on me a time or two, but I'd always stopped him before he went too far. Lera was not either man. Her calling against my skin was like silk running against my breasts and between my legs. Featherlight strokes of air slid over my too sensitive skin.

"Let yourself go," she whispered huskily, and my eyes slid shut.

Lera's soft lips molded to mine, and I felt myself slipping deeper. Her nails scratched against my skin as she slid her fingers beneath the waistband of my pants.

The door crashed open, and slowly, Lera moved her mouth from mine. I heard arguing outside the gaping door and my eyes struggled to stay open. The lag had set in and the strength I'd used to keep my hands to myself sapped me. It had been a long day.

"Lera, what the fuck!" Slate roared, and I felt her hand slip from under my clothes and her calling stop.

I sucked in a deep breath and opened my eyes. I was looking at the gold textured ceiling and Lera had climbed on top of me. My eyes went wide. I didn't remember falling over. Slate stood over the side of the couch glaring at Lera, who sat calmly next to me.

My mind was thick and slow, and I clumsily sat up trying to button my pants with Brass in the doorway, barring Chafer from interfering. I felt like some evil witch had cast a spell over me. Maybe she drugged my dinner.

"I am only helping the girl. I share well, Slate. You know that. I was only introducing her to what could be when you are both tired of one another," Lera said smirking and crossed from the couch to sit in her high-backed chair. "You and Brass —"

"She is my mate. Mine. My wife." Slate grabbed me roughly by the arm. He yanked me up to my feet and held up my ring and his own.

Lera narrowed her eyes. Clearly, her spies hadn't informed her of that.

"She will not be shared," Slate growled, lowering his tone.

"Except with Brass," Lera purred, regaining her composure. Slate's hold on me tightened.

I looked to where Brass stood, his strong dark honey jaw clenched. "Do not cross that line, Lera. You are perilously close as it is," he said smoothly. It took a lot for Brass to get riled up.

Before I knew what was going on, Brass was taking me from Slate and leading me through the door. As I walked away, I saw Lera rising from her seat with a big welcoming smile for Slate as he crossed around the desk.

The easiest way to get to Slate was through me.

NINETEEN

Brass and I didn't speak as he took me back home. I changed into a pale blue and cream satin halter slip and pulled on my robe as he went to retrieve where Slate had hidden the rousen. I sat on our plush beige couch with my legs drawn up so I could rest my chin on my knees and stared blankly out into the sitting room.

My mind wandered as I waited for Brass to bring me my poison and wondered what Slate could do that would take so long. Brass sat down next to me on the couch and held up the purple vial that I despised and craved. I plucked it from his fingers and held it in my palm.

"Take it before you cannot move," Brass said softly, and I nodded absently and pulled the cork.

"What did she mean by sharing me with you?"

I turned to Brass. His dreamy amber eyes dropped, and his dark hair swung forward as he leaned on his elbows. The ebony and copper beads clicked. "I promise to explain it one day, Scarlett, but today is not that day. I should get going."

When he rose, I grabbed his hand, stilling him, and he sunk back onto the couch. My favorite thing about Brass was that I didn't have to ask. He literally read my mind when he pulled me against him and slung his arm over my shoulders.

Brass handed me the nix torque, and I lifted my hair so he could put the icy pewter around my neck. I poured the rousen down my throat, leaning against Brass again. His hand rested on my elbow as we sat in silence.

"What time is your date?" I asked, remembering he had plans with Katydid.

"Do not worry about it. You know, Lera has extensive experience in dealing with rousen addicts. Try not to be too hard on yourself, Scarlett."

"Your aunt had her hand down my pants, Brass. She told me her and Slate had threesomes and gods know what else she implied. I feel so weak and disgusting. First, Quick this afternoon and your aunt was aiming for... I don't know, third base, maybe? I think she planned for you to tell Slate what was going on so he would go in there. If he was remotely up for it, she would have taken it all the way."

Brass's presence was comforting. He radiated this calm and warmth that made you want to be close to him. Katydid was a lucky woman.

"She manipulated you. It is what she does and she is very good at it. I do not make any excuses for my aunt. She wants what she wants, and she does not like losing Slate to you. They have not been together for some time because he spends all his time with or chasing you."

I sniffed. "I never asked him to chase me. I told him many, *many* times not to. There is this part of me that hates him. Please don't tell him that. I resent that he's dragged me in kicking and screaming. Now I'm here and every day is a battle."

"You love him, Scarlett. You have for some time, or I would never have kept my distance," Brass soothed and thrilled me with his words.

He wanted me.

"I don't have a problem fighting for love, but I don't enjoy competing with other women. We're together or not. There can't be a blurred line with a man like him. He'd exploit it."

"He called you his wife tonight. Does that not make things clearer for you?"

He had. He had shocked me with that exclamation. "I suppose. He was strange today."

"You are becoming more independent, and he needed to test you. You will not depend on him for as much soon and it pleases him as much as it disturbs him."

I pushed off him and turned to look at Brass. His lids were low over his eyes as he gazed down at me.

"You always defend him. You're such a good friend, Brass. I might have to sway you over to my side," I said, laying back down against him.

"Our friendship is strained lately. Has no one told you Tawny and Indigo were against letting Slate care for you?" Brass asked.

"What?" I tilted my head back from where I leaned against his chest, my knees in his lap.

I felt safer and more comfortable with him than anyone, even Slate. There was always this nervousness with Slate, or worse, anger.

"Amethyst and Steel also sided with them for me," he said without hesitation.

My eyes widened. "Did they even ask you first, or did they just offer you up as a sacrifice?"

Brass chuckled, making me shift with him, and the first wave of heat from the rousen rolled over me. "It would have been the sacrifice of my friendship, but if it had to be someone else, I think Slate would have preferred it to be me. As long as it was not Ash."

"What did you say?" I asked, out of curiosity.

My hand had slipped between his thighs to knead his muscles. If I didn't go any higher, he'd grant me my horrid need to touch.

"I said if no one else, then I would."

"You would?"

Brass cocked a brow with a dry smile. "I hardly needed my arm twisted, Scarlett. I would have taken you the night I introduced you to the competitions, except your bond with Slate was active as it was the night of your birthday. I worried about how you would feel and if Slate would forgive me, but it worked out. Here you are *better*, and he is happy."

I closed my eyes and nestled back against his chest. "If not Slate, then you. I trust you; you make me feel... *better*. Be glad it wasn't you. You might have been stuck with a stalker," I teased.

"I welcome your attention," he said so softly I wasn't sure if I heard him.

"You should get going. You'll miss your date. After today, I bet you're wound up as tight as a drum." I could feel myself sink away into the darkness.

"You would not mind me being with Katydid that way?" he murmured.

"I want you to be happy," I said tightly.

The idea of Brass with Katydid felt like a knife in my stomach, which I knew a lot about.

Brass stroked my hair, and I felt him call and I fell asleep.

"She is on rousen, and you stayed?"

"You should have been here with her. What were you doing?"

Slate hesitated. "I had a long talk with Lera."

"I bet you did. I am going back to headquarters. If I discover you did anything, so, help me, Slate, our deal is off and I will take her from you." Brass had never sounded angrier.

Slate chuckled softly, "I would like to see you try."

"No. You would not. She suspects you are always up to no good. The second she finds any proof, she will leave you. If you are telling it true, then keep your nose clean. Do not mess this up. She cares about you, and I am not the only one you will have to answer to if you fuck this up," Brass whispered harshly; his chest moved against my head.

His hand rested on my shoulder; I must have slid down when I fell asleep. I couldn't have been out for long because I could still speak, and my thoughts were still relatively clear. I balled my hands into fists to keep from touching Brass inappropriately and lifted myself off his lap into a sitting position.

"Brass, your date," was all I could manage before the rousen woke in my system.

Brass jumped from the couch, seeing my pupils dilate, and I knit my brows. I just wanted to be me again. I started crying. I couldn't help it, my friends had to run from me because I would molest them and even though I was upset about it, I still wanted to do it.

"Just go. Thanks for staying with me so I wouldn't have to be alone," I choked out.

Brass stood beside Slate, who watched me pensively, and I curled in on myself trying to fight the urges. Brass watched as if mesmerized as I panted on the couch and made noises no normal person should make.

"She fights it harder with you," Slate said, turning to Brass.

"I can see that," Brass said, "What do you want me to do?"

Slate turned back towards me, and I closed my eyes. My day's torture was ongoing. I fought harder. I hated admitting it to myself, and it was because I cared more about how I looked to Brass. I wanted to still be the sweet girl from Chicago that could count on one hand how many dates she'd been on.

I gritted my teeth. "Please don't," I ground out.

Brass looked to Slate who shook his head. "Fight it, Torch. It is for your own good. Maybe you can start taking half doses tomorrow if you can last longer."

I was running my own hands over my arms, satin sliding along my soft skin reminding me of Lera's calling and I moaned aloud at the remembrance. The next ten minutes were painful, my skin felt hot and only a firm touch could soothe it. The following ten were hellish, I tried not to knead myself or do any other inappropriate things with Brass's eyes on me and tears streamed down my cheeks at the effort.

Slate watched with his hands balled into fists, like he wanted to put an end to my agony. I wriggled and fell onto the floor where I forced myself back into a ball so I wouldn't leap at anyone.

"Why are you fighting so hard?" Slate rumbled from where he stood at the ready.

I shook my head. It wasn't fair to ask me questions while I had to be honest. My brain couldn't come up with the sugarcoating I needed not to be brutally honest.

"Why?" Slate demanded and Brass looked at him.

"Gods, give her a break."

Slate gave one slice of his head in negation, and I moaned aloud. "I don't want him seeing me like this." It came out haggard and breathless, words were getting harder to remember.

"Why?" Slate demanded again.

Tears streamed as my pants became more pained. "I care," I rasped.

"Care?" Slate asked, furrowing his midnight brows.

"Please," I mewled, "Care that he sees me as good. That he loves me back."

Brass let out a long breath, and they had a silent communication. Slate tone softened as he knelt still out of my reach, but closer to my level.

"Scarlett, I see you as good. We both do. You are not any less, you are more. Stronger, wiser, and we respect you for how far you have come in such a short time. Do not get caught up in what other people say about you," Slate said tenderly, and I cried all the harder.

"Those who matter, know. Nothing could diminish you, Scarlett. I would never judge you," Brass echoed, and I raised my head to see him.

Brass's dark honey brow drew together as he watched me struggle in an expression of distress that mirrored Slate's own. I closed my eyes and rolled onto my back trying to hold myself still. They wouldn't be saying that if they could see what Brass must have seen in my mind.

"Date?" I uttered.

"Long past. She will forgive me," Brass reassured me, and I laughed with a semi-hysterical edge.

"Go," I said roughly and got to my feet.

I looked between the men and could feel part of me deciding between them. They seemed to sense it too and the two men looked at one another. Slate's eyes flared to silver when he looked back to me, and I looked to Brass.

Brass backed out slowly, which was good, or I would have snapped and chased him. When the door closed after Brass, I turned to Slate. My chest was heaving, and I started removing my robe and slip.

"Did you?"

Slate shook his head once as he watched my body move while my clothes billowed, falling to the floor. "No. I needed Lera to understand she can never include you in her games. You are mine. I have never wanted to hurt Lera so much in my life, not even after I caught her with Jett. Seeing her with you — I wanted to crush her throat in my fist for touching you," he snarled, remembering.

"I won't always need you," I started and Slate stiffened, and I help up my hand, the very air from the movement against the tiny hairs of my arm made my skin prickle. "But I will always want you."

I launched myself at him and started tearing at his clothes. Slate tore his own shirt off his chest as I unbuckled his blade belts and pants. He was kicking off his boots and unbuckling his wrist blades while we started towards the bedroom.

"You chose me over Brass for once," Slate rumbled as I kissed along his neck.

"Husband."

It was more than enough for Slate who lifted me onto the round dining room table with a growl of satisfaction and pulled my backside to the end before driving into me.

I knew we wouldn't make it to the bed.

CHAPTER 20
JETT

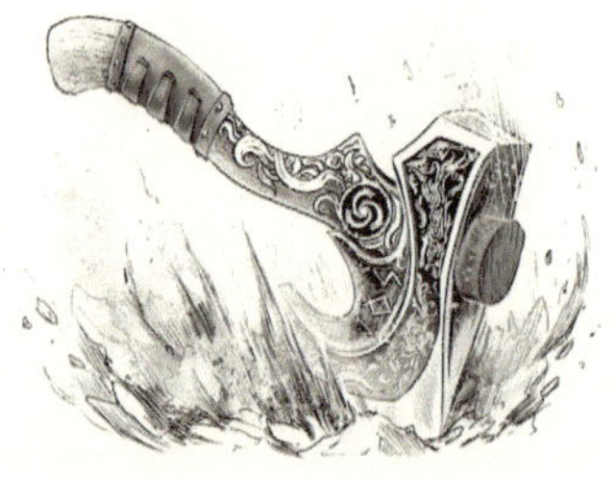

"What a gods be damned train wreck this is going to be," Jett said, thrumming his fingers on the tabletop.

For once, Jett and the girls were the first ones in the dining room waiting for the others. Slate and Scarlett had been at breakfast, and it looked like something had been resolved between them.

Amethyst smiled at Jett. He thought she should be irritable and nagging now that she was showing, but she seemed blissfully happy, and her hand almost never left her stomach. If it did, then it was Cherry's hand on her stomach. Jett hardly ever got a turn between the two of them. They had forced Amethyst to sit up in bed so Cherry and he could rest their heads in her lap and talk so the baby would know their voices. It was what he looked forward to at night.

Cherry looked ravishing in a clingy red dress that made her plump naturally stained lips stand out against her fair skin. Amethyst opted for black and open backed since you could not tell she was pregnant from behind. They were both gorgeous, as always.

"I think it's romantic. He nursed her back to health and now they've fallen in love," Cherry said with cobalt eyes glittering in her vulpine face, his vixen.

Jett snorted. "Nursed. You're using that term loosely, babe."

Cherry made a face at him, and Amethyst laughed. "Worry about Indigo. Scarlett is being looked after, while Indigo hasn't hardly spoken to anyone since she and Quick ended things."

She'd spoken to Sterling. Jett had watched the two sneak away during Alder's funeral. He was going to have to say something soon. Diamond would be at the university now and things would have to change. Too many mornings he'd seen Indigo ducking out of Sterling's room which he shared with Ash, Sage, and that other blonde kid Hunter. Jett didn't know Hunter well, but if he hung out with Ash and Sage that was two strikes against him.

"You're right. Indigo needs to find a husband now that Scarlett is out of commission. That'll be easy," Jett said dryly, all the greater families knew about Sterling and Indigo.

Funny thing was, Gypsum had seen Diamond last month, and the two had left the club after Scarlett's birthday together. That marriage was doomed. Sterling with Indigo, Diamond with Gypsum... they were a palace full of home wreckers. You couldn't talk about home wreckers without mentioning Slate and Scarlett. Slate was the penultimate, rivaled only by Quick. Though breaking up a Straumr/Tio engagement should get Slate some kind of medal, or at least a plaque.

Indigo came walking in white satin that draped at the small of her back giving her a small train. She looked lovely and Jett told her so. Tawny and Steel came down with Gypsum, Sparrow, and Hawk. Tawny and Sparrow always favored deep reds and purples, the shades looked good on the dark-haired women and Hawk and Steel dressed to match them. Hawk and Sparrow were moving out in the next week. Sparrow had been miserable for some time. Getting away from all the memories would do her some good. They would always be a brief trip away if they got the Dagr portal door activated again.

Pearl's short, voluptuous figure sauntered in with swaths of emerald fabric flowing behind her like a goddess and Jett rose to give her a kiss before she started greeting the others. Then Scarlett came in on Slate's arm and it was like a spotlight had come on and the rest of the room darkened.

Her turquoise eyes were smoky, glowing back at him. Her hair fell over one shoulder in big loose curls. A glittering comb held back the hair on one side of her head. The black slinky dress was very un-Scarlett like. The neckline crossed over her shoulder blades with long sleeves, but it was completely backless. Rows of black glittering beads hung from one side of the dress to the other along her back in graduating lengths, dangling at the curve of her back.

She still had those fetishes in her hair as did Slate, who was head to toe black with leather pants and a waistcoat embroidered with gold damask over a black shirt and matching cravat. His hair was plaited so the front didn't fall into his face. Jett could see his knife belts crossing his chest under his shirt. Jett himself had knives in his boots.

Normally you didn't wear weapons to Valla events, but things had changed since Scarlett was captured and Alder was murdered. Someone was targeting their family, though from Scar's story it sounded like she was collateral damage and was simply at the wrong place at the wrong time. Jett had to confess — she was proving a tougher nut to crack than he'd suspected. She'd had her moments, which she was entitled to, but all in all, her recovery was astounding.

Slate had taken over Jett's worrying over Scarlett for the most part, but Indigo was truly on her own. That's who Jett worried about now. Alder was her rock and now that he was gone, she didn't have a shoulder to lean on with Scarlett needing her own shoulder and Jett dealing with his pregnant wife.

Scarlett's arm looped through Slate's and an arrogant smirk played on his lips when he entered the room. Apparently, it was their coming out party and Jett had missed the memo. It wasn't their proximity that made them a couple, it was their body language. The way Slate seemed to move around her protectively, the way she expected where he wanted her to be so he could best care for her.

Scarlett's lips curled into a drop-dead gorgeous smile as she took in the group. "Everyone cleans up so nicely, you all look stunning," she purred, and Jett didn't think she meant to.

Hawk and Sparrow shared an uneasy glance, to Pearl's credit she returned Scarlett's smile. She seemed to approve of the two even though everyone else struggled with it. He could count Gypsum in the *for* column; he idealized Slate for some unknown reason. The ceremony would be a cruel punishment for both Indi and Gyps. Thankfully, at least the two got along well and could keep one another company.

Steel slung his arm around his tiny wife, as if anyone would be foolish enough to cross Tawny and suffer her ire. She had an impressive glare she mostly directed at Slate.

"Anything you would like to tell us, darlings?" Pearl asked in her cultured tone.

Slate and Scarlett stood in the domed room gazing at one another and broke out into smiles that made Jett must look around at the others to make sure they saw the same thing. They had been so wrong about how she would react to Slate being the one to care for her.

"Scarlett and I are together," Slate said cryptically, and Jett's inclination to snort overwhelmed him.

They exchanged more furtive glances. Steel got in on the action. Might as well send up a flare, but Scar and Slate were oblivious. Good thing too, Jett didn't want to yell at anyone for upsetting his baby sister so early in the night.

Jett and got to his feet. "Well, now that you two are done braiding your hair, we can get to the party. I'm famished."

Scarlett gave him a sympathetic smile that would've made the coldest hearts melt and Jett helped the girls up from their seats around the table.

The procession made its way to the portal room, Jett regretting standing behind Scarlett and Slate. Slate rubbed the bare skin of her back as he led her through the halls, as if she didn't live here for the last year and needed his help. Bastard.

Indigo and Gypsum walked together near Tawny and Steel, with Pearl right behind them. Sparrow and Hawk spoke in hushed tones at the tail end, and Jett hoped they waited a while before dropping any bombs on Scarlett. She needed a little happiness, everything else could wait.

The blue light glittered off Scarlett's dark beads and the shimmering threads in the girls' dresses. Jett furrowed his brow at the shadows that Indigo's dress cast across her front. Gods, hadn't she a bra she could wear with that dress? Gypsum caught Jett's scowl and shot a dimpled smile. He'd clean house at Valla U next year.

Throngs of people stood in circles in the Valla University portal room, even more people flowed throughout the rooms. The yellow stoned castle was ancient. Intricately carved arched doors opened and closed with a flash of bright light for each arriving guest. Pewter sconces were lit between each door with enormous tapestries at either end of the long room. Hawk guided them into the hall, where Jett caught a few people glance their way.

Alder and Wren dying within months of one another had been no coincidence, and they had given their family the black mark so to speak. Yet another reason finding Indigo a suitable husband would be near impossible. It could have also been that garbage proclamation Ash put out airing Scar's business to the world and here was the infamous woman now, all swaying hips and sultry smiles for the equally scandalized Slate.

They made their way from the hall to the ballroom, down the stairs and more halls until we were finally outside and headed towards the tent. They decorated the billowy white tent in frosted branches of garland and twinkling white lights. Enormous chandeliers hung from the top of the tent and candelabras lined the tent walls. Last year's induction ceremony had been the first time the whole family went to an event together and Jett had left with Viper's approval to marry Cherry and a stomach full of stones at having to then face Moon Straumr and ask for Amethyst's hand.

People were making their way into the tent. A steady flow of families looking for tables around them. The Sumar table was in the same spot as last year, which meant the Var table was on the opposite side. Tawny and Steel would only be a table away at the Vetr table. Pearl looked hesitant.

Indigo and Scarlett had a silent communication. Twin talk. Jett didn't think they knew they did, but they both turned to him in unison.

"Where are you sitting, Jett? We won't sit at the Var table without you," Scarlett said with a little crease between her brows.

Indigo nodded, "Without dad, I feel like an outcast."

That was the most she'd said about their father's death and Scarlett slid her free hand into Indigo's. "I must sit at the Var table. Come on girls, don't let them scare you away from your birthright," Jett said.

The girls gave him sheepish smiles and Scarlett checked with Slate who led the way over to the Var tables. The girls said goodbye to the others, Gypsum stayed with Pearl as did Hawk and Sparrow for now. One day Dagr might have their own table again the way the Natts got their own table.

They had split the Sumar table in two last year; that year, the second table wouldn't be needed.

Orion came in and Tawny gave him a wave.

"I guess I'll see you all after the ceremony," she said, taking Steel's hand in her own and leading him towards the Vetr table.

Steel gave Pearl a peck on the cheek before heading off. Pearl was watching, eyes full of something unreadable, but it wasn't happiness. Jett gave Pearl a kiss before leaving and she offered a wide smile, they were all growing up. She'd always have Gypsum and eventually his wife and children. Gypsum seemed to sense that as soon as he sat down amongst the empty seats and his dark eyes met Jett's. He'd be married off within the next two years for sure.

They sat at the second of the now two Var tables. Their march was watched by the first Var table which sat Canis, Cygnus, Ruby, and Sage. Delta had sat with her mother at the Natt table, which hadn't surprised Jett since both women had been estranged from their husbands. They felt no need to keep up pretenses now that all the Guardians knew it. Slate pulled out the chairs for Indigo and Scarlett and waited until they sat to seat himself beside Scarlett.

Jackal Var was coming back from the bar with an entire punch bowl of the traditional wassail drink. Their tall knave of an uncle placed the bowl at the center of the shimmering white tablecloth pushing the stark white poinsettias to the side and nearly knocking over the votive candles around it. His blonde hair was neatly combed, and he was looking much healthier than he had at Alder's funeral.

"We are going to need it. Well, hello there Mr. Slate. Escorting our fair Scarlett? What a charming couple you make. Perhaps some of your linguistic skills will rub off on her, she has no ear for languages. It is rather appalling to hear her try to speak it." Jackal looked around the table. "My, my, no one to second that. The rest of you are in the Ask course, only Scarlett is in the Embala. Wonder how that happened." Jackal said raising a brow at Scarlett and she blushed.

Ash was how. His father, Basil, was the one who made out the classes and since he was brother to Moon Straumr, he could do whatever he wanted. Basil Straumr was sitting with his wife, the pinch faced strawberry blonde, Dahlia Natt, sister to Cassiopeia and the lesser of the two evils. There were two Straumr tables this year. Quartz sat with Ash and his parents and the three Straumr brothers sat with their father and River's family.

Crag Straumr saw Jackal sit down at the second Var table and while he should not have, being the heir to the Straumr family, Crag stood and made his way to them. Crag was the most like his father. Stoic, ebony skinned, of an average height, though Moon was barrel chested now in his older age, Crag cast an impressive form. His head was shaven where Moon's had tight short curls.

"Is this seat taken?" Crag asked in his deep croaking voice.

Jackal smiled impishly up at Crag, "Welcome to the table of misfit Guardians!" he said spreading his long arms out wide.

All the girls had a good chuckle at that. They were misfits. Jett had two wives, which would have gone unnoticed if he were someone else or if Amethyst weren't Moon's daughter. Scarlett was the disgraced ex-fiancée of a Straumr, and Indigo was the real daughter of Alder that Delta had been fooled into raising. The three of them were disgraces in and of themselves, add in their gay uncle and his lover, the Straumr heir, and the Lothario orphan who had slept with most the daughters in Tidings as well as their mothers and they were easily the most gossiped about table there. Jett loved every one of them, except maybe Crag, but anyone Jackal liked would warm up to them in the end.

Crag was older than their father had been, while Jackal was only eight years older than they were. There was a significant age difference between the two men, nearly fifteen years by Jett's estimation. Before Crag and Jackal had come out together, Crag had dated a few of the prominent women in Tidings. Jackal never made any pretense of what his preferences were. They had been quite the scandal themselves three years earlier when they had shown up at the induction ceremony together.

Crag was greeted by the others, curt nods exchanged between Slate and him and he sat beside Amethyst. He doted on her as much as Moon did, she had been spoiled rotten when Jett met her. She'd come a long way in a short time.

"Another small group of Guardians were sent into Ostara?" Jett asked Jackal.

"Yes, only a hundred more for now until we can convince my father and uncle there is a real threat. The council was satisfied with the information from the Jorogumo empress, she will not be bothered further. The real threat lies in whether their portal door can access one place or all of them. Otherwise, they could show up here or any number of the palaces or town centers. It is a serious problem." Jackal could be serious when the occasion called for it.

The idea that half of a thousand Jorogumo rogues could storm into Valla U at any moment would give anyone nightmares for a lifetime. Jett ignored the unwelcome thought and looked about the room. Ruby Geol gave them a small smile and Jett noticed her big dark eyes twinkled magnificently; maybe they would have two allies in the Var family. Jett didn't think she knew anything about their births before Alder had moved out.

Moon walked across to the podium in his dark sleeveless robe with silver and gold thick trim, the three interlocking triangles emblazoned on the back. The crowd quieted. Moon looked even more run down, his hair was grayer than ever, and his ebony skin was lackluster. He could still command a crowd though. Reed, Fern, and Dahlia joined him on stage. Reed Tio was the disciplinarian while Fern and Dahlia were headmistresses. Boa Sunna and Sky Tio followed, the headmasters of the men's years. The red headed Tio was also the heir to the Tios.

"Welcome back to Valla Guardians!" His deep voice projected as the crowd cheered.

"For those who do not know me, I am Moon Straumr. Prime of the Guardians and Overseer of Valla. Tonight is the fourth anniversary of the reopening of Valla University for Guardian Mastery. I would like to take this opportunity to have a moment of silence for the ones we lost those many years ago and the recent loss of the heir to the Var family, Alder, as well as Wren Tio."

Jett hadn't been expecting that and a lump sprung to his throat as the girls' hands sought his. Scarlett slid her hand into Indigo's who had instantly started to tear. Gods, someone should have warned them. Jackal clenched his jaw sucking in a deep breath. Slate wrapped his arm around Scarlett's chair, and she gave him a watery eyed smile.

Moon continued, "During this time of gathering, I would remind you to stay strong. The provosts are expediting the tests as fast as possible for those of you who are eligible. Soon all will be as it should."

Jett thought about Wren's Ragnarök and how many more Guardians would need to complete it to get their gold torques. Jett rubbed his bare wrist. One more year.

"I would now introduce this year's inductees to Valla University for the Mastery of Guardians, and the future of Tidings! Please come to the stage as your name is called," Moon finished and started calling the names.

Reed stood next to him as he did for their inductions handing out leather folders while Fern placed Yggdrasil necklaces on each of the students, the sigil of Valla University.

A year ago, life was much simpler. Jett had been nervous about meeting his mother the first time as well as the sister who knew nothing about him, but it had been easier than he could have hoped. They were lucky, his mother and sisters all shared that same warm, welcoming attribute that made people want to be close to them.

Halfway through the ceremony, Diamond Natt walked across the stage. She was smiling, she stopped to give her mother a kiss and wave to her dad. She took her folder and her necklace hung around her neck. Jett noticed she spared a glance for the Sumar table and not the Haust where she had been sitting with Sterling. Maybe Jett should've invited Gypsum over to the misfit table.

Diamond walked past their table and leaned down, "We should talk."

It took just a moment for her to whisper into Scarlett's ear and keep going. To anyone else it would've looked like she adjusted her dress or shoe. Jett noticed Dahlia was looking at them.

Moon was shaking the hand of another student; Jett could almost hear the words he'd said to him last year. "Be strong when you are weak, be brave when you are scared, be humble when you are victorious."

"Thank you everyone for coming. Let the merriment begin!" Moon said with his hands thrown wide.

It was the same thing he did every year. Staff with platters hurried out and started serving dinner. When Dahlia and the rest left the stage, Jett saw the others start to relax. Jett didn't know how long it would last, but he hoped to make it through dinner. Scarlett was doing exceptionally well on the rousen, but already it was pushing it. She had maybe another hour or so before she would have to leave, by Jett's estimation.

While they ate, Jett noticed others around them whispering. It set Jett's nerves on edge and he and Slate met eyes. Fuck 'em. They could take their pick of rumors and gossip until their ears bled. Jett hoped they would and then their wagging tongues would rot out of their mouths.

There was one set of eyes he didn't expect and didn't initially dart away. Flowing dark hair was the backdrop to emerald cat eyes that felt vaguely familiar. Jett thought she was Tawny at first and his brow knit before someone obstructed his line of sight and the girl was gone. He shook off the eerie feeling. He had enough problems.

Jackal pushed goblets of wassail across the table at the three siblings and Jett inclined his head. Scarlett and Indigo, both picked theirs up and guzzled.

"Whoa. Take it easy. I would like to get a dance in tonight, but not if I have to drag you around the floor," he teased, and they both giggled nervously.

How could he ever have thought they weren't twins?

"I'm not feeling well," Scarlett said.

"All in your head." Slate told her under his breath, and she investigated her goblet as if the answers to her life resided at the bottom of it.

She certainly drank like they did.

"I suppose you should start addressing me as Uncle Jack." Jackal cocked an eyebrow at us and smirked lightening the mood.

Indigo beamed prettily at him. "I've never called you Uncle Jack."

"Never mind, that sounds terrible. Need another bucketful? You will if you are sitting here." Jackal smoothly glided from his seat and headed back towards the bar with Crag in tow.

Dessert had been served and Tawny had been making small talk with Orion, Steel being the only other person at the table looking like the good sport. Tawny would be the only female head of her family; Steel was a good match for her. She'd tamed his wild streak with no effort whatsoever and Steel had taken to being her supportive husband like a fish to water. Jett wasn't sure if Tawny recognized the power of her new position, and the responsibility.

The stage had been cleared away and the dance floor erected in its place. A band set up at the back of the tent and when the music started to play with not a soul on the gleaming wood floor, Slate stood towering over Scarlett and offered his hand. She stared at it as if it might bite her. She took it biting down on her lower lip and looked at Jett out of the corner of her eye.

"Would either of you ladies like to dance?" Jett asked, getting to his feet.

Amethyst rose and placed her hand in his, she glided on the dance floor like a dark swan. Scarlett shot him a veiled look of relief as she placed her hand in Slate's, a mocking smile on his lips. He knew how uncomfortable she was with it. Their bond must have been activated. Jackal made his way over to Indigo and followed them onto the dance floor.

The ethereal music of Tidings swept across the tent. Amethyst was lucky Jett had been forced in dance lessons or he would have looked like a stomping elephant next to her. Slate had been subjected to the same lessons and Scarlett's glittering beads swung from her tan back as Slate moved her body with practiced ease. They were on display, and he meant to show her off. Other couples joined them, and it grew crowded quickly so Jett led Amethyst back to the table before she was elbowed, and he'd have to strangle someone.

Cherry held her hand out at the ready and Jett smiled down at her before he kissed Amethyst and took Cherry onto the dance floor. Oh, the pains of having two beautiful wives. Jett turned to the dance floor with Cherry on his arm and slowed. You couldn't push a nickel hunt coin between Scarlett and Slate. He held her tightly to his body as they swayed, their bodies flushed as she seemed to be speaking to him with a smile on her full lips. Slate's eyes glittered from where Jett stood as he gazed down at her. Whatever his response, it tickled her fancy, and she threw back and laughed in her full gravelly voice that made a chill shoot up Jett's spine.

People would be jealous. What they had was so fragile. They should've kept it locked in a box until it was strong enough to flourish, away from the prying eyes of those who would see their... was it really love? It looked like it.

Oh gods!

Cherry gripped Jett's arm as he almost tripped over the edge of the dance floor. Slate didn't just place a kiss on Scarlett's lips, Jett saw tongue. Out there, in front of everyone. Jett gave himself whiplash as he looked towards the Straumr table. Sure enough. Ash had seen it. It was all fine and well for Ash to move on, but not for Scarlett. By the Mother, what was Slate thinking? He might as well wave a red flag at the bull.

CHAPTER

TWENTY-ONE

Whomever said heaven was white was wrong. It was fragrant and colorful, and you were held in the arms of whomever you loved.

The tent smelled like pine sap and ginger, and the twinkling lights wrapped around the garland made light reflect off Slate's glossy waves making him look like an angel, or a fallen one. In any case, he had swept me off my feet.

After our exceedingly rough day yesterday, the night had been all lovemaking and sweet words...so had this morning. I'd had a lot of apologies to make and while Slate trained, I'd made the rounds. I'd gone to Quick and apologized to him, found Brass, thanked, and apologized for making him stay with me and missing his date. I went to Katydid's salon and practically begged her not to be upset with Brass because it'd been all my fault. The blonde was upset at first, but when I explained he'd been doing me a huge favor, she seemed to lighten up a bit and I'd seen her walk over to the Regn's table while Slate led me around the dance floor.

While I was at Shadow Breaker headquarters, I'd stormed into Lera's office and told her that if she ever tried anything again, I'd leave, taking my manipulation talents with me. Then I'd told her that Slate was more than happy with our, um, marriage, and if she tried to be anything less than professional with him I'd be back and very unhappy.

I may have quoted the Hulk once I got started, it was a kind of blur.

She'd been surprisingly amenable and wanted me to join her to go over a contract later in the week. I had left feeling like I over did it, but whatever, she deserved all my ire. Brass gave me a high five as I left the Shadow Breaker's headquarters and I felt like I was on top of the world.

The hardest part came when I went to Indigo's room and told her what happened with Quick. It would tear me apart if my lack of control came between us, but she forgave me even though I felt that she missed him.

She missed him.

I stored that nugget for later. Indigo was alone, and she didn't need to be.

I'd never seen Slate like he was that day. Ever since I'd attempted to utter the word husband, he'd been sweet as pie. I could get used to that. He hadn't wanted me to leave the room, but I had things to do. Bronze was nice enough to come up to our apartment to help me with my hair and makeup. I'd gotten dressed despite Slate's "help" and we'd walked downstairs together and let our family know we were going as a couple.

It was awkward at when we arrived at the induction ceremony, but our saving grace was our uncle. Jackal was a good man. He'd broken the thick ice that prevented us from feeling welcome and I'd caught Jett and Ruby smiling at one another. Things were looking up and then Slate kissed me.

It was unfair to the rest of the world to have to bask in my affection for Slate and I was always nervous about it, but *ugh*, that kiss. The world around me had evaporated as his velvet tongue met mine, sending my skin singing that had nothing to do with the rousen. I didn't care that everyone had been watching us since we'd arrived or that most of the families thought I was a khoraz, not as long as I had Slate. He made everything else tolerable.

"I would do a great deal for that smile," Slate purred when he broke the kiss.

I smiled moronically up at him opening my dreamy eyes. "Love me. That's enough," I whispered, and pressed my cheek to his chest as we danced.

That could've been my last minute on earth and I would've died happy.

Unfortunately, while I felt like Slate and I had been together forever, it wasn't the case and my betrothed from two weeks past was making his way towards us. Ash's lightest green eyes were focused on me with iron determination.

"Ash is coming. Please don't make a scene, it'll be fine," I whispered, pulling away to dance more appropriately with Slate and he squeezed my fingers almost painfully until I shot him a pleading look.

"May I dance with my former fiancée?" Ash said with every ounce of charm he could muster.

I had to give it to him, it was an obscene amount.

Slate glared down at me, and I nodded. He didn't even look at Ash before walking off the dance floor, his bronze face hard as granite.

Ash took Slate's place with graceful ease. That was how I was lured to Ash to begin with, his charm, his gorgeous looks, and the way he moved on the dance floor. Ash was a phenomenal dancer, and it felt like my toes barely touched the floor as I floated across it.

"You have decided to court the orphan. More's the pity, but you will not be able to find a suitable husband in your condition. Better him than being alone, though I was certain you were meant for more," Ash said with a cocky smile.

I pasted a sweet smile on my face, I knew people were watching to see how we would get along now that it was over. "Ash," I said dryly, "I hope your engagement is proving better than ours. How kind of you to pay we little people your attention. Slate and I are doing very well, thank you for asking. It's funny how losing my ability to birth children can be so... liberating," I said in a honeyed tone.

Ash's smile hardened on his face and his hand crushed mine. "How is the rousen, my love? Still fucking anything you can wrap yourself around?"

"Anything, but you," I retorted with my fake smile.

My smile faltered when something passed through Ash's eyes that I had seen go through Slate's eyes on many occasions. On Slate, I expected it, but in Ash it didn't sit right. He laughed heartily and my smile slipped completely. The fine hairs on the back of my neck rose. I couldn't put my finger on what was wrong, but there was.

"We shall see about that, my love. I wonder, have you given any thought to becoming my paramour?" Ash said it so casually I thought I must have misheard him.

"Excuse me?"

"You are perfect for the position, no bastard children I would have to give to the Valkyries and we both know you are stunning, Scarlett. I imagine the Merfolk taught you many things during your extensive stay. Perhaps you could teach me a few things." His sensual lips curled at that, and I swallowed at my dry mouth.

Every day I was stronger, Ash hadn't counted on that and his carnal appetite for me was palpable. "I have no intention of being anyone's paramour — ever. I think the song is coming to an end. Thank you very much for the dance."

He let me go without a fuss and I hoped my cheeks weren't as red as I imagined they were. I made a bee line for Slate whose back was to me where he stood at the bar. I placed my hand at the small of his back and he stiffened at my touch. I understood why when I moved to his side.

Amber was standing in front of him. She was a little curvier than I was, especially now since I'd been on a diet of little food and plenty of *sexercise*.

She had strawberry blonde hair that came down to the middle of her back and big blue almond eyes. She had a full mouth, her upper lip nearly fuller than her lower lip just like mine. Her blue eyes were narrowed at me when she saw me appear from behind Slate.

"Oh, what fun, you two are catching up," I said sarcastically, and walked between them to get a goblet of wassail at the bar.

"Amber was just leaving." Slate rumbled, and I nodded, swallowing my wassail.

"Were you now?" I asked, batting my lashes.

Amber pressed her full lips together. She had been one of the girls to cross the stage, she'd be at Valla U with us. Wonderful.

She looked up at Slate.

"You know where to find me. I am looking forward to a repeat of last year," she purred before walking away.

I closed my eyes and counted, praying they wouldn't be hot coals in my skull when I opened them. Slate led me away from the bar by my elbow and stopped near an empty table.

"She approached me at the bar."

"I don't want to talk about it, one ex down, four hundred to go. I'm having a fabulous night by the way. I especially love that we've both been propositioned within the first two hours," I said dryly, and Slate growled.

"What did Ash say?"

"Only that he wanted me to be his bed warmer when he wasn't busy with his wife because I couldn't have children and that was perfect for whomever he would keep on the side." I snorted. "I dodged a bullet there."

Slate growled deep in his chest, and I gave him a lopsided smile. "We promised no arguing. Why don't you take Indigo out on the dance floor? She looks miserable. I'm going to see if I could force Gypsum out there." I stood on my tiptoes and gave him a chaste kiss before walking to find Gypsum.

I rolled my eyes to the heavens when I saw who he was with. Ama and Shale, who were both wearing dresses for once, had snagged Gypsum and he didn't look upset about it at all.

"Goodness, you look gorgeous, Scarlett." Ama's big round eyes sparkled with delight.

"I almost didn't recognize you two without black from head to toe. How did Ama manage to convince you to wear an actual color?" I teased Shale whose hair fell in a raven sheet over her shoulder.

"Trust me, you do not want to know," Shale answered with a devilish grin making Ama giggle.

Gypsum's dimpled smile flashed his white teeth, and I knew I'd never get him away from those two, they'd all but declared him for the night the way they stood to either side of him like guard dogs daring another smaller animal to come take their ribeye.

"I would like to dance," Brass said, coming up behind me.

I turned around with a ready smile. When I'd seen him earlier, he'd started to get ready, and I'd seen what he planned to wear tonight, similar to Slate's outfit but with a copper waistcoat and black paisley embroidery and ebony buttons. His dark hair was knotted at his nape which was almost at odds with how formal the rest of him looked, but he played it off as I knew he would.

"I'd love to," I said, flashing him my very best smile.

Brass offered his elbow as we walked onto the dance floor.

Let the temptation begin.

It'd been so long since I could smile in other people's company other than Slate's and my immediate family. The night was magical, and I stayed on the dance floor until I started to feel the lag. Hawk, Steel, and Jett twirled me around as did Jackal, Fox, and somehow Gypsum broke free and made it out to me.

I was walking off the dance floor with my arm looped through Gypsum's when Quartz appeared in front of me. Before I had time to react, she threw her drink on me. She was drinking the maroon concoction of warmed wassail and it ran in rivulets down my face before dripping off my jaw. Gypsum stepped between us immediately and I grabbed a napkin off a table and dabbed at my face.

"Khoraz." She spat at me. "Never proposition Ash again."

My mouth fell open in disbelief. As she walked away, Gypsum turned around and wrapped an arm around my shoulder leading me out of the tent so I could go freshen up. Most of the Guardians had been drinking or were up mingling so not many had seen the interaction, but enough had. By the end of the night the newest rumor would be that the notorious khoraz Scarlett Tio had tried and failed to seduce her ex-fiancée back.

Fantastic.

I looked around for Slate and I waved off my family members, Ama, and Shale before telling them I just needed to wash my face. I left Gypsum at the tent opening and told him to go back to the party, he couldn't come into the bathroom with me, anyway.

I sighed and wound my way back into the sprawling castle hoping I wouldn't run into anyone else who had something to say about my life, but as usual, my luck was against me.

I rounded the corner to the bathrooms and saw a petite brunette leaning into Slate whose back was against the yellow stoned wall. Heat rolled through me, if he betrayed me again, I'd have to kill him.

With a jury of my peers, I was sure I'd get off.

Slate's head turned as I came towards him, and I realized I knew who the brunette was. It was the woman from last year's feast, — Lynx he said her name was. His exes dropped out of the sky.

He placed his hand on her shoulders pushing her back a step and when I walked right past him, he called out, but I ignored him and slammed the bathroom door after me. Luckily the bathroom was empty, so I didn't make a scene.

I stormed over to the cream marble sinks and started to dab away my runny make up. Ash must have lied to her, or she assumed something along those lines would happen and chanced that it was true. In any case, Quartz believed the worst of me as did many other people there.

I heard the door crash open and from the almost imperceptible steps, I knew it was Slate. He rounded the corner eyes flashing and saw what I was doing and furrowed his brows.

"What happened?"

"If you weren't cavorting with ex-lovers, you'd know," I snapped.

"Who threw their drink on you?" he asked, bewildered.

I placed my hands to either side of the sink and turned to him, telling him the story and he very nearly rolled his eyes.

"I am done here. How are you feeling, Torch?"

I shrugged. "So-so. Slate, what was she saying to you?" I turned to him, leaving the napkin on the sink.

"Same thing she always says and this time I told her no," Slate rumbled as he stepped forward. "Frigga's sweet grass, I never thought I would have to worry about ex-lovers. I am glad you only have one here, I would not be as collected as you are."

I laughed wryly, "Collected is not what I am."

Slate's lips curled as he wrapped his arms around my waist. "Have you seen my bedroom here? No other woman aside from Shale has, but Shale is Shale," he said as if that explained everything. Oddly it did.

CHAPTER 22
JETT

Scarlett disappeared after Quartz doused her with wassail. Quick said he'd seen her leave with Gypsum, but Gypsum said he'd left her at the tent exit. No one had seen her since, and Brass couldn't pick up a read from either Scarlett or Slate. Quick and Jett had gone to the palace and searched the rooms while Brass had gone to headquarters. Nothing.

Neither had activated their tracker, so Jett was hoping for the best. If Slate had gone off with one of the dozen women who had approached him, Jett would skin him alive. Scarlett had handled Quartz better than Jett would have expected from the way she'd been blowing up at people, but it could've been because she'd been so incredulous by Quartz's accusations. Scarlett wouldn't proposition a man on her worst day. From what Brass had told him, Scarlett was doing better than ever. Jett had seen that with his own eyes.

We searched the university; it was two hours since the mini soap opera. Brass, Quick, and Jett hadn't told anyone else what was going on, they had all been under enough stress from... everything else. Some of the Guardians were still dancing and drinking and would be until the wee hours of the morning, which was typical for a Tidings feast.

They moved silently through the halls hoping no one would notice that they had a purpose in mind, Scarlett had more than enough publicity.

"He owes me for this one. Someone had better be maimed or unconscious. Garnet was primed," Quick said grouchily as they walked the long corridor of the men's wing.

Jett didn't bother rolling his eyes. Garnet was as deep as a puddle and Quick could hardly stand to be around her more than a few hours at a time.

"That one's more froth than ale," Jett muttered, and Brass chuckled.

"Does not matter. She has a tight ass and a warm bed. That is all I need to know," Quick said with a roguish grin. "How was Katydid?"

Jett's arched a brow at Brass whose lips curled, but he kept his eyes on the door on the right. "I have been forgiven. Scarlett went to her early this afternoon and sorted things out for me. I merely had to show."

"Really? She must have thought you needed to get laid as badly as we did," Quick teased as they came to the door.

"Not everyone feels the need to have meaningless sex, Silver," Brass said smoothly, leveling his golden eyes at Quick.

Jett groaned internally. Brass had last been with Scarlett seven weeks past. He hadn't seen any other woman, though Jett knew he had been propositioned a few times. It was as if he was holding out for her.

"Suit yourself." Quick shrugged as he opened the door to their shared room.

Jett, Quick, Slate, and Cyan Tio, one of Reed Tio's grandsons, shared a room again the coming year. Cyan was one of many red heads that went to Valla U, the place was teeming with them; provosts and tyros.

Quick was busy looking at Brass when he walked into the room when his feet flew out from under him. He hit the wood floor with a grunt. Jett and Brass chuckled and helped Quick to his feet. Jett noticed the black glittering beads on the floor of the almost dark room and kicked one watching it roll across the room, the beads were everywhere.

"What the…?" Quick asked, getting to his feet picking up a swath of black glittering fabric torn apart.

Brass called a flame to his hand and the three men looked about.

They didn't have to look far. In the four-poster bed directly in front of the door were Slate and Scarlett. She was tucked tight to his body, his arm around her waist and a big hand covering her chest. A grey sheet was flung over their waists, but there was no question that they were nude.

Jett furrowed his brow and looked to the other men. "How have they not woken up?" he whispered, concern superseding the inappropriateness of the situation.

Brass was unable to pull his eyes off the sleeping couple. They looked peaceful, not injured or like they'd been bashed over the head. Could they have been drugged? Anything was possible nowadays.

"Aren't you picking anything up?" Jett asked Brass, and he shook his head.

"They are passed out," Brass murmured.

Scarlett stirred and Jett let out a gusty exhale. Then she turned around and Jett dropped his eyes until he heard Quick gasp. Jett's eyes darted back up and in Brass's firelight her pupils were huge. She wasn't wearing a nix torque either. Jett didn't care that the other men saw him cover his groin. The memory of her warm, wet calling sucking and swirling over his body like a multi-mouthed tentacled monster gave him nightmares no matter what pleasure he'd unwillingly derived from it.

The three men took a collective step back in case she went after them.

She didn't. She blinked dreamily at them, her caramel hair a wavy tangle around her tan face, the sheet not doing much good down at her waist, but she acknowledged them as they held their breath and she pushed gently at Slate's shoulder turning him onto his back.

Slate made a noise deep in his throat and Jett dropped his eyes again when Scarlett swung her leg under the sheets and straddled Slate's semiconscious body. Brass's light winked out the men scrambled to get out, with Quick making choked noises of suppressed laughter.

Jett would never get the sound of what he'd witnessed out of his head. He could add that scene to his nightmares.

They fell out into the hall and Brass closed the door softly before looking back at the other men with color in his cheeks. Jett thought he must mirror his look. It wasn't her fault, she was on rousen. At least she hadn't attacked them, and from the noises she was making, Slate couldn't have been that deeply asleep.

He stuck his fingers in his ears and wiggled them around praying he could erase those sounds of moaning and the shadows of movement. Jett dry washed his face.

"They should have told us," Jett admonished.

"Yeah? Like what? 'Excuse us, I am going to go give your sister the squeeze and squirt.'" Quick laughed, and Jett narrowed his eyes at him.

"Silver?"

Jett stepped out of the shadows in the dimly lit men's wing and frowned at Indigo. Brass was smirking and Quick was devoting too much attention to the way the shadows bent over her thin satin dress.

"Indigo. What are you doing in the men's wing?" Jett growled, and her pace slowed as her cheeks flushed.

"Jett. I didn't see you there. Things are dying down in the tents." Her powder blue eyes peered up from under her lashes.

"Were you looking for someone?" Brass offered with a warm smile that was much more appropriate than Quick's intense gaze on Jett's little sister.

She smiled brightly, and the sun seemed to rise at night. Quick shifted and Brass looked at him.

"There aren't many dance partners left downstairs," she said, pressing her pink lips together.

"And?" Quick asked, Jett furrowed his brow at the other man.

Her eyes softened, and she ran her fingers through her corn silk hair that fell over her slender shoulder. "Silver, I don't want to dance alone tonight."

Quick seemed to inflate as he stepped forward. Jett mumbled a curse. Quick slid his hand into Indigo's and she followed him with her eyes as he turned back.

"We are done tonight, right?" Quick asked, sparing a moment to peel his eyes off Indigo.

"Yes," Brass said with amusement lacing his voice.

"Fantastic." Quick dazzled Indigo with a smile and then lifted his eyes to Jett with a mischievous gleam. "I am going to take you sister to do the four-legged frolic." Quick led her away swiftly after that and Jett growled.

"I know what that means!" he shouted after them and heard Quick laugh.

Jett swung his eyes to Brass who was suppressing a laugh.

"Your brother is a bastard," Jett said.

"That he is, but in that relationship, it is Silver who should beware. He could not prepare for her coming down his path in life," Brass said thoughtfully watching the two disappear around a corner. "We are all destined to have our hearts broken at least once."

"I have never had my heart broken," Jett said distractedly, and Brass faced him.

"It is not always a lover who breaks it."

"Have your heart broken yet?" Jett asked as they walked back towards the tent where he was sure Indigo and Quick would not be.

Jett thought Brass hadn't heard his question he took so long to reply.

"Daily," Brass said softly.

Jett only nodded and tried to keep his thoughts clear so Brass wouldn't pick up on them. The look on Brass's face in the firelight of their room when he looked down at Slate and Scarlett wasn't jealousy or anger. It was longing, he was a man biding his time and miserable in the process.

TWENTY-THREE

We were back in the apartment when I woke up. Slate must have carried me while I slept, and since we had attacked each other once we got up to his room, it didn't surprise me that I hadn't woken. Slate had been a man possessed. As soon as he closed the bedroom door, he'd gripped the arms of my dress and ripped it asunder sending beads flying everywhere and leaving the dress in a pile of rags on the floor.

Thinking about it gave me delicious chills. I had taken the rousen while we were still in the bathroom and by the time, we'd reached the room it was slowly kicking in, but it was so much more manageable now. Until that numb hour I was so deep under I still couldn't communicate.

Jett, Brass, and Quick had been in the bedroom with us for a mortifying moment. At first, I thought it must have been a dream, but Slate had been real enough. I blushed at the memory. I had mounted Slate like my own personal pogo stick right in front of them.

Knowing Slate, he'd pulled his shirt over me and carried me bare chested through the university like a barbarian. I hoped we hadn't been seen by anyone. Today was our last day before classes started again, I was looking forward to my last year as a tyro until I became a Guardian and hopefully became an ambassador.

In the meantime, there were the Stygians. My life couldn't move on while they were out there in the world doing the things they did to me, to others.

"I do not want to leave bed all day. I will tie you to the frame if need be," Slate purred as he ran his hands all over my skin while we laid in our big white bed.

"We have the feast in town tonight," I said pointedly, and he groaned dropping his head to my chest.

When he lifted it, his silky waves slid over my skin making it prickle. "I suppose you wish to train as well?" he asked with lazy grey eyes.

"We can do that here. Go for a swim after, eat lunch, climb back into bed... or have a picnic," I said, smiling down at him.

He raised his brows. "Be seen in public with me? Will I bore you if you do not feel the need to hide me away?"

"First of all, I've been seen in public with you many times before. Now that I let you touch me, you do it constantly usually in inappropriate ways. Secondly, nothing about you is little, though I do find you to be very dirty." I told him with a coy smile.

Slate's full lips pulled into his rare cheek creasing smile as he laughed richly making my toes curl under the blankets. "Picnic it is. I will have the kitchen pack a basket after our swim."

"Deal." I slid off the bed narrowly missing a swipe of Slate hand as I danced away to dress. "I'm going to grab a swimsuit from my room, and I'll meet you at breakfast," I told him as I dressed hastily, and came back into the room and attempted to jump onto him while he laid prone under the mound of blankets.

Silly me, Slate was never prone.

He caught me in the air and rolled me onto my back, so he laid flush over me. His midnight hair spilling around his bronze face. A blue-black stubble covered his jaw as his silver eyes peered down at me from between his thick long lashes, that would have been more at home on a woman. I was envious of those lashes.

I cocked my head at him as I ran my fingers through his hair. "Why are you looking at me like that?" I questioned curiously; his eyes were glinting.

"Forgive me my moment of mawkishness. By no means are things easy. Yet, with you they feel painlessly uncomplicated. I am thankful you have shown me this side of you," he rumbled.

Butterflies. The man gave me butterflies.

"I love you," I whispered as I pulled his face down to mine.

I didn't wriggle away when I'd hoped, but it was well worth the extra time I'd spent in our big white bed. I hurried through the halls to my old room and dug out my favorite sea foam bikini with fringe that hung over the halter top.

I heard the shower running in the bathroom and walked in without a second thought. "Indi, I'm going to train here today with Slate if you want to join me. Sorry I left early last night."

I hopped up on the pearlescent countertop next to the sink and faced the cascading water fall that blocked my view of the shower. I could only see a blurry outline of a body.

"Did you ever run into Quick?" I asked over the running water. "He was alone, well... Garnet, but boring. He did look very handsome. Which of course, he knows," I laughed. "Do you think he practices that smile of his in the mirror? I bet he does. It's a potent smile. Not on me. I think we know which Regn is far too potent for me," I sighed. Indigo laughed from within the shower, and I hopped off the counter. "Can I take that as a yes?"

The blurred shape split, and a man's hand slapped the energy plate. My eyes widened, and I spun around only to face a wall-to-wall mirror. Quick smiled rakishly at me from his reflection and I dropped my eyes to the floor as he wrapped a towel around his waist and passed one to Indigo who came out of the shower blushing. I was much redder than she was.

"I... sorry," I said stupidly, and started to crab walk towards my old room.

"We will both join you for training. Do not worry, Scarlett. We are covered now," Quick chided, and I turned around keeping my eyes on the floor.

Indigo did an impressive job of trying to act natural while she blushed down to her toes to Quick's never-ending amusement. I winced at all the things I'd said.

"Okay, um, cool. I'll just let Slate know. Then you're coming to breakfast too then, right? Cool. Cool."

I wanted to die. I thought I'd rather be walked in on the do the walking in.

"Yes, *cool*," Quick teased, and came up behind Indigo as she dried her hair at the counter.

My eyes widened again as he ran his hands through her hair taking over her hair drying for her with his hips pinning her to the counter from behind. I needed to leave before I saw more than I could forget.

I stopped just outside the door and turned to them. "I don't suppose you two have plans later? Slate and I don't get out much so we could use a buffer for lunch."

Indigo lifted her head as Quick stopped drying and they looked at one another. Indigo looked hesitant, but Quick didn't seem to be taking no for an answer.

"After training, we will be there," Quick said, hitting me with that dazzling smile, the panty dropper I called it and it worked. "Oh, and Scarlett."

"Yes?" I asked, poking my head back in.

"There is no need to practice, it is effortless," he said, laying on the charm so thick my cheeks heated again.

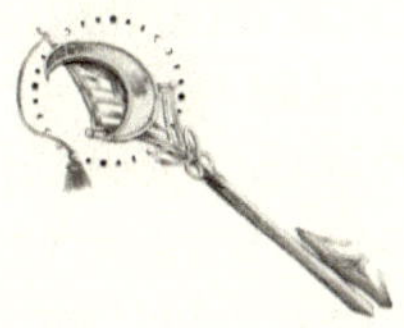

No one looked particularly surprised to see Quick at breakfast. Jett did do a great deal of scowling, but he hated anyone Indigo and I showed interest in. Training went by in a blink. I started to see all the little ways we were interconnected and realized Tidings was a small world. Cherry had been with Quick when Amethyst and Jett stole her away. Which was peculiar because Quick liked blondes. Gypsum and

Quick had apparently "dated" some of the same girls already, and Gypsum had been inducted into their club of sorts. Gyps was not at a level with Slate or Quick, but more like Brass. I hoped it stayed that way.

Tawny was kinder to Quick than she was to most men, which was kind of hilarious since Quick was one of the worst womanizers I'd ever met, but he was charming. It made for an interesting morning. Indigo was trying not to pay Quick too much attention and hadn't known about Cherry and Quick, or that Quick and Tawny were friends. I kept picking up the slightest spike of jealousy coming from her, though she stamped it out fast. Quick had been ignoring her, but it was a game. Gods, I hated games. Funny thing was, Indigo needed that game. If Quick paid her too much attention, she shied away, at least in front of the others. So, when he was ignoring her while keeping an eye on her out of his periphery, she stewed.

The whole situation was sigh inducing. I didn't invite the others to the picnic. Indigo would have a hard time enjoying the double date without adding more eyes to it. Slate wore a white sleeveless shirt and lent Quick some fresh clothes so we could picnic next to the Sol River outside the palace.

Once we were away from everyone else, Quick redirected all his focus to Indigo and since she'd been deprived of it all morning watching the other girls laughing and joking with him, she accepted it and repaid it in kind. I had brought a tan throw blanket for us to sit on and Quick nestled his head into the pale pink chiffon folds on Indigo's lap. Her hand rested across his chest as he ate our packed lunch and sipped sweet fruity wine we'd brought out of a thin glass.

Slate was my own personal recliner. I sat between his outstretched powerful legs leaning against his chest we I fed him bites of whatever I was eating. Things just clicked, and I was glad we'd decided to do it. Quick and Slate got along, and Indigo was one of the few who didn't give Slate a hard time. There was so much right in that afternoon I kept feeling the impulse to cry out of happiness.

The hot Thrimilci sun heated our skin and caused us to laze about well after our meal was eaten. Slate stood taking me with him and crossed to the river where he unzipped my mint green dress and let it fall to the ground before carrying me into the river. His magnificent body held me effortlessly, not a single qualm about his nudity in front of Indigo and Quick.

Not that they were looking. The moment we left the picnic, Quick had lifted himself off Indigo's lap and pulled her down in front of him so she disappeared. We could only make out Quick's back laying on the tan throw from the river. I could not have dreamed of a better way to spend my afternoon.

"I almost don't want to go back. We could convince Indigo and Quick to marry and build a hut out here so we could live this way forever," I told Slate while he floated in the cool river with my arms and legs wrapped around him.

"Forever is a long time," Slate purred, the river water pooling along the ridge of his collarbone.

"Only forever will do," I said before I slanted my mouth over his.

I tightened my arms around his neck and felt him shift inside me. "Happy, Torch?" he whispered roughly against my lips.

"Mm-hmm. You?"

"Very," Slate purred, kissing me again.

"Slate, tell me about your mother. Don't say you don't remember. I know you do. I don't care that you lied. I know you have your reasons."

I pulled back to look at him when he went rigid. "I did say that. You are right, I have my reasons for not being honest with you. The same reasons I have for everything I do. I swear it," he said soberly, and I kissed along his jaw.

"I want to know more about you." I pushed his jaw up with my own kissing along his throat.

"You know all that matters, Torch." His sculpted chest rose and fell against mine as he sighed. "I remember them both. My mother and my father." He rested his forehead against mine. "You remind me of her. Sweet, but feisty. It is more of a dream of her that I remember and what my father told me of her. Dark of hair and eyes, with a pouty mouth. She radiated a warmth and love unsurpassed in the moments after my birth."

Slate was silent for a few moments, and I waited patiently for him to continue. I doubted he talked about her often if ever.

A small smile played on his soft lips. "I look a lot like my father. Eerily so. He loved my mother fiercely; I believe if he had lived he never would have been able to love another woman the same way he loved her." He smiled again and raised his grey narrow eyes to mine, droplets clung to his lush lashes. "Though there was one woman he had always loved that could have blossomed into more." He gave a rueful smile, "It is a hard legend to live up to."

"He would be proud of you, they both would. You've saved me...in many ways. Sometimes the greater strength is in the living when you'd rather die." I chewed on my lip; I was hitting too close to home.

Slate tipped my chin up to look into my eyes. "Alder wanted to live, Scarlett. He may have missed your mother, but he loved you and your siblings more. Do not ever think he wanted to leave you."

My heart twisted. "He welcomed death. You didn't see the look of peace in his eyes when —"

"Peace, because he had his family after all those years, he had finally done the right thing by Wren and was a father to his children. He had your mother and was trying to reunite his family. It was likely the happiest he had ever been. Your mother would welcome him back to her if she knew how he went against the Vars and claimed you."

I nodded and swallowed against the lump in my throat.

"I know you keep a lot from me." I stopped his denial with a finger to his lips. "That's okay. I know you'll tell me in time, I only wanted to say that I'm ready to hear it when you're ready to tell it. Nothing could change how I feel."

Slate's full lips curled, his grey eyes flashing to silver, so they reflected the sunlight. "I have exceptional sight, smell, and hearing. For instance, since you have been sharing my bed, your scent has changed. Not the way you smell, but your scent. It has matured."

I quirked an eyebrow smiling. "Matured," I repeated. "And your sight?"

Slate looked towards Quick and Indigo, we could still only see Quick's back and that he was moving, but nothing discernible. "The pulse at Quick's throat, they will be finished soon."

I looked at him incredulously and back at Quick. "No way."

Slate nodded. "I will be able to hear it as well."

"That's kind of creepy."

I scanned my mind for all the snide remarks I'd made under my breath in his presence, and he smiled knowingly as if guessing my thoughts.

"Okay. I'm going to swim over there. You stay here, I'm going to say something, and you tell me what I said."

Slate laughed and let go of my waist as I pushed off him, feeling him slip from between my legs. He arched a brow at me with a salacious grin and I splashed at him making him run his hand across his face and over his long midnight locks that curled when wet. Gods, he was beautiful.

"Quit staring, Torch." Slate shaking me out of my revelry, and I scowled before swimming further away. I stopped a good distance, and he smiled with a flash of perfect white teeth. "Challenge me. Go further."

I rolled my eyes. Now he was just showing off. I swam further and stopped to look at him and he nodded. I whispered, and he smiled one of his rare cheek creasing smiles.

I shouted to him, "What did I say?"

"I do not think you want me to shout it," Slate laughed, and I blushed.

No way he could have heard that.

"Try again. Keep it suitable for children," Slate laughed, and I chewed my lip.

Perhaps my first comment had been more than a little vulgar, but it was something I could not have normally said that's why I had said it when I was sure he wouldn't hear me.

"Okay. Ready?" I shouted, and he nodded.

I whispered again and his face changed. He smiled softly at me, and I raised my brows pushing my wet fringe to the side.

"Well?"

Slate pursed his lips as he smiled. His lips moved, but I couldn't hear him. It was easy enough to read though. I smiled and bounced off the riverbed.

"Louder! My hearing isn't as good as yours!" I shouted.

"I LOVE YOU!" he roared and dove into the water after me.

I had enough time to squeal before he appeared in front of me shaking his mane like a dog with a blindingly bright smile. Slate grabbed me around the waist and pulled me up to kiss me deeply as I giggled.

"Gods. About fiddlesticking time," I breathed against his lips, and he chuckled, kissing me again.

"We should head back. Quick and Indigo have fallen asleep," Slate chuckled.

"Really? With all that shouting you're doing — I don't know how," I teased.

Slate pulled me under the water calling a bubble of air around our faces so we could breathe and kissed me slowly. His hair floated around his bronze face in shimmering waves. I had no idea how I'd resisted him for so long.

TWENTY-FOUR

Townsfolk were everywhere, they were setting up a dance floor along the shimmering white roads of Thrimilci's town heart and long tables with benches for a feast. Watching them work was mesmerizing. They used calling for everything. No hernia surgeries there. The women brought out steaming platters of food for the feast in Grecian style dresses common to Thrimilci and a band started to set up next to a square lit overhead by strings of lit bulbs.

Night had fallen in Thrimilci, and it was the day before classes, the last big hurrah before everyone got back to the grind. The atmosphere was relaxed, and laughter rang through the air. Children ran past, chasing one another around the adults. Things like it didn't exist outside of Tidings, a camaraderie it felt good to be a part of.

Slate and I had climbed out of the river to find Indigo and Quick asleep, as Slate had said they would be, with his chin resting on her head and their arms over one another. Quick didn't seem like the cuddling type, but then again, neither did Slate and we did it all the time. Slate had got the brilliant idea to lay down under the sun and let our hair dry like lions on the savanna. We fell asleep in minutes.

It had been a quiet, comfortable walk back to the palace after we all woke. Indigo seemed embarrassed they'd fallen asleep, but Quick had pulled her under his arm and wouldn't let her get weird on him. I understood now why people stared at Slate and me. I was doing the same thing to Quick and Indigo. When Indigo let him, Quick anticipated her wants and needs as they sat at the long wooden bench with our family.

"What's Brass up to?" I asked, making conversation.

"He is with Coyote, Butterfly, and the kids," Quick told me with a nostalgic smile. "My grandfather dotes on his great grandkids."

The band had started to play, fun light music meant for lines of synchronized dancers played in the background of our meal. The air had cooled under the full moon, cool for Thrimilci. Coyote was the eldest Regn brother, intense with striking good looks. His red-headed wife was the provost of Tribal Affairs at the university, and Reed Tio's daughter, Butterfly Rot. Small world.

"They have celebrations like this in Ostara too?" I asked, using my fingers to pick up a chicken drumstick.

Indigo gave a nostalgic smile. "Yes. Very similar to this one, though we — the Vars — rarely celebrate in the town like Pearl does. I don't think the family is as well liked and the Thrimilci folk seem to want to get to know its heirs better."

Indigo nodded to where Gypsum had been dragged away from his meal by a gaggle of giggling tweens.

"Look at those dimples," I smiled. "He's approachable, girls flock to him. It's so funny. It was the same way he started at our high school."

Tawny groaned. "It was only slightly better than when girls would wait after class for my dad."

I laughed. "Hawk had no idea why so many girls had questions after class."

"You two need to stop babying Gyps. It's the fatal flaw of the Guardians, babying their heirs. Makes for arrogant leaders. What?" Jett asked defensively when we all started snickering.

"Jett, I love you, but the night I met you... well, you were about the most arrogant person I'd ever met. Then I ran into another man who surpassed even you. Pearl spoiled you two rotten. Steel and Hawk are the only ones with an iota of modesty," I teased and Slate squeezed me tight to his side kissing the top of my head.

"Look how well that turned out," Slate purred with a knowing smile.

"I'm starting to think that arrogance is a Guardian trait, like people from a specific region having an accent, Guardian men are possessive and cocky."

Indigo and Tawny nodded with my assessment.

Once the dinner was over and we helped clean up the tables, the dancing began in earnest. I'd remembered to wear flats again, and the men treated us to some of the traditional dances of Thrimilci. Soon, my hair had fallen free from its pins as I was spun and jumped around kicking my feet to try to keep up with the steps. My face hurt from smiling.

Sparrow and Hawk had come out onto the dance floor, it was their last night in the Sumar palace until they rehabbed the Dagr palace. She was looking more like herself already. Hawk's arm was on the small of her back, Gypsum on her other side as they danced in a circle around a smaller circle rotating as they went. She was smiling for the first time in what felt like ages. Steel pulled Pearl out to join us and our table was soon empty, even Amethyst got in on the fun.

Glistening with sweat, I led Slate off the dance square for a breather. I lifted my hair in my fist while I fanned my neck.

"You realize you can call to dry your hair," Slate chuckled, and I scowled at him.

Movement caught my eye past him, and my breath caught.

"Torch?" Slate asked, low and dangerous.

I wished Slate had Brass's ability to read my mind. My voice had failed me and a wave of nausea chilled my hot skin. I stared into the space I thought I saw a cloaked man with a beard, but I must have imagined it.

"It's nothing. I thought I saw one of the Stygian Knights that captured me," I rasped.

My whole body was trembling. I hadn't expected my reaction to leave me so frazzled. It was all well and good planning my revenge, but coming face to face with one of them scared me. I was afraid.

Slate stepped so his body was against mine. "Where?" he growled.

His posture changed, and I swore his skin darkened. It was predator Slate. Primitive and savage with the primordial need to protect his mate. I nodded to the edge of the dance square, and he pulled me back into the fray.

Instead of taking me with him, he shoved me at Steel and grabbed Quick and Jett off the dance floor. I stood gaping after him. I could have been wrong. It seemed like an overreaction, but Quick and Jett had almost run after Slate's retreating back telling Steel to watch over the women. Gypsum saw the commotion and started towards us.

"I'm sorry. I thought I saw one of them," I mumbled after Steel led Tawny, Indigo, and me off the dance floor.

Gypsum danced with Cherry and Amethyst, but his eyes constantly scanned the crowd. A brown beard was hardly enough to go off, there were a dozen different men there that fit that description. Still, there was something about this one that made my hackles rise and I was going to start trusting my gut.

Tawny wrapped her arm over my shoulder, I was still shaking. "Slate will hunt him down. That guy's got a nose like a bloodhound, but he's built like a lion or a sabertooth or something enormous and feral."

A nervous giggle escaped me, she was right. If one of them were out there, they'd catch him.

"Sorry for ruining your date," I said, giving Indigo an apologetic smile. She waved a dismissive hand at me.

"I've spent every second with Silver today. I'm not used to it," she said, wrinkling her forehead. "I don't have the first clue what to do with him either. I don't want it to become a thing, but he's very..." Indigo trailed off.

"Charming?" I offered.

"Sexy?" Tawny chirped, and Steel leveled his eyes at her making her giggle.

Indigo smiled. "Persuasive, and both those things." She groaned. "He has so much baggage. Not that I don't, I just don't want to deal with someone else's."

"I can understand that," I murmured. Tawny mumbled an agreement and fastened Steel with a glare.

My uncle gave her a poster boy smile of pearly whites and she defrosted. She would never stay mad at Steel, those two balanced one another out better than anyone I'd ever met. I strived to be that equal.

Jett came jogging into view, his face red and out of breath. "Come now. You're all to go back to the palace. There was someone, but they took off. Quick and Slate are after him," Jett coughed, and I handed him a goblet of water.

He guzzled it as it spilled off his square chin and down his tan throat.

"I don't know if it was your guy or if it was someone up to no good, but in any case, it is good someone caught him before he acted."

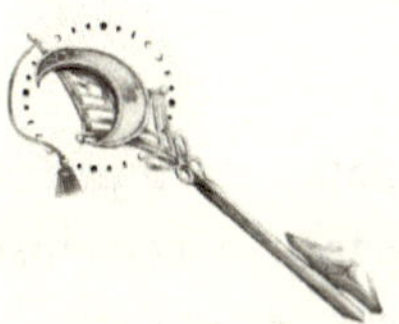

After I showered, I waited nervously in bed for Slate to return. Slate was the last person who should have gone after the man. If it was a Stygian, could he have lured Slate into a trap? I should have waited with Indigo. My thoughts had gone down a very dark path, and I was beside myself with worry. I'd activated my bond so Slate would know that I was okay, if extremely concerned.

The door to the apartment swung open, and I leapt from the bed and stumbled over myself, tangling in the blankets, as I hurried to the sitting room. Slate stalked into the bedroom before I had a chance to make it to the door. He was filthy, covered in sand and sweat, his eyes wild.

"Wha —"

I didn't get a single word out. He flipped me onto my stomach on the bed and tore my white silk nightdress from my body with the panties underneath with one sweep of his hand. My toes brushed the rug as he pushed me down.

I gasped at the sudden nudity, and then he was in me. He went fast and hard, my cheek against the white sheets as he panted in my ear. When it was over, he pulled out and turned me back around on my wobbly feet. He fell to his knees in front of me and nuzzled his face against my stomach.

I blinked down at him, not understanding what had just happened. What was still happening? I stroked his tangle of long wavy hair and started to pull out the braids and beads.

"Is Quick okay?" I asked hesitantly.

He bent his head back, so his chin rested below my belly button and looked up at me with gunmetal eyes. "Scarlett, if anyone hurt you, or took you from me, I would raze the world in blood and ashes," he growled deep in his chest.

I swallowed against my dry throat. How easily I forgot about this side of him.

"He got away."

It wasn't a question. Slate would not be this upset if they'd caught him. The hard planes of his face looked chiseled from a cliff side.

"He dropped this. He was one of them."

Our Condolences, We look forward to your first competition.
Stygian Knights

Slate rose to his feet, his pants still pushed down past his hips and started undressing after he handed me a piece of crumpled paper. Fear bubbled in my stomach as I ran my thumbs over the paper. I could not read it and be blissfully unaware, or I could face these monsters and one day put an end to them. I chose to face my problems head on.

The paper shook in my hands, and I balled it in my fist. They knew who I was, where I lived, and where I'd be. I was a danger to all those around me. I looked to Slate who was in danger all on his own, but they had grown brazen since I'd entered the scenario.

Slate pulled me into his arms reading my mind and kissed the top of my head. "I will not let anything happen to you. You are safer with me than without me. Do not try to leave, Rabbit. I will chase you and I have ways of keeping you we have not yet begun to explore."

I nodded. I wouldn't run. Not today anyway.

"What's the point of taunting me? It doesn't make any sense," I said distractedly as he led me into the bathroom.

"Could be to get me to retaliate before we are ready. It would work — threatening you," Slate said and placed my bare bottom on the countertop and turned his back to me.

We'd done it enough times that I knew exactly what he wanted. I finished removing his braids and fetishes and hopped off the counter.

"Did you have to tear off my pajamas?" I said, looking at my back in the mirror to see if he sliced me.

Slate looked down his nose at me, pulling himself to his full height. It was so hard to reason with him when he was like this. Most of the time I relished in his untamed animalistic ferociousness. Then again, those times I was feeling a little feral myself. Tonight had been different, there was no warmup.

He came, he saw, he claimed.

Mine. His body had roared. Mine and no one else's, no one can touch what's mine.

He needed a serious lesson in manners. It wasn't the time and, if I was being honest with myself, I'd been forceful on more than one occasion while on rousen. He'd needed healing more mornings than not.

Whoops.

I held up my hand to silence him before he growled at me. "Do not tell me how to fuck you," I said in a mock bass, and an uncanny imitation of one Slate Sumar if I did say so myself.

A slow sexy grin spread across his lips, and I let him lead me into the shower.

CHAPTER 25

JETT

Slate had brutally tortured the man once he'd caught him. Quick had tried interrogating the man, who had in fact been there to deliver a message to Scarlett, but had bitten off his own tongue before Quick could get any real answers. Slate had lost it. Jett had to leave to make sure one of the girls didn't get worried and try to follow them out of town. They hadn't gone far. The man did have a beard, but he wasn't one of the men who kidnapped Scarlett, Quick got that much out of him.

When Jett got back, Slate was dressing again and Quick was disposing of the bits and pieces of what had been a man. By the Mother, hadn't he ever heard of not killing the messenger? When it came to Scarlett's safety, they weren't taking any chances. Jett might have killed the man himself, but in a faster, more humane way.

Quick had been splashed with blood and had to rinse his pants and incinerate his shirt. The bottom line was the man was a Stygian Knight. He was part of the group who killed Alder and had Scarlett raped, plain and simple. Jett only wished he could've partaken in the killing.

They had been painstakingly careful not to use the 'R' word in front of Scarlett. She knew what happened, it wasn't her choice. The rousen made her think she wanted it and forced her to be a willing participant in it. If she wanted to acknowledge the extent of it, that was fine with Jett. He wouldn't know what to do anyway. Slate seemed to be erasing all memories of what they'd done to her by making new memories with his own, and retribution would come. They could count on it.

Slate wasn't the avenue Jett would've preferred, but you worked with what you had.

They'd all agreed to let Scarlett have the letter. If she found out they withheld it, she'd be doubly angry. Hopefully, she'd never find out about the murdered man. Slate said he would just avoid answering, he didn't want to lie to her anymore. Why stop? Omission was just as well as lying and Slate was the lord and reigning master of omission.

"They're all back at the palace. He was a diversion. If we hadn't left Steel with her, I hate to think what would've happened," Jett said, trying very hard not to growl in frustration. Slate was doing enough roaring for a pride of lions.

"Fucking foolish," Slate growled.

"You did what you thought best. Everyone is safe. That is what counts," Quick defended and Slate growled again.

"The real message was that they could find her whenever they want. I do not know if it is a warning for me, or a threat to her," Slate said through gritted teeth.

"Both," Jett snorted. "We've got your back and they'll have to climb over my dead body to get at Scarlett again." Jett narrowed his eyes at Quick. "Are you planning on hanging out with Indigo for a while or not? I think she may need eyes on her just in case. Amethyst will be safe in the palace and she's a Straumr, they'd be crazy to mess with her and I'll be with Cherry."

Orion had put a man on Tawny the moment he realized who she was. She was probably safer than any of them. Orion had taken no chances in the welfare of his heir. There was at least one staff member at the palace who was Orion's and one of the local shop owners always happened to be around her when she was in town. They were good, damn good. Tawny had no clue she was constantly followed, though Steel did, but he didn't think it was a bad idea.

Quick licked his lips. "She is with Sterling during the day. She is not likely to be with him most nights now that Diamond will be at Valla U, but I will see what I can do."

Jett thought he sounded like a robot. His tone was flat and without inflection.

"Well, don't do me any fucking favors," Jett growled.

Quick gave Jett an impish grin. "It is my pleasure. Really."

Jett growled and Quick chuckled. "I only meant Indigo does not always want me around. Especially if there is a chance Sterling will be there. I am not sure things will continue when we get to Valla U," Quick admitted.

Jett nodded. He hadn't been thinking clearly, of course that's what Quick meant. Jett felt like a shit for making him admit that he was Indi's second choice. No one liked being second. Case in point, the glowering brute that had been so covered in blood when Jett had walked up that all he could see were the whites of his eyes and the flash of clenched teeth. A complete sociopath and Scarlett was blind to it.

Gods, his sisters had horrible taste in men.

TWENTY-SIX

I stared at the blue morning glories on the wall of the informal dining room dreading the day to come. I hadn't begun to think about how Dahlia would treat me this year. Ash's mother was rude on her best day, and I wasn't likely to get her best anymore. The sooner Ash married Quartz the better.

"Scarlett, darling, you have not touched your breakfast. Is there anything the matter?" Pearl asked, lifting her delicate brows.

Slate wanted the bond always activated during classes, no more taking chances. If I went to headquarters, I had to be with him or Quick. There weren't any other Breakers at Valla U now that Shale was proven tried and true at the Ragnarök. I understood the precautions, but they chafed, and it had only been an hour since he'd laid them out for me.

"I haven't interacted with these people since things ended with Ash. They'll all be gossiping, and that'll just be the friendly ones," I brooded.

All my classes were with Ash, and he would not be cordial. I expected things to get bad and for me to have to hide it so Slate wouldn't lose it. Gone was the sweet, tender man I tricked into telling me that he loved me. The captain-knuckle-dragging-me-Slate-you-mine-obey-or-else barbarianism was back. If I was looking for sympathy, I would have to look elsewhere. Jett had the same expression on his face like he might handcuff me to him or Quick, who had stuck to Indigo like flypaper.

Tawny was the only one who looked to be feeling my pain and it would only get worse. Quick would be oppressive in our classes, but at least Tawny and I would have him to hide behind when Ash and Sage were being particularly nasty.

Slate squeezed my thigh under the table, and I looked up offering him a weak smile. I wanted to go back to our room, back to our bubble. To pretend the rest of the world wasn't happening. I was thinking it again when his lips curled in a knowing way, and I sighed. Things were much easier when he didn't know me as well, when my thoughts were more private. Now, he could guess by my expressions alone what I was thinking. It was frustrating as sugarfoot.

I was already wearing my black caftan dress trimmed in gold with a wide yellow belt that was the women's second year uniform. The men were head to toe black with a thin yellow belt. First years had fire engine red belts. There would be at least a hundred new students this year, Garnet, Amber, and Diamond among them.

"What are the plans for tonight?" Indigo asked. Her long light blonde hair pinned up on one side, her light blue eyes always seeming so happy.

That perked me up. Jett's was twenty-one. Our parents had had a busy year a while back.

"I thought we'd save it for the weekend, head out to the cottage. Get away from it all," Jett smiled.

No smugness whatsoever.

"Sounds romantic," Tawny gushed, she folds her hands with her elbow on the table, chin resting on her laced fingers.

Tawny turned to Steel, her wide mouth split into a beautiful smile. He gave her a chaste kiss. Gypsum rolled his eyes, Hawk looked down at his plate, and Sparrow looked on fondly, lost in memories of her own.

"I want to throw a costume party Saturday night. Real costumes, not that masquerade garbage. No costume, no entry. I think we could get three cottages for people to crash in." Jett looked to Steel who nodded.

"Leave it to me. I've got you covered." Steel turquoise almond eyes glittered in his tan face and Tawny quirked an eyebrow at him.

Jett was basically Steel's little brother. Always had been, and Steel planned Jett's birthday celebration every year since he was old enough to have them away from Pearl. Last year had been the first time I spent the night with Ash. This year I'd have a much better night, with a much better man.

"How can you lay out a costume party and not have warned us? Where will we get costumes at the last minute?" I chastised Jett.

"Be creative." Jett jutted out his chin arrogantly as he chewed. I pursed my lips with a smile.

"We will be back most weekends once the portal door is up and running. Hawk will still be at Valla U most of the time, so you won't miss him. We'll have guest rooms set up for anyone who would like to visit as well, so don't be shy," Sparrow announced looking down the long table at all of us gathered.

Once the portal door was working it would only take a second to reach them. Until then, it would take a few hours. The Dagr palace was in Thrimilci which explained why Sparrow and our mother had been so close. They spent all their time together as girls, just as Tawny and I had. Tawny and Gypsum didn't seem perturbed by their parents moving. We'd all be so busy with classes, we'd barely notice their absence.

"There will be a master suite ready for any Dagr heirs that happen to be found," Hawk added, "We are hoping one will come forth."

I furrowed my brow, "What makes you think there are any?"

"We have it on good authority that there may be one still in Tidings. You haven't heard anything, have you?" Sparrow asked.

Her eyes were so hopeful it made my heart hurt. "I'm sorry. I wish I could help. I don't really know anyone. The people I do know... most of them I don't know their last names. Indigo, do you know anyone?"

She shrugged and shook her head. "Do you have any idea what they would look like or how old they would be? If they're our age, we could ask around and see who doesn't know their birth parents. Or do they know and not want the responsibility?" Indigo asked.

Sparrow sighed, "It's my family line. Dark featured, around your age. Don't trouble yourselves, girls, I appreciate the sentiment."

"Mom, what's up?" Gypsum frowned at his mom.

"Don't worry about it, Gypsum," Hawk interjected, running his hand over his silver hair.

The tension in the room had grown thick, I gave Pearl a questioning glance knowing she must feel it too. She sliced once with her head of coppery coiffed hair, and I knew she meant it wasn't for me to know. I let it go... for now.

Quick must have brought his uniform with him to our palace because he had put it on this morning. "Perhaps the Dagr heir, whomever they are, is happy the way they are living their life."

"One can only hope, darling. How very observant of you, Silver," Pearl said, directing a fond smile his way. "There is plenty of time yet. No need to grow desperate."

Indigo and I shared a confused look. I'd always thought my mom and Sparrow looked like sisters. Were they speaking so cryptically because one of us might be the Dagr heir? If we were, there was no way we would know without them telling us. Hawk only gave a tight quirk of his mouth in return.

Quick blended right in with the rest of us, just as Slate said he would. I hadn't believed him. Men like Quick weren't made for blending. Shadow Breakers were though, and he was a Breaker to the bone.

"Can I make a trip to the U.S. and get a costume this week?" I asked, feeling giddy just thinking about being back stateside.

"No," Slate said brusquely, and my eyes snapped wide.

I turned to him with an incredulous look. "I wasn't asking you."

"I would have to arrange for a car to be brought. Your license is still valid?" Hawk asked, and I nodded vigorously with an idiotic grin on my face.

"We can make it a girls' trip." I looked animatedly at the other girls and Tawny had stars in her eyes like I did.

"You go, we go," Slate growled, and I turned to him for the second time.

I kept my voice low, "No one will know we're going to the U.S.; we'll go straight to the costume store and back." I whispered even lower, "I'm not taking a needless risk."

It rankled my pride, but sometimes people needed to be managed and I was getting good at dancing around other people's egos to get what I wanted. Namely Slate's. The man would keep me in a gilded cage if I let him.

A muscle leapt in his jaw, but I saw what I needed to in his eyes. I faced Hawk again.

"Thursday? Is that enough time? We can pick up costumes for you guys too if you like," I told the men.

"Would you mind?" Quick asked Indigo who blushed but nodded.

"I'll get you one too," I said to a sullen Slate, and he lifted a brow.

"I do not wear costumes," he growled low, for my ears only.

"Exceptions must be made, lover."

It was barely audible. Slate would hear it, and the corners of his lips quirked at my words. There should be an all-encompassing word for all the things between Slate and I, but lover scraped the surface.

Sparrow, Steel, Pearl, and Gypsum said their goodbyes to us in the blue starry portal room. Amethyst got a bit weepy, but Pearl took her in hand and told her they had much planning to do for the nursery so she would hardly notice Cherry and Jett's absence.

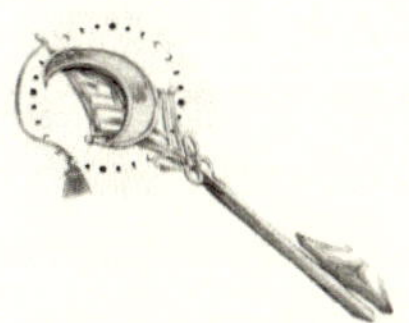

The yellow stoned room with its intricately carved vines on the wooden doors was brimming. First year tyros in their red belts chattered excitedly with their families, while second-year students roamed, looking yellow-belted friends. We were easy to identify.

Indigo kept looking out the of the corner of her eye. I followed her gaze. Sage stood there with Sterling and a young blonde man I had seen around them before but I always forgot his name. Hunter, I thought.

"Have you spoken to Sage since?" I left it at that, and Indigo shook her head.

"Not even at the funeral. I think they'd rather pretend I don't exist." Indigo gave a weak smile and Quick moved closer to her to place a comforting hand on the small of her back.

"Good luck to them. It is no easy feat," Quick said low near her ear, and I smiled idiotically at the dazzling smile he flashed her when she looked up to him.

Slate bumped me from behind and I snapped myself out of my stare and slid my hand into his. He didn't like hand holding, but he did make exceptions. All the usual suspects were around: Diamond was with her mother, Dahlia, near Garnet and Amber and their families. I had no idea the two girls were cousins.

Ash stood nearby, and I shifted uncomfortably. I wasn't used to having exes or an ex. I've never needed to worry about running into a man I'd been physical with. Sure there was Chris, but we had both graduated high school and I could count on one hand how many times I'd seen him after that. I would see Ash every day. His head swiveled and our eyes met. He gave me his cockiest, most charming smile that had always made me relent before. Now I noted he was a gorgeous man, but not the man for me.

Slate bumped me again, and I broke my gaze with Ash to look up at a glowering Slate. I smiled a little at his jealousy and stood on my tiptoes to place a kiss on the corner of his mouth. He relaxed visibly; it wasn't often I gave out P.D.A..

We moved to the front of the room near the doors to the hall and waited for the second-year headmistress and master. Fern Rot was second year headmistress and our great aunt. She was a bubbly redhead and mother to all the red-headed provosts at the university, the grandmother to all the red-headed tyros. She had that warmth and patience of a grandmother that made you feel at home with her.

The red bearded Sky Tio entered the room and looked about with sapphire eyes. The eldest Tio son was the headmaster and provost of Counter Casting. He wasn't the shouting type. He'd wait patiently until he was noticed and take his tyros to their new quarters. Indigo nearly stammered when Quick ducked his head and pressed a kiss to her cheek before walking to Sky. Jett did the same to Cherry before leaving her with us, and Slate let go of my hand and kissed the top of my head before joining the men who were slowly gathering to Sky. Sky's hair brushed the collar of his dark blue jerkin while he nodded at the younger men.

Shale's uncle, Boa Sunna, came in after him. They had the same haughty bearing. His dark hair was slicked back from his olive face, and his tilted eyes took everyone in before he moved deeper into the portal room. Fern came in last, looking remarkably similar to Pearl, except with fiery red hair and stunning blue eyes that crinkled in the corners of her fair face when she smiled, which she always did.

She spotted our group of girls at the front and gave a sunny smile before hugging each of us. "Last year, ladies. You must make it count."

We nodded like bobble heads and waited for the other girls to gather. We knew where the second-year wing was, but not which room they had transferred our things to. I looked around as we waited, taking in the smiling faces of the new excited students and their happy families. That had been us last year. I looped my arm through Indigo's, needing to be closer to my sister. She understood and gave me a commiserating smile.

Jonquil and her minions gathered to Fern, and I wanted to bare my teeth in a snarl. The platinum blonde's head was shaved on the sides, which didn't diminish her looks at all. Her wide blue eyes met mine and she gave me a smug grin. Tidings was too damn small. She was Cherry's cousin. They weren't close, their mothers had been sisters but Cherry's mother had passed away a long time ago and was raised by her father Viper Enox in Mabon. Their two families hardly spoke, but they were both Kaldrs. They had the same tall slender shape, same big cobalt eyes, and same red stained pouty mouths.

I rolled my eyes and waited for the day to start. The sooner the better so I could lose myself in my work. I'd taken my smallest dose yet of the rousen, and Slate had woken me in the middle of the night to give it to me. I'd fallen asleep without it; he said it was a good sign. He had felt my lethargy through the bond. We had very little sleep after that.

My eyes scanned to where I would find him, and I cringed. Ash was standing closer than necessary and the constant hum of aggravation through the bond told me Ash was doubtlessly antagonizing him with something nasty to say about me. I tried to send reassuring emotions through the bond until I saw Amber sauntering over to him like a ship to harbor. She wanted to dock in Slate, or him to dock in her.

I took a step forward, but Tawny put her hand on my shoulder. "Let him handle it. You deal with his sugarfoot all the time, Scar. It's time he sets his old lovers straight."

Amber had reached him, and Ash was looking amusedly between them. I could only imagine what the brazen girl was saying to him. Focus. I needed to focus. I couldn't let some boys get me all worked up. It was my last year at Valla U. I had to be proven tried and true, and I needed to do it with little to no complication. I didn't think I could handle another year like last year. I'd have to be committed to a padded room if that happened. Slate was a big boy. If he wanted to be with me, he would be.

End of story.

Four flights of stone stairs led to the second-year girls' wing. Valla University was a sprawling castle twice the size of the other palaces or castles in Tidings. You were transported to the dark ages when you walked through the halls and grateful that, at some point, they had installed plumbing.

"This wing is dedicated to the young women training here at Valla University for Guardian Mastery. The entire fourth floor is for the second years it is four girls to a room."

The center of the hall opened out into a large room with several sofas and tables spread out across large Persian looking rugs as a parlor of sorts. Two fireplaces were lit on opposite sides of the yellowed stone wall room, it looked ancient. It had been the same on the first-year floor.

Our room was the first one on the right; Cherry, Indigo, and Tawny went in before me. Tapestries hung on the windowless walls scones or mirrors didn't occupy. Across from the door were two cherry four-poster beds nestled in a large arched alcove. Braided pillars divided the room's three alcoves, another bed to the left, and one to the right. We took the same beds as we did last year.

"They are obsessed with Wind and Storm," I said, looking at the tapestry of a light-haired woman lying in the arms of a dark-haired man on something that looked like an asterisk.

Indigo walked up beside me. "It's our only civil war. A legend about power, love, and betrayal. It doesn't get any more provocative than that. Their depictions are wrong though. Historically, Natt's have light hair, so he would've been blonde with fair skin and Dagr's are from Thrim-ilci, which usually means dark hair and olive skin."

"Yeah, but they die. That sucks." Tawny made a face as she made her bed.

"Mother Nature took away the elemental powers of the Guardians and separated the lands with the hope that with more space and less power, we would never war again. The Natt and Dagr lines have only been women since. We have created the council, named Guardians to separate tribes, and have worked together as a people much better than those in our history. It was the only time the energy Mother Nature was seen by a Guardian," Cherry chirped in and the three of us turned around as one.

Cherry wasn't the brightest crayon in the box and that may have been the smartest thing she'd ever said. She shrugged with a giggle.

"I love a good love story."

I widened my eyes at Indigo and Tawny, and we set about arranging our room.

TWENTY-SEVEN

Magical Beings with provost Ford Tio, another of the red-headed brood, was our first class for the Embala course. Quick had met Tawny and I in our usual spot by the stairs and we walked the hall together.

"Your ex is determined to get himself killed this year," Quick said.

"Oh yeah? I saw him nettling Slate earlier when Amber came to chit chat," I retorted and Quick sniggered.

"I told him you saw that. Jett was there, so Ash kept his comments to a strictly jerky nature, but I'm willing to bet they will turn perverse with time until Ash gets the desired reaction."

Tawny snorted. "He can try to provoke Slate all he wants, but we all know you never laid with him. I bet that pisses him off so bad," she chuckled.

"He has seen me undressed though, and that is enough to make Slate want to tear off his head and drink his blood like a fountain. Ash has touched me. That's more than enough."

"Slate is not as dumb as he looks, he knows what Ash is after," Quick said with a dazzling smile, and I leveled my eyes at him with Tawny laughing in my ears.

Slate did not look dumb, he looked deadly and capable. I knew for a fact he was manipulative and shrewd. What a lovely man I'd chosen.

The halls were filled with students. Girls in their floor length black caftan dresses trimmed in gold and wide red or yellow belts cinched at their waists. The young men in their black 'V' neck linen shirts and black pants tucked into black boots. They walked in groups completely oblivious to the five hundred Jorogumo loose in Tidings.

I let go of Quick's arm since it was drawing attention, or very possibly I was drawing attention. I couldn't blame them when they averted their eyes or spoke in hushed tones. I would probably talk about me too.

The barren khoraz who cheated on a Straumr with Merfolk. That was me.

We walked through the open door of the Magical Beings class and nodded to Ford who looked just like Sky without a beard and shorter hair. He was ready with a friendly smile as we took our seats.

"Good morning," he said as we passed.

I had only ever sat in two seats in each classroom. The room was designed with stone stadium seating, cushions covering the seated portion. Wood desktops collapsed into slots in the front of each seat that pulled up into an L shape. Last year it was always Sage, Ash, me, and Tawny in the seats. I thought it might be time for a new start. Ash was bold enough to sit next to me if I didn't choose a new spot.

Tawny read my mind and gestured to three empty seats in the front row. Quick shrugged his big shoulders not caring where he sat and placed himself between Tawny and I, so I sat in the aisle seat.

Ash, Sage, and their blonde friend, Hunter, walked through the door, and I felt myself tense. Sage's big blue eyes met mine. The smile he gave me with his pouty lips was vicious. I felt chilled. I wasn't close enough for an accurate emotional read, but the *We Hate Scarlett Tio* fan club was in session.

Crimson Rot, the pretty red head who was a distant cousin of mine, followed them in and took the seat next to Ash. I wondered how Quartz felt about Ash keeping his groupies now that they were engaged.

Ford turned on his projector and started to lecture about the Jotnar.

Last year we had learned about the blue-skinned giants that lived in Elivagar. This year we were getting more in depth on all subjects, and I found myself looking forward to it. I was a firm believer that knowledge was power.

Ford's class easily kept our interest. Besides his detailed slides depicting the lifestyles and traditions of the Jotnar, he spoke animatedly about them as though he thoroughly enjoyed teaching the subject.

The bell tolled signifying the end of class and we walked down the steps to leave. Ford's head lifted from his desk to find me. "Scarlett, a moment."

"I will be just outside the door," Quick whispered as he passed me.

Ford came around his next and leaned against it, people were still leaving the class behind me. Ford was tall, the tallest of the Tio/Rot siblings which wasn't much at six feet. He had a broad forehead his short red hair didn't quite cover up, his features more on the rugged side. He seemed like he would spend a lot of time outdoors.

"I will not keep you; I am sure there are enough rumors going around. I wanted to make sure you were well." His eyes flitted down to my ring and back to my eyes. I wasn't even sure he noticed he did it, but my hand went immediately to it.

"I am. It's been... difficult, but my family is very supportive and have taken very good care of me. It helps that I'm a Tio and have met someone already," I joked and Ford smiled.

"Yes, I see that. Good for you. We Tios are resilient."

"Are we going on another field trip this year?" I asked, changing the subject.

Last year's trip was to the troll and fairy community in Mabon. I wouldn't mind going back even though that was where I discovered Ash with Crimson. I had met Baboo and made friends with a Centaur I would've liked to see again.

"You enjoyed it?" he asked skeptically.

Ford and Butterfly had been there when Ash had stumbled into camp nude with Crimson because my Centaur friend had stolen their clothes while they were in a stream.

"I did. Mabon was beautiful," I said honestly.

He rubbed his hairless chin, "I will look into it and let you know." He smiled and sat behind his desk.

Quick and Tawny were in the hall talking rather close. I had completely forgotten about their flirting.

I walked in between them. "Nature and Focus next," I said obnoxiously.

They looked up with twin cat with cream looks and a part of me grew angry. Steel was one of the best men I'd ever met. Maybe I was overreacting.? Quick walked between us, Tawny and him talking about all the pop culture Quick didn't know with Tawny poking fun at him. I could hardly stand it.

Nurture and Focus took place in the green house at the very back of the school. We'd have to go all the way done to the first floor to get there. We walked past the open doors of the other classes. I rubber-necked into Wisteria Rot's class, the Ask course would be there and I caught sight of Slate, Cherry, and Jett moving up the steps of the stadium seating. Indigo was already seated in the second row with Sterling. Out of the corner of my eye, I caught Quick's mouth turn down.

Whatever was between Sterling and Indigo ran deeper than the carnal appetites. I wouldn't want to be in Quick's boots, but I hoped he wouldn't give up on her. We Tio women tended to be mulish when it came to our hearts. We made a choice and stuck to it even if we knew it was wrong. Since I'd given over to Slate, the weight off my shoulders had been remarkable. I didn't know how I ever thought if I kept turning him down, he would eventually get the message. Quitting wasn't something he was capable of.

We walked through the vine covered tunnel that led to the greenhouse, which was enormous. Really enormous, more like ginormous. Every flower and tree imaginable resided here. It even had home-grown ponds. I took the opportunity to bring up Steel.

"Which way is the pond Steel brought you to?" I asked.

She smiled, I guess I should have expected it, but I thought she'd feel guilty. "It's over there. That was a magical night." She breathed.

"Oh yeah? What was so magical?" Quick asked, he must have felt that she was telling the truth.

"It's where we made love for the first time. Where I made love for the first time."

Her eyes had gotten dreamy, her smile softer. I wondered if she knew she'd said it out loud.

"I would have love to have seen it," Quick said.

I slapped his arm. Tawny just laughed, full and feminine.

Tawny had changed since we'd arrived at Tidings, and it wasn't just that she got married. She was more mature or something. I couldn't put my finger on it, but she had come around on the Guardian's culture. They were erotic, not that I could blame them. I mean, they were all exceptionally good looking in one way or another and worked out all the time. The Mother literally handpicked them for their beauty and power. I learned that in Dahlia's class, of all people.

Provost Boa Sunna taught Nurture and Focus; it was always nice to have a break from stuffy classrooms to sit amongst the exotic flowers of the greenhouse. Boa's tilted eyes lingered on me a second longer than the rest of the students. I was willing to bet that would be happening a lot today. His hair was slicked back away from his face as he paced around us with his hands clasped behind his back. He was strict, but fair as an instructor. I could deal with that.

Asp Sandr was Shale's mother and Boa's sister, she also taught at the school. I had her class next in fact, Calling. I didn't have a problem with it anymore. Once I learned to call the first time, something Ash had taught me, I could do anything they asked of me with little effort. They always said what you could do with calling was limitless. Of course you had to deal with power restraints, but I had the most powerful calls that I knew of.

After a lot of meditation and growing lotus flowers, we headed towards Calling, which was back in the main building. "I've got to make a stop in the lady's room. You too can go ahead without me," I told Tawny and Quick.

Quick hesitated, eyes serious for a moment, but let it go. I hurried to the bathrooms on that floor, it took so long to walk from the greenhouse to the classrooms, I didn't want to be late.

I closed the stall after me and relieved myself. No period. It took me a second to remember I wouldn't be getting one anymore now that all my business had been eroded. I twinge of the deep sadness that I went through great lengths to avoid crept up making me swallow hard.

"Um, hello?"

"Yes?" I asked, feeling like a complete fool.

"Would you happen to have a tampon I could use, please?" Asked a familiar voice.

"Yes, of course," I said, and a caramel-colored hand reached under the door taking my offer. I still had one handy just in case, Slate said sometimes our bodies healed slowly, it was wishful thinking.

"Diamond?" I asked hesitantly.

"Scarlett?" Diamond asked. "Thanks for the... tampon."

Finding out that they had tampons in Tidings was like discovering there were dragons, well, it would've been that cool if there had really been dragons. Of course, the tampons were just about as organic as you could get, but it was better than nothing.

I walked to the sink and washed my hands when she exited the stall. "I did not get a chance to speak with you the other night."

"That's all right. I know you're busy planning a wedding and all," I said with a sympathetic smile.

"Scarlett, what Ash did... I want you to know that you are far better than Quartz and he should not have put all that... stuff on the announcement."

"Yeah, what's done is done. No point dwelling on the past. I wouldn't take it out on you, Diamond. We're cool."

"And Amber, she — I feel like I should warn you. We are friends, best of, but she has her eyes set on your Slate. They were hot and heavy for a few months last year and then he stopped seeing her out of nowhere. I think she thought they were getting back together this fall, but now he is with you, and she is very mad." Diamond knit her brows together.

I sighed. "She's welcome to try. Slate is a grown man; he can make his own decisions. I noticed you and Gypsum aren't seeing one another any longer," I said giving her a disapproving look.

Her brows leapt to her hairline. "We are. That is... it has been more difficult to hang out, but we try to make time. That older blonde has a thing for him, so it has been awhile."

She meant Ama, and I almost laughed. "It's probably better if you don't, I should know. You wouldn't want anyone blasting your indiscretions all over Tidings."

Diamond's full mouth pursed. "Sterling has been seeing Indigo since they were twelve... thirteen. Before even me. I am not upset about it, but when will that end? Sterling was my first, too. I do not know if she realizes that." She gnawed her lip and my stomach dropped.

"I don't know, but she's been seeing Silver Regn. I can talk to her if that's what you want," I said cautiously. I couldn't figure out why she was telling me this.

"Quick." Diamond shook her head, "Garnet has her heart set on him. Everyone knows Quick does not stay with one girl for very long. She would be better off finding a suitable man to marry since she must continue the Tio line."

"Do you know any single normal men?" I self with a self-deprecating smirk.

Diamond shook her head. "What about Hunter? He is a Snjar, a lesser family like the Regn, or your friend Brass? I have not heard anything bad about him and Butterfly married a Regn."

I did not like the idea of Brass and Indigo together. He wouldn't be into it anyway since Indigo and Quick had... whatever they were having, and we had... but Diamond was on the right track.

"Thanks, keep your ears open. I'll find a husband for Indigo yet," I told her.

"I would have really liked to have you as a sister, Scarlett," Diamond said as I opened the door.

"I wish more Guardians were like you. Be careful with Gypsum, I don't want to see what happened to me happen to you," I told her in all seriousness, and she nodded.

TWENTY-EIGHT

Counter casts was taught at the last room down a side hall. We faced one another while working casts against each other. I was decent at it, calling against other people wasn't instinctual for me so I was always a second too slow.

I saw Provost Sky Tio's red-bearded face addressing the class, and I knew I was late. I opened the door and his blue eyes met mine as his lips pressed into a firm line. Sky liked me under normal circumstances.

"Come in, Scarlett. You are late. I will have an extra assignment for you tonight." I groaned internally. "Does anyone not have a partner?"

My eyes met Quick, and he nodded towards Tawny who beamed at me mischievously. Curse those two.

"I do not."

I was so thankful it wasn't Crimson I could've done a jig. She wouldn't pull any punches.

Then I saw who it was, Sage's blonde friend. I wondered if it was a set up and he would mop the floors with me. Ash and Sage looked at him with raised brows and I felt a little reassurance at their surprise.

Sky gestured for me to move down the aisle and stand across from him down the long room. I sighed and resigned myself to my fanny pack kicking. There were plenty of cushions and other things around the room to help with calls that got out of hand, but they wouldn't help in the moment.

I stood across from Blondie. He smiled, he had a fit build like most guys our age, not nearly as big as Slate or Jett, but ripped. The veins in his arms stood out prominently. His skin was tanned which darkened his hollowed cheeks. His forehead seemed permanently furrowed above his hawk like blue eyes. He was good looking, but in an obvious sort of way.

"We have not officially met, I am Hunter Snjar." He held out his hand, and I shook it.

It was uncommon to shake hands, so I was surprised for a moment. "I remember you from last year. Scarlett Tio," I smiled.

He seemed friendly enough. If he'd meant to pummel me, he'd hardly have needed to introduce himself first. He crossed over to his spot in the line opposite mine, hands at the ready.

Sky walked down the line telling us what to call. Hunter's line went first. Hunter nodded at what Sky told him and before I could blink a fire ball hurled at me. I absorbed it. Someone gasped. Sky looked confused. I fidgeted. I didn't even know I could do that. Apparently, fire could no longer be used against me, my body just soaked it in. I thought back to the times I crossed the Crash Course, and the geyser had grazed me but left no evidence behind. I figured out why.

Hunter's eyes had widened but seemed determined to try again. Sky whispered to him again, gain Hunter nodded. Air flew at me, but I countered it with a wall of air around myself that deflected it. Sky moved on to the next person. Hunter arched an eyebrow at me, and I shrugged.

We went back and forth all class long, I had been doused with water and knocked on my fanny pack with air, otherwise I'd countered all of Hunter's calls. I hoped he wasn't taking it easy on me. Sky handed me a list of calls that I had to describe ways to counter. My punishment for arriving late.

Hunter peeked at the sheet. "That is not so bad. Boa wraps you up in a tree for the entire class if you come late, which happens frequently since the class is further away." I was pleasantly surprised by the laugh that bubbled up. "You did well today," he said.

"You were taking it easy on me," I countered.

"Not at all." He gave me a knowing grin.

Quick and Tawny were waiting for me at the door. Quick widened his eyes at me.

"I've got to go. Thanks for being my partner," I told Hunter.

"Any time, Scarlett," he said with a courtly bow.

It would have been ridiculous on some people, but it looked right when he did it.

"Green — Hunter green," I said musingly.

He winked. Ash and Sage walked to where he stood facing me and Ash's celadon eyes met mine, narrowing. How could he be upset with me when Hunter volunteered to be my partner?

I turned and hurried after Quick and Tawny. "Adding another broken heart to the trail, Scarlett?" Quick asked arching an eyebrow.

I rolled my eyes, "Trail of what?"

"Broken hearts. What else? Slate, Ash, Brass, Solder, now Hunter?" Quick teased.

"Oh, please! First of all, I had no impact on Ash's heart. Slate maybe, his is far from broken. Solder is a friend, maybe he thinks I'm attractive," I defended.

"Truth. And Brass?" Quick questioned.

"His heart is fine," I sniffed.

"Oh, lie. A fat one," Quick rebuked.

"Brass can take care of himself, Quick. Don't worry about him," I huffed.

Meals and battle training were the only times all the students were in one room together. This year we'd be sitting on the left-hand side, right-hand side being for first years. Platters waited for us at the long tables and benches. Jett was already sitting with Cherry at a bench and waved us over. Indigo looked grouchy as she sat next to Slate. Quick slid in next to her and Tawny sat across the table by Cherry. I beamed a smile at Slate when I lowered myself onto the bench next to him.

Moon sat at the center most table with my great uncle Reed, Fern, Dahlia, and Basil with them. Sky and Fern sat directly in front of the second-year section. At the head of the hall was a fireplace, with long windows to either side. The head tables for the provosts in front of them. The dining hall was teeming with movement. Only the headmistresses and masters wore black sleeveless robes with gold trim. Moons had both, his three interlocking triangle sigils designed with both silver and gold.

Long tables and benches strategically lined the room's marbled floors. The walls were ancient, yellowed stone. Sculpted pillars lined the rooms and sculptured people lined the edges of the ceiling looking down at us. Chandeliers were on each side of the hall, two by two all the way down. Between chiseled rafters were circular stained-glass mosaics depicting the phases of the moon.

"How's your day going?" I beamed at Slate.

Slate had no use for words. He slid his hand into my hair and kissed me none too chastely until I couldn't stop smiling against his lips.

"That good?" I breathed.

"Gods, I thought Steel and I were bad," Tawny joked.

I giggled and then blushed for giggling like a schoolgirl. "I would do a great deal for that smile," Slate purred, and I melted against him.

"Mm. I love you."

It was word vomit. I couldn't stop it from bubbling up before it was out and all over everyone. Jett dropped his fork, and it clattered to the table. I said it out loud. It wasn't in my head. Sugarfoot.

"Truth." Quick mumbled and my face burned with embarrassment.

Slate's eyes opened to look directly into mine and they were silver like mirrors that saw through to my soul. I didn't need to see his lips to know he was smiling one of his rare smiles.

"You're enjoying this," I whispered.

"Immensely," he purred.

I faced the table and confronted the gaping faces of Tawny and Jett. Indigo was looking past Quick, but she looked less astonished at my outburst. She did see us at the river together.

"Like Quick said," I said, daring anyone to comment.

Jett was tongue tied; he focused his turquoise eyes on Slate was impossibly smug. "What did you expect after all those long nights?" Slate chided Jett.

I laughed and Jett's tan face turned an unhealthy red. Slate was so close on the bench that his big shoulder was behind my back so I could lean slightly on him. The electricity thrummed between us.

"Aww." Cherry batted her lashes and looked to Jett. "I love you, babe."

Jett gave her a look, but he mumbled the words back to her making her preen.

Meals in Valla U were served family style, and I filled my plate with steamed vegetables and slices of honeyed ham. The great thing about getting into shape was being able to eat whatever I wanted again since I worked out for hours a day.

Chocolate cake would be next.

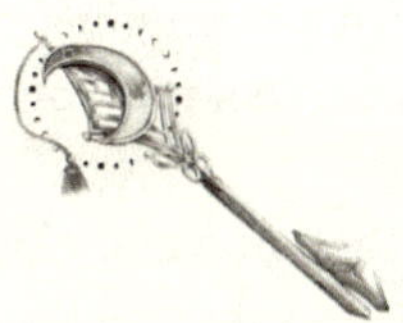

I got a very different dessert when Slate pulled me from the dining hall and into one of the abandoned classrooms. It was the very same one I'd kneed him in the groin in, which wasn't by accident. He sat me on the empty provost's desk and pulled my legs into the air before burying himself in me in a quick tryst before our return to classes.

"Do you regret your words in front of the others?"

Slate's mane fell in front of his face as he dressed. He lifted his soft grey eyes to mine. I had found my panties hanging off one of the desks.

"No. Why would I? It'll all come out in time," I said, shimmying into the undergarment.

"All of it, Torch?" Slate's smile mocked me.

"Don't you want it to?" I asked, feeling very insecure.

Slate crossed the room to where I stood trying very hard not to fidget. He fisted my hair in his hand and pressed me against him.

"What do you want? Tell me your heart's deepest desire," Slate purred.

"I've only had the same silly dreams since I was young. I wanted to be an author, a wife, and a mother. Simple things really — to be loved and have a family." Slate could see the sadness in my eyes, and I felt him delve and close his eyes putting his forehead to mine. "No change?" I asked.

"A little, Scarlett."

I didn't expect there to be. There was a protracted silence, and I kissed him deeply, running my fingers through the dozens of braids letting the beads flit through my knuckles.

"I wish we didn't have class right now and we could go back to our big bed. Are we going home tonight?" I asked.

"We need to go back. I do not know if I can control you if you are on rousen here. Gods forbid you get loose in the men's wing," he teased, lightening the mood and I laughed.

"Would you be okay with a ceremony?" I blurted.

"Ceremony?" Slate asked, looking down at me and his grip in my hair loosened.

"A small one. None of that glitz and glamour, just close friends, and family. Not any time soon. I need some time, but next winter maybe," I rambled nervously, feeling like the shy girl I used to be.

Silver eyes searched mine. "You want to claim me, Torch?"

I rubbed my lips together. "In a way. I want the world to know you're mine and I want to celebrate what we have."

Slate chuckled. "First you need to be comfortable telling them that things are more serious than they appear."

"I'll get to that. Can we just plan in our minds, or you can let me plan in my mind and you go along with it?"

Slate slanted his mouth over mine and I knew it was a yes.

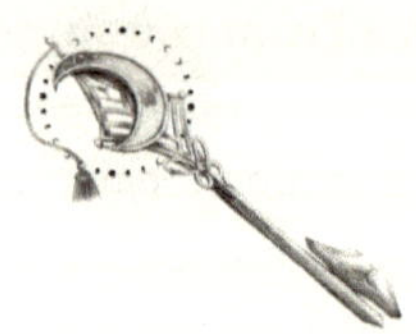

The two days before my competition, I took my lowest dose of rousen to date. The urges weren't as strong and I could convey thoughts the entire time in broken sentences, but still. Slate thought maybe another week, and that was it. He was letting me compete since I wouldn't need the rousen for Vegas, also known as the patron room.

We'd passed up training at headquarters that week until Quick said Lera wanted me to come negotiate a contract with her. I was expecting it and asked Slate to come with me. I wanted him around every moment of every day. It'd only been two weeks to the day that I'd been Slate's sex slave. Slave was probably a harsh word. It would be better suited for him after the way I'd treated him on rousen so many times, I'd lost count.

I could see the balance of power shifting in unexpected ways. I'd been the aggressor in the bedroom for the first half, now Slate was. It told me a lot about him. I didn't think he had let a woman push him around as I had before. It would explain a lot of the struggle I'd seen in his eyes those times. Now there was a better balance, he gave as good as I did. I was a different person with Slate when we were undressed. I didn't think I would ever be insecure like I had been the first time with him, so in awe of him and his body — the things he did to me with it.

My body squirmed as I thought about it.

I had my first contract to negotiate with Cordillera. I was eager for my first negotiation; I hoped it was something easy like needing a merchant guard. Not even Cordillera knew what clients needed before they met, the first meeting was the one and only meeting and Cordillera decided on the spot.

Cordillera's downstairs office door was open, and I knew she was waiting for me. Chafer leaned on the wall beside her door. His brown hair deliberately messy, his eyes like a laser beam beneath his thick straight eyebrows. A wicked grin spread over his face when he saw us come in.

Chafer had guessed Brass's feelings for me and since he was Tiding's biggest sugarfoot disturber, Chafer felt it was his personal mission to antagonize them both. He crossed the room with a fluid like grace I now knew came from being confident and dangerous.

"Cordillera wants to prep you." His grin spread, "That is, if you are done with your boyfriends?"

My hands found both Brass's and Slate's wrists and I held tight. I didn't have a third hand for Quick's. Quick walked up shaking his head.

"You just do not know when to quit. My aunt will only protect her boy toys to an extent, and I believe you are reaching yours." Quick's smile chilled me to my core.

"Silver, I believe you should be training," Cordillera said, standing in her doorway. "Chafer, please bring my delegate here." Her short, dark hair swung as she turned back into her office.

"You will have to stop holding their hands if you are going to come with me," Chafer said, wicked grin never faltering.

Slate hadn't known I was holding Brass's wrist, and I felt him tense beside me. I turned to Slate and leaned onto my tiptoes to give him a kiss. He didn't bend to me, so I called, and a solid stair of air pushed me up to meet his lips. He didn't smile, but his eyes glittered as I kissed him.

"No need to be so difficult all the time," I said as my feet hit the floor again. Not everyone could use calling like I could, but Slate and Brass knew what I was capable of. I felt Chafer's astonishment. "Lead the way," I said, smirking at Chafer.

I knew Chafer was thinking something particularly dirty when Brass took a step forward radiating indignation. Slate was actually the one who stopped him. "We have training to do," he growled. Brass narrowed his eyes at Chafer but let Slate lead him away.

"You're going to push too far and they're both going to pummel you." I told Chafer as he walked next to me.

He chuckled darkly, "I know."

Cordillera was seated by the time Chafer, and I closed the door to her office. I took my usual seat across from her on the blood red couch. She took a deep breath and stood crossing the room to sit next to me. She smirked when she noticed I was wary of her after she tried to seduce me.

"Meetings are clandestine. Chafer and another will meet them at the portal gate and lead them here blindfolded and cloaked. We will also be in cloaks and wearing masks during the meeting. They may elect to wear a mask once the blindfold is removed, but a record of their name is kept in our records once the contract is accepted." Cordillera assessed my clothing. "I shall provide you with something more appropriate. Come along. We have much to discuss."

With her heels on, Cordillera was my height. They clicked on the stone stairs we climbed to the top floor where her rooms were, the same floor her outside business office was as well. Her heels echoed through the hall until we reached one of the intricately carved wood doors. She opened it and Chafer and I followed her in.

Red, red everywhere. Red velour bedding with a matching canopy on a cherry wood pillared bed, tapestries over walls with red as the prominent color, dark wood floors so polished they reflect the light from the gold sconces along her bedroom walls. I half expected whips and chains to hang from the walls. She was classier than that, though there was probably a secret compartment for what was inevitably there.

My heart twisted imagining Slate in the red bed.

Cordillera had gone into a room I suspected was her closet, no doubt the size of our entire bedroom had been in Chicago. Chafer made himself at home sprawling across a maroon couch in her sitting area a dozen feet from her foot board. She came out of her room in her under-wear, and I tried not to stare.

Tattoos wrapped around her rib cage on both sides. I didn't remember seeing them in the images she had seared into my mind, but they were not new. I knew she was around forty, but there would be no way to tell by looking at her. Her stomach was taut, her arms and legs toned to the point of being muscular, and in her red bra and panties she looked, well, she looked hot.

My insides burned, I didn't know if that was her way of reminding me of what Slate had got to see, what she wanted me to see, or if she was just getting dressed. I decided to give her the benefit of the doubt. I made note of her Valla U Yggdrasil necklace and torques as she stepped into a black dress, her chin length hair fell forward to brush her bright red lips. She turned around, and I zipped her up, automatically closing the dress over her olive skin.

She pulled another black dress off a hanger and her thick arched eyebrows raised, waiting for me to undress. I looked at Chafer from the corner of my eye who didn't make a move to look away but wasn't leering either. I sucked it up and kicked off my boots, pulling off my black pants, and tugged on the drawstrings on my shirt so I could pull it over my head.

I stood before her in my pale pink bra and underwear. My body was toned, tan, and I was blessed with generous curves. That didn't mean I was comfortable with Cordillera appraising me as she was, lips pursed as if searching for flaws.

"I should have guessed pink," Chafer said from where he sat smirking.

Cordillera turned to him, and her lips curled as well. "Brass must have loved it. I am surprised Slate does though."

I held my hand out for the dress and she handed it over. I stepped into the floor length dress that was identical to the one she was wearing, but in my size. It was one of her clingy numbers with a low scoop neck that barely covered my shoulders but had wrist length sleeves. The material was slinky and stretchy and feel surprisingly comfortable.

"You look better now that you are not so... innocent," she said, dropping heels in front of me.

There was no inflection in her tone, and I wasn't sure if I should be complimented. I stepped into the shoes she provided, and she moved behind me to pin back the front of my hair. When she finished, she walked in front of me and applied a red lipstick to my lips, gripping my chin tightly between her thumb and index finger when I resisted.

"Why the make over?" I asked, irritated that my normal appearance wasn't good enough.

"We present a certain image; you need to fit that image. Not the happy sunshine little girl you usually are," she snapped.

"I am not happy sunshine," I said, defensively crossing my arms.

She pursed her lips again and approached me with her hands up. She stuck her hands down the front of my dress and adjusted my breasts, so they spilled over the top of the neckline.

"That wasn't inappropriate at all," I mumbled.

"You have assets. You should use them to your full advantage." Her tone was matter of fact and left no room to argue.

Again, I wasn't sure if she was complimenting me.

Chafer stood and left without a word, and I could only assume he was going to pick up the client.

Cordillera headed back into her closet and pulled out two black cloaks and two black half masks, she handed me one of each, long elegant fingers placing them delicately in my hands. She opened the bedroom door, and I followed her into the hall.

We moved along the hall to her office. Her real office, not the one she used day to day. She clasped the cloak around her throat and sat at the high-backed chair behind her desk. I blinked at the second chair behind the desk on her right side. She gestured towards it with a red nail, and I mimicked her actions.

She was giving me more responsibility, trusting me to carry out her wishes. I hated to admit it, but I wanted to impress her. I wanted her respect.

A knock on the door broke me from my thoughts and we pulled the half masks over our faces and the cloak hoods over our heads, so our faces were covered by shadows, the lights in the room dimmed so it looked almost as if it was lit by candlelight.

"Come in," Cordillera said.

All you could see within her cloak were her red lips, and I understood why she had wanted me to wear the lipstick.

The heavy door swung open silently, Chafer removed the blindfold, and a short, feminine looking form beneath a black cloak glided across the room. Floral perfume wafted from her when she sat down on the couch across from us. I recognized her immediately, she was Slate's brunette, Lynx. I was sure Cordillera knew as well, she wouldn't miss something like that especially if a few months ago, she was the one fooling around with Slate.

The only way I could tell she recognized her was by the purse in her lips as she sized her up. The brunette's cloak spread from her chest exposing the infamous bosom that rose and fell dangerously in her low neckline. Chafer had taken up post against the wall watching us, looking as threateningly as he had the first day I'd met him.

The woman slipped across a piece of paper that I reached for as per Cordillera's instructions. My eyes scanned the paper. She wanted an armed escort through Ostara. I fought back a scoff when I saw that she wanted a specific Shadow Breaker. I passed the paper to Cordillera, and she pinched it between her fingers as she took it from me, the gesture looked irritated.

I didn't think she even read the paper before she incinerated it. Cordillera felt denial, as in, there was no way on the planet she would let her choose her own Shadow Breaker.

"You may not choose your guard. Are you still interested in the contract?" I asked.

The short brunette's face pinched and then she recovered herself. "I was really hoping to have certain ones, ones I know I would feel safer with. It is a dangerous journey after all. A long, difficult journey. I am sure it is expensive."

My cheeks burned, and I wanted nothing more than to throw my seax at the woman. I waited for Cordillera's response. I felt compromise, and I pressed my lips together firmly before I spoke.

"How many guards?" I asked, trying to maintain my emotionless tone.

The brunette smiled as if she'd already won. "Two — Savage Storm and Quick." She didn't even think about it, I fought back my elemental fire that threatened inside me.

I already knew the answer, "They are not available for journeys at this time. You may choose another."

Slate couldn't go on journeys unless it was during one of his breaks from Valla U, that would all change next year.

Her smile fell and her brow furrowed, she thought I was lying to her. I couldn't care less.

"You are sure they are unavailable? I will offer Storm a bonus for a job well done." Her smile coaxed — just this once.

I gritted my teeth, and I thought she must be able to hear it. "I did not lie when I said he was unavailable. If he was, he would be assigned to your guard," I said flatly.

Slate told me I was a bad liar.

"I meant no offense," she spat. "I am sure whoever else you have will be good. I know I will be in Heat's good hands." My fingers squeezed the arm rest until I heard it crack.

I released it quickly and opened the drawer with the contracts, my jaw clenched so I wouldn't say anything to spoil the deal. I asked her about the length of time and haggled the price, which I manipulated as strongly as I could, but she was firm since she wasn't getting Savage Storm. Cordillera still seemed pleased with the amount, so I filled it out as Cordillera had taught me. I wrote in the mission, the Shadow Breakers assigned to it, finally I stabbed my thumb with the end of the athame that was razor sharp and pressed it to the section marked Delegate. Cordillera took the athame and pressed it to the section to the section labeled Grand Mistress. Then, I slid the pen and contract over to the woman.

She picked it up and nodded at it before taking up the athame and pricking her finger with the end and pressing it to the line marked Client and then she signed her name, it was done.

"You know, Lera. I resent you making me jump through hoops. I have done you favors, too," she said getting to her feet.

Lera coolly regarded her. "You are a khoraz, Lynx. Men pay you to bed them. I pay twice as well for no questions. You did me no favors. The men you have helped me with always return to you. It is not my fault Slate has stopped sleeping with you. Taking him out on a journey would not have changed that. Good day."

Lynx sniffed and Chafer walked up replacing the mask and taking her out of the room. I carefully shifted the contract over the desk and handed it to Cordillera before sinking in my seat.

I pulled the mask off my head and unclasped the cloak and took a deep steadying breath. Cordillera filed away the contract in her desk and handed me her computer where I filled out a digital contract and filed it so we could keep an electronic record, the actual paper would go to the file room once completed.

"You did well. Better than I expected," she said as we returned to her room dropping off the cloaks and masks before heading to the Crash Course where the Shadow Breakers were gathered.

I would not seek that woman's approval, I told myself. But a part of me was proud.

"I wanted to throttle her. Her intentions were so transparent." My voice was as hard as nails, each word clipped and cold.

I could feel Cordillera watching me from the corner of her eyes, a small smile on her red lips. "Still. You were honest and professional. A lot of patrons come in trying to buy more time with competitors. When I weaned Slate off rousen, he was little more than a boy. I thought multiple partners would help his attachment. Someone skilled in dealing with... I paid her well. It was not my fault she never charged Slate once he left my care."

Skilled in dealing with what? Rousen?

More secrets.

"Constructive criticism?" I asked her.

"Yes, trust your people. If they are going to sleep with clients, patrons, etc. then there is nothing you can do to stop them. There is no use in getting upset over it, Brass will sleep with her if he wants."

Ouch.

Her words sounded rehearsed, she'd either said or thought it before. I took a deep breath, and she stopped on the stairs landing to look at me. Her thin face almost level with mine in her ultra-high heels.

"The hard part is not over," she said weighing me.

I steeled myself and nodded. "I'm ready." Chafer snickered behind me, he clearly thought I wasn't.

Cordillera turned to me and pulled the pins from my hair before readjusting my breasts again and spreading my hair out so its golden locks framed my face. I looked down and my necklaces were almost visible so much of my cleavage was spilling from my neckline. I had more to work with than Cordillera did, and she must have expected me to act like it.

She opened the doors, and I walked next to her, Chafer at our backs. Ama was sparring with a girl I didn't recognize and stopped open-mouthed to stare at us. Slate was barking orders to Quick and Brass who were shirtless and bleeding from what appeared to be knife wounds from one another, their chests heaved as we walked up. Part of Cordillera's training was teaching me to keep my thoughts guarded from Brass, it felt like a betrayal, but if he and I were ever going to be friends, then he couldn't know every time I had a single thought about him. I could tell it disturbed him that he couldn't get a read off me.

Slate's eyes were hard as he watched us approach. Shale was standing next to Slate. She had her arms crossed and a thin eyebrow arched. I could see other Shadow Breakers milling about down the course, the most I had never seen.

I kept my face smooth, and my eyes hard. If I was ever going to be someone of respect to the Shadow Breakers, I was going to have to start acting like it. Not grind on them at clubs, and not flying off the handle at Slate in public.

It could have waited until they were in the rumpus room. She wanted to supervise me though, she wanted Slate to see his pet was her pet, too.

She regarded me with narrow dark eyes, and I walked past Slate and his team to Hopper and called him over.

"Brass, I need you." I called and gestured over by the prep room.

Slate's fury flared in my mind. Poor choice of words, but true none-theless which Quick was as good as his namesake to point out.

Hopper's eyes never reached mine as he locked in on the impressive amount of cleavage I was showing. Impressive since I wasn't aware I had that much.

"You've been assigned to a week-long escort mission to Ostara. You leave Monday," I told them without preamble. "Any questions?"

"What are we guarding?" Brass asked.

"A woman," I said more brusquely than I meant to.

Hopper snorted and tossed his ponytail over his shoulder. "One of *those* missions."

I pinched my lips together as Hopper walked away and watched Lera and Chafer leave me with Brass a few feet away from where Slate and his team watched us.

Amber eyes searched my face. "Not very happy?"

"I've been happier," I said peevishly and walked into the prep room.

Lera and Chafer had already flown the coop. I walked to my cubby with the intention of changing and going to dinner, but Brass came to sit next to me on the marble bench.

"I do not always sleep with the clients."

I bristled. "I didn't ask."

"You did not need to, even though you are trying to block your mind, you are not accomplished at it yet. You are angry the client wanted to use us," he said matter of fact.

"Savage Storm. I know he's slept with her before... at our home." I looked up at the ceiling wondering why I was letting it bug me.

I felt lust.

My eyes went wide as I looked at Brass. Instantly, my face went a red as a tomato. Those warm amber eyes had taken advantage of my daydreaming and had hitched on the neckline of the dress where a sliver of my pink bra was showing. My hand twitched to cover my chest and Brass slowly brought his eyes to mine.

"That is a very flattering dress," he said in his smooth deep voice. "I like that you favor pink."

"Brass." I blushed deeper, saying his name while looking at the floor.

"Your scent is so strong; I can smell you from here," Slate rumbled from the swinging metal doors.

Brass got to his feet with his lips spread in a puckish grin. "Can you blame me?"

Slate arched a brow. "No. Get on with you, I am taking my woman home."

Brass chuckled, "But not directly. Good night, Scarlett. Captain. Sorry for ogling."

I gave a little wave not sure what to say. That's all right? No, Slate would become apoplectic. Slate's body moved with a fluidity that didn't match his size. Rippling muscles flexed under his dark shirt.

"I do not like other men seeing what I should only see, Torch," Slate growled from where he stood before me making my neck crane back.

"Are you getting a good look now?" I asked taking a deep breath and his eyes glinted.

"Do not tell Brass you need him again. Who do you need, Torch?"

My mouth had gone dry. He fixed me with his predatory gaze, and I knew he'd either tear out my throat or tear off my dress. The darkness that lurked below the surface rippled more wildly these days. As if me giving myself to him had awakened it. There was no middle ground with him anymore, all or nothing. If I wasn't fiddlesticking him, I was fighting him.

I reached my hand up and cupped the hard bulge level with my mouth. "I need you," I told him as I tugged on his belt.

TWENTY-NINE

Slate was buckling his belt when a slim dark-haired woman with grey eyes and an open mouth passed through my mind, and I felt a sharp pain in my hip. I gasped and my hands gripped my inguz tattoo I'd gotten last year to cover the KHORAZ Jonquil had carved into my skin. Within the Celtic ropes that made up the rune, was a Shadow Breaker tracker.

I heard someone in the Crash Course howl as if in pain and I looked to Slate who hung his head. "What was that?" I asked.

"We lost a Shadow Breaker. Polecat. One of mine," he rumbled softly, and I got to my feet and wrapped my arms around him. "Aside from the ones you know, there are only four men left on my team."

"I'm so sorry, Slate. Can you find out more? It was so brief."

"We will send a few Breakers to go where her mission was and see if we can retrieve her body."

"Are you sure she's dead? Maybe she's lost, or captured?" I grasped at straws.

Slate lifted sorrowful eyes to mine. "No, Torch. She is dead."

Slate and I walked side by side to the common room. The familiar crack of pool balls greeted us as we stepped into the purple walled room, wood flooring with a few dark rugs covered the floors there were no windows to speak of. Large industrial lights hung from the loft like ceiling, I took a deep breath... leather. All the Shadow Breakers wore black on black, leather being their fabric of choice.

We ordered our dinner. Shadow Breakers were already gathering around the bar to celebrate the life of Polecat. Just like that, they lost one and mourned her.

Before I could sit down Chafer gestured me over. I apologized and walked over to Cordillera's main office. Cordillera leaned back in her chair pressing her fingers together as if in prayer.

"I have another project for you. If you are up to it," she offered, raising her chin, "We have lost three Shadow Breakers recently; I want you to find new recruits. Possibly Valla U might have some to offer. Screen them, then we will give them an audition. If you find more than three, I will consider swelling our ranks."

Hiding my excitement was impossible, "I can find you some new recruits. I'm sorry about Polecat," I said, and she inclined her head.

"No recruits from the greater families, they must have a talent, preferably not married, and do I have to tell you that they should be physically appealing?" Lera arched a single dark eyebrow and smirked.

"No, I got it. Strong, butt-kicking, good looking, nobodies. *Check.* I was curious about something." I leaned forward on the blood red leather biting my lip. "What if I can find a good amount? Say — ten or so? I want to make Brass a captain. I think he has the right temperament for it and people respect him. He trained me and he's one of the best I've ever had. Trainers," I said, glancing away to pluck invisible lint off my dress.

She leaned back and the corner of her mouth quirked. "You want Brass to leave Slate's team?"

"If he is to get his own team, then yes. I get the impression Brass was passed over. I'm sure you had your reasons," I said knowingly, and her smirk deepened.

We both knew Slate shouldn't be a captain when he wasn't even a Guardian. He might have been the best, but he was young.

"Done. You can tell Brass tonight and begin recruiting as soon as possible. Brass could help you screen them if you wish, since he will be their captain. Happy hunting, Delegate."

Cordillera dismissed me and Chafer followed me out.

"The pet will not like this," Chafer chided.

"Why not? They're friends." I countered and Chafer laughed darkly at me.

"Who do you think men are most competitive with? The pet's woman promoted his man out from under him. I do not think he will like that. In my opinion, you are right. You can tell them that."

I snorted. "Your opinion in favor of mine will count against me."

Chafer laughed and gave me a nod as I walked away.

Slate's team was already gathered around tables pushed together. A steaming plate of savory salmon and rice waited for me next to Slate, as did a mug of pilsner beer. Beer was not a common drink in Tidings.

Ama was crying, and I sat down awkwardly next to Slate and offered them my condolences. I started to eat because I was famished and was relieved when the others had food brought to the table as they drank.

"I have some good news," I said, trying to perk everyone up.

They lifted their heads with halfhearted smiles, and I tried to make my brighter. "I spoke with Cordillera, and she charged me with doing some recruiting... so we have decided to make Brass a captain. Congratulations." I stated with a small smile and his eyes slid to Slate who stopped mid drink of his ale and slammed it down on the table making it slosh over the mug.

"Whose idea was it?" Slate asked.

"Mine. Why?" I asked, feeling like I did something wrong, but not having the first clue why. "Slate, I'll find you good people. Don't worry. Oh, and Brass, Lera said if you want to join me when I recruit, that you could. I get the impression she wants to keep this very hush-hush."

Slate lifted me out of my seat by my biceps and I yelped as he dragged me into the exit hallway where he pinned me against the wall and lowered his face an inch from mine.

"Do you want Brass?" he growled.

"He deserved the promotion. He didn't sleep his way to his position, not that you don't deserve it, but did you when you started? I doubt it. You should be happy for him. He's your friend," I said in disbelief.

Slate slammed the wall to either side of me and I knit my brows. "You tell him you need him. You fuck him. You make him a captain. What else are you planning to do with him, Torch?"

I sighed and brought my hands up to his face tucking his wavy hair behind his ears. "Don't be jealous because I'm paying Brass attention. I go home with you every night." I displayed the emerald ring on my finger and looked up at him through my lashes. "Don't you think it's overdue?"

Slate's lashes were so long they touched his midnight brows. "It is. I do not want my mate to be the one gifting him with favors."

I gave him a lopsided grin. "I only want to help. It's not a favor. He earned it."

Slate pushed his body against mine and kissed my neck. "You have trampled my rules and unintentionally forced your way into my life. There are moments I rage just because you are away. When you return, I find my way back."

"If you're lost. I will always find you."

I bent my head so I could kiss him and led him back to the dinner table.

Slate patted Brass on the back and the tension dissipated.

"Thanks, Scarlett," Brass said with a genuine smile.

"Don't thank me yet. We still need to find you a team."

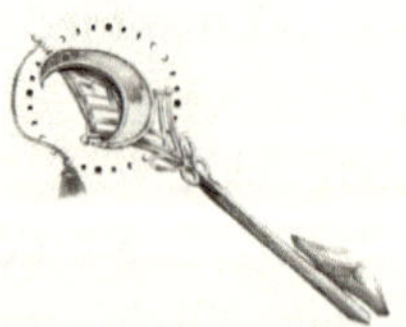

We mourned and remembered the lost Shadow Breaker and Slate, Quick, and I stumbled our way back to Valla University after a lot of drunken wandering around Valla. The boys' wing was empty, it was a Wednesday night so everyone was already in their rooms sleeping. Slate produced a vial of rousen, and I knocked it back before letting him pull me into their shared room.

Quick made himself scarce getting ready for bed and fighting off a smirk before climbing into his bed. I saw the sleeping forms of Jett and Cyan as Slate dragged me to his bed.

My resistance was halfhearted. "What if my brother wakes up? Quick is still awake. What if I lose control?" His mouth swallowed the rest of my protests as he backed me into his bed, which happened to be in the left corner, next to Jett's and adjacent to Quick's, directly across from the door.

It was pitch dark in the room, but it didn't stop me from blushing purple when he started nuzzling my chest, pulling my dress off easily before we even reached the bed. His lips traced along my clavicle before he tossed me onto my back, leaping on top of me in the process. A small squeak escaped me, but the squeal that threatened quelled.

He pulled out a blindfold we used on newcomers and put a finger to my lips before I could protest. He slipped it over my eyes, and I felt him replace his body with a blanket. The blankets lifted and Slate eased his bare body over mine. Air pulled off my panties and bra.

"I am going to fuck my wife. Do you want to tell me how to do it, Torch?" he growled into my ear.

Wife.

I bit my lip and shook my head. I felt him smile against my ear before slipping something over my head and into my mouth. He pulled it tight effectively gagging me.

His lips moved along the skin below my ear. "So, we will not wake the others."

My skin prickled, and I was squirming.

His mouth moved south, and I knew straightaway from my involuntary moans that the gag was a good idea.

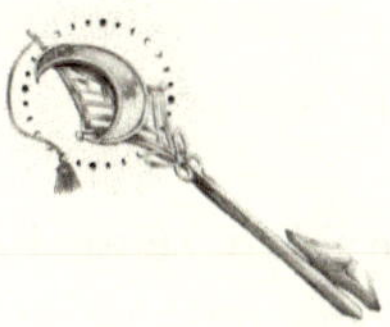

I woke up tucked to Slate's naked body. I was still blindfolded, and I dreaded lifting it. I wasn't sure our mission to be as quiet as possible was anywhere near the realm of a success. Something about the possibility of being caught and having to be quiet had me bursting at the seams even with my more subdued version of me on rousen. Thank goodness Slate had thought of the gag, which was hanging around my neck. I peeked out from under my blindfold to look at the gag. A simple black cravat he had knotted over my mouth, I was so glad it wasn't something gross like a sock.

Slate stirred next to me, and I turned in his arms. "Good morning," I said, pulling my blindfold off.

He pressed against me, and I felt just how good a morning it could be.

"Scarlett?" Jett's voice sounded confused, and I threw the blanket over my head.

I heard Slate chuckle and the distinct sound of Quick's snigger. Bastards. I was completely naked under Slate's blankets; I might have spoken a little too loud. I wondered what Jett was thinking. All I could feel was confusion.

"Give me my clothes," I whispered to Slate.

He peeked to where I hid under the blankets his amused lip curl playing on his full lips. "He already knows you are here. Might as well come out."

"You did this on purpose," I hissed.

He chuckled. His look said, *maybe I did, maybe I didn't, doesn't matter now*.

I scrambled under the blankets and used air to slide my bra and panties into my hands. I pulled them on under the blankets, much to Slate and Quick's amusement. I reached down again and felt around for my dress.

"Where's my dress?" I whispered harshly. It was beyond mortifying; I was taking forever to get it together.

"Here it is."

Jett was standing at the side of Slate's bed. The jig was up.

I poked my head out and pushed my hair away from my face. I grabbed my dress away from Jett's outstretched hand and pulled it over my head hurriedly. Slate laid on his side, elbow propping up his head and watching us. He didn't seem embarrassed at all at our predicament.

In fact, he seemed to be in rather good spirits.

"Scarlett. I'm surprised at you. Out of all the girls in our family, I never expected to find you in the men's wing," Jett said in mock disapproval with his arms crossed over his expansive bare chest.

I slid out of Slate's bed throwing back the blankets and revealing a bit too much of Slate's lower half which he calmly covered.

Jett's brow furrowed. "You took rousen last night and stayed in here with us?"

"*Um*, yes. I don't use as much anymore," I answered.

Jett gave me a hug. "I'd give you a kiss, but I don't know where your mouth has been," he said in a way only Jett could get away with knowing I wouldn't slap him, but I still thought about it. "Can I assume the best?"

"Or the worst depending on your standpoint." Quick said chidingly before standing up to reveal his perfectly sculpted behind.

"Put some pants on Quick, my sister is here," Jett said somewhat jokingly gesturing at his own low slung navy linen pajama pants.

Quick gave a dazzling smile over his shoulder and sunk back onto his bed, supposedly looking for pants. "She has seen her daily quota of man meat for the day it would seem?"

I would have shot him a glare, but that would men risking another eyeful of Quick. "She should be off the rousen in a week or so. My mate has no interest in seeing what you have to offer," Slate said from the other side of the bed.

He was pulling a pair of black pants identical to Jett's over his bare bottom. Not that Jett didn't know what we were up to, but now there was no denying it.

Jett ran his hand over his close-cropped blonde hair and looked dazed. "Gods, that's got to be a record. Things are almost back to normal, damn it's about time. Scar, I'm glad you won't need that trash anymore."

"Me too." I told him and Slate lifted his head. "I meant, I don't like to be dependent on it."

Jett rolled his eyes at Slate who was shirtless exposing countless hard bronze muscles and two perfect, dark pink nipples.

"Come. I will walk you out," Slate said.

I hesitated. "Maybe Jett should, you know, so people won't talk."

"You don't think they'd talk more if I walked you out?" Jett said with a sarcastic glint in his green eyes.

"Ew. Jett," I said, scrunching my face.

Quick and Slate chuckled and Slate wrapped his arm around my waist, leading me to the door.

"Oh, and Scar, next time try a bigger gag. I could hear everything," Jett said with a wink.

Jett's abs flexed as he laughed, he didn't feel the need to wear shirts around me either.

My skin felt on fire from embarrassment. "You just couldn't let it go, could you?"

Jett was incorrigible. Boundaries meant nothing to him. I was one to talk.

Slate closed the door on their laughter and led me through the hall which was crowded with half-dressed men walking around. The women's wing was the same way; girls in their boy shorts or night gowns. Apparently, men did not wear shirts to bed often, or pants for that matter as I noticed more than few men in boxer briefs who didn't look the slightest bit embarrassed about my presence.

"All the other girls who snuck in last night know to leave earlier," Slate said in a growl as he held me closer.

I was getting than my fair share of bawdy looks, the dress did not help matters. I tugged at the neckline and felt Slate's approval.

"Have you ever led a girl out of here before? Maybe that's why they're staring."

"I never let women into my beds, whether at home or here. That is not why they stare. It is because you are lush. I do not miss your innocence, but I do not like the added attention," Slate growled.

I chuckled. Me? Seductive?

"I could hunch. Drool a little?" I offered with a playful grin.

"Stop smiling. Gods, when did you start smiling like you knew the most delicious secrets?" My smile fell into a pout, and he chuckled wickedly, "That is much worse. I will get a bag for you to wear over your head," he teased, and I slapped his bare chest with an audible whack.

Slate stopped in the arched hall that separated the stairs from the men's second year wing and pinned me with his body against the wall, pulling my lip with his teeth.

"No pouting either. These lips are mine." He slid his tongue into my mouth, and I inhaled him deeply — cloves, fall, and sex.

I made a noise deep in my throat more animal than woman. "You smell like me, like us."

"Do you like it, Torch? The scent we make together?" he purred and my insides pulsed. "You do."

He could smell my arousal. I hated and loved it. I felt like I wore a sign with my every emotion scratched across it in bright red bold print. HORNY, the sign currently read.

"I should get ready for class." I fought all the hands he'd suddenly sprouted and smiled moronically as I walked back to my room.

I cast a glance over my shoulder to find Slate still standing there, adjusting himself for my benefit. I whipped back around and walked faster. I was that man's khoraz. I should have left the scar on my hip, it was true.

THIRTY

"Did you hear? Lavender was found in the girls' prep room beaten to a pulp," Cherry said sliding onto the bench across from me.

The only reason I remembered Lavender was because she was one of the girls that had jumped me last year with Jonquil in the very same prep room where she had been found.

"You're kidding," I said wrapping my roasted chicken tighter in its tomato basil tortilla.

"Crazy, huh? She was alone supposedly, no one saw anything. She's still knocked out, so you know they'll pump her for info when she comes to." Cherry started to make her own wrap from the platters on the long wood table.

"Good," Jett muttered raising his eyes to mine.

I hadn't forgiven Jonquil. I didn't know when a good time would be to exact my revenge, and I wasn't the plotting type. Well, except for that night.

After we grabbed our costumes and dinner in the U.S., I did not plan on coming straight home with the other girls. I didn't know how I would pull it off, but I had to. Slate or one of the other Shadow Breakers were always tailing me, and if I was going to talk to Styg alone, they couldn't be around.

I arched my brow at Slate who was feigning distraction. No one's food was that interesting.

"And you know nothing about this?" I whispered.

Slates sliced with his head once. Liar. He may not have done it, but he knew who did. He could keep his secrets.

I sensed Tawny's anger before I saw anyone approach. Amber felt smug and desire ripped through her, as if it wasn't obvious from the way she gazed at Slate with hunger in her blue eyes. I'd rip those eyes out and wear them as earrings. She stood with her back to me facing Slate. He sighed as she approached, placing down the wrap he'd been eating.

"Slate..."

His name in her mouth drove me to crazy town, it was a one-way street.

Quick grabbed my hand and brought me back to the now enough to realize my eyes were on fire. Whatever Slate had been saying to her, she wasn't getting the message. I stood up from the bench and Indigo's eyes went wide. I was carefully harnessing my elemental fire so I wouldn't unleash, but Slate was under my skin. Normally, I could act like a grown up and not a psychopath, but that time had passed.

I stood right behind her and leaned into her ear. "I can do this here, or you can step out into the hall with me. If you say another word to him, it'll be your last because I'll tear your tongue out with my bare hands and feed it to you."

My voice was low and gravelly, her body gave an involuntary shiver as she walked down the aisle of tables towards the door.

"This won't take long," I growled as I followed her.

"Maybe someone should... make sure Scar doesn't kill that girl?" Indigo stammered, and I heard several someone's get to their feet.

I'd only need a minute.

She waited for me a few feet away from the door, her arms crossed under her bosom. Gods, we looked a lot alike. I sucked in a breath calming my roiling insides. My instinct was to pummel her like I had back at the nightclub. Slate was mine though, there was nothing for her to fight for.

Her eyes were cool as she regarded me. "If he does not want me, then you have nothing to worry about," she said snidely and I agreed she had a point, internally at least.

"Look, you had your chance. He left you. It's over. Save your pride and go find someone who reciprocates your interest in them," I patted myself on my back for putting on my big girl panties.

Amber's too full lips spread into a sneer. "You think you will be better than me when he leaves you? You will not. You will take him any way you can get him just like the rest of us. You know how special he is, how he makes you feel. What would you be willing to do to get that feeling back if he took it away? There is nothing I would not do to get him back."

I blinked at her. "Are you in love with him?" Morbid curiosity got the best of me.

She laughed condescendingly, "I love fucking him."

I made a face. Did not need to hear that. Ever.

"Whatever. Just back off," I said dismissively.

She'd caught me off guard with her blunt honesty.

Before I came to Tidings, I would've licked my wounds and hid with Tawny until she dragged me out to some house party or another. Tawny would try to peer pressure me into hooking up with some rebound guy and I wouldn't do it, then we'd go home and talk about the guy she'd made out with.

My world had been rose-colored and full of petty worries that had no real impact on the world. They'd barely affected me, but that didn't stop me from whining about them. My mother kept the hardships of the real world from me. She hid her bottomless sorrow, and I believed in fairy tales and happily ever after. That wasn't the real world, not the one I was living in. It was possible that I wouldn't get my happily ever after with Slate. I didn't like that thought at all.

"Amber. I will not tell you again." Slate was behind me the entire time.

"You do not mean that. I can wait until you tire of her." Amber smiled smugly and walked back into the dining hall.

She had jarred me. My happiness was temporary. He had promised himself to me, but a man like Slate lived by his own laws. Blood oaths be damned, he'd find a way around it if he could. If he wanted to. He walked around me, and I heard someone follow Amber back into the dining hall. Quick, I guessed.

Slate leveled his grey eyes framed in those long, lush lashes at me. "That is not going to happen, Torch."

My bond with him broadcasted my emotions loud and clear to him. A wary cynicism had risen in me. What made me so special that he would want to change his whole life to be with me?

So, he had some prophecy that included me, so he'd dreamed about me his whole life. Semantics. I didn't believe in prophecies. Slate had also said Ash and I wouldn't get married, but that was because I'd been captured by the Stygians, and my baby maker had been defunct.

"For now, promise me you'll let me down easy when it comes time to go." I searched his eyes as they hardened.

He crossed his corded arms over his broad chest. "Absolutely not. We are not discussing this, Torch. It is an impossibility, and I will not waste my time."

"Humor me."

"No. Subject closed."

It was, he wouldn't discuss it further. He'd shut up tighter than a clam shell and I wasn't feeling any better. I knew exactly what Amber was talking about. I felt it too. That invincible, powerful feeling that seeped into me from being with Slate was worse than the rousen. What did one do to recover from him? Amber's strategy of throwing herself at him did not seem to work.

"Come. Finish your lunch," Slate ordered, and I placidly walked back into the dining hall.

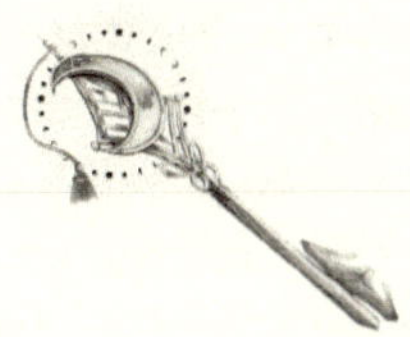

Classes went quickly while I was in my gloomy daze. I didn't even enjoy my excursion into the U.S. like I had hoped to. We all found costumes, but my dour mood was a damper on the day. No one asked what was wrong which told me they had expected me to brood, either now or some time. A well-deserved brood. A long overdue stew.

I pulled the SUV back into the blue starry portal room and the girls hopped out. I grabbed my bags from the floor of the backseat and instead of walking towards the hall as the others had done, I made a bee line for the portal door behind me.

Amethyst turned back at the last moment and her dark eyes went wide as I was swallowed by the bright light. I had been careful to deactivate the bond with Slate before leaving to the U.S. knowing I wouldn't want him following me where I went.

My destination was one I'd been to before, the Iron Maiden. I'd gone in search of Styg there before and found him. I'd also gotten myself thrown out. I was hoping that I wouldn't be recognized or if I was that Styg would think I was a khoraz and he would get his chance with me.

Guardians walked about Valla's town heart as the shops closed. It was getting late, and since it was a bitterly cold January night, none of the vendors were still out. I didn't get cold like a regular human anymore, not since I triggered my elemental powers.

I found a dark alley and while calling shadow, I changed into the clothes I brought. A hot pink bandage dress and black thigh highs. Jackal had told me the Iron Maiden was a pub, but what it was really an underground dubstep club. Styg had a private booth and was well known there. It was foolish to return knowing people were out to kill him, but the man had specific tastes, and he liked the variety of vapid women that frequented the club.

As I approached, I heard a series of locks and the filigree door opened to a blue lit hall and a man as big as Quick stood to the side, the universal gesture for come on in. He'd seen me coming and decided I would fit right in — my, how things had changed.

I swayed my hips as I walked past the coffee-colored man with the shaved head and stony face and felt the first vibrations of bass. He was the same bouncer as last time, and he hadn't recognized me at all. Maybe it was the bangs.

At the end of the hall was a metal catwalk that lined the huge room that had people dancing all over it. Metal stairs led down to a platform lit from underneath and was constantly changing colors while people danced atop it. Below the platform was a bar that spanned three solid walls and tables for mingling. The fourth wall, the V.I.P. area, held roomy booths with impeccably dressed people drinking amber drinks and others that held a hint of purple. That was where I'd find Styg.

The club had an industrial feel and cool air constantly blew from big fans that hung from the ceiling amidst the flashing lights. I took off my cloak and got a Bay Breeze. I fit in much better this time around and while I still got looks, they were ones of interest and not wondering how I'd stumbled into the joint.

I slid a nickel hunt to the waitress, and she beamed a smile at me. I was still terrible at the local currency. I turned around and rested my elbows on the slick metal counter as I scanned for Styg.

His real name was Civet, but no one called him by it, which put him at an age with Jackal and Fox. I spotted him right away; he was hard to miss. Styg wore white that glowed from the black lights above the booths. He was rail thin and towered over the women who sat around him. He looked cultured with short brown hair combed into an undercut and you could see the hollows of his cheek bones even from across the room. Those dead eyes penetrated everything.

I'd have to be smooth. Last time we interacted, I cut off his hand, and he'd had me tossed out. Then I followed him to headquarters, and he had wanted Brass to kill me, but Brass knew who I was. I'd just met him and he kissed me. I'd made love to him in that same spot months later. I thought about that every time I passed it.

I chastised myself and focused.

Styg had said some nasty things about me and had gotten punched by Brass first, then beaten to a pulp by Slate. I didn't ask for it and had even healed Styg afterwards. Men had such short tempers. If Styg was feeling jerky, he could have me thrown out before I reached him.

Cordillera's advice to use my assets came to mind, and I put down my drink and fluffed up my breasts. I shrugged at the bartender watching me with an amused look in her eyes. We women did what we needed to. The electronica music pounded over the speakers and the laser lights slid over me in bright green and red.

I gave my best sultry look as I walked to the chained off area that led to the V.I.P. booths. The burly man removed the chain and held out his arm and I walked the thin metal catwalk that led to Styg's booth.

Sometimes, it was all about how you presented yourself. If you looked like you belonged there, then people believed you did.

Styg was taller than any man I'd ever seen. He would have been good-looking if he gained a little weight, and if his grey eyes didn't scrutinize everything with an air of superiority. I caught his eye and watched him measure. The slightest hint of a smile curled his lips, and he stood to greet me.

"Do you have somewhere private we can go?" I purred.

His grey eyes glittered and the girl to his left grudgingly moved to let him out. I needed to get him alone, away from his guards, and to question him about his black-market dealings with the Stygians. That was my only chance of getting to them before the Stygians got to me, or worse, Slate. He wouldn't make it to his prophecy if the Stygians killed him first.

The burly man who'd escorted me off the dance floor saw us coming and led us along the catwalk. We went deeper into the club and down another hall with Styg's hand groping my fanny pack the entire time.

He opened a side door, and I entered with Styg behind me. It was a narrow room with plush blue couches that lined the mirrored walls. The room had a sweet fragrant smell that covered up the mix of bodies and booze from the greater room of the club. He'd taken me to the same room last time, I wouldn't be surprised to find his blood on the carpet.

Styg didn't waste any time. He grabbed my wrist and yanked me to him, and his lips closed over mine, shoving his tongue into my mouth. I almost gagged. Instead, I smiled, giving him a shove, and he fell into the door. His eyes glittered. He loved a good fight. He removed his white suit jacket and laid it carefully on the couch revealing a modern crisp white collared shirt.

"Take off that dress and let me see what we are working with."

I wanted to vomit. Calling wouldn't work on Styg, he had nix torque bracelets that nullified all calling. My only chance was to get him vulnerable and interrogate him. He would never volunteer the information willingly, that much I knew.

"You first," I said and took a seat on the blue couch crossing my legs lazily as my fingers ran the length of the back of my seat.

His grey eyes lifted from my long legs and back up to my face and my breath hitched. If he recognized me, he'd shout for his bouncer and tonight would be a bust. He didn't. His boney fingers unbuttoned his long sleeve shirt, and he carefully folded it over the jacket. The man was a type-A. Styg unbuckled his belt and unzipped his fly and looked at me.

"I will show you mine if you show me yours," he said with a smirk that didn't touch his eyes.

I'd expected it and fighting in the dress would be the same as fighting in my bra and panties anyway, so I leaned forward and pulled the dress hem over shoulders until my hair fell around me in a cascade of waves. Styg sucked in a sharp breath as he walked over to where I sat.

My arms were still hung over the back of the couch, and he knocked my knees apart with his own. A little closer…

Styg wasn't even bothering to kiss me, he went straight for the panties, which was fine since my arm concealed my clutch which I'd hidden several feet of silk rope in. Before he knew what hit him, I leaned forward making him think I was going to finish undoing those pressed white trousers, but instead tied a knot around his legs. I pulled him forward as I moved off the couch and straddled his back as I tied his arms at the elbows. I shoved my discarded dress into his mouth with one hand while I tied the rope from his elbows to his feet and proceeded to hog tie him.

Thank you, Non're.

He was fuming, but hopeful I was just some kinky weirdo. He had no idea.

I faced him towards the mirror on his stomach and stood behind him in my black bra and panties and black thigh highs. The same thigh highs I'd worn when I was last with Brass. I looked like a morally bankrupt super villain.

"I need to find the Stygian Knights and you're the only person I know who might be willing to help me find them because you don't care if I live or die."

His grey eyes narrowed, and I straddled his long arms over his back as I carefully removed my dress from his mouth.

"You," he cursed, "Untie me, and I will not kill you."

I grinned at him pertly, "I only want to know where they are, and I will let you go. I don't want to fight. I only needed to get close to you to ask you a question or two."

He snorted, but he wasn't struggling, nor did he look like he was going to shout for his bodyguard. Probably because he'd been disarmed by a half-naked woman more than a foot and a half shorter than him at least than half his weight.

"What do I get in return?" he asked as if we could strike a bargain.

"My thanks and your freedom," I purred at him in the mirror.

He snorted. "I do not think so. What is it worth to you, girl? That is the price, or you can wait around and see what happens. Time is a ticking."

Styg looked so smug, I wondered if he had some device that would alert his lackeys, or if there was a camera in the room with a room full of men watching to see what happens.

"Can you tell me where their next tournament will be or where their headquarters are?" I asked.

His neck strained to lift his head and his brow furrowed as he met my eyes. "I know the next tournament and I know one of their Knights. I could tell you where to find him... for a fee."

"You're hardly in the position to haggle," I snapped.

"Have you seen yourself?" he countered, laughing.

I looked up at the semi-nude wild woman that had a man tied up between her legs. I learned quite a few lessons about ropes with Non're I hadn't thought I'd put to use, but there I was.

"Just tell me already," I said, exasperated that I wasn't on my way home already to my big white bed and my big bronze man.

"Information is expensive. What is your name again?" he asked, cocking his head to try to face me.

"Scarlett. Quit stalling. Tell me what you want and don't make it something I wouldn't pay. That'd be wasting my precious time and wasting my time pisses me off. When I'm pissed, I get stabby. Your hand reattached just fine I see." I chided, and he bared his teeth in a snarl.

"Roll me over and wrap those lips around my cock. That's my fee. A cheap one, just for you. Any one of those girls out there would do it for free."

I made a face. "No fiddlesticking way, dude. Try again."

"I do not know what you have other than what I can see, so how can

I tell if you can give me what I ask? I see a body, I will take it. This does not have to be so difficult, Scarlett."

Styg spoke to me like I was an imbecile. It would be easy to do as he said. Somewhere in my mind it asked, what's one more? That voice was a dirty khoraz, and I was only a dirty khoraz for Slate.

"I can get you in with the Shadow Breakers. Become one of them, or someone you less than hate." I doubted he had anyone he actually liked.

"How is that?" Styg asked skeptically.

I turned him over loosening the rope that tied his feet to his elbows and let his legs go straight, but still stood over him. He wasn't going anywhere.

"I'm recruiting. Do you know someone or not?" I snapped, squatting down near his chest.

His cold grey eyes scanned my face for a possible lie. "Swear a blood oath." I nodded impatiently. "Cousins. A boy and a girl. I want them both in."

"Are they talented? They'll have to pass the screening process."

"They are. They will. Now untie me so we can speak like civilized adults." Styg ordered, and I smiled knowingly at him.

"Tell me who this Stygian is and where the next tournament is," I countered hating that they called themselves Knights as if they served some noble purpose.

"Tournament will be held in Ostara; I will write down the directions for you. It is in a few days. Let me up and swear a blood oath, I will tell you the rest. That is the deal."

He held up part of his bargain so I agreed, pulling at the knots I'd tied and freeing his elbows so he could untie his legs. I sliced my thumb with a blade from my boot and tossed him the knife, so he did the same. We pressed our thumbs together, and I promised to recruit his cousins. I snatched the knife back and secured it in my thigh high as he flexed his arms and legs.

"Onyx. He is at Valla U; he has recently been recruited to the Stygian Knights and will be competing in the upcoming tournament."

Styg pulled out a kerchief from his pocket and wrote the directions to the tournament spot in a thin trail of his blood. I frowned as he did it, he could have been using a pen for all the reaction he gave. He dangled it above his head, and I arched a brow at him.

"Give it over. I'm tired. We both got what we wanted, let's call it a night," I said with irritation, watching my hopes of finding the Stygians flutter several feet above my head.

"Jump for it. The other part of my price," he cooed.

I snorted. "How high?"

I stepped onto the couch and reached for it with no intention of jumping when Styg wrapped a spindly arm around my waist like an iron band. He dove on top of my body as we landed on one of the couches. The thin fabric was in my hand and my arm pinned above my head. I called sending it over to my purse and out of harm's way as I grappled with Styg.

"Get off me!" I ground out, trying to head butt him and keep his hands off me at the same time.

The problem was, Styg liked a good fight. It got him going and his bulge was pressing against my thigh. The other problem was, I was a rousen addict and sex was my come down of choice. Styg's scent intoxicated me, and I struggled with him and myself.

Then the worst happened.

"I have rousen in my pocket. I know you need it. It is in your skin, your walk, your face. I can give you what you need. All of it. No holds barred, just between you and me. No one else will ever find out."

My breath caught as I felt the wave of temptation pull me under, drown me, and leave me gagging on the shore.

"Which pocket?" I ground out and his smile touched his eyes for once. "No!" I shouted. "Just get off. You don't even like me."

"What does that have to do with a few hours of pleasure?"

Styg's body was wiry and pale, his muscles were tight and lean, but by no stretch of the imagination could I be attracted to him even if he was Adonis. The man was a ruthless fiend with the morals of a guinea pig, and I would never ever sleep with him. Still... I could really use the rousen.

Styg pressed his hip to my thigh. "This pocket. You can get it yourself."

I bit my lip and looked down to where his pocket pressed against my bare thigh. We'd stopped fighting one another, and I had both his wrists in my hands. My eyes flitted to his only a few inches away, and he nodded lifting his hands up in surrender so I could safely procure the rousen. I licked my lips and loosened my right hand's hold.

The door busted into splinters and the burly bodyguard flew against the mirror to shatter it on the far end of the wall. Styg ducked into me to keep the debris from hitting anything vital. He also managed to cover most of me while he did it.

"What the f —" Styg started to say before he was lifted off me.

The dust was still settling in the room, but I didn't need a clear view to know who it was. Who *they* were. I jumped off the couch and flung myself between Slate and Styg, who was about to go the way of the bodyguard, but not before Slate dismembered him.

"Stop, Slate. Please! It's my fault. I needed something from him," I said, trying to make myself taller, my five-inch heels only helped so much.

Slate's silver eyes held raw menacing rage. I wasn't even sure he saw me. His body seemed to grow swallowing up the space in the room to the point of claustrophobia. Brass and Quick appeared behind Slate and looked like twin walls of cliff side looking at me.

"I will deal with you later," Slate ground out and nudged me aside with his arm.

I narrowed my eyes and set my jaw calling so much that I stole the sound from the room. The men's eyes all widened. I could steal energy from my surroundings and make myself stronger. I'd only done it a few times, and it never ended well. Now I managed to do it because I was pissed. So pissed.

Dust hovered in the air as if I stole the gravity from the earth. I clapped my hands and the air thundered from me, knocking all the men down. I ran to Styg and helped him up telling him to get lost and I'd see him at Shadow Breaker headquarters about his cousins. The cache hole didn't apologize, didn't thank me. Just got up and booked it but remembered his white shirt and coat.

By the time I turned back around, Slate was on his feet and Brass was helping up Quick, whose fanny pack had gone through the wall.

Slate hadn't looked at me like that in a very long time and my heart sunk. His silver eyes ran over my dusty boots to my black panties and bra and up to my face with my hair wild around it.

"It wasn't as bad as it looked. I had it under control," I said crossing my arms.

Slate closed the distance between us so fast I gasped in the floating dust and stumbled backwards. He caught me and lifted me off the ground so my head nearly touched the ceiling, then pinned me to the mirrored wall.

"What do you think it looked like, Torch?" he ground out.

"Like something intimate. I had to ask him a few questions, that's all. It was the only way I thought he would see me."

"Truth," Quick said, coming to stand behind Slate.

Brass had never looked disappointed in me like he did then. He crossed his dark honey arms over his chest and watched Slate interrogate me with a glacial expression. I had thought he would try to talk Slate down as he always did, but he seemed to concur with Slate's manhandling.

"Can I at least put my dress back on? Then you can interrogate me as much as you want, I promise."

Slate's thick fingers dug into my biceps where he held me, and he let me slide along the wall to my feet so I could hobble over to my hot pink dress. I turned my back to them as I pulled it over my head before facing the firing squad once again.

The three men took in my dress and their faces turned ever harder. It shouldn't have been possible.

"You were better off undressed. At least then you could pretend you were not up to no good," Brass remarked.

I stuck my fists on my hot pink hips and glared at them. "I'm getting information. How did you find me? Do I have another tracker I don't know about?" I snapped.

My ire would normally cause a bit of flinching, maybe a cringe, but I got nothing. Slate glided over to me, face tight, muscles bunched as he prowled around me.

"What information did you need so badly that you tried to hide from us, those who would protect you?" Brass asked.

"I'm not hiding, merely... eluding," I corrected and Quick scoffed.

"Truth, but just barely, Scarlett."

"How did you find me?" I asked again.

"Amethyst said you ran off, there's only two places you would go,

Thrimilci or Valla. Styg activated a tracker we gave him in case he was in trouble. You missing plus Styg in trouble. It was fairly obvious what was going on." Quick chastened.

"He wasn't in trouble." I mumbled and Slate dangled the white silk rope in front of my face from behind me and my stomach flip-flopped.

"Teaching Styg a few lessons you picked up, Torch?" Slate growled, and I flinched. "Leave us."

Brass rubbed his plump lips together, Quick had already started climbing over the busted down door. Brass's amber eyes met mine, and I wondered if I should be afraid. The better I got to know Slate, the more fear I knew I should have for him. Brass walked out through the door and vanished into the hall.

"That was a low blow," I murmured, "I knew my calling wouldn't work against him, so I needed a way to bind him until I got my answers, that's all."

"You would have fucked him. Tell me now, Torch," Slate growled so deep in his chest it sounded like he spoke from within a cavern.

"That's a low blow. I didn't want to," I snapped.

Slate was still behind me. He grabbed my wrists in one of his big hands and I felt the silk rope slide tight along my arm.

"What are you doing?" I gasped.

"Giving you what you need," he growled.

I felt lightheaded as he called, moving the knocked-out bodyguard's body to a couch behind us. He pushed me onto my knees, holding the rope around my wrists. I kneeled in front of the mirror and felt my insides clench.

Accepting that I was a khoraz would be too much for my delicate state of mind. Admitting that I was willing to do anything Slate wanted to do to me was humbling enough. Amber's words flitted through my mind, but I didn't care in the least.

Slate stroked my hair with a gentle hand, but I had no delusions that it would be gentle. He was just deciding what to do first. My nipples were so hard they cast shadows through my dress. Slate ran his hands over my shoulders, pushing the fabric of my clothing down until they trussed up my chest. The callouses of his hands ran over the soft swell of my breasts as he tugged gently at my pearled peaks.

"What am I going to do with you, Torch?" he said almost inaudibly.

"I have a few ideas," I purred and his hand stilled.

Slate walked in front of me and began unbuckling his belt. "Give me your smart mouth," he said, clenching his jaw, and I did so with enthusiasm.

Slate was shuddering into me when I heard the arguing in the hall. My dilated eyes had been fixed on the mirror, watching Slate behind me on his knees. His hands on my body, the only things keeping me upright after he'd pushed my panties down my thighs and rucked up my dress. I'd immediately decided we needed more mirrors in our apartment.

My body still felt heavy and tingling when he began untying my arms and helped me to my feet. The silk rope was much better than Non're's rough woolen ones. After he tucked himself into his pants, Slate helped me collect myself.

"How are you feeling, Scarlett?" he asked, watching my face carefully as he pulled up my top.

"Good," I said distractedly and adjusted my sopping panties.

Slate clasped the cloak around my throat and tilted my chin up. He hadn't kissed me even once, he did now and deeply — crushing me to his hard body.

"You can say no. You know that, Scarlett," he whispered.

I shook myself out of it and met his gaze levelly, "I don't want you to stop. That worries me more." I told him bluntly and his lips curled.

"Your turn when we get home. Lady's choice," Slate murmured.

"You have a lady in your pocket because I don't see any here."

His lips twitched with amusement and the voices in the hall grew louder. I opened my clutch and placed three gold daymarks on the couch hoping that would be enough to fix the room and then walked over to the unconscious bodyguard and healed him. Slate watched me work and when I was done, he wrapped his arm around my shoulders and led me into the hall.

Two bouncers were blocked by Quick and Brass a mere ten feet away from the busted door. My face burned with embarrassment, I thought they'd be further away. I'd done nothing to stifle my moaning.

"We are finished here," Slate said, pulling me to him as the bouncers narrowed their eyes at us.

They'd be crazy to try to stop Slate from leaving. He pushed between them with Brass and Quick on his heels. The club was still packed for a Thursday, but it was how Guardians unwound after their long days of keeping nature in balance.

All work and no play...

I was led out by a dark shadow, I felt invisible. The crowd parted for Slate without him having to nudge a single person. He was raw power, and the people felt it and hurried away. When we walked out of the club Brass and Quick stood to either side of Slate. I barely counted I was pressed so tight to Slate.

"Did you ask him about the Stygians?" Slate asked, picking up their interrogation from earlier as if our time in the back room hadn't even happened.

"If I did?" I asked cocking my head, not feeling up to another fight.

"You did not ask us about them," Brass said from my right.

I smiled sardonically, "Yeah, right. Like any of you would tell me how to find the men who captured me. Please. I know I look soft, but my mind isn't."

Slate sighed. "We will include you from now on if you promise not to go offering yourself on a silver platter," Slate said and my back went rigid as I stopped in my tracks, or tried to since I was under his arm.

"Keep your fiddlesticking secrets, Slate. I'll get my information any way I can. I have a blood debt to repay those men, and my body is mine to use as I please. It's free to me to get what I want with it, and I won't have you or anyone one else trying to tell me what I can or can't do. You have no idea what I am capable of or how far I'll go to achieve it. I'll do anything to destroy those men, with or without you." I snapped hands on my hips.

"With, Torch. We are always with you," Slate said, and I blinked.

"Everything we do is to protect you. Any secret we keep is not because we do not want you to know and enjoy lying, Scarlett. It is to keep you safe," Brass said softly, and I felt disarmed.

My anger was the only thing shielding me and they'd taken it away. "I'm tired," I murmured and Slate pulled me against him again.

"Home it is."

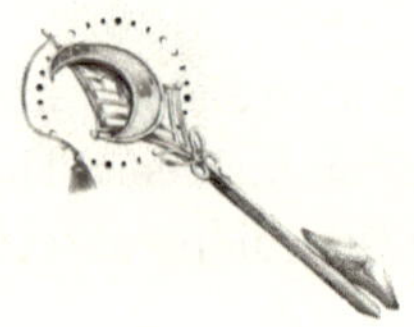

Brass went back to headquarters while Quick, Slate, and I went to the Valla portal gate. I had to find the alley I changed in and grab the bags I'd hidden there before going home. Quick went back to Valla U to see if Indigo's bed needed warming. Slate had said the two were together most nights this week which I took as a good sign.

Slate opened the double doors to our apartment, and I walked to the bedroom feeling worn and dim-witted. I should have asked Slate first, let him turn me down, and only then go to Styg. I would've spared myself a lot of embarrassment tonight and having Styg's gross tongue in my mouth.

Slate stopped me at the door to our big white bed and slid his hands around my stomach. "Let us handle the Stygian Knights. I do not want to risk you, Scarlett."

"You'd risk yourself instead?" I asked.

"We face very different dangers if taken. Please. I cannot do my job if I know you are in jeopardy." Slate nuzzled the crook of my neck and I felt myself melt.

Tender Slate got me every single time. "I won't investigate it alone and I won't get in too deep. I promise. I'll leave all the action and fighting to you, but don't shut me out."

Slate's breath tickled my neck, and I shivered. "Deal. I expect you to stick by your word, Torch. I do not like to make compromises."

I turned in his arms with a wry smile. "Really? I hadn't noticed," I said pertly and squealed as he tossed me into the bed.

CHAPTER 31

INDIGO

With Scarlett spending her nights at the Sumar palace while she was on rousen and Tawny staying with Steel every night. The only time my room had all four of us in it was during the day. Even Cherry had decided to stay in Jett's bed tonight. When the door opened letting in the dim light of the hallway, I cracked open my eyes to see who it would be.

I never guessed which man it was for fear I might be wrong. Sterling or Silver. It was a weeknight though, so it could only be Silver. Sterling would never risk Diamond witnessing him leave my room. That was what our weekend rendezvous were for. Until a month ago, I had only ever been with Sterling. Now the renown Lothario 'Quick' Silver Regn was trying to get me tangled in his web.

His scent of patchouli, sandalwood, and cedar wafted from him after the heavy clunks of his weapons hitting the floor before he climbed into bed behind me. His hand snaked around my stomach to cup my breast as he kissed along my ear.

By the Mother... his kisses.

"Wake up, Dove. I have missed you."

His whisper sent a shiver through me, and he smiled against my ear. I bunched the jersey fabric of my nightgown in my hands and rucked it up against my hips. I felt him sigh at my nape.

"Not like this. You can be on top," he said defeated, and I used my calling to slide off my underwear before sitting up to straddle his hips.

Silver shifted on the bed and reached for me, but I knocked his hands away while I lowered myself onto him. I would've sucked in sharply, but I wouldn't give him the satisfaction of knowing how much I enjoyed him.

I knew I was changing. I could feel myself growing colder and segregating myself. I didn't want to, but I felt like I'd lost everything. My father was the only person in my life who had shown me unconditional love and he had been murdered. I found out I had a real mother and when I was supposed to meet her, she was killed. I couldn't take anymore.

The only family I'd known had disowned me. My own brother, half-brother hadn't said two words to me. He was never nice, but now I didn't exist. My life had been torn from me and I was alone.

Diamond was around all the time, so I'd lost Sterling too. I hated that Silver offered me so much comfort. It gave him power I couldn't afford for him to know he had. With Scarlett recovering and Jett busy with two wives, Pearl was trying to reel me in so I wouldn't get lost, but it was too late.

I had lost everything and each day it grew harder and harder to remain the perfect, sweet daughter my father raised. Happiness with Silver was temporary, and I knew once I grew too comfortable he would rip it away. I had to keep my distance.

I rocked myself on top of Silver, his hands groping at will. None of it was breaking my rules, but it was only a matter of time before he pushed my limits. Only our first night together had I not set any for him. I didn't plan on seeing him after that, but he just never left.

He'd brought clothes into my bedroom and a gods' cursed toothbrush! As if we were a couple! I'd had to set him straight and told him we would never be, that we could sleep together, and he could stay the night, but that was all. Sterling would never be okay with me dating Silver. They were cousins, though neither family recognized it.

I could feel Silver tensing beneath me and lifted myself to catch his seed with my calling then incinerated it in the air. He clenched his jaw and the cords in his neck stood out in the light from the stained-glass windows.

"I hate... when you do that," he panted, "You are distracted."

I shook my head and swung my leg back over him to lay on my side away from him. I listened to him sigh again and roll towards me, sliding his hand under my nightgown. He'd be ready again in moments. He never stayed sated long.

"Let me kiss you, Dove," he whispered. "Throw your cautions to the wind and let me make you feel better."

I squeezed my eyes tight. The man was so gods be damned tempting.

Tonight was especially bad. Amber was thoroughly pissed off at Scarlett and had elected to casually mention Diamond's blissfully romantic first time with Sterling while strolling past us at dinner.

I'd known he was with her, but not the details. That he'd gone out of his way to make it special, when our first time had been after we found out he would be betrothed and that we would never be married. So, we'd hid in my bedroom and made painful awkward love for the first time for both of us. No romance, no candles and flowers like Diamond had gotten. Being the adopted daughter, I was used to being snubbed, but Sterling had always been different. It had hurt more than I thought.

I choked down a stupid girlish sob that made me feel frail. Silver lurched up in bed and rolled me onto my back despite my struggling to stay on my side. His devilishly handsome face was a mask of anger and his nostrils flared before he spoke.

"Did someone hurt you? Tell me, Indigo." His usual impish charm went out the window and the rare serious side of him surfaced.

"No. No one. Someone said something I shouldn't have heard is all." I assured him knowing lying to Silver was impossible.

His face grew harder. "It is about him. Freya's burly boar, Indigo. How long are you going to —"

"No one asked your opinion. You got what you came for, you may leave."

If he hadn't been leaning on my stomach, I would've rolled over. His brows drew together in an expression of hurt. So sensitive, the woman-izer was. He swallowed visibly as he looked down at me. It was his tell. He was going to ask for something he was unaccustomed to asking for. I pressed a finger to his lips before he started pouting.

"You can stay the night if you want to. Your choice," I said and watched his dark eyes glitter.

"Please," he said, pressing a kiss to my finger.

I took a deep fortifying breath and nodded. You'd think I gave him all the Sumar wealth by how happy it made him. He yanked me into a sitting position and pulled my night gown over my head and began kissing my lips before my hair fell over my shoulders.

It was hard to think with his lips on mine. They may have been laced with rousen. I'd have to ask him.

It would have to wait though because he was already knocking my thighs apart to fit his hips. "Do you want to play a game?" he asked, sucking on my throat so it would leave a love bite.

My mind swam as my toes seemed to curl and uncurl at his talented tongue. "What kind of game?" I asked, temporarily regaining enough sense to remember I had a tongue of my own.

"Truth or lie. I ask, you answer. I determine whether you are full of it," he said, muffled against my skin.

"I don't care. As long as it doesn't require much thinking," I moaned as Silver went lower and he started smiling again.

"Do you think I am attractive?" he asked as his tongue slid around my belly button.

"Yes," I breathed, curling my fingers into the sheets.

"Truth. Good girl. You have played this game before," he joked. "Do you like having me in your bed?"

"Yes."

His fingers slid under my thighs as he settled on my stomach as the torture began. "Do you like other people knowing you are with me?"

"I'm not with you, Silver. We just sleep together and you're at my family's home all the time because you're friends with my brother-in-law," I panted as he placed his mouth over me.

"Truth. I will take that as a yes. Do you bear any feelings for me?" he asked before returning to his devious work.

My back bowed on the bed. "Yes. Of course," I ground out.

"Do you love me?" he asked, abruptly stopping, and I groaned.

"This is a stupid game."

"It is simple really, just say it." Silver wiped his lips on the inside of my thigh.

"No."

"No, you do not love me or no you will not respond?" he asked.

Words were everything to Silver. He was an interrogator, always picking up on truths and lies. It's what he did.

"I am sorry. I don't love you," I said, leaning up on my elbows to look down at him.

"Say it then. Say that you do." he told me, not meeting my eyes.

"What for?" I asked, staring at the top of his head.

"Please, Dove." He turned his gold-flecked eyes to me, and I groaned as I fell back.

"Fine. But I don't like you torturing yourself. I'm only trying to be honest with you."

"It is a stupid game but humor me," he agreed and I jolted as his tongue rubbed against me.

"I love you, Silver."

My insides burned at saying it. My stomach flip-flopped and even my cheeks flamed. My father and Sterling were the only two people I'd ever told I'd loved them.

Silver's tongue was causing me to black out. I might faint. My fingers and toes curled as he held my thighs still.

"Ooh, ooh." I cooed, and he shifted so suddenly he was kissing me again and thrust to the hilt.

The self-proclaimed master of the multiple orgasm struck again until I was a useless limp body under him. It didn't stop him from kissing me as I started to doze.

"You are right it is a stupid game," he said, smiling as he kissed me.

Why was the idiot smiling then?

He laid his head on my pillow beside mine and contented himself to fall asleep inside me. You couldn't give him an inch or he'd take ten miles.

"Oh, Indigo. I missed you," he said again before his steady breaths denoted his slumber.

Silver was a dangerous man to become intimate with. One could almost feel special with his sweet words and talented body. Still, it wasn't the first time I'd let him fall asleep inside me. I used my calling to help roll him onto his side and I curled against him. In his sleep he rested his chin on my head and roped his arms around me making sure I couldn't escape.

I wouldn't. He was much easier to deal with when asleep.

THIRTY-TWO

"You look beautiful," Bronze gushed as she lowered the white glittering mask over my eyes.

We all wore masks to hide our identities while we competed. My face had a permanent stony look to keep from vomiting up my dinner everywhere. She had done a very good job with what she had to work with, I thought.

"Perk up hun, you are going to be great."

"Thanks Bronze, looks good," I told her mechanically.

My limbs felt shaky and awkward like I'd been reanimated from a death-like state. I could hear a thousand or so fans taking seats in the Breaker's arena.

I got up and went to my cubby and changed into my white leather outfit. Cordillera had outdone herself. It was like a bathing suit; its front piece was completely open, exposing half my breasts and my stomach down to my belly button. It was all held together by white lacing across my skin. She had even gotten me white thigh-high boots with a hint of a heel.

My makeup was very dramatic and my whole body had been dusted with shimmering powder, kind of like a morally bankrupt angel. I was going against Ama. Battle of the Blondes they were calling it, even though my hair was more brown than blonde. We were the main event and Ama was excited to be a headliner. I didn't share her excitement. I knew Cordillera had made sure I would win. It was hardly a competition, but I'd still do my best.

Brass was competing as well. He was going up in the match before ours against Hopper. He sat in his leather briefs, body oiled and ready on the benches near the doors. I'd had to watch Katydid oil him which took twice as long as it took to oil Hopper. I didn't have to watch, but when I looked away my imagination of what she was doing was far worse.

I was nervous for so many reasons. I didn't know what would happen with the patron once I won. I didn't know how it would make me feel with all those people cheering, watching me. I patted my necklaces, which were visible in my white leather monokini monstrosity.

Ama came to sit down next to me in her usual black leather bandeau top and shorts. Her hair had been teased, her curls framing her cherub face.

She patted my thigh, "Just have fun."

I nodded and twisted the ring on my necklace. My emerald ring hung from the stone pendant necklace; I didn't want to risk it getting damaged in my run. Slate wouldn't be happy I wasn't wearing it. He hadn't even come to see me before my competition. He'd stoically kissed me goodbye in the rumpus room before watching me walk downstairs to the prep room with Brass.

I'd have to show my face at the after party, Cordillera would make sure I did. Slate was going to have to wait and he was not a patient man. I kept imagining him bursting into Vegas and torturing the patron for looking at me.

I jumped as the announcer started up. He called the first match and two older girls headed out into the arena. When the doors swung open, I heard the roar of the crowd that made my stomach knot. Slate had activated the bond before leaving me and he must have hated me. The thought of Slate feeling sick from my upset stomach was a little funny and perked my mood some.

Hopper sat down on my other side. "Ready for some fun, sweetheart?"

I sniffed and looked at him from the corner of my eyes. "I think I'm going to barf."

Hopper chuckled and tossed his dark blonde ponytail over his burly shoulder. Fine blonde hair covered Hopper's torso to his snug black pants. I'd done my training all month with Hopper. He was a good captain, if an unequivocal pervert.

"They are not going to let anything happen to you. Try to not look like you are being tortured." He barked another laugh and Brass forced his way between us.

I could only imagine what Hopper was thinking to make Brass do that. The first match was over. The girls ran in and jumped in the showers quickly before one of them was remade by Bronze and Katydid for her patron.

Katydid kept casting glances at Brass, he must have known it, I wondered where they stood these days since they hadn't been making much small talk. I hadn't seen Brass talk to her hardly at all. She had always been sweet to me, and I'd gone out of my way to repair things between them at the expense of my red-hot jealousy.

Brass's hair was pushed back from his dark honey face he arched a brow at me, peering at me from the corner of his amber eyes and I shook my head.

... For once, I was not thinking inappropriately. Don't give me that look...

Brass chuckled and I looked everywhere but at his oiled flexing abs. I had a bad habit of rogue thinking in Brass's presence, so thank the gods Slate didn't possess Brass's gift. I wouldn't have made it past my first week with him before he exploited my thoughts. Though, it was hard to be in the prep room with him and the oils and not think about all we did after the massage he gave me the first time I ran the Crash Course.

My insides were squirming. He'd given me the impression he'd never made love to another Shadow Breaker. My memory of us with the oils was making me doubt he hadn't used them outside of Breaker HQ. That dumped an ice bucket on my lust.

"Things with Katydid are complicated. Are you in such a rush to see me settled down?" he asked.

I ran my teeth along my lower lip. It would clear the lines between Brass and me. I was with Slate, that was clear, but somehow Brass had snuck in there — always in the back of my mind. There was this indescribable thing between us that Slate resented, yet didn't discourage. Like I said, I didn't understand it.

I hoped his question was rhetorical because I didn't have an answer for him.

I watched the small screen light up. Red digital numbers ran across it. The numbers were steadily going up. Cordillera wanted me to try to get people to bid higher. I wasn't sure if it would work from inside the prep room, but I told her I'd try.

The victorious girl was stuffed into a revealing blue dress that matched her eyes and she waited until the room number appeared. 200-1 Flashed across the screen, she took a deep breath and smiled as she walked back out through the prep room doors. I heard the crowd cheer as she was walked through the stands and to her assigned room. Vegas. What would happen there, would stay there.

I took a deep breath, the waiting had to be worse than being out there. It was agony.

The announcer started again. "For our second match, our first competitor stands at an even six feet and weighs in at two hundred and ten pounds... BULLSEYE!" Hopper stood up and gave me and Ama a wink before running out of the prep room, his ponytail swung along his back.

"Our second competitor and former champion, the ladies' favorite... HEAT!"

... Good luck, ladies' favorite...

I teased with only a slight amount of scorn.

Brass's head swung to meet my eyes and smirked. He wanted to say something but turned back towards the doors.

"Good luck kiss?" Brass asked a flustered Katydid who closed her eyes and tilted her head back.

My breath caught and my stomach soured. At first, I thought he'd asked me. It dawned on me that I would've granted it and I couldn't begin to dive into what that meant.

Brass, tall and muscular, gleaming from the oils, cupped the blonde's face and pressed his plump defined lips to hers. She melted. Who wouldn't? Her hands seemed to go limp, and a comb clattered to the floor. The room seemed ten degrees warmer, and I shifted on the bench next to Ama.

I hated myself. I hated how wrathfully jealous I was and how I felt like Brass was rubbing it in my face. He wasn't. He was an *extremely* attractive single guy living life, and I was married to his best friend. I needed to quit being such a terrible wife.

"Sometimes I miss dating men. Not usually, but sometimes," she murmured.

When Brass broke the kiss, Katydid's eyes were still closed, and he kissed her cheek before heading to the metal doors that led to the Crash Course. that was terribly romantic; I sighed as I watched him go. Katydid collected the comb off the floor with amused expressions from Bronze and Cricket. No one would fault Katydid for going weak in the knees over that kiss.

Slate would probably question what had gotten into me just before competing. I had no right whatsoever to be feeling.... how I felt. Good. Brass was finding a girl of his own. He was an amazing man and deserved happiness. Really amazing.

I needed to keep reminding myself — good for Brass. Live your life. Good for Brass. It would be my mantra.

I could hear the women screaming as he smiled. Poor Katydid.

I knew that feeling.

"How are you doing?" Ama asked. "I know you are nervous, but besides that."

"I'm good, just nerves. I'm a little scared of whoever my patron is going to be. I hope if he's going to try to get in my figurative pants that at least he'll be good looking," I joked.

Ama squeezed my hand. "You don't have to pretend with me."

I pulled my lips between my teeth. "Ama, I don't want to unload on you. Especially not now. I have so much pain in me, sometimes I feel like I can't breathe. I forget it for a time, Slate helps..." I shook my head. "He helps so much with that. I don't know what I'd do without him," I confessed.

"Whenever you want to vent, I'm here," she said soothingly, her hand holding mine. "I hope you do not think I am overstepping, but... I cannot help but notice how you have fallen for Brass."

I sucked in air so sharply I choked as I looked for Katydid to make sure she hadn't heard her. Ama patted my back.

"Amalgam. I'm not in love with Brass. It's just regular love. Like... well, I don't know," I whispered, "I'm in love with Slate."

Ama knit her brows. Was that pity?

"Scarlett, I see your aura. You love them both. I am here when you need to talk. I will tell you something, though. I am certain they both know."

I glanced back to Katydid. My mask felt like it was blocking my airways. Ama must have been hitting the sauce earlier because I was not in love with Brass. It was a crush. That was all. Harmless. Who didn't have a crush on him? They'd be crazy not to.

The crowd was going wild, it must have been a close one. Then they roared, stomping their feet. Women were screaming again, and I assumed Brass had won. Hopper and Brass ran in and went straight to the showers. Bronze came back around to Ama and me for touch ups as Brass dried himself and pulled on his clothes waiting for him. Katydid dried and styled his hair quickly. I was shocked at his open nudity, even Katydid was all business for the moment.

I looked at the screen as the numbers went higher. 500 - 2 Flashed across the screen. Five hundred gold daymarks, completely unassisted by me.

Brass came over to me and leaned to my ear. "Happy, Scarlett?" he paused.

No, I wanted to snap. He smelled like a meadow after a spring rain shower.

"Good luck." He turned and headed through the door.

My emotions threatened to wiggle free, and I locked them down once more. Show the slightest bit of weakness and everyone saw a window in. We were up next. Ama put her hand to my stomach, and I felt her call, my stomach stopped twisting and I could breathe again. I hadn't even realized how shallow my breathing had become.

"We have a very special main event planned for tonight," said the announcer. "The Battle of the Blondes! The first beauty, our... RISK!" The crowd went wild, and Ama stood up and ran out with her blonde curls bouncing. I stood up ready to go. "Our second competitor is our newest recruit and youngest member. You could say tonight will be her first time, the breathtaking... WILDFIRE!"

I swallowed hard and headed out the doors. The spotlights were swirling, my shimmering skin glittered under the bright lights. The crowd was deafening. I sashayed onto the course, raising my chin and letting my hips sway as I walked. When I got to the start of the Guillotine, instead of waving I bent over dramatically over one leg to check my boot. The cheering grew louder, and I let my fingers trail back up my leg and flipped my hair back dramatically before I'd fully straightened.

They ate it up. I was Wildfire, not Scarlett.

"Are the ladies ready? I know I certainly am," said the announcer, drawing a laugh from the crowd.

Ama gave a thumbs up and I gave a wink in the direction of Cordillera's suite. I had no idea where the announcer was, but he took it as a GO sign. The boom sounded, and it was even louder down here than it was in Cordillera's suite. My instincts took over, and I was running into the Gauntlet before my mind could catch up.

I was fluid. I was grace.

I had gone through great lengths, once I had learned the course to a 'T', to make it an erotic dance for the crowd. My every movement was intentional. I slithered between the blades, rolling and leaping to best display my body's natural gifts. I didn't stop moving when I came to the treetops. I could flip from treetop to top, back flipping off the last tree, and the crowd screamed.

I had trained a year for it. First, conditioning myself. Then, gaining the skills. Finally, I fine-tuned and honed what I learned.

I ran and flew across the earthquake section. I made landfall three times as I twisted and turned, leaping gracefully through the shaking grounds and falling boulders. I reached the lava and front flipped onto a lava rock passing by. The crowd gasped and clapped as I landed. I checked for Ama, it had to look good.

Ama was reaching the end of the earthquake zone, so I leapt to the next rock, and kept at it until I reached the end, twisting midair to avoid a geyser. The water was in front of me, I took it at a jog and propelled myself with the force of both of my feet off the edge of the lava rocks spinning till I landed on a raft going by.

I widened my stance to keep my balance. Another raft came around and I hopped over, teetering dramatically before righting myself. One thing Hopper had taught me that Slate hadn't was the art of showmanship. Cordillera wanted a show pony, so I trotted for her.

Ama was on the raft behind me. It was time for me to win.

I had got my finishing move from an idea Brass had given me. I hopped over two more rafts so I was close enough for it to work. I jumped on the back end of the raft, sending the front-end angling up dangerously, though I had no intention of staying on it. I rebounded off the airborne section and flipped. My hands gripped the edge of the dock as I did a handstand on the edge. I brought my legs down slowly one at a time and spun around to face the crowd. I didn't smile, I let the end of my lips curl as I sashayed further onto the dock to make room for Ama. She leapt gracefully after me, running into me and gripped me fiercely. She hadn't seen the new routine I'd been practicing. It was all choreographed.

I'd won. I was doing a little showboating, but the fans forgave that when I embraced Ama and smiled a genuine smile at her. There were people on their feet clapping and cheering. Cordillera must have had flowers for sale because white flowers flew from the stands. I stretched down and picked three up. I broke off the stems and tucked one behind Ama's ear, one behind my own, and kissed the petals of one before throwing it back into the stands. The surrounding fans dove for it, making them look like a human implosion.

Ama and I walked back, our arms around each other's waists. I manipulated the bidders as much as I could as she waved brightly to everyone, urging them to bid higher and higher. We reached the prep room and scrambled into the showers. I washed as fast as humanly possible and slipped into a silk white halter dress that was completely backless. The skirt gathered at my backside giving it a two-foot train. It was low cut, and the sides were exposed as well, the skirt attached by a single glittering silver clasp below my breasts. I couldn't wear underwear with it.

Bronze and Katydid hustled to dry my hair and redo my makeup. My hair was piled up in romantic curls exposing my back. They dusted my body again in shimmering powder and I slipped on my silver strappy heels after I patted my necklaces and squeezed my torque. I wore my ring, not caring if the patron didn't like it.

"Gods," came Ama's awed voice. I turned in my seat while Bronze put another mask over my eyes.

1000 - 3 flashed on the screen.

I squeezed my eyes shut. No way some guy was paying that much for my witty conversational skills. Ama knew it as she turned towards me with her brows knitted.

"You do not have to do anything you do not want to. Maybe you will want to, though. You never know." She shrugged.

I gave her a lopsided grin before sauntering back out into the arena. They went crazy. It could be addictive. No wonder they didn't mind it. People were stretching out just to touch me as I passed. I let a smile play on my lips as I went through the crowd. Two black garbed men had to come out and clear the walkway because I was being bombarded by fans that were grabbing at my thin dress and sensitive skin.

It was all so overwhelming. I went from nobody to superstar in thirty minutes. I was being pulled by one of the men in black, I'd seen him before around the rumpus room. He was on the third team of Shadow Breakers, whose captain was a woman I hadn't met yet. We made it into the hall and he locked the door behind him.

"Never had that happen before. You really got them going," he said excitedly. He picked up a white rose that followed me in and broke off the stem before slipping it into my hair. "There. Perfection. She should have called you the Angel, you do not seem fiery at all."

I smirked and let my eyes go red, they blazed. "Don't I?" I asked, seductively. He gasped. "Where's room three, if you don't mind?"

"First door on your right," he stammered.

I blinked, and the fire was gone. I smiled genuinely at him, a Scarlett smile. "Thanks. Thanks for out there too." I turned around and snapped back into character.

If this guy wanted Wildfire, he would get her. Assuming it was a guy. What if it was a woman, I wondered belatedly?

I opened the door and a wine-colored curtain hung in the way. I pushed it aside, the gold tassels swinging as I stepped into the room closing the door behind me. The room was lit by candlelight, the wall directly opposite was a two-way mirror so patrons could watch the competition after they went to their rooms. A bald man sat back on a couch at the far end looking out through the mirror.

I stepped down onto the black and wine-colored rug, a fruit and cheese spread sat on a low table in the center of the room. There were couches on either side of the wall and a bar against the window, which looked to be fully stocked. I made a beeline for it.

The bald man turned as I approached. "Dhole?" I asked in disbelief.

I could make out his smile through his long brown goatee. "I hope you are worth it," he said gruffly, taking me in. "Scarlett, right?"

I hadn't expected anyone I knew, it made me completely off balanced. I slipped off the mask seeing as it hardly mattered anymore. I had gone in thinking I'd be my alter ego and pretend none of whatever occurred here happened to Scarlett Tio, I wasn't sure that was possible with someone who really knew me.

I moved to the bar. "Can I fix you a drink?" I asked.

I was flailing, I had no idea what to do next. Did he want me to do things to him?

"Relax. Yes, a drink please," he said before sitting back down on the couch.

I poured him a whiskey on the rocks and myself a cranberry vodka, thinking I was going to need the hard stuff. I sauntered over and sat down next to him, handing him his drink.

Make conversation Scarlett.

"I didn't think you liked the Shadow Breakers very much. I must admit, I am surprised to see you."

All true. I was shocked, and still hadn't recovered.

"I came for a friend. I had no idea you were such a hot commodity or I would have asked for your autograph." He smiled again and sipped his drink.

Was it really going to be this easy or was he getting my guard down? I stood back up and downed my drink as I walked back to the bar pouring myself another one, stronger this time.

"I didn't think Guardians did autographs," I told him making small talk. "I could maybe plug your shop if you like. I don't know the name of it though."

He shook his head. "No, thanks. I like to keep it exclusive. If you want to come back though, you are always welcome."

No kidding. After how much he just spent on me?

"My friend wants to get Valkyrie wings on her back. I hoped to take her sometime after her birthday in a couple months. I thought about getting a pair myself," I told him.

I could do it. I would do this with him in his tattoo shop, he didn't need to pay me for it. I wondered if it was some weird novelty of his.

"Normally, I would encourage body art, but I would not want to mark such flawless skin. I only agreed to do your inguz because of that scar," he leaned in conspiratorially.

I curled my lips. Was I supposed to flirt or was that plan over now, and I only had to keep him entertained? I stood back up and downed my drink on the way there. I poured myself another, this one only had a hint of pink.

I felt amused.

"Would you like another?" I asked, glancing over my shoulder.

His glass was still half full, he shook it at me.

"Do you normally drink this much?" he asked jokingly, but it rang with truth.

I sat back down. "I rarely do, but when in Rome." I held up my hands gesturing to the velvety wine room.

Rome or Vegas. Didn't matter.

A knock sounded on the door, and I nearly jumped out of my skin. Dhole stood up.

"Excuse me," he said, pushing past me and heading to the door.

I had locked it behind me, it seemed the safest thing to do so I wouldn't be ambushed. I stood again and slammed my drink and poured myself another with a shiver as the liquor warmed my belly. I sipped on it and faced the two-way mirror, taking a deep breath.

Headquarters' staff was cleaning up after the crowd which meant they had moved on to the club. I hoped Jett, Steel, Indigo, and Tawny were having fun. They'd come to see me compete and no amount of arguing could get them to back down.

I heard Dhole approach from behind, but he felt wrong. I knit my brows and he put his hand against my exposed back. There it is, I thought, confirming all my assumptions. I turned and prepared myself to wriggle out of as much physical interaction as possible. My drink fell out of my hand. My mouth hung open.

Slate's silver eyes drank me in. "I could not let your first time be with a stranger," Slate rumbled.

My knees went weak. I leaned against the mirror.

"You had Dhole bid on me?" I asked weakly, my relief was palpable.

Slate towered over me, and I felt limp in his arms. The alcohol hit me like a truck the way I'd been guzzling it and suddenly I was drunk on it and intoxicated from Slate's possessiveness, which I didn't mind for an instant. He could've peed a circle around me and I'd have welcomed it.

My husband came for me.

"I did. You are mine, Torch. Another night a patron will be with you, but not tonight." His fingers dug into the shimmering skin at my waist.

"You paid for me. That was a lot of daymarks, Slate." I twisted my lips into a coy smile. "I hope you didn't think I would have sex with you, sir. I know my time was expensive, but I'm not that kind of girl."

Slate threw back his head and laughed rich and heartily, making my toes curl. The hard planes of his face creased in a rare smile and his silver eyes glittered.

"I happen to know that is a lie, sweet woman. No matter, I can be very persuasive," Slate purred and lowered himself to his knee.

His hand trailed over the slinky white fabric to the silver clasp and with a twist of his fingers, the bottom half of the dress billowed to the floor. I gasped and gripped his head for support at my rubbery knees. Slate made a noise of need in his throat that nearly made my eyes roll back in my head.

Did I just swoon?

THIRTY-THREE

We laid on top of the wine-colored rug of room number three, our limbs entangled, both our bodies glistening from the exertion we'd put forth in our several rounds of love making. It had started out fast and frenzied and ended slow and passionate. Two lovers familiar with one another's bodies, knowing exactly how to bring each other the most pleasure possible. Orgasm after orgasm had ripped through my body until I thought I'd faint, only to be brought back by Slate's skillful kisses.

We were well past our hour and a half. I was sure Jett, Tawny, Indigo, and Steel would start worrying.

"We have to go to Dark Shadows," I told Slate again.

I'd said it at least twice before, but he didn't want me leaving, or getting dressed for that matter.

I sat up next to him and smiled down at his outstretched form. Strawberry juice was smeared along his stomach as well as my breasts, we had come up with creative ways to eat the assortment of foods laid out in lieu of plates.

He leaned forward and ran his tongue across a pink streak over my breast sending shivers through me.

"How can we leave when you are so filthy? I must help you clean up," he said, his teeth gliding along the soft skin of my breast.

He sucked hard against my skin, licking away the juices. "Decadent." His voice was guttural.

I had to push him back or we'd never leave.

I called, dampening cloth napkins and wiping his stomach down while he paid keen attention to my own body. I had to stop him again from getting carried away, and he chuckled darkly sending a spike of pleasure through me. He was insatiable.

My hair was down as I slipped back into my dress, still without panties, and Slate got dressed in turn and slid my mask over my face for me. He wore a black waistcoat over his all-black clothing. He looked dark and dangerous and all mine.

We left the room and saw Brass at the end of the hall. A woman with blonde hair had her hand down the front of his pants as he pressed her against the wall, kissing her passionately. His hand held her wrist high over her head, the other squeezed her breast as he gave her a final goodbye kiss. Slate and I had stopped in the hall trying not to interrupt.

A strange little grunt punched from my lungs.

The woman had a mask on, but something about her was familiar. Gharial — she'd cornered Brass before. Brass and Quick apparently had a thing for blondes. She slid her hand out from Brass's pants and gave him a lewd grin before walking away. Her statuesque form nearly glided as she walked. I knew the competitors slept with the patrons and, technically, I'd just done the same thing. Never did I think I'd actually see them together, especially Brass. Somehow, he seemed better than that.

They had to be in there for hours for them to only be leaving now. Longer than Slate and me. I tried not to judge. Who was I to judge?

Yet, there I was judging.

A crush, a harmless tiny crush. I had to lock it down.

Brass turned to us and adjusted himself. I averted my eyes my face burned, and not just from seeing Brass touching himself. Slate led forward, his hand on my exposed back.

"Dhole did well," Slate said as we met him in the hall.

Brass nodded slipping his mask over his eyes, he had love bites along his dark honey neck that his long dark hair didn't cover. My blood boiled inexplicably.

"Good. I see it worked."

I averted my eyes trying not to look as sour as I felt.

I could hear the warm smile in Brass's voice. "We did not think it was a good idea to have Slate bid. It is not against the rules, but Lera would not want Breakers bidding on Breakers. It defeats the purpose of the patron."

"You cannot keep doing that whenever I compete. It's too expensive," I said brusquely looking down at my heels as they kicked the skirt of my dress in a hurry to be away from Brass, whom I itched to slap.

Both laughed. "You did go for more than I anticipated. But worth every daymark," Slate said, growling into my ear.

It may have been the first time Slate had no impact on me. It wasn't fair to him, but I couldn't help how I felt. I just had to get away from Brass and his unabashed affair.

"The most anyone has ever gone for," Brass said matter of fact.

I wanted to inquire about his blonde. I bet she was married. Rancorous words waited on the tip of my tongue begging for release. My mood had spoiled. He'd kissed Katydid downstairs and slept with Gharial all within the same hour! Would he now bed Katydid? The night I saw him with Gharial, did he meet her after I left his room?

I could feel Slate and Brass both looking at me with amusement. Those two spent too much time together.

"Someone's mood has taken a turn," Slate mused, "Noble Brass too red-blooded for you, Torch?"

Fiddlestick! How much further?

"I would not sleep with one woman and then another in the same night," Brass said walking alongside us confirming my suspicions about the night I slept in the guest room.

"Did I say something?" I asked, feeling querulous.

Slate didn't stop me when I picked up pace to leave them both in my dust. Pretending I was fine without the help of my liquid courage wasn't happening.

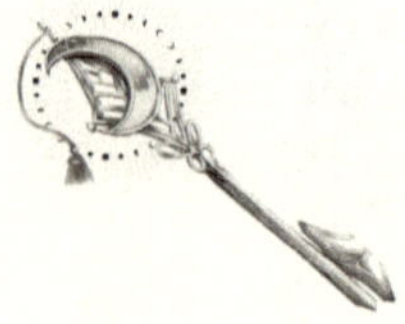

I serenaded the Breakers.

Dark Shadows was an ultra-chic night club, complete with purple velvet V.I.P. area and black tiled dance floor. More purple velvet couches lined the walls with free standing tables. A spiky-haired man stood behind what could only be described as a DJ booth.

Haarder was the Dark Shadows DJ I'd met at the Iron Maiden the first time I'd gone. He remembered me and played my favorite songs and I danced with wild abandon. My dance partners constantly changing from Slate, to Quick, Jett, and Steel. Tawny, Shale, and Indigo were even dancing with us. Tawny, Jett, and Steel seemed amazed by my skills on the Crash Course. When Brass attempted to join me, I suddenly needed a refill that very second. Poor timing on his part.

"You were like an acrobat out there flipping and leaping. It was insane!" Tawny gushed.

"Slate must be proud," Jett agreed since Slate trained me first.

"I'm afraid to touch you, your dress might disintegrate," Steel said, ignoring my chest area.

Tawny back handed his chest, and he smiled at her.

"I didn't pick it," I said in a rush, appalled at the thought.

Jett laughed, "If the patrons had seen you in it beforehand, you probably could have gotten more."

"Glad she did not. I could hardly afford her," Slate teased.

I rolled my eyes as the others laughed.

At the end of the night, Cordillera had come to see me. I sat between Slate and Tawny, Slate's hand on my knee.

"Walk with me," she demanded and started off before I could even stand.

We walked briskly to a side room that held cameras and a desk where Chafer sat watching the club from the monitors. Not just the club though, cameras displayed every nook and cranny in HQ except for the showers. I could see the massage tables where Brass and I had made love, even the dead end where we'd made love.

I could see Quick in a corner monitor between Indigo's legs, her head thrown back as they moved in a rhythmic motion in what they must have assumed was a dark corner. Nothing was hidden from the night vision cameras. And I blushed as I looked away. I had wondered where they'd gone off to.

"You did exceptionally well tonight," Cordillera said without preamble.

"Thanks."

"Brass informed me that you are looking for the men who captured you. They have a tournament the day after tomorrow. On occasion, they invite me even though we rival for the same contracts. They have invited me to pit my Breakers against their Knights a few times. I always reject their offers since I have nothing to gain from it. The Shadow Breakers bring in much more revenue than the Stygian Knights and their work is... of a more unscrupulous nature," she said, sitting on the plain wood desk.

"Okay?" I asked, wondering where she was heading with it.

"You may come with me. Masked of course, and I will dress you." She scanned what I wore with approval. "If they are pleased with your appearance and ask to have you compete, would that be something you are interested in?"

I fought to contain the thrill that shot through me and schooled my face. "Can Brass hear what you're saying now? If so, I might as well say no. He'll tell Slate and they'll never let me go through with it."

Chafer snorted but didn't take his eyes off the cameras. "The pet has his own pet."

I shot daggers at Chafer, which he ignored, and Cordillera continued. "Not my problem. That is my offer take it or leave it."

"I'll take it," I said a little too quickly, and she smirked with her bright red lips.

"Good. See you then, Delegate. Oh, and you will be competing next month as well. As will Slate, so he will be unable to bid on you... so will Brass. Quick too, if necessary. Do not make it necessary, Delegate." Cordillera looked at the closed door.

I considered myself dismissed and walked back into the luxurious lounge. I kept my head clear and sauntered through the crowd, having to stop every few feet to speak to another new fan. The whole thing was overwhelming. The mask gave me a certain amount of anonymity, but it wouldn't exactly take a rocket scientist to figure out who I was from the people I was with.

I went out onto the dance floor and said goodbye to Steel, Tawny, and Jett. I knew where Indigo and Quick were, so I wouldn't waste my time trying to find them. Brass and Slate drank amber liquid out of snifters, Ama and Shale were nowhere to be found. Silver and amber eyes followed my walk over to them, making me acutely aware of my lack of undergarments. If they were respectable gentlemen, they would look away, especially after my skin prickled.

"I am going to head home," I said, looking down at Slate expectantly. I was waiting for one of them to bring up my talk with Lera.

Slate's tongue licked along his lower lip, and I felt myself mimic the action like a monkey and gave myself a mental kick. Brass chuckled, and I fought the urge to snap at Brass. It was an entirely foreign feeling to me. Slate got to his feet, and I took a step back. A smile played on Brass's lips, making me bite down on the inside of my cheek.

"Torch, are you angry Brass saw two women tonight? One might say it was hypocritical of you since you have kissed me and other men in the same day before," Slate said smugly, and I pursed my lips.

Slate was feeling my irritation and Brass, well, he could read my mind. Brass was the untouched subject. I wasn't going to break that rule right in front of him.

"Are you joining me or not," I asked stiffly.

Brass got to his feet so they could both tower over me. "Holding me to a higher standard, Scarlett?"

I nocked my chin up an inch and gave them both measured looks. "Who cares? Honestly."

I hated that they made me talk about it at all. I turned and left the club alone stewing with anger until Slate caught up and slid his palm against mine. I sighed.

Maybe he needed to discuss it.

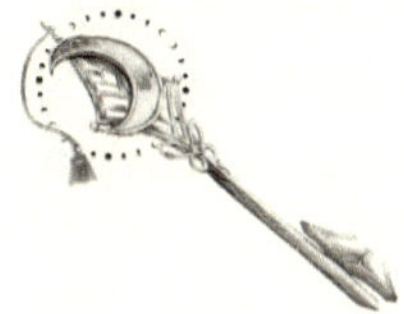

Slate and I went back to the apartment, showered, and climbed into bed like a normal couple. Slate handed me a tiny vial of rousen, and I fell asleep in his arms. I didn't wake up to molest him in the middle of the night and when I did wake up, Slate was watching me sleep.

The white sheets pooled around our hips. I had a leg slung over one of his powerful thighs with my fingers grazing the hard ridges of his abs. My cheek was pressed to his hard pectoral as his hand slid under my cream satin nightie to run along my spine.

"You made it through your first night." Slate's morning voice was deep and raspy, making my insides pulse in the most delicious way.

"Only because I was exhausted."

I pulled myself over Slate's nude body, he made a noise deep in his chest that sounded like a purr. He was rock hard against my stomach, and I shifted to get comfortable. I inhaled his heady scent deeply as he gazed down at me with sleep swollen lips and hooded eyes.

"I love you," I purred, and he pulled me up to his face so he could slant his mouth over mine.

"You did well last night," he murmured against my lips.

"Yeah?"

"Mm."

"Lera wants us to compete next month. She knew you bid on me; he said you're going up against Brass and if Quick tries to bid on me, she'll make him an opener. I don't think he'd be very happy about that," I told him with a small conspiratorial smile.

Slate ran his fingers through my hair. "No, he would not."

"Are you going to be okay with that?" I asked, looking down at him.

His strong jaw clenched and unclenched. "No, but you will have to endure it yourself. I have never lost." My stomach twisted and the corner of his mouth quirked. "No, it will not be easy for either of us."

"Slate, are we... would you..." I scanned his face.

It was too early in the morning to have such a serious conversation.

"I will not have relations with the patron, Torch. That is what you wanted to hear?" Slate rumbled.

"At all, right? Nothing? I only ask because —"

"Because you think Brass is so honorable, and if he would fuck a patron then you know I would? I have. I had no reason not to, now I do."

I grimaced, "You promise?"

Slate pushed my legs apart, so I straddled his hips and he rocked against me. "You are mine, and I am yours. No other woman can have what is yours. Do you understand?"

I nodded.

He only wanted me.

"Why?" I asked, not understanding.

His grey eyes softened. "Because you are my mate. Do you know why I call you Torch? It is more than your elemental power, or your fiery nature. You are my torch, as in the flame I carry for you. A torch song is one of love lost, as you will inevitably lose me to prophecy. A torch singer has a sultry voice, like yours. I told you I was lost. You are my torch in the darkness. You are my hope."

My heart thundered in my ears as he continued.

"On my Northwest coast in the midst of the night a fishermen's group stands watching. Out on the lake that expands before them, others are spearing salmon. The canoe, a dim shadowy thing, moves across the black water. Bearing a torch ablaze at the prow."

I swallowed hard. It was as close as Slate would ever get to telling me he loved me without me tricking him into it.

Torch.

Such a silly little nickname I never paid too much attention to. I did notice that Slate called everyone else other than Gyps by their name or competitor's name.

I leaned back and pulled the nightie over my head and Slate's hands slid up my body unfettered. He drew in a sharp breath as I lowered my mouth to his and rubbed myself against him.

"Pinch me," I said, huskily as I sheathed him inside me.

Slate laughed deliciously with one of his rare smiles and I pushed myself up so I could gaze down at him. "If you had told me last year that this was where I would be, I would've called you a liar."

Slate's hands cupped my backside, guiding my movements. "I am sure you would have come up with something much more colorful than a liar."

It was my turn to laugh.

After a morning of lounging in bed with Slate and a skipped breakfast, Slate and I met with the others to go to the cottage in Valla. We had a large group making the trek into the country. Tawny, Steel, Jett, Indigo, Cherry, Amethyst, Gypsum and Slate met with the Shadow Breakers. Brass, Quick, Ama, and Shale dressed in their heavy cloaks to make the five-hour hike past the Verdandi gate.

"That's everyone. Ready?" Jett asked, excited to start his birthday extravaganza.

I gave a strained smile. "One more."

Slate looked at me speculatively feeling my mischief through the bond, but I was carefully masking my thoughts from Brass.

"Who might that be?" Slate's smile was infectious.

"Hey! Sorry I am late." Katydid smiled shyly at the bundled bunch and her blue eyes hitched on Brass.

Brass's eyes slid to me and back. "You're not late. Don't worry." I told her and her smile brightened.

Katydid's big blue eyes shifted to Brass as he leaned in to kiss her cheek expectantly and we started out down the cobbled road. For once it wasn't snowing. Slate hung back to walk with me, and I got the feeling he wanted to have a discussion.

"You seem keen on pairing Brass off. Any reason for the sudden interest?" he asked softly with his big hand on my shoulder to keep me close.

"Only that he's always the only one without a date and I thought it might be nice for him to have someone," I said pertly.

Katydid was wholesome. The image of him groping the old married cougar was seared to my eyelids and all the unwelcome feels with it. If I had to see Brass with another woman, *er*, a woman, then I wanted it to be with someone I approved of, and didn't want to light on fire and cackle wickedly as she burned.

"So, it has nothing to do with you being uncomfortable with your attraction to him? That you are not trying to set him up so there is less temptation for you?" Slate asked point blank, and I blinked at him.

Thank goodness he held my shoulder, or I would've tripped and went sprawling into the road. "Slate, the point is moot. I'm with you. I never want to discuss him with you."

If Brass was any other man Slate would never have let him close to me. Frankly, I was surprised he did. If I were in Slate's position, I wouldn't want another woman hanging around him that I knew he would be interested in if I weren't around. Then again, I never asked, maybe he did. I was glancing around the girls suspiciously when Slate chuckled.

"What's so funny?" I asked as we passed the hurrying townsfolk.

Just because it wasn't snowing, didn't mean it wasn't bitingly cold.

"You, Torch. You think for one second that Brass would not court you if I were to leave you, you are wrong. Did he let another sneak time away with you the way he did?" My brows quirked as I remembered all the little dates we shared while I was supposed to be with Ash. "Why I doubt he would let another man have so much as a single date with you. I do not blame him; I would do the same. You are a rare woman," Slate said, pulling me in tighter to his body.

"This is a stupid topic; I don't know why we're talking about this. What's gotten into you today?" I asked then lowered my voice. "Is it because we didn't make love last night? I was honestly tired, and it was refreshing to get a full night's sleep without waking up because of the rousen. Besides, we more than made up for it this morning," I said, unable to stop the moronic smile that bloomed on my face.

Slate made a deep purring noise in the chest and placed a kiss on the top of my head. "That we did," he replied with a lecherous grin I hoped my brother didn't see. "I will pretend that your ardor was not stolen when you witnessed Brass with Gharial." He knew all along, the cache hole. "Scar, when this prophecy happens, whenever it will be, I would not want you to deprive yourself of happiness. If your heart should lead you to someone we both knew, I would not begrudge you."

I'd stopped walking. Torch was what Slate called me. Sometimes, when he was serious, he called me Scarlett.

"I'm not discussing this. I won't talk about your death or your stupid prophecy, even in the hypothetical. You may have been right about Ash and me, but that's because the Stygians got involved. If it wasn't one thing, it would've been another. It wasn't meant to be. I won't go around talking about what I'm going to do after you. So, knock it off." I scowled at him, and he urged me forward to catch back up with the group.

The exit to the Valla countryside was guarded by two Guardians in thick black cloaks with the three interlocking triangles on the back. They nodded as we left, and Slate pulled me close again.

"We should talk about it. While you may not believe it, it is a truth you will have to address one day. I prefer to go over it with you than leave you alone with not having a plan in place," Slate said in a business-like tone, his eyes far ahead towards the horizon.

"Fine. I agree to go where my heart takes me, but Slate..." I found his gloved hand on my shoulder and gave it a squeeze. "It would hardly be fair to any other man I'd be with when they'd forever be in your shadow."

Slate gave me an arrogant grin as he looked down his straight masculine nose at me. "I would expect no less from you."

I rolled my eyes, and we continued our walk.

Ash and I had made the walk last year about that time. Behind us were the ridge of mountains that spanned the entire city. At the very top of the highest mountain was a castle, Valla University. You could make out rounded stained-glass domes of the green house.

We walked on flat land as the road disappeared, the city behind us slightly elevated. Ahead there was another hill I couldn't see past yet, but it had the promise of more rolling hills to come. The group of us rotated around as we walked and talked without breaking. The sooner we got there, the sooner we'd have lunch and get the cottages ready for the costume party.

The hills were mostly devoid of other people. It was peaceful out there, quiet. I now knew that somewhere on this trip was where Tawny and Sparrow had been attacked with her birth father, Ridge Vetr. I wondered if Tawny thought of that at all while she smiled at Steel, his tan cheeks carrying a hint of red from the cold wind. I was willing to bet those two would have found each other sooner if Tawny never would have left Tidings.

We crossed over a stone bridge, and I could make out a dark forest straight ahead. It was seldom traveled; Slate said the Valkyrie compound was beyond the trees and hardly anyone ever went there. We walked along the river until I could make out a small woods and cottages nestled against the river. Steel had managed to get the Tio, Sumar, and Vetr cottages prepared for the weekend. The cottages were private yet still within sight from one another.

In the summer months, I imagined big leafy green trees and blossoming bushes covered the bare branches that surrounded the stone cottages. Smoke swirled up from the chimney of one of the nearest. I recognized it and pursed my lips.

"Looks like someone heard about our shindig and decided to have one of their own," Jett said with an edge to his voice.

"I invited Diamond," Gypsum admitted.

It was the Straumr cottage that was occupied.

"Diamond might have told Ash and her friends," Amethyst sighed.

Her friends. I was more upset about the fact that Amber and Garnet might be there than Ash. Ash, I could handle. Amber unnerved me and Indigo wouldn't fight for Quick. If Garnet pursued him, Indigo would back down. It'd all be on Quick to decide what he wanted.

"The more the merrier, as long as they don't start anything," Cherry chirped as she started towards what must have been the Sumar cottage since it had a blazing sun carved into the front door.

"How many rooms in a cottage?" Ama asked, pushing the hood from her curls.

"Master suite, three double beds, and a room with two single beds," Steel answered.

"Dibs on master suite at the Sumar cottage," Jett said with a smug smile.

Jett and the girls took the master suite at the Sumar cottage, Ama and Shale took a double, Gyps took a double that I doubted he'd use, Brass took a double, Katydid did not say where she would sleep, but I had a pretty good idea. Tawny and Steel took the master suite at the Vetr cottage, Quick took a double at the Vetr's, as did Indigo. Again, kind of redundant. Slate and I decided to take the Tio master suite since I had to take the rousen at some point and while I was doing better, I didn't want to put anyone else at risk.

I pulled off my pack and handed Katydid the costumes I'd picked up for Brass and her.

"Thanks," she said with another shy smile.

Brass's amber eyes glittered at me, but he didn't say a thing. Katydid grinned when she looked into the bag. I'd gotten them a couple's costume. Nothing crazy, but I loved me some princesses. Katydid would be Rapunzel, and Brass her reluctant savior, Flynn Rider.

After we put our packs down in our rooms, we moved the furniture around in the Tio and Sumar cottages so there would be more room for dancing and drinking. Then we began to get ready.

Slate laughed, deep and rich when I gave him his costume. It wasn't much of a costume. A red shirt I'd found in our closet, a set of horns and a pitchfork. I thought it was self-explanatory, and I would be an angel, complete with feathered wings.

Slate pulled me to him as I started to change. "I could have gone as myself and it would have been just as effective."

I wrapped my arms around his trim waist. "Don't I know it. I knew you wouldn't want to wear much of a costume, so I thought this would suit you and keep in tune with a costume."

He hooked his finger in the dress I'd laid down on the bed and held it up. It was slinky and white with spaghetti straps.

"Angel is a stretch these days, Torch," he mused, and I found myself being slowly undressed and laid across the velour bedding.

It was hard to find the words to dispute Slate when his silken waves slid over my thighs.

THIRTY-FOUR

Haarder, the DJ from the Shadow Breakers was in the Tio cottage playing music for the fifty different people who had shown up for Jett's birthday bonanza. Jett had dressed as JFK, Amethyst as Jackie O and Cherry as Marilyn — they were probably going to hell. Slate and my costume got more than a few chuckles. Indigo had surprised us all by doing a joint costume with Quick — Sandy and Danny Zuko.

My speaker played some tunes while we drank in the Sumar cottage.

The cottages were quaint for a greater family's abode, but more extravagant than any place I would have been to in Chicago. We gathered around the fireplace in the front room and sat on the couches as we played random drinking games.

As we suspected, the Straumrs were there and so were all the usual suspects. They'd even worn costumes. A normally possessive Slate was even more so with Ash around, even with Quartz on his arm. I spent a good amount of time sitting in Slate's lap since every time I tried to sit like a grown up, he pulled me back. I didn't get my own drinks, Slate got them. I didn't leave his sight at any point. I got the distinct feeling that whatever Ash was thinking, Brass had warned Slate and that was the reason behind it all.

Sage had come with Ash, as did Diamond and her friends, Sterling came with his evil twin sisters. Hunter was there, he smiled and gave me a nod while Slate got us drinks and I smiled back. I hated feeling like Slate's property, but I didn't feel like arguing and while Slate was keeping me in his lap, he wasn't being too touchy feely. He must have a good reason; it could have been for my own protection. I'd seen a few little purple vials floating about and now I was always at risk.

Sterling and Diamond drifted away from one another, and I saw Gypsum disappear. Quick seemed to be waiting to see what Indigo would do. If he thought that she would suddenly vanish after taking a bathroom break, he was right. Technically, Indigo and Quick weren't an official thing. Still, I couldn't help but be disappointed Indigo left Quick to be picked up by Garnet. She'd been biding her time waiting for Indigo to leave.

Amber saw her blonde friend slide into Indigo's place on the couch and her eyes rested on me in Slate's lap. Maybe Slate had more than one reason for keeping me close.

Jett was deep in his cups with Cherry at his side and Amethyst playing the diplomat. She wandered from the Straumr's group of people to ours bridging the hostilities in a way that would have made her family proud. Fox hadn't come to the festivities, but Nova was there. They'd been smart enough not to invite Jonquil; there was only so much I could take. Especially if I was tolerating Quartz's presence after she doused me with her drink just last week.

Tawny and Steel wanted to head to the Tio cottage for some dancing. Brass, Katydid, Jett, and the girls joined Slate and I where Haarder was playing the latest hits outside of Tidings. You wouldn't find any of that ethereal Guardian music here.

"You don't think Quick will invite Garnet to stay the night, do you?" I asked Slate in a low voice.

He shook his head once. "The better question is where will Indigo spend the night and how bad will it be in the morning between them."

Good point. Quick wasn't likely to invite Garnet to spend the night. It wasn't his style, but Indigo would stay with Sterling if he asked. I looked to Brass who was dancing with Katydid, her smile lit her face from ear to ear.

I might have had ulterior motives for choosing the Tio cottage.

Jett had managed to pull Amethyst away from her ambassador duties and out onto the dance floor doing things sandwiched between his wives that made me blush. My debauchee of a brother.

"You're in a weird mood tonight," I finally said to Slate.

"Brass told me that Ash is looking to catch you alone, and the same goes for our friend Amber. I do not feel like getting upset tonight, nor letting them spoil your night. Besides, there is plenty to look at when you are sitting in my lap in that dress." Slate's eyes dropped to my low neckline and gave me a lewd grin.

I rolled my eyes. "Then I suppose you want to join me in the bathroom when I go," I teased, and he arched a brow at me.

"Are you inviting me, Torch?" Slate growled low, and I looked around the group to make sure no one was listening.

I gave one nod of my head and pulled my lips between my teeth. Slate lifted from the couch taking me with him and I was glad Brass was occupied with Katydid on the dance floor so he wouldn't see what was in my mind.

My fingers fumbled in their rush to strip off Slate's shirt. "Leave it. I want you now," Slate growled, his teeth running along my exposed throat.

His fingers firmly spun me around by my hips and rucked up my dress. I gripped a fistful of his hair pulling his mouth to mine over my shoulder and I kissed him deeply as he pushed his pants over his trim hips. Slate's hand slithered around my hip, and I gasped as he pushed into me. The back of my head rested on his chest as he thrust in tune with my moaning.

It was fast and hard and ridiculously hot. Slate had bit his lip and slid his bloodied tongue along my lip so our bond activated, and I could feel what he felt. There was no line where Slate ended and I began; we were one and the same. My body, his body, our feelings, our pleasure. I lost myself with my husband, in myself.

The door to the bathroom crashed open, and I cried out amidst my shuddering and Slate spun me from the sink and blocked my body from view of the door. I heard snickering as Slate slid from within me and a low growl started emanating from his chest. Slowly, my mind cleared from its fog and my cheeks heated as I straightened my clothes.

Sage cultured voice taunted me. "The khoraz and the orphan."

I heard Ash chuckle. "I knew once you had been plucked, you would spread like butter," Ash said smoothly to more laughter.

Slate had tucked himself away and whirled around. His rage was palpable. Through the bond, Slate felt like some primitive wild animal. I shifted my head to find his body bunched with tight bronze muscles. I reached out to touch his back and his skin tensed under my fingertips.

"Ash, what do you want?" I said, trying to sound angry, but all I could muster was embarrassment.

"Outside, Straumr," Slate growled.

"Orphan." Ash obliged, and I heard footsteps sound over the wood flooring.

I couldn't see past Slate until he left the bathroom, then I noticed Brass, Jett, and Steel standing alongside the hall. Ash's entourage had followed him out and the three men spoke in hushed tones to Slate who shrugged them off.

"Slate," I called after him and he stopped in his tracks.

I rushed to his side before he stormed outside. His knot of emotions in my head told me I wouldn't be able to coax him into staying.

"Don't let him goad you. We forgot to lock the door, it's the bathroom. If not one of them, then someone else."

The expression on Slate's face gave me chills. Chiseled from granite and as cold as ice, ever since the feast in Thrimilci Slate had been domineering and more possessive than I thought possible. I didn't mind it any other day, but today it threatened Slate's life. Even if Slate didn't lose this fight, Ash would never forget it and Ash wasn't the type to forgive. It would forever divide Ash from us. He already despised us, but he would surely hate us if Slate won.

"I did not forget to lock the door. They will not speak of you that way again," Slate ground out and I fought against the shiver that prickled my skin.

I felt bereft without his affection. I needed his kiss, his arms, but he gave me his back and walked past Haarder playing his songs and the dancing crowd. Brass and Jett moved past me following Slate out. Tawny approached with a frown furrowing her fair face.

"What happened?" she asked with wide hazel eyes.

She was dressed as Olive Oil with Steel as Popeye; Steel came alongside her and removed his hat. "Maybe you ladies should stay inside."

"Not a chance," Tawny said pertly and grabbed my arm, pulling me outside.

"Ash walked in on Slate and I."

Tawny groaned as our feet crunched on the snow. "That cache hole."

"It was fine. People laughed because they're drunk and being childish," I explained, "It was just embarrassing."

A thick layer of ice covered the river that bent just outside the cottage. Ash was removing his hat, vest, and tie as well as the other items from his costume while Slate tossed his red horns to the snow-covered ground and tugged his shirt over his head. His crisscrossed blade belts were strapped across his chest, and he removed them with care. I walked up to him and took them from him, slinging them over my shoulder and walked back to Tawny.

The moonlight shone on Slate's bronze skin, the silver beads in his hair glinted, his eyes reflected the light. His face was hard and shadowed as he set his jaw looking at Ash. Word of a fight was spreading through the party goers, and they had started filing out onto the crunching snow in their costumes.

"I don't think there's much I can say to stop this. Ash shouldn't have come," Steel said, his turquoise eyes stressed.

I sighed. The party for the Tio cottage was out in the freezing air watching as Ash removed his shirt revealing his tightly muscled torso. Quartz's curvy petite frame was by his side speaking low and harsh until she folded her arms under her generous bosom and glowered at me.

Jett and Brass were speaking quietly to Slate. Quick, Garnet, Indigo, Sterling, Diamond, and Gypsum were all missing. It took little effort to guess where they were. Brass and Jett quieted as I approached, neither were as drunk as they had been acting.

"Don't do this," I pleaded under my breath sending the emotion through our bond.

His silver eyes glinted back at me from where he stood, even when the feral beast was scraping the surface, he dripped sexuality. Slate stalked across the circle that was forming and let the corners of his full mouth quirk. He wrapped a muscled arm around my waist lifting me off my feet and crushed his lips to mine deactivating the bond.

"Come upstairs. I don't care that they saw us. Don't play their games," I breathed as he set me down.

"I know you care, I felt it. I am through playing their games, Torch. No man sets eyes on you while I please you," he growled, and I opened my eyes to find his had gone gunmetal hard again.

I glanced over to Ash. Sage, Hunter, and the twins were at his side, holding his weapons for him. There wouldn't be any weapons, and no calling, they would probably fight until one of them could no longer stand. I didn't want to watch; I wanted to go inside and ignore this ugliness. I couldn't leave Slate, some insane idea of honor or whatever it was. Maybe it was just a pissing contest, but I had to stick by his side. My costume made a mockery of me with its wings and halo in white. I should have been in the red devil horns.

Slate and Ash stalked forward as the partygoers made a ring around them. Slate stood several inches taller than Ash, but the few inches in height didn't diminish Ash in any way. The Straumr and possible future Prime had presence. Ash and Slate traded insults no one could hear, but judging by the tensing in their muscles, they must have not pulled any punches. I felt like my ears were burning, it was worse when they looked over at me making me feel like reversing into the cottage.

"Did he beg you not to lay with me, Scarlett?" Ash taunted as they prowled around one another.

Oh yes, they were trading barbs about me.

Slate bristled, "Do not speak to her."

Steel stepped forward and discussed something between the men and took a few steps back. Ash chuckled.

"He wanted to be the first to breach your portcullis," Ash chided and Slate growled.

Slate and Ash were blurs. I didn't see either of them move when they attacked one another. Tawny looped her arm through mine and winced with my flinches. Their hits were brutal, the sounds of flesh hitting flesh brought bile to the back of my throat. I felt a hand on my shoulder pulling me back and Jett's chiseled face looked down at me.

"Back up or you'll be trampled," he said, and we moved just in time to be missed by Ash and Slate.

Blood sprayed from a right hand hit to Slate's strong jaw and I gasped as it spread over my white dress. Slate's emotions bloomed in my head, and I swallowed the lump in my throat to keep from shouting out and trying to stop them from fighting. Jett kept his hand on my shoulder as he spoke.

"Slate is holding back, baby sis. He won't be using anymore force than necessary to teach him a lesson." Jett murmured roughly and gave me a reassuring squeeze.

Tawny winced again, and I brought my eyes back to Ash and Slate. Their hard faces bore snarls underneath the blood that poured forth from the wounds. Slate's wavy mane clung wet with his blood to spots on his skin, bruises and swelling was already beginning to show over Ash's trim torso. People were cheering, and I saw that they had started to grow sluggish.

I lost track of how long they were fighting, their bodies steamed in the winter air. I gnawed my lip, so my tongue probed my raw skin. Sage's eyes slid to me and Tawny and his pouty lips sneered. I imagined Amethyst went to bed with Cherry.

Slate and Ash slipped in the snow, raining blows down on one another and, finally, Ash fell. Slate didn't let up for an instant, Brass and Jett pulled Slate off Ash and my heart skipped when his face darkened.

My instinct was to check on Ash to make sure Slate hadn't done anything irreversible, but I stood frozen. Quartz and Sage were already by Ash; he was sitting in an instant, healed, and shooting a murderous glance at Slate who had refused to be healed and spat blood on the pure white snow.

Party goers sensed the end to the best part of the fight and began to head back into their drinks and dancing with the hope that they might find someone to warm their bed tonight. Slate prowled back and forth with bunched shoulders; he wanted Ash to come at him again. He was nowhere near finished.

"Maybe you can convince him to go inside now," Tawny said, floating over to where Steel checked on Ash and went back to Slate.

Slate's eyes swiveled on me, and Brass ducked his head and murmured a few words to Slate. Slate's corresponding smile grew full of salacious intent, but it wasn't a kind smile with the amount of blood staining his white teeth. My feet backed away of their own volition when he fixed his predatory eyes on me. I could feel his intentions through the bond.

"Party is over, Torch," he rumbled and I shook my head.

"Offer's expired," I retorted and Slate's chuckle was deep and hearty.

"I can catch your scent from here," he replied and started to stalk towards me.

Ash stood in my periphery, and I saw Sage and Quartz try to hold him back, but he stalked towards us.

"When, Scarlett?" Ash asked and I knit my brow.

Slate spun towards Ash with the intention of pummeling him, but I held up my hand. "When what?"

"When did you give yourself to him? Did you not think he tried harder than necessary to keep us apart? That the moment he sensed your weakness, he pounced? You were not thinking clearly then, and you are in too deep to see clearly now. He has you..." Ash stabbed his index finger into his palm and clenched it into a fist.

It was the first time Ash had shown anything other than arrogance and disdain concerning what happened between us since I caught the glimmer of hurt when it ended, and it shocked me. Most of the party goers had gone back to their drinking and vanished inside; the few who remained were busy recounting the fight or watching us like a train wreck.

I took a step in Ash's direction. "Ash, I'm sorry."

Ash shrugged off Sage and Quartz walking to where I stood holding Slate's weapons. Brass and Jett stood in Slate's path preventing him from coming between us. Ash's light green eyes locked on mine.

"He saw how pure you were and could not help himself. It is in his nature to defile; you should have been smarter." Ash leaned forward so only I could hear his words. "You were untouched when we were together, Scarlett. That is why I waited until you were ready. You shamed yourself and me by lying with that humorless wretch," He spat.

My stomach heated as the acids within churned. "Slate wasn't my first, Ash," I whispered.

"What?" he snarled. I told him I had been with someone, he assumed it was Slate. "Who?" he ground out.

My eyes betrayed me. Brass stood with Slate and Jett. It could only be one person.

Ash scoffed incredulously. "Him? The middle son of a lesser family? A *Regn*," he said Brass's family name in disgust. "I was wrong about you. All Tio women are the same."

My face was on fire, the insides seemed to be melting my brain since I just stood there mutely staring at him. "What's done is done. There's no point —"

Ash's hand whipped about, and my cheek stung. Not hard, but enough to do what he'd intended. I'd never been struck by any man unless we were sparring, and I'd expected it. It shamed me. I heard Slate roar and Ash glanced up to him before stalking off into the night towards the Straumr cottage. Jett could barely hold Slate back from going after Ash.

Brass had a look I'd only seen twice on his handsome face as he briskly walked after Ash. I leapt in front of his path until he was dragging me over the ice.

"Please don't," I squeaked.

Tawny ran to my side and her healing warmth flooded me, but it hadn't been needed. The sting was there, but I wasn't injured.

"He slapped you," she said wide eyed. "I can't believe he slapped you!"

Steel had gone after Ash, and I could hear him arguing with Ash and Sage. "... tell the council about your abuse." Steel bit off and Ash rebuked in a snarl.

The men glared at one another before Steel walked back to where we stood. "How's the cheek?" Steel's dark blonde hair was haphazardly tousled as he looked down at me with concern.

My fingers lifted to the soft skin of my cheek where a phantom sting lingered. Slate grabbed my wrist roughly, turning me to him and he pressed his lips to the spot I was struck. Brass faded into the background.

"He took his anger out on you. Why did you not strike him back, Torch?" Slate's lips brushed my ear as he pulled me close. Despite the freezing air, his hard body was hot.

The others trickled back inside leaving Slate and I alone in the moonlight. "I'm sorry. Where's Brass? I didn't mean to oust him."

"Come inside. I believe you were the one who wanted to keep him a secret. He is not the kiss and tell sort. While being the first man to have been with you may have occurred sub rosa, Brass is hardly ashamed. Your timing could have been better."

Katydid. No one wanted to hear the man they were with had been with another woman *ever*.

Slate slid his arm around my waist and brought me into the cottage as I fell into a deep puddle of self-loathing.

I let him lead me up to our master suite; he grabbed a carafe of wine as we went. Slate closed the door behind us and took his weapon belts from me, tossing them over a jacquard chair. He undressed himself until his tall muscular body was bared before me. His calloused finger rubbed at the spots of blood on my dress before he took the hem and pulled it over my head and brought me over to the bed.

Slate climbed on top of me forcing my body onto the bed. "Having regrets about your former lover?"

"Don't ask questions you don't want to hear the answers to," I said pertly.

"You thought that boy from the theater took your maidenhood?" he asked, looking down at me.

I nodded as I let myself relax beneath him. Slate popped the clasp between my breasts and slid my arms from its loops before lowering his head to my hips.

"I deserved Ash's slap. I was supposed to marry him. I never should have slept with Brass. I cheated on him with you."

Slate's teeth grazed my skin snagging on the elastic and he tugged down slowly, like he'd down our first night together. "Do not let the Straumr boy's words bother you. I told you he broke hearts. When the portals to the islands were opened, he deflowered half the lesser family girls without a second thought. Crimson, Jonquil, her younger sister, Quartz, as well as a few others. It is his favorite sport. I could not let you give yourself to him knowing all that and I could not tell you without sounding petty." He looked at me speculatively. "You finally admit it?" he asked in a low, dangerous rumble.

I lifted my hips from the forest green velour bedding as he tugged my panties over my backside. I didn't regret it; if I hadn't been with Brass or Slate, I would never have slept with Ash either. My first time would have been with the Merfolk king. While that made for an interesting story, I never regretted Brass for a second. He was the right choice my first time, or the first dozen, and I was in love with Slate. He overwhelmed my senses every minute I spent with him, he always had. I was ashamed to be that foolish girl blinded by a man, but here I was.

Slate saw whatever answer he needed to in my eyes when he crawled up my legs and closed his eyes, his long thick lashes fanning across his bronze cheeks before he lowered his mouth to mine.

"Thank the gods you gave yourself to me, Scarlett. That you relinquish your body to my keeping. You are mine," he purred.

"You are mine," I breathed.

We melded together and my thoughts vanished. Slate had taken Ash striking me remarkably well, too well. I hoped Ash and his group would be gone before we awoke. Though judging by how amorous Slate was, it would be a late morning and I was glad for it.

CHAPTER 35

INDIGO

Sterling and I were well practiced at sneaking away, but that was before Silver. He'd been so supportive I was having a difficult time leaving his side no matter how many looks Sterling was giving me to follow him.

Silver was the only man I'd been seen with in public. It was mostly uncomfortable for me, but I did get him a matching costume. When I'd brought it out for him, he'd stripped me down where I stood in the Vetr guest room and taken me up against the wall with Tawny and Steel walking down the hall.

I had never been with them both in a day. I didn't know if I could.

Sterling's violet eyes met mine again, and he gave a nod towards the door. Silver's hand was laced through mine and my stomach twisted. Diamond sat on the sofa chair Sterling leaned against, speaking to Garnet and Amber. If I left Silver's side, Garnet would jump on the opportunity to take my place. I'd been watching Silver intently to catch him making eyes at her so it would alleviate some of my guilt, but he never did.

The urge to relieve myself granted me an opportunity to think without Silver and Sterling in my line of sight. I stood and ran my fingers over Silver's short hair at the back of his head. The only part of his hair he'd let me touch. It was the only affection I'd give him in public.

"Be right back. I'm going to the little girl's room," I told him so he wouldn't think I was sneaking off with Sterling.

"Truth," he beamed that smile that maddened me and melted me all at once. "Hurry back," he said, and his eyes flitted unwittingly to where Garnet and Sterling were near.

I gave him a reassuring smile before fluffing my blonde curly wig and sashaying over to the bathroom. He chuckled until I turned the corner were my whole body seemed to slump once the tension of being before them both dissipated.

After I relieved myself, I pulled up short when I opened the bathroom door and Sterling filled the door frame. "Oh!" I averted my eyes. "You surprised me."

"Come. We will go out the window," Sterling rasped, grabbing my hand and leading me to the nearest bedroom.

I laughed, thinking he was joking. "Right. Silver would love that."

"Garnet sat in your seat before the bathroom door shut. He is who he is. You knew his reputation before you laid with him." Sterling hadn't even looked back as he dragged me into the bedroom.

He opened the window and slung his legs out one at a time before hopping out and reaching up for me. My brows were knit. Silver had let her fill me spot before it had even grown cold. I'd been letting him do whatever he wanted. All my rules out the window and he knew how hard that had been for me.

For the gods' sakes, I had let him persuade me to take me to a darkened corner of the Shadow Breaker night club. I braced myself on the window's ledge and Sterling smiled as he lifted me through. He didn't set me down on my feet before he began kissing me. We'd been together once since Silver and I started... whatever. The day of my father's funeral when I had been a complete wreck.

"Frigga's sweet grass," Sterling murmured pulling on my spandex pants.

"Sterling!" I hissed at his recklessness. "Anyone could walk past."

He rested his forehead against mine as he collected himself. He couldn't afford to be caught with me.

"You are right," he conceded and grabbed my wrist as he started to jog towards the Tio cottage.

"Sterling!" I yelled as I slipped and slid over the ice behind him.

"Indi. I need to be inside you. I missed you. Quick is not the man for you," he said slowly to shake his head at me before he continued his ankle breaking pace.

I couldn't agree more.

"I must go. I have stayed too long as it is." Sterling ran his hand over my bare back, rousing me from my slumber.

Since I started seeing Silver, Sterling acted as if he had something to prove. He didn't. I would love him forever and a day. Our affair had worn me out and I'd fallen asleep, missing most of the party.

"Okay. Be careful on the ice," I warned him and he bent down to brush his lips over mine.

"I love you, Indi," he said, brushing my brow.

"I love you too, Sterling. I promise I'll make more time for you."

"That is all I ask," he purred before leaving me alone in the Tio guest room.

I fumbled around in the dark too exhausted to summon a globe of light and searched for a something to wear. I found a pearl buttoned nightgown that could have belonged to my mother. It smelled like her; jasmine and roses.

I sighed as I opened the bedroom door and let out a yelp when I came face to face with Silver. He glowered at me. He must have just gotten there, or I would've heard an altercation between Sterling and him. Unless Silver hadn't spoken. Sterling would ignore him.

"How are you going to spend more time with him?" he spat.

"By spending less with you. You hardly missed me. He said Garnet was all too happy to sit in my spot before my back was even turned," I snapped, pushing past him to find a bathroom.

"You were sneaking off with Sterling!"

I whirled on him and pushed his hard chest with both hands. "No. You knew it was the truth when I said I had to go to the bathroom. You lied to yourself to justify doing what is in your nature." I shook my head. "Forget it. We're not discussing this. Tomorrow we can pretend like tonight never happened. It holds no bearing on us whatsoever."

I climbed the stairs ahead of Silver and he growled in frustration, following me. Gods, I did not want to do this right now.

THIRTY-SIX

The night was still high when I snuck into the bathroom. Slate stirred and groped the empty bed but fell back to sleep before fully rousing. I crept out into the hall after I pulled on the night dress I'd brought but hadn't worn.

I was on my way back to the master suite when I heard footsteps in the hall. I froze with the door partially open and the lights off.

"He is going to marry her this year. She was here tonight, and you fucked him anyway."

"It's none of your business. Garnet was a fine substitute; you don't have any reason to complain," Indigo said harshly back to Quick.

I covered my mouth to mask my breathing and stepped into the dark room. I wished I could see them. It sounded like Quick punched the wall and I flinched.

"Garnet is a girl. Not a woman. Why do you waste your time? You waste *my* time," Quick said fiercely.

"You knew what you were getting into when you started coming to my bed. I haven't made you any promises and I don't want any in return. You're blowing this out of proportion. We have fun. What I do with Sterling is my business and has nothing to do with you. I don't ask what you do with your women; Garnet, and Ama, and Shale and all the others. I never ask," Indigo defended.

"Ama and Shale? Just fun, they know it. Same with Garnet —"

"I don't care, Silver," Indigo interrupted. "I'm in love with Sterling. I like you, Silver. I thought we were having fun; you don't want anything serious and neither do I."

"I am a distraction for you," Quick said in disbelief.

"A welcome distraction. I care about you, Silver, but it doesn't affect what I have with Sterling."

"What happens after he marries her? What then, Dove? You become his paramour? Who will continue your family's line? Would you have bastard children just to keep him?" Quick said in a rough tone.

"When they get married things will change. I have a year to figure things out. What are you doing?" Indigo's voice whispered.

Shifting fabric and boots on wood floors scuffed. "What does it look like, Dove?" Quick said, and I shifted uncomfortably in my hiding spot.

Indigo moaned, "Silver, we shouldn't... We can't."

Her protests sounded feeble even to me and I heard fabric tear, and something bounce onto the floor and roll away. "I am capable. Are you?" Quick growled, and I heard Indigo gasp.

"Gods, this is so wrong," she breathed roughly and he chuckled low and dark.

"Does it feel wrong?" Quick's voice was gruff and strained.

I bit my lip and chanced a peek into the darkened hall. Moonlight poured through the cottage window, and I could make out the outline of Quick pressing Indigo's back against the wall, her long legs wrapped around his waist as he moved. Those had been her nightdresses buttons that rolled away. One pearl button sat at the threshold of the bathroom door where I stood hiding. I felt like a pervert trying not to hear their lovemaking and thanked the gods I'd not taken the rousen yet.

They eventually stumbled their way into an unoccupied bedroom, and I ran from the bathroom and back into the master suite to find Slate with his big arms crossed behind his head with an amused smile on his lips.

"They always make up," he rumbled as I climbed back into bed.

"Yeah, but is it usually after they'd both slept with other people? Honestly, what is Indigo thinking? I feel like I should say something to her, but where do I start?" I rolled onto Slate's midsection, and he produced a dreaded purple vial from behind his head.

"Few more days at most," he said as I uncorked it and drank it down.

"You might need to do some of that coercing now that I don't need to be drugged," I teased.

Slate growled biting down on his lower lip as he pulled me up to his face. "Did I ever tell you about the part of my prophecy that concerned you? How would I know for certain if it were you if I did not already know?"

I frowned as he kissed me chastely, "No, but I remember you mentioning it."

"The girl from the prophecy would fall in love with me." He smirked, and I narrowed my eyes at him.

"No wonder you're so arrogant. Everyone would be if they had a guaranteed lover waiting for them."

"Love strikes the Time; Tide loses a bride.

In lust and distrust, her heart turns to dust.

Beg and Plead!

Fight for the light!

Else, fade to the shadows and welcome the blight."

Like Time was a translation for Tio, so was Straumr for Tide.

He wrapped his arms around me, and I settled my ear against his sculpted chest. "That's the prophecy about Ash too," I noted. "You should have told me before."

"I thought you would assume I made it up so you would bed me. Prophecies cannot be stopped, Torch. It would not have done any good."

"I suppose you think you're done enough begging and pleading?"

Slate chuckled, "I only do one thing well on my knees."

I smiled as I melted into my complicated man.

CHAPTER 37
GYPSUM

"Chief. That squirrel of yours is watching us," Diamond panted.

I cursed. Drill-tooth was his name. He was on the lookout for me. If he was there, Sterling and Indigo had either fallen asleep or he was already on his way to the Haust cottage where Diamond was not.

Diamond placed her hand over mine at her hip and I sighed ceasing my movements. "They are done. I must go wash before he catches your scent on me."

I fell back on the bed as she shifted to face me. She didn't though. She slid right off the bed and collected her costume. I waved to Drill-tooth in the window and the fuzzy squirrel jumped from the window. He didn't care if he saw us nude. It meant nothing to him.

"Sorry. You know how it is," she said zippering her dress.

I did. It was only okay while Sterling did it, though I did see her more often than Sterling saw Indigo. I never thought I'd be hoping Indigo left Silver. Diamond said it had been like a game of Double

Dutch. Diamond didn't know what Double Dutch was, but as she described it Sterling was always waiting for the right moment to approach Indi and get her to come back to his bed. Silver had been occupying too much of her time.

"Don't marry him. You're a grown woman, make your own choice. I'm heir to the Sumar Patriarch."

I realized the implications of my words, but she turned with a slight smile and came to sit next to me. My marriage proposal meant nothing to her. She kissed me softly and tucked her thick chestnut hair behind her ear.

"It is inevitable, I will not disgrace my family. Nothing must change between us. We have been together for over a year now." She looked down the length of me and her smile turned suggestive, "I could finish you off."

I pulled the sheet over my hips and turned on my side, "No thanks."

I didn't care if I was pouting. Diamond only sighed and left me where I laid, feeling used and stupid. I was her retaliation. She cared about me, but she didn't take me seriously.

It was no picnic being in love with someone knowing they didn't see you as you saw them. That she never once thought about a future with me beyond the bedroom.

I kicked off the sheet and checked the wound clock on the bedroom wall. It wasn't even midnight. I could hear the party still going on. I grabbed my Captain Jack Sparrow costume off the floor and dressed. The night was young.

Ama and Shale were dressed as a mouse and a cat, they spotted me coming down the stairs and Ama beckoned me onto the dance floor. I held up a finger as I went into the kitchen to get a drink winding my way around the drunken tyros.

I took a shot of something a girl passed me that burned going down and poured myself a glass of whiskey on the rocks. I leaned against the far kitchen wall, slamming my drink and hoping to numb my rampant brain.

"You took her maidenhood, Brass." I could hear Katydid's soft words that ended in a sniffle. "I do not understand why she would be trying so hard to get us together. Why am I here?"

"We were not together then, Katy. We have not been together for over a year. You could not make up your mind and I did not fault you. I told you we would remain friends and encouraged you to be sure I was who you wanted. You are here because she likes you and thinks you will make me happy. She wants me to be happy. I have always enjoyed your company, Katy. You know that."

"You want me here?" she asked cautiously, with another sniffle.

"I want you here if you want to be here. Are you having fun?" he asked.

"I am. Kiss me, Brass. I want you to make love to me tonight," Katydid pushed.

I thought I heard Brass sigh. "Katy, I would be doing us both a disservice if I gave into our urges."

"One last night. Something to remember you by." Katydid's tone had changed, from wounded to wanting.

I didn't wait for Brass's response. I'd eavesdropped long enough, and Ama was crooking her finger at me from the entrance of the kitchen. I poured myself another drink and strode over to her.

"Shale wants to lose her virginity to you," Ama said, looping her arm through mine.

I spit my drink out at a passing guy who Ama apologized to for me as I collected myself.

"She is not really a virgin. Fox got as close as any man has gotten after a late-night training on the battle grounds and I have used... well, it will not be typical. She has just never had —"

"Yeah, Ama. I get it," I spluttered.

Fox Straumr had apparently given a lot of late-night training to tyro girls. Still did, if rumors were to be believed. I almost felt bad for Novac-ulite. Almost, but not really.

"Why now?" What I wanted to ask was why me.

Ama pulled my arm against her considerable bosom. If she'd been in the States, she could've been one of those half-dressed models in the magazines and she was all natural. Rare for one whose waist could be circled by my hands with my fingers touching.

She was leading me back upstairs. "Because she knows how much I love sleeping with you and she finds you attractive. The only man she has found so. You also know how to keep your mouth shut. I do not think she wants anyone knowing she has slept with a man. She's the Sandr heir and their little secret does not want a husband, but she will eventually need a child."

Ama laughed when I balked.

"Not with you. Practice. I am going to be there. She is my girlfriend, after all."

Ama opened the door to the bedroom I'd been in with Diamond and light shown on Shale's back. She laid on her side across the bed and when she turned around, her sheen of black hair fell across her shoulders.

"Take off your clothes. I have seen all the ways you have taken Ama. If I am going to try this, I want it all done. Tonight," Shale said, turning her cool gaze on me.

Ama was already undressing me around my drink, giggling all the while. "Do not worry. You will not be disappointed, Shale. Will she?"

I stammered. "I'll try my best."

Shale's lips pulled to the side in a knowing smirk. "Yes, that is what I am hoping." Her eyes dropped between my legs, and I fought the urge to cover myself. "Freya's burly boar." Shale cursed.

"You are not a true maiden, Shale." Ama giggled.

I was a prop. I was *always* a prop.

Ama gave me a little nudge, and I lifted each foot so she could take off my boots and pull off my pants. I still had my drink, so I downed it before Ama took it and placed it on the dresser.

Ama gave me a shove forward, and I staggered forward, aware that despite my bewilderment, I was ready for Shale. She was a striking woman and while I had not done much interaction with her while we had both been with Ama, I had kissed her several times before.

She rolled onto her back and looked up at the ceiling before I reached the bed as if she was talking herself into it. Shale adjusted her legs as I climbed onto the bed.

"You really want to do this?" I asked dubiously.

Shale's eyes rested on my face and then darted down to my lap. She sucked in a breath.

"I am twenty-three years old and have never lain with a man. I trust you. Ama trusts you. And you are pretty with girlish hair. I have also felt your skilled mouth. If the rest of you is half as skilled, it will be good." She waved to me to crawl up her tautly muscled body.

"Chief." Shale shook me awake.

Ama was asleep on my other side, my arm held in her hands at her chest. Shale searched my eyes in the dark and I carefully slid my arm from under Ama's head. Shale was so petite I thought I would crush her when I rolled on top of her.

Her hands wound through my hair as she pulled my mouth down. She had fully emerged herself into trying out a man for the night.

"Slowly." She coaxed, guiding me into her.

Ama had grown jealous. I had no idea how to deal with two lovers being the third wheel. Shale had been a maiden in name only and had relished being the focus for once. Ama had thought she would be needed to help Shale along. Shale had taken charge telling me exactly what she wanted me to do, and I had incorporated my own knowledge. It was awkward with Ama watching and not participating so when she started pouting with her arms crossed at the edge of the bed, I was grateful she wanted to join us.

Shale took Ama's usual position, and we'd continued.

Shale pulled me until our bodies were melded. It was love making and Shale was encouraging it. I felt Ama stir and her hand slide over my backside as she turned Shale's mouth away from mine.

I'd slept with three women in one night. Who the hell was I?

CHAPTER

THIRTY-EIGHT

Surprisingly, Amethyst, Ama, and Shale woke up early and made breakfast in the Sumar cottage. Quick and Indigo were back to their normal awkward tension. What I hadn't anticipated was Brass and Katydid. Katydid was moon-eyed and gooey at Brass's side. He must have been very apologetic last night.

I wondered if I was equally obnoxious since Slate was determined to treat me as a tavern wench. No, Slate was the obnoxious one. Odd thing though, I couldn't stop smiling.

With Ash completely forgotten, eating as one big family, with laughter bouncing off the walls and smiles all around. I never thought I would've felt complete after my mom died, after my father died... but I felt... better. Not great, but good.

Even the walk back under the bright morning sun reflecting off the snow was a joy. Slate spent a good deal good of time smiling his rare smile that was infectious. Jett was in a terrific mood, extraordinary for him as of late. He'd been in a sour mood ever since the Wild Hunt chal-

360

lenge. None could blame him. He spent a good amount of time rubbing Amethyst's ever-growing belly in a way that made my rotted womb ache. Cherry and Ama had become fast friends, which was a recipe for disaster, as they walked together.

Gypsum was the only one whose happiness looked forced. Whatever happened between Diamond and him last night must have gone poorly. Since Indigo didn't spend all night with Sterling, I only needed one guess to imagine what that must be. They were playing a dangerous game. All of them.

After a brief lunch in Valla, we went our separate ways. My family went back to the Sumar palace where we showered and lounged about until dinner. I had my rendezvous with Cordillera, and I'd been masking my thoughts from Brass all afternoon. I made love to my domineering, bronze god and concocted a plan to evade said god.

We all sat down to dinner in the informal dining room; Hawk had come to spend the evening with us having ended the reconstruction for the day. Slate and I rivaled Tawny and Steel with the affection we paid one another at the table, which the others had chosen to ignore. All except Sparrow.

Sometimes I thought maybe I wasn't as observant as I fancied myself. I didn't like truths I wasn't ready for, so I avoided them like a Jorogumo web. That night was no different; discussions with Sparrow while I was with Slate had begun to take on an uncomfortable tension.

Sparrow was brimming with impatience at the table. Pearl felt it too. We both kept glancing at her waiting for her to speak. Hawk seemed to be frustrated as well, but it seemed directed at Sparrow. While Gypsum went on about his first week at his school, it built until I shifted in my seat uncomfortably, hoping it would end soon.

"The Dagr palace should be fully functional at the end of the month. Have you given anymore thought to moving in?" Sparrow asked abruptly at the end of Gypsum's story.

Her brown eyes fixed on Slate.

I swung my head to Slate, furrowing my brows. I knew Sparrow and Hawk had asked Gypsum to move in with them, and gave Tawny and Steel the option, too. Tawny and Steel were moving into the Vetr castle once Tawny was proven tried and true, so they had declined. Why Slate would move in made no sense to me.

Slate went rigid and shifted his eyes down the table towards Sparrow, who leaned forward to meet his gaze.

"I have a home here," he said in a low, measured tone.

Jett and Steel seemed to understand something the rest of us didn't. Pearl pursed her lips but kept silent. I watched with silent irritation at being kept out of the loop.

"Of course. We only feel that since the situation has changed, your heritage does not need to be guarded any longer," Sparrow hesitated, "Then there is the matter of continuing the line."

Slate went impossibly still. "We should discuss this in private." He and Hawk started to rise, but Sparrow persisted.

"Scarlett should know."

"Know what?" I said quickly. I needed to know.

It was eating me alive, not knowing what they were talking about.

"No," Slate growled.

"Scarlett, Slate is —"

"NO!" Slate slammed his hands on the table, making everyone jump. "She has been through enough. She does not need this over her head as well."

Jett fell back in his chair and ran his hand over his face before looking at me with something in his turquoise eyes that looked like... an apology? My stomach grew heavy as if the food I'd dined on had suddenly hardened into heavy stones.

"I can decide what I can handle. Thanks for your concern, Slate, but I'm a big girl. What should I know?" I asked Sparrow.

Sparrow's eyes looked at Slate whose body was bunching with tensed muscles in anger and she sucked in a deep breath. "I love you like a daughter, Scarlett. I would never want to do anything to upset you, but I cannot do this on my own. I need Slate's help and perhaps you can help convince him."

"I can try..." I said warily and lifted my eyes back to Slate, who was still standing.

"I will not, Sparrow. It is not up for discussion," Slate ground out.

I put a hand on his and he tensed further. Gods, what was this secret?

Indigo's blue eyes were wide with worry as she looked at me, but in them I saw she would comfort me if it was as bad as they were making it seem. Tawny let out a groan of frustration.

"Out with it already, Mom."

"Slate is Slate Haust, a Dagr. Slate Dagr since you took Vetr's name. His children would be the heirs to the Dagr family. He's my nephew, my sister's son, and your cousin," she told Tawny and Gypsum.

My mouth fell open. A Haust? A Dagr? The last Dagr able to reproduce and have an heir.

Lark Haust's son with Sea Dagr? My mother had adopted her Guardian husband's true son and raised him as her own. There were secrets on top of secrets with that one admission. My mother had known and Slate had outright lied.

My blood ran cold as realization dawned on me.

I couldn't have heirs. Slate was the Dagr's last chance to continue their line. Slate needed to have children and not with me. The Stygians had taken away my chance at giving Slate an heir. My shoulders bowed as the pain in my heart was almost too much to bear.

"You're as white as a ghost, baby sis. Need some water?" Jett said, his handsome chiseled face etched with concern.

I shook my head. I felt betrayed. Again. Slate should have been the one to tell me. I should not have said the blood vow to him. He definitely shouldn't have said it to me.

"Can you use a surrogate or something? People do that outside of Tidings all the time," I said sounding weak and despondent.

Slate's silver eyes flew to Sparrow, but she met them levelly. "I do not want children. We have gone over this. Nothing has changed."

Lie.

It was the one thing Slate couldn't hide from me when we made love. I could feel his need to fill me with his seed and to bear his children, it was a deep sadness in him when we laid intertwined in one another's arms that I'd ignored countless times. Perhaps it was his way of mourning the one we lost, but it was there. My stomach was doing flips causing the acids to splash, burning in my gut painfully. I couldn't give him what he needed.

"We could try that," Hawk said, forcing a smile onto his olive face, but his eyes said otherwise.

Sparrow looked anguished when she spoke. "In truth, the chances of a woman willing to give up her rights to a child that would be heir to the Dagr family is slim and the more children, the more secure the line's future."

Another woman having Slate's children. That was what it all boiled down to.

"That makes sense," I said feeling defeated.

"No, Torch. No children. I do not want the Dagr or Haust name. It will not leave this room." Slate glared around the table at anyone daring to say otherwise and was not met with any objection.

"It is something to consider, darling. That is all. Sparrow means well. It is her family we are speaking of. You have been raised as a Sumar and a Tio, but the Dagr line was once proud, and you could keep it strong. It was your mother's line, her family and Sparrow's. We loathe to see it disappear. Indigo and Amethyst are faced with the same problems," Pearl said, her torque clinked on the wood table as she gestured to the girls on the opposite ends of the table.

Amethyst looked to Indigo. "If I have a girl, she will be a Geol, my mother's line. The last Geol."

Indigo chewed her lower lip. She was the last Tio female. The closing of the University had caused so much damage to the families. A shortage of marriages, ambassadors, and training had stretched far. An appalling thought popped into my head before I could stop it.

Maybe Indigo and Slate could solve one another's problems and we could raise the children together. The thought made me so sick to my stomach, bile rose into my throat.

No, better a stranger than someone I had to face.

I needed to get some fresh air. The emotions in the room were oppressive and I couldn't look at Slate for another second. I rose shakily to my feet and Slate grabbed for my elbow to steady me. I flinched away from him, and he pressed his full lips into a hard line.

"I need to be alone," I said with a tremor in my voice.

"Do not do this. Do not run, Rabbit," Slate said in a low rumble so only I would hear him.

"Scarlett, I am so sorry," Sparrow said, rising to her feet to comfort me and I held my hand up.

I didn't want to be touched. I couldn't stand the idea of being touched. If someone placed their hand on me, I would scream. The others looked at me with expressions that ranged from horrified to somber. Everyone understood the implications of Sparrow's words.

Slate and I were not meant to be.

I could not be the matriarch of his home; another woman would be. Another woman would have everything I ever wanted with the man of my dreams. Literally. Without warning, I was livid. Slate should never let me get so close, to lull me into this false sense of happiness and security that didn't truly exist.

He was not mine.

My ears heard, but voices sounded underwater. I leadenly left the dining room and headed towards the portal to escape the inescapable. My heart had double-crossed me. My brain knew Slate was just about the worst a decision as I could make, and my heart had somehow won.

Stupid foolish heart.

The blurred starry lights welcomed me as I walked to the blazing sun door. The bright white light engulfed me, and I closed my eyes as I walked through.

CHAPTER 39
JETT

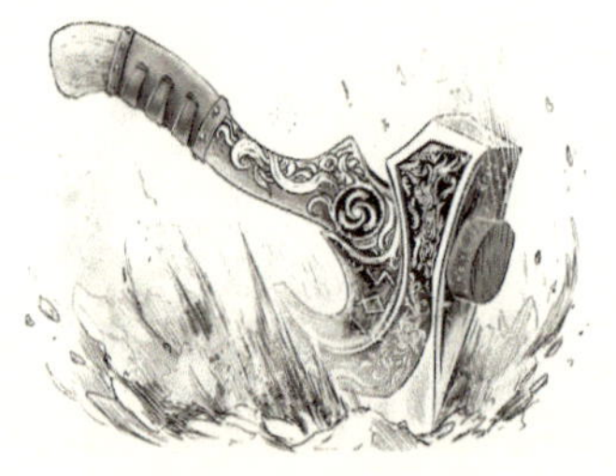

"Well, that was handled with all the delicacy of a bull in a china shop. Now Slate, go find a suitable wife, forsake my sister, and have lots and lots of babies you don't want with a woman you don't love. Excuse me." Jett rose to his feet, his tanned cheeks red with fury and Amethyst grabbed his hand.

"Let her get some air," Amethyst clamped down on his wrist and he sighed nodding.

"I'm sorry, Slate. We are well past our age of fertility; it is the simple truth. We need you. Tidings and the Guardians need you to continue the line. Don't let the Dagr die out, please. The line won't continue without you," Sparrow pleaded rising to her feet.

"Without Scarlett? Abandon her as Ash did because she could not bear children?" Slate ground out.

Steel and Jett met eyes and they started carefully rounding the table. Slate's head was canted towards his plate, but they knew what would happen next. Slate could not contain his anger when it came to Scarlett. Ash was lucky that Slate hadn't torn out his throat after he struck her. Only Brass and Jett kept Slate from attacking him again. Them, and

Scarlett keeping him company all night so he wouldn't break into the Straumr cottage and kill them all. They had no idea what they were dealing with.

Hawk sighed and ran his hand over his silver hair. "We will help Scarlett find a husband if she wishes. You choose the woman; we are not trying to force you to marry now. A marriage would be ideal, but not necessary if she would be amenable to a different arrangement."

"I can't believe what I'm listening to. What about Scarlett? Fine. Slate goes off and marries one of his floozies, but who will she find? Everyone knows what she's been through."

Tawny's eyes were brimming with tears. She was no fan of Slate's, but he made Scarlett happy so she would fight with everything she had for her happiness.

"He's already married her," Jett said, sinking into a chair to Slate's right.

He heard a few of them gasp and leaned forward taking a goblet, sloshing wine over the top before he put it to his lips. Drinking deeply before looking at the top of Slate's head.

Pearls coiffed copper curls shifted as she gazed at Slate with anguish in her emerald cat eyes. "Slate?"

"It is true," Slate rumbled.

Tawny and Indigo let out twin gasps and covered their mouths while Hawk hung his head. "You married Scarlett without permission from your family?"

"We said blood vows."

Sparrow let out a little groan and covered her face. The secret was out, and Scarlett didn't even know. As far as Jett knew, she hadn't told a soul. Judging from Tawny's face, he was right. Scarlett was not going to be happy. Jett doubted she knew yet just how deep she was with Slate.

Sparrow removed her hands from her face and shook her head. "No one else knows. There is still a chance we can find matches for you both."

"Mom! This is Scar we're talking about. She's married, and you want her husband to have children with someone else?" Gypsum was incredulous and staring at Sparrow as if he'd never seen her before. "How'd you like if Dad had to do that to you?"

Sparrow cringed at that; Hawk put his hand on Sparrow's. "If I were

the last Sumar and your mother could not have children, we would do
what we had to. That is why Ash turned Scarlett down in the first place,
it's why she'll have to be with someone who does not come from a
greater family. We don't like it any more than you do."

"No. I do not want children. I will not be with another woman. Scarlett is mine and no other man will have her," Slate said roughly before
standing and balling his hands into fists.

"You won't let your mother's family line die off," Steel said.

"Leave your wife and let her have children with another man; then I
will listen to your argument," Slate growled. "I have nothing left to say
on the subject. It is closed."

"Scarlett will listen. She already has," Indigo said and turned her
face to Slate. "I may not know her very well yet, but I saw the look in her
eyes. You should have told her, Slate. She should have known before she
promised herself to you." Indigo shook her corn silk hair. "She won't
stay with you. Not until you have an heir and likely not after, since that
reminder that she could've had your heir will be ever present."

Slate growled and Jett flew from his seat and grabbed Slate from
behind as Steel moved in front of Indigo. "Before the Merfolk took her!
When she can have another, so will I!" Slate's chest heaved as he calmed
himself. "She will forgive me, she always does."

Slate shrugged Jett off and stalked from the dining hall. Jett took
Slate's vacated seat and pulled his goblet over to him as Steel sat in
Scarlett's seat.

"You're right," Jett told Indigo, "Scar won't stay with him now. Not
how he wants. He keeps too many secrets from her."

"He does not think he will live long enough for his secrets to be
revealed." Pearl fretted. "My poor darlings, I will try to speak to Slate.
Scarlett may wish for her things to be returned to her room." She
pushed back from her upholstered seat, the flowing fabric of her bronze
dress draped off her shoulders. "I will see some of her clothing is back in
her room and have it prepared in case she returns."

Jett watched Pearl leave and blew out a long breath. Sparrow and
Tawny were having a heated argument across the table from one
another that Amethyst was starting to get in on.

"Sparrow is right. None of us chose who we were born to, but it
comes with responsibilities. Slate, you, me, Gypsum, Indigo, and even

Jett have an obligation to continue our family lines. Dagr, Vetr, Geol, Sumar, Var, and Sumar, all in one household. Your family was born to privilege, the only thing you need to do that no one can help you with is have a child or two."

Jett closed his eyes and let the back of his head rest on the chair. Amethyst would have been betrothed much younger if her mother had been alive. Dahlia might have tried, but Moon would never deny Amethyst anything.

"Okay. Since we're all plotting behind their backs anyway, who do you have in mind for them. Don't say no one, that's not how plotting works," Jett said leaning back in his chair. "Brass will help ease Scarlett's heartache. She's never gotten over him."

One look at Sparrow confirmed his suspicions.

FORTY

Valla was dusted in a powdering of snow; I was wearing a thin chiffon dress and no cloak, but I didn't feel the cold. I could thank my elemental power for that. I numbly walked the cobbled roads past the closing shops to the dead-end alley that hid the entrance to Shadow Breaker headquarters.

Once I was down the polished wood steps, the temperature grew warmer the closer I grew to the rumpus room. I stood beneath the low hanging lamps from the ceiling and smelled leather of the room. The sound of pool balls cracked against one another. My mind floated in a fog; every time my thoughts tried to gasp at anything, my fingers caught wisps of nothing.

Breakers played pool and sat on the scattered couches around the expansive loft room. There were card games going on, and people at the polished wood bar. My eyes scanned the room, and I spotted Ama and Shale playing darts against a set of muscular men that weren't Brass and Quick.

Before they could approach me, I walked across the wood floors and the dark rugs to the stairs at the far end of the room.

I walked up the stone steps running my hand up the wood and wrought-iron balustrade. It was cool to the touch and my heels clicked on the steps as I climbed to the highest floor.

I wasn't due to arrive for another two hours, but I had nowhere else to go. Chafer opened the door after a few minutes and his brows raised when he saw me waiting.

"Look what the cat dragged in," he said, confirming how bedraggled I was looking.

My lack of wit made the corners of his mouth turn down. Chafer kept his mouth shut as he opened the door further so I could duck beneath his arm and enter the long narrow hall. Walnut floors reflected the warm light of the sconces that lined the navy walls. Cordillera's bedroom door was open, and I knew what Chafer and she had been doing before I came.

If I had any doubt, walking in on Cordillera as she draped a red satin robe over her bare back put it to rest. She cast a dark glance over her shoulder us as we entered the room. She turned around and tied the sash, but not before giving me an eyeful of her flawless body and her unique tattoos.

"You are early," she rasped and disappeared into her closet.

I crossed the room to sit on the red couch that faced the wall. Chafer came to sit down next to me and crossed his ankle over his knee. He didn't bother to pretend like he wasn't staring at me.

"What happened?" he asked.

"Do you care?" I asked as my eyes slid to his.

He pointed at me with his index finger. "Good point."

Cordillera came out of her closet with two dresses; one black, one red, both long and slinky with long sleeves. She laid them on the big red bed and arched a manicured brow at me. I got up from the couch and went to the bed. She came back out with shoes, and undergarments for me. A black corset and a black pair of pumps were placed on the black dress.

I looked at Chafer, he was facing the far wall, his way of being kind. My clothes fell to the floor in my daze as I started hooking the corset and slipped the black dress over my head. The sleeves were off the shoulder, the bodice had heavy boning to prop up my... assets.

Cordillera changed and checked me over with scrutinizing eyes. "Sit," she ordered.

She gestured towards a chair near her vanity and I sat, lethargically styling my hair, and doing my make up. Cordillera came up behind me and started pinning my hair up in a loose chignon and tapped me on the shoulder with a tube of lipstick before walking away. I took the top off and applied a fire engine red lipstick to my full lips.

My skin looked paler than usual; my turquoise eyes red rimmed even though I hadn't cried yet. Yet. It was coming, I could feel it. I couldn't go back to our apartment, our bed. Make love to a man that I couldn't keep.

Like a tongue poking at a sore tooth, I recoiled from the painful thoughts, but I couldn't stop.

I rose from the seat and found Chafer and Cordillera watching me from where they sat on the couch. "Are you up for this?" she asked, pursing her lips.

Her room was warm with her rich musky feminine scent. My eyes were glazed over, I needed to divert my attention. Focusing on the Stygian Knights and revenge for my father, that I could fully divest myself in. They had stolen the life of Slate's heir and given me to the Merfolk rendering me unable to birth Slate's children, my children.

"I'm ready," I said blankly, and they got to their feet holding out a cloak and mask for me.

My mind was far away as I followed to the next room over. A studded wood carved door was against the dark grey wall. Chafer walked to it and turned the knob to reveal a bright white light. I gasped. It was a portal door.

"This has been here all along?" I asked, and Chafer chuckled.

"And now you know, that makes... six Shadow Breakers," Chafer said.

"She is not a Shadow Breaker; she is my delegate," Cordillera said, and started forward.

I internally rolled my eyes and walked through the portal door with Chafer.

My heart ached to be in Ostara. The smell of flowers in the air and fresh rain reminded me of my father and Brass. My mind recoiled again from the thoughts.

The Var castle glistened in the moonlight, making it look spun of white glass up on its pillar of stone. The globes that lined the bridge glowed blue in the night. Cordillera walked ahead of me with Chafer. I guessed it would be the three of us. The Stygians knew me and Chafer well. Chafer had been infiltrating the Stygian Knights' ranks for a year when he had been discovered. Brass and I had been there when it happened, and they only released us because I fought against a bies and killed it.

The crushed glittering white stones that made up the road crunched beneath our feet as we walked between the pastel homes and shops of Ostara. In the darkness, I couldn't make out the vivid flower beds that lined the road, but I knew we were coming to the purple flowering arches that led deeper into Ostara.

Cordillera turned down a road that wasn't lit and the atmosphere changed. Chafer's blade pommels stuck up over his shoulders. He slid each one into their sheath before stopping at a plain wooden door of a two-story home. They painted a red skull with a sickle onto the center of the very top of the door.

I checked my mask and repositioned my hood to cover my hair before Chafer tugged open the door. Red light filled a narrow hallway just as it had the time Brass had taken me. The fighting hadn't begun yet. We could hear the rabble jostling and shouting at one another. The very air felt tense and wrought with hostility. The crowd that came to the Stygians' fights were not as civilized as the one that came to watch the Shadow Breaker competition. These people wanted to see blood.

A flight that led up a floor emptied into a wooden arena of sorts with a pit at the bottom for fighters. They must have thrown it together at the last minute. Aside from the roped off area, cloaked men sat quietly with masks and the ring around the top level. The arena was completely different; not the dirty concrete and stone, but wooden. The house had been gutted and reconstructed recently to accommodate the pit and stands.

The topless waitresses holding trays of ale wandered about, being groped the same as last time, but it didn't stop Lera from removing her cloak and displaying her petite curves. I followed suit and felt the emotions rise around us. Chafer took Lera's arm and led her nearer to the roped off area as I followed behind.

I was wondering what the plan was when an arm looped through my arm and kept me walking. "Was there not a discussion about staying out of Stygian business?" Brass's smooth, deep voice growled in my ear.

"I didn't think you'd be here. That any of you would be here," I said, following behind Cordillera and Chafer.

They knew Brass was coming. They hadn't cast him so much as a second glance when he slid beside me. We were on his home island. It made sense that Brass would be there, smelling of spring rain and cinnamon. I kept my gaze straight ahead on my destination, not meeting the eyes that followed me. It wasn't often a fully dressed woman walked through Stygian Knights' pits.

"Here I am," Brass said simply and took my cloak from my arm.

Cordillera took a seat a level behind the roped area and Chafer sat down beside her, looking cruel with his sharp angular face. Brass walked before me to sit next to Chafer and sat me down next to him on the wood bench. Brass kept his arm around me as a topless woman offered us flagons that I shook my head at, but Brass took, flipping a coin onto her tray.

"What happened? You are as stiff as a board and masking your emotions from me," Brass said, leaning towards me so his ebony and bronze beads clicked in his thick dark hair.

"You'll find out soon enough. No need to rush it," I said, facing the pit, trying to ignore the rowdy crowd and the men who had likely orchestrated my father's death.

More masked men filed in around the top level to line the wall and I recognized one that started down towards the pit only to angle towards us and the roped off area. His brown beard framed his mouth under his mask and when he saw me even with my mask on, his lips parted in a lewd smile that made me feel as naked as the day he'd sliced the clothes off my body.

"You are a terrible actress, Scarlett," Brass whispered into my ear.

"They knew I would come. They don't even look surprised."

My mind ran through a million thoughts per second. I could kill the bearded man. I might kill a few of them before they realized I was an elemental. They were guilty by association, if not outright. I'd make their deaths swift. Brass shifted my shoulders and his amber eyes locked on mine.

"Your eyes," he whispered harshly, and I knew they were glowing like two hot coals. "Relax, Scarlett."

I tried to focus, tried to get it under control, but the more I thought, the hotter it burned. The noisy crowd made me feel like I was suffocating. Chafer cursed when he saw me past Brass and I shut my eyes. Then I felt Brass move closer.

I was still inhaling when his full lips pressed against mine. Brass's hand cupped my face and his nose rubbed against mine as he deepened the kiss. A whimper escaped my parted lips, and I felt the tears prick the back of my eyes. Brass's hand slid into my hair and his velvet tongue caressed as he swallowed my cry.

"Do not cry here," he breathed as he tugged on my lower lip with his teeth.

My fire was out, but the tears were going to fall.

"Stand," Brass said, and he took me by the elbow and hurried me to a shadowed hall. "You are leaving him," Brass said, propping me against the wall, covering me with his body so no one would see my tears.

Brass pulled a kerchief from his pocket and handed it to me. I dabbed at my face and a cloaked man started towards us. Brass nearly growled as he pushed my hand away gently and ducked his head, tilting my chin up to his. My lips molded to his as he kissed me again, deeper that time, forcing my mouth open wide. His hand slid to my nape while the other ran down my spine. Brass's emotions assailed me, and I gasped.

"Oh," I breathed as I pushed Brass softly away.

Brass rested his forehead on mine and apologized.

"For kissing me?" I asked, and he lifted his head with a warm smirk.

"No. For everything else, but never for kissing you," Brass said and lifted his forehead from mine. "Better?"

I nodded, "Better." I lifted my mask and wiped underneath at my tears.

Amber eyes searched mine, and I reached up to his stubbled jaw. Brass could read my mind easier when I touched him willingly, I could almost feel him scanning through my memories and when he was finished, he pulled me tight against him, letting me bury my face in the crook of his neck.

"He should have told you before anyone else had. He meant well, Scarlett. We thought you would be safer not knowing," Brass said, and I nodded.

I'd thought of all that myself. It didn't matter. Slate should have known better. He shouldn't have married me.

"Come, we will do this, and I will find you some chocolate ice cream after," Brass promised with a warm, genuine smile.

"That man with the beard by the roped-off section, he's one of the men —"

"I know. Ignore him. We are here to glean as much information as we can and see what they want. They invited Cordillera for a reason," Brass said, pushing my loose strands away from my face when I withdrew.

"Slate won't be happy you kissed me," I said, turning away from his big hand.

"He would be less happy if you were captured again. Not much makes Slate happy these days but you. He will not be happy that you are leaving him."

"What choice do I have? Stay with him and be responsible for the end of the Dagr line? I can't do that. I won't, and I won't be the other woman. Whoever he finds has a right to her happiness as much as I do. He's more than your friend. He's your cousin."

My words broke as I strangled them out of my rapidly closing throat. Brass's hair fell to graze his cheek when he cupped my face again and slanted his mouth over mine. It was a chaste kiss full of warmth and affection and none of the lust and frustration I felt earlier. It was like the kisses he'd given me before Slate and I were together. The kind that reaffirmed that I had given myself to the right man.

I whimpered as I felt my body melt against his. Was I never supposed to be with Slate? Should I have been with Brass the entire time?

"You needed to be kissed. Try not to think too much about it. I doubt Slate would forgive me for that one," Brass whispered and my cheeks heated.

"He wouldn't forgive either of us." I turned my head away from his lips that brushed mine when he spoke.

The first fight had begun. We could see some of the crowd on their feet and the sick sound of flesh hitting flesh of the combatants in the pit in tune with the punctuated cheers.

I licked my lips and looked at Brass, his dark honey face shadowed by his hair. He didn't look upset, only curious, and I pressed myself further against the wall, taking my hand from his face.

"I should have fought harder for you. When he broke into my room looking for you, you were going to be with me. Were you not? I sat by and let Slate take you after you came from the Merfolk. If you had taken me on that shore, Scarlett, I would never have let him have you."

I gasped, eyes widening as he continued.

"I live with it every day. I knew you loved him before you did, but I know you love me as well. It is the curse of being able to read others' minds. I do not need any heirs, and I know you may always be in love with Slate. Do not answer now. Take as much time as you need. Nothing else need change, it is only an offer I hope will make you happy and put your mind at ease. You will not be alone, Scarlett; I will always be here for you," Brass said and took a step forward so he pressed his body against mine.

I wouldn't be alone, I'd have Brass. Good and honorable Brass, who wouldn't have children of his own if he wanted to be with me. I could never do that to him. Brass would be a wonderful father.

Words failed me. I turned away from him and strode from the hall and back to our seats on the wooden bench. Cordillera and Chafer stared into the pit, not making a sign of noticing my return. Brass sank down next to me, close enough so our thighs touched, and I stared down at the fighters. Blood already sprayed the wood panels, but we could not tell who it was from since they were both wearing facial distorting rings they'd obtained from Styg.

The two men were bare chested and since there was no referee, there were no holds barred. They were skilled fighters, every kick and hit struck in quick precise movements, doing as much bodily damage as possible.

"I am not sorry," Brass said.

"What about Katydid?" I asked, not taking my eyes off the fighters.

"Katydid and I are not together. She has always had a hard time deciding. I told you once, if I were with someone, I would not go around kissing another woman. I do not kiss you whenever I want, you let me when I try. There is an enormous difference between the two."

"Guardian men and their words, how you love to play with them. You were with her last night, and this morning. With her," I said and watched the combatant go down after a roundhouse kick to the head.

I winced at the crunch the man's body made as it slid down the wall, leaving a streak of blood as it reached the floor. Money exchanged hands, and I grimaced as the victor spit blood on the ground before leaving the dead or dying man to bleed out.

If someone would approach us, it would be now. There would be a few minutes between matches.

Right on cue, the bearded man leaned back to smirk at me.

"I told them you would come. They did not think you survive Non're, but here you are. Stronger than ever, all that softness beat out of you." The bearded man stood and climbed up in front of Chafer, whose hand rested on his sword.

The bearded man scoffed. "Down, boy. We only wish to speak to the girl." He looked at me from under his cloak and Cordillera cleared her throat.

"Here she is," she said with a hint of irritation.

My heart pounded as the man placed his hand on my shoulder, gesturing for me to move. It would be a false sense of security to bring Brass with me, but I needed it anyway.

... Come with...

Brass rose as I did and nodded. Cordillera must have sent him a message. We didn't go far. A small room off the darkened hallway Brass and I had spoken in held four wing-backed chairs and nothing else. A second bearded man waited in the room and his eyes glittered from beneath his mask when he set his eyes on me.

"I almost did not recognize you with your clothes on," he said flatly and gestured to the seats.

I sat in the stiff chair across from the second bearded man while Brass stood behind me. The first bearded man crossed to sit in the other vacant seat and smirked at Brass.

"How are you these days, Scarlett? We know your engagement fell through. We expected the other one to escort you," the second bearded man said.

"As much as I appreciate the interest in my love life, get to the point," I spat.

The first one, who led us there, pressed his fingers tips together and smirked. He had a million-dollar smile that belonged on a red carpet, not making seedy deals in darkened rooms.

"Are your urges under control, Scarlett? I am surprised the other one lets you out with this one." He nodded to Brass, "I bet he does not even know you are here, much less together." He snickered. "I would not trust you two together. You can hardly keep yourself from jumping him. You think about it constantly. I can see it in your big khoraz eyes. Have you carnal knowledge of him, Scarlett? Where have those lips wandered over him? We can leave the room and return when your needs are fulfilled. You might be more amicable sated."

He was painting me a picture, trying to get the wheels turning so my pupils would dilate and my ceaseless fire would be stoked into a frenzy.

"Once again, get to the point," I ground out, barely able to control my rage.

The second's eyes darkened. "We want you to join us. Leave the Shadow Breakers and we can help you do things you have never imagined."

I pursed my lips as I glared at the two men and got to my feet. I met Brass's eyes as I turned around and he got the door for me.

"Think about it," one man said before I left the room.

I stopped on the threshold and pulled up my mask. "The day I join you is the day I sign over my soul."

The men chuckled and leaned forward with eerie synchronicity. "We helped make you who you are. Pushed you to your limit, and you survived. Think on it, Scarlett."

Brass closed the door after me and took my elbow in his hand. "I will go tell Cordillera we are leaving if she has not already left herself."

I nodded numbly and leaned against the wall of the upper level. A match was still going on in the pit, but my sight blurred. I felt light-headed. My world was coming down around my ears and there was no way the Stygians were going to let me go so easily. Just what they wanted with me eluded my grasp.

Brass startled me when he came to my side and started guiding me around the upper level past the crowd and topless ale girls back to the entrance. Did the Stygians want me to be one of their ale girls? Nothing was making sense.

"Scarlett?" Brass's face came into view, a crease formed between his thick dark brows.

My body swayed and Brass scooped me up off the floor as my lips moved, but nothing came out.

"I have you," he murmured.

I squeezed my eyes shut against the dizzying effect my eyes were having. He put his cloak over my lap when we came out into the floral scented night air. When I opened my eyes again, I was staring at the bright moon and the star filled sky. His home island's fragrance amplified Brass's scent.

"Don't take me home," I squeaked and Brass sighed.

"I must, you know I do. I cannot take you to my family's home. I will not take you to headquarters. Slate will be worried. Your family will be worried." Brass was making too much sense.

"Take me to Valla U," I pleaded, and he looked down at me with regret.

"Better to face your problems than run from them. You nearly fainted. Do you want me to tell you why?"

"No. I know why."

"Do not run, Scarlett. If you want to get away, you can come stay at the Regn manor when you are not at Valla U." Brass started towards the portal gate.

Brass's mind reading had its downfalls. "Don't rifle through my thoughts, Brass."

"Wait. Give it time."

Brass carried me through the portal gate and the blue starry lights of the Sumar portal room. I felt Slate's electricity the moment we entered the room. His presence was a punch to the gut. Brass stopped on the other side of the door, and I knew his eyes settled on Slate.

"Why are you carrying her? Where have you been?" Slate growled, and his footsteps came towards us.

I patted Brass's arm, and he set me on my feet. I held his arm to steady myself and gave him a grateful smile.

"She came with Lera and me to a Stygian competition. She is not feeling well, so I carried her home," Brass confessed.

Slate stood before us, and my heart lurched. I couldn't look at him, just seeing the black leather boots hurt knowing his feet would eventually turn into his powerful legs, and trim waist, hard torso, and chiseled face. I wasn't ready. Too much had happened that year, and I felt like a raw, open wound someone kept tearing the scab off and dumping salt into.

"Thanks, Brass," I said and looked at him through my lashes.

Brass's hand lingered over my arm as he left without saying another word to either of us. The bright light enveloped him, and he left me with Slate.

I slowly lifted my head and settled on his full lips. A muscle in his strong bronze jaw leapt and his mouth opened.

"Look at me, Torch," he said.

I slid my gaze to his sad silver eyes and felt my chin wobble. "I'm tired."

"Fine. Can you walk?" he growled.

I nodded and only flinched a little when he took my elbow and led me upstairs to our apartment. He opened the door and led me inside. We'd walked all the way in the silence that ate at him as his frustration mounted.

"For the sake of the gods, Scarlett. Say something," Slate pleaded as I walked into our shared closet and changed.

"Is it because you didn't trust me to keep your secret, or I wasn't important enough to confide in? Good enough to warm your bed, but not share your life?" I said, pulling on Slate's favorite nightie, the pale pink satin with ivory lace.

I glided past him to the bathroom and got ready for bed. Slate changed and followed suit; his white drawstring pants hung low on his hips as he brushed his teeth at the sink next to me. We wouldn't be doing it anymore after that night. I was moving out, back to my room.

"Warm my bed, share my life, my secrets are my burden —"

"You're a Dagr! Have children! I am physically unable to do this for you, but you married me anyway! I feel tricked and betrayed. You never should have let me do this." I shouted and stormed out of the bathroom.

"I'm moving out. I don't want this to become a drama. It is what it is. I'm leaving. Nothing you say can convince me otherwise."

Slate grabbed my shoulders, spinning me around. "What did he promise you? He would be there for you? He would love you? What won you over, Torch? Tell me that much." His fingers dug into my skin.

"Stop, you're hurting me. You already knew your cousin had feelings for me. He's looking out for me is all. I'm not leaving you for Brass. I'm leaving you because you need to find a wife who can provide you with heirs whose family isn't against your match."

His fingers loosened on my arms, and he grabbed my hand, holding my ring in front of my face. "Man and wife. You and me. We are a match. You are my mate, mine. I am sorry you found out this way. I would have told you one day."

"This isn't a discussion; I'm telling you facts. Tomorrow I'm arranging for the staff to remove my things," I said matter of fact.

Slate bared his teeth. He grabbed my arms and carried me to our big white bed before dumping me onto it. "What would you have me do then? Court other women, find a wife? Fuck my way through suitable matches until one of them gets pregnant?"

"One wife, fuck one of them. Get her with child, many children, and be happy, Slate." I said, scooting up the bed and away from him.

He moved like a dark beast up the bed, rippling with muscle. "No."

"This isn't a debate."

"What will you do?" he asked, pulling the strings of his pants.

"Stop. I can't have sex with you, Slate. Never again. I'm only here because Brass refused to take me anywhere else. I don't know what I'm going to do," I choked and Slate dropped his hand from his pants and climbed on top of me and rolled onto his back, pulling me with him.

He held me tight as I bawled.

"I hate you," I whispered against his hard pecs, and he stroked my hair.

"It only feels that way," he murmured.

I sat up and pushed at him with my fists.

I punched him weakly as I cried. "Why, Slate? Why couldn't you let me be? Instead, you chase me down, wear me out and for what? To get me to feel all these things and I can't keep you. You're not mine. I only borrowed you. If I had known you were the last Dagr..."

"What? What would you have done differently? Not have said a blood vow? You wanted it as much as I did. I only pushed first."

"What does the blood oath change about the marriage vows, Slate?" I asked tentatively.

"It means you can never say the vows to another. The blood oath prevents it."

I gasped and blinked down at him. He'd taken my limp punches without even bothering to stop me, but now I slapped him hard across the face. His jaw was made of steel.

"You bastard," I hissed.

"I never wanted to be with another, Torch. You knew this."

"You said you would die. You wanted to make sure I would never remarry. You didn't have to trick me into it." I dried my eyes with the back of my hand.

"And now?" he asked, grabbing my wrists and pulling me down to his chest.

I didn't fight him when I placed my cheek on his silken skin and let his arms wrap around my back. I fit so perfectly in his arms; how could he not be mine?

"Now I don't know, Slate. The only thing I know is that I can't be with you. Not if it means the end of your mother's line, of Sparrow and Tawny's. I won't let that happen, but I also know I can't be your mistress. It would make things even worse to watch you go home to your family after you were with me."

I lifted my head and looked down at Slate. His hair spilled over the white pillows and peered up from his lush lashes.

"I love you, but this is it."

"I refuse to believe that," he said.

I ran my hands up his chest to his face and ran my fingers along his chiseled features. He was beautiful.

"Let me go. Do the right thing."

"I am a selfish man. I do not want to do the right thing. I want to have you whenever I want you, to lie down with you at night and to wake up next to you every morning. That is all."

"This is the last time I'm taking the rousen. I don't need it anymore," I said, and he sighed.

"I will not give up, Scarlett. I need you more than anything else under the sun. Living without you is an unacceptable option."

"I'm not giving you a choice. You won't do the right thing, I will," I said, and Slate's jaw clenched.

"We shall see. It will not be so easy to keep away. I will not go gently," he promised, leveling his eyes at me.

Of that, I had no doubt. "When we wake tomorrow, it won't be as a couple. I'm Scarlett and you're Slate. Two separate parties."

Slate slid the thin sleeves of the nightie over my shoulders and his lips curled when I didn't stop him. "Tomorrow, but not tonight," he purred as he continued pushing down my nightie.

My greatest weakness was also where I drew my strength. I got little sleep and was woken up early by Slate. The morning continued in the shower before we went to breakfast. Slate was the epicenter of my life and I relied on him for everything.

Breakfast was wrought with a quiet tenseness, even with Sparrow and Hawk back at the Dagr palace. Slate ignored my silent plea for him to sit in his previous seat across the table from me and boldly sat next to me. We were both wearing our rings as well. From outside, it looked like nothing had changed. I supposed it hadn't.

After Slate had fallen asleep last night, I devised a plan. It required help from a few people and keeping Slate in the dark for a long time. The hardest part would be acting like everything was right as rain. I'd said a lot to Slate last night, and I'd meant it, but he was right. I could never deny Slate anything. Least of all, my love.

Our family walked on eggshells around us. No one mentioned dinner or our predicament, but I knew better. It would come up again. I only needed to buy some time. Get my affairs in order and keep my head low. That was the plan.

Once we were readied for Valla U, I joined Tawny, Indigo, Jett, Cherry, and Slate for classes. From the outside, we were unchanged. Tawny and Indigo tiptoed around how things were. Slate never moved too far away from me.

We walked to the second floor where most of the classes were held, the other tyros in black with their red and yellow belts and Slate cornered me. With narrowed eyes, he pinned his hips against me so I couldn't move past him. I tried to hide a wry smile as I looked through my lashes at him.

"I do not know your game, but I know when I am being played. Last night you were determined to leave me, this morning you have never made love to me more fiercely. It was not goodbye sex, was it?" Slate rumbled, sliding his hand up my arm.

"Every time I make love to you it feels like the best time. Can't I be enthusiastic in the morning?" I purred and rose to my tiptoes to plant a kiss on those full lips.

He sliced his head once to the right and let his lips curl. "You are up to something, and I am going to find out what it is."

"Good luck with that, love." I told him and pushed him back by his hips when I saw Quick coming.

Tawny had already gone into class and had studiously ignored Slate and me. Quick would probably have to be brought in on my plan, but not before I spoke with Pearl, Lera, and Brass. Those were my key players.

"In one piece. When Brass told me you nearly fainted after you spoke to those fuckers, I thought you would be out of it today." I widened my eyes at Quick and he grimaced.

Slate grabbed my elbow. "You spoke to them? What did they say to you? Brass said you were tired."

"Thanks, Quick." Quick ducked his head as he and Tawny went inside our Magical Beings class. "It was nothing. They want me to join them. I felt dizzy."

His eyes turned wary, and he ran his tongue along his lower lip. "Did Brass kiss you last night?"

I nodded and swallowed.

"For distraction or for his own pleasure?" Slate's voice was low and dangerous, and my eyes flitted to Sage and Ash walking into the class beside us.

"Do I ever give displeasing kisses?" I asked, folding my arms as I followed Ash and Sage into the class.

Slate gripped my chin and pulled my face back to his. "I think you are used to letting Brass kiss you whenever he pleases, and he takes advantage of it. Why is Brass afforded unconditional trust?"

"You sound jealous, Slate," I said slyly, and his upper lip twitched.

"As long as I know you are mine," he growled.

I masked a sigh. "I love you. Forever and always. Yours, mine, the world's, for all time. I'll see you at lunch." I pulled his mouth to mine, and he lingered, not kissing me back.

"Do not do it," he whispered.

"Do what?" I asked, feeling the butterflies in my stomach turn into pterodactyls.

"Whatever you are planning. You cannot hide the sadness in your eyes from me."

"Go to class, Slate," I said with a sigh, and turned into Ford Tio's class.

I nodded with a smile at the provost and walked to my seat next to Tawny and Quick. "Thanks a lot," I said, giving Quick a dry look.

He grimaced again, "How would I know you are keeping secrets from him?"

I ran a hand through my hair and sighed gustily. "You have no idea."

The day dragged on for an eternity. Feigning happiness was going to be a lot harder than I expected. My heart would likely explode before this was over. We were at Battle Training with Fox Straumr when we got the news.

They had found Jonquil dead.

It was such a shock that someone our age could die. Many of the tyros started crying at their own mortality rather than Jonquil's death. She was Cherry's first cousin and, even though the two of them disliked one another, she cried on Jett's shoulder.

"It was a clean death. She did not suffer," Crag noted, and I slid my hand into Slate's.

He squeezed my hand back, and I leaned on his shoulder. Slate was my light in the darkness as much as I was his.

CHAPTER 41
JETT

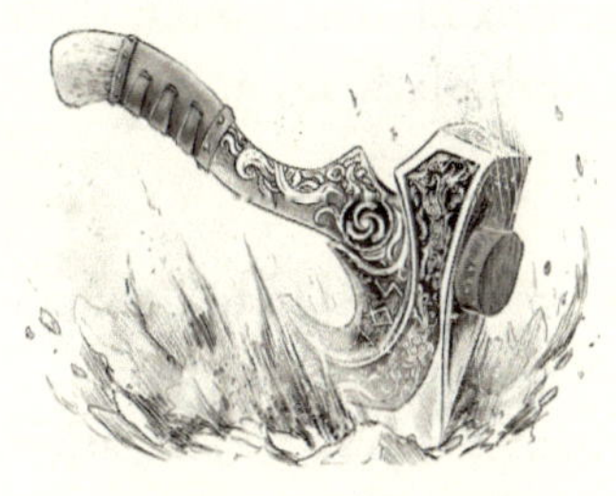

"You bastard. You killed her, didn't you?" Jett accused Slate after Scarlett had gone down to dinner.

Scarlett was staying in their apartment, but he saw a change in her. She was plotting, and Jett wanted to know what. Slate seemed to sense it too and didn't let her get more than a few feet away.

Slate sneered, "I should have killed her when she stabbed Scarlett the first time. I allowed her to live against my better judgement and she attacked Scarlett a second time. It never should have happened."

He didn't deny it. Not even a token protest. Jett dry washed his face with a scratchy palm and eyed his adopted brother.

"Is it true? She didn't suffer?" he asked, resigned to the fact that Slate was a killer.

Nothing would change his nature, not even with all the love Scarlett brought out in him.

Slate cocked a brow. "It was quick in the end. Before that, she may have experienced some fear." His smile was vicious, and Jett's lips turned down.

"What is wrong with you?" he breathed, and Slate growled.

"Given half a chance, she would have murdered Scarlett. We all know it. She was scheming since Scarlett came into Ash's life. It was a matter of when. Now we no longer need to play that particular game."

Jonquil had been the source of many of the nastier rumors that concerned Scarlett that Jett had debunked. Slate was right, of course, but that didn't make it okay to go around killing women. He didn't discriminate — male or female. Slate was an assassin, one of the best. Jonquil was vengeance. Slate might not admit to it, but Jett knew what drove him to it after so long was Ash's slap to Scarlett. Slate would tear apart Ash's entire family if he ever truly hurt her. He had resorted to his old ways. Kill first question later. Scarlett did not know who that person was.

Sparrow revealing his past had only worsened things. Scarlett and he had been happy, and they'd pulled the rug out from under them.

Never corner a badger.

Slate wasn't a badger; he was the biggest baddest thing out there and they'd stuck him between a rock and a hard place, leaving Scarlett to make the hard choice.

She would leave him.

How far she would flee would be Jett's problem. How to get Slate not to drag her back kicking and screaming would be another.

"Who are you going to make your baby's mama?" Jett asked abruptly, and Slate's face fell and hardened.

"Go fuck yourself," Slate growled, and moved past Jett to head down to dinner at the Sumar palace.

Jett had come back home so he could speak to Slate. He'd stay the night with Amethyst and would go back to Valla U in the morning. "Better you choose her than the family sends their choices to happen by the palace when Scarlett is out."

They had already discussed potential candidates after Scarlett and Slate had left for dinner. Crimson Rot, having been disgraced but still from a great family, topped the list. Cordillera and Lynx were too old to have children. There was always Amber. She was from a lesser family. She would've been a good match under normal circumstances, but that would be a slap in the face for Scarlett. Besides, how do you explain Slate's inability to say the marriage vows? She'd be a wife in name only.

They could exchange no vows. Slate physically could not say them. Funny how that backfired on him.

Slate stopped and narrowed his eyes at Jett. "Do you know what she is planning? I should know, but she either has not fully figured it out herself or is keeping it uncharacteristically tight to her chest."

Jett shook his head. "Nah, nothing. Not a word to me. She's up to something, though. She's going to break your heart. It's the only way you'll let her go as I see it. She'd tell herself it was for your own good. Beware, brother."

"That is what I fear most. That she might take Brass or Solder to our bed." Slate closed his eyes and ran his hand over his forehead.

Jett's breath caught as they started walking. He would never survive without his wives, if one of them were with another man... No. Just no. But Scarlett? Maybe. If she thought it would force Slate to do his duty. Jett knew she would. Brass and Solder were very good guesses.

"You'd forgive her," Jett murmured almost inaudibly, and Slate grunted.

"I would do a great deal to keep her. If she wants me to have this child, I will. After, I would win her back," Slate promised, and Jett blew air through his mouth.

"It's not so simple. The names have changed, but you're our in our father's position. She's our —"

Jett stopped in his tracks, and his eyes widened. He knew what Scarlett was planning.

"What?" Slate insisted.

"Nothing. Scarlett won't be the other woman, that's all. You're damned if you do, damned if you don't. Scarlett will push you away to free you to do what is necessary. Then you'll be without her, but even if you do it, she'll never take you back while you have another wife and child." Jett rested his hand on Slate's shoulder. "Whatever you need. I'm here. I can help you screen wives, have the girls round some up, keep tabs on Scarlett once she moves out of your wing. Name it."

Jonquil's death was long forgotten in the grasp of Scarlett and Slate's dying love affair. Slate frowned at Jett and rubbed his thumb along Alder's ring.

"I cannot lose hope. I cannot lose her," Slate murmured, and Jett's chest felt as though a Jotnar had squeezed it tight.

CHAPTER
FORTY-TWO

Privilege. Duties. Obligations. Expectations.

I wasn't ready to reveal my plans to anyone, but I had plans to recruit with Brass while Tawny said Sparrow had a girl coming over to the Sumar palace to eat dinner as a prospective wife for Slate. The heartache was unimaginable. I thanked Tawny all the same and made my excuses for Slate. He'd been peculiar. Slate had managed to be everywhere at once and yet give me more space than ever before.

More rope to hang myself.

I'd sent a messenger to headquarters to make sure tonight would work for Brass and, since I knew I never really went anywhere alone, I figured it would let my bodyguard for the night know he or she wasn't needed. Brass had agreed, and I kissed Slate goodbye with a stiff upper lip and had to pry my eyes from him, knowing another woman would eat dinner with my love.

After I changed into a red ribbed tank and black leather pants tucked into black boots with a four-inch heel, I reapplied my Deeply

Adorable maroon lipstick, buckled on my knives and took the portal to Valla.

Brass waited for me, cloaked in the shadows just inside the road to the Urd gate.

"I told Slate you kissed me," I told him when I stood a foot away, so close I could catch his scent.

He gave me a lopsided grin and pushed the cloak from his thick, dark hair. His amber eyes glittered at me.

"And?"

"And you'd better not do it again," I said, and started down the cobbled road.

"Who are they bringing to meet him tonight?" Brass asked swiftly, catching up to me.

"I don't know. Don't want to know. You can choose not to help me, but you won't be able to stop me." I paused and placed my hand on Brass's arm, turning him towards me. "I don't want to do it alone. It's hard enough as it is, but I can't leave things undone here."

Brass knit his brows and rubbed his lips together. I smiled and pulled on his chin, tugging his lip free, and he smirked.

"You are only telling me this because I would read it in your mind, anyway."

"And I trust you. Totally and utterly, as Slate is quick to point out. Help me fix my life, Brass," I implored him.

I thought he would kiss me; he stepped forward and put a hand to either side of my face and looked deep into my eyes. A passer-by walked close to where we stood alongside a shop front and his amber eyes cleared.

I felt love.

I sucked in an open-mouthed breath and knit my brows. "Brass," I breathed.

He placed his thumb over my lips and smiled. "You do not have to run. You can be with me."

My fingers softly wrapped around his wrist, and I pulled his thumb from my lips. "In a different life," I whispered, "It would hurt too much and you're one of his best friends." I let out a heavy breath. "His first cousin. Your mother was his father's twin sister."

It explained so much of their physical resemblance.

The hand he still had on my face slid into my hair at the nape of my neck. "You did not say because you did not feel for me."

"I also didn't say that no matter what, I'd love Slate for the rest of my life."

"So, I would not have to say that I believe you could make room in your heart for me."

I took a shuddering breath and kissed the inside of his wrist. "You're too good for me, Brass."

"That is not true. If I were good, I would not be trying to get my friend's wife to run away with me."

I chuckled out of the ludicrousness of our situation, and Brass smiled. "Stop hitting on me. You're better than that. I'm not running away with you."

Brass lowered his hand from my face and chuckled. "You cannot blame me for trying. Come let us recruit me some minions. We have a quick stop to make before we recruit. I had an idea."

"I'm all ears," I said with a smirk.

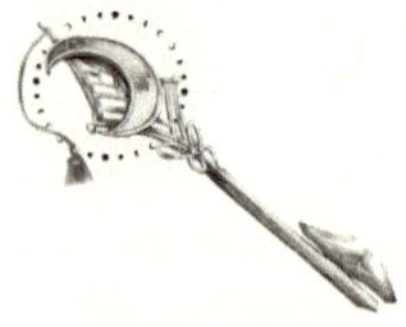

"Tattoos?" I asked as we approached the metal slotted door to Dhole's underground tattoo parlor.

"A quick one. We will need to find one another while we work on your scheme."

Brass knocked on the door, and a slide shifted to reveal a slot. It slid closed, and I heard locks tumble and the door swung open. Dhole gave us both a smirk through his goatee that hung on his chest and led us deeper into the building. Tattoos snaked up to Dhole's chin and around his neck to where his hairline would be, if he had any.

"I did not expect to see you so soon. What can I do for you?" Dhole asked in his gruff voice.

He led us down a narrow hall with a high stone ceiling to a larger carpeted room. It was wall to wall designs with hanging catalogs. There were four little cubicles behind a stone counter. It must have been a slow day. Only one other artist was working and there were no clients.

"Bonds. Here," Brass told him and pointed to his ring finger.

Dhole's dark blue eyes glittered when he looked at me. "You know what a bond is now?"

I smirked, "It's hard to gain knowledge when you're unconscious."

Dhole laughed, "I require a hefty price to ignore the mental state when tattooing my victims. Brass is a good man. I trusted he would not have asked me unless it was for a good cause."

Dhole sat in a modern black chair that looked softly padded and rolled easily across the floor. He gestured to the reclined seat in the center of his cubicle. I scoffed and pulled off my emerald ring so he would have access to my ring finger.

"The tiwaz rune."

Brass walked to the counter and pulled out a thick book of runes and thumbed through the book until he found the one he searched for. He brought it to me and pointed to a little upward pointing arrow. Dhole looked into the book and started taking out the syringe and inks for our tattoos.

"Success through sacrifice?" he asked, looking at me.

How very apt. I nodded in agreement.

I knew there was more to Dhole than met the eye that made him capable of infusing ink with calling. That was why it was so exclusive. His Celtic designs were so intricate were impossibly small and the ink never drew together.

Once my half of the bond finished, Brass replaced me in the seat as I perused the walls filled with designs. Dhole and Brass spoke in quiet tones as I moved about. Under the emerald ring was probably the only part of my body that Slate wouldn't see without having to shave any part of my hair.

"You are lovely when lost in thought," Brass said so close behind me I could catch his scent.

Every inch of my skin seemed to pull tighter all at once, even my scalp, as I fought a smile. "What else do we have to do to establish the bond?" I asked and turned around.

Dreamy amber orbs gazed down at me, and he took my hand in his, lacing our fingers together. "A binding," he said in that smooth deep voice made for late night whispering.

Dhole appeared behind him holding up two ribbons, one that was navy with a grass green border and another that was gold with silver trim. Brass held my hands and moved so we faced one another before Dhole.

"You love me," Brass asked, and I swallowed.

"Was that a question?" I squeaked.

Dhole and Brass both chuckled, and I blushed.

"Yes," I said, just wanting them to stop laughing at me.

"And I you. Our bond is as long as love lasts," Brass explained.

I smiled wryly. "I hear love transcends death. Are you sure you want to be bound to me that long?"

"Forever," Brass whispered, and I opened my mouth to question him, but Dhole interrupted.

"Will you honor and respect one another, and seek to never break that honor?"

"We will," Brass said, and I blinked dazedly before answering.

Dhole draped the navy ribbon over our hands.

"Will you share each other's pain and seek to ease it?"

"We will," we said in unison and Dhole draped the second strand of ribbon over our hands.

"Will you share the burdens of each so that your spirits may grow in this union?"

"We will."

He draped another corner of ribbon over us.

"Will you share each other's laughter, and look for the brightness in life and the positive in each other?"

"We will."

Dhole wrapped the fourth end over our hands. "And so, the binding is made. As your hands are bound together now, so your lives and spirits are joined in a union of love and trust. Above you are the stars and below you is the earth. Like the stars you love should be a constant source of light, and like the earth, a firm foundation from which to grow."

Brass leaned in to kiss the corner of my mouth. I belatedly returned it. Quick and Brass had a bond. I had a hard time imaging them holding hands. It was an awful lot like wedding vows, but none I'd ever heard before. Dhole had said bound as in bond, not man and wife, so I let it go.

Brass took the ribbons from Dhole, tucking them into his pocket and taking out a gold daymark. "Thank you, Dhole."

"Congratulations," Dhole said as Brass ushered me out.

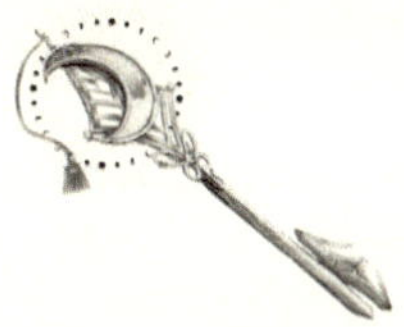

There was a promising-looking pub on the road we walked on. They gathered Guardians from all walks of life in the low-lit den of wood paneling and low hanging-stained glass. Booths lined one wall and stools were along the bar, which stretched from the door to the wall we faced when walking in. Nicer than a dive, but not as nice as most places. I wasn't sure what I was looking for; some place quiet where I could drown my sorrows and find some talented Guardians.

The bartenders were an attractive brunette and her male counterpart. He had an easy grin that made his eyes squint when he found something funny. I didn't guess his age — turned out I was usually a decade off. I bellied up to the bar with Brass, slipping onto the wood high backed stool before placing my hands on the varnished bar top.

The male bartender spotted me and flashed me that easy grin as he headed over. He was good looking with stylishly tousled dark brown hair, hazel eyes, and broad shoulders. I didn't have to fake my grin.

"You have a fan," Brass mumbled, and I flashed him a wry grin.

"Not seen you here before, what can I get for ya?" He wiped the spot in front of me with a dish towel he'd had slung over his shoulder and tossed out two coasters that I stopped with a finger.

"A pilsner, please. I haven't been here before. Name's Wildfire." That affable grin spread over his face, and I gave him my best lip curl.

"Wildfire? Nickname?" he asked as he filled my glass.

Pilsner on tap. I had found my new watering hole when I couldn't go to the Shadow Breaker's any longer.

"You could say that," I said coquettishly, batting my thick lashes at him.

He seemed a little less sure of himself then but gave me another grin before getting Brass a whiskey neat.

The bartender, or Cocktails, as I called him since I couldn't remember his name, turned out to be an omnilinguist.

"An omni-who-ist?" I asked.

Cocktails wasn't doing much bar tending since he had occupied the stool next to me for the last hour. I found myself interested in his story and chatted him up, refusing to let him buy me any drinks. I'd slapped down a silver crescent. Its moon shaped glinted even in the low lighting and he joked about how much I'd intended on drinking — as long as his shift was.

"Omnilinguist. I learned no languages besides those they teach at Valla U, but I never needed to. I have always understood all of them. I rarely realize I am speaking a certain language; it happens on instinct."

I'd hit the jackpot; talented, good looking, and after checking his ring finger, unmarried. Cordillera was going to be pleased.

"So, why do you bartend? You go do anything with that skill set. I'm hopeless at languages." Jackal was my language provost, and he teased me ruthlessly about how hopeless I was.

He shrugged, "I get to work with my sister here. We are close."

He pointed to the pretty brunette tending bar alone, but mostly leaning over the bar having chats of her own.

"Does she have a talent too?"

Oh please, oh please, say yes!

He laughed nervously, "Yeah, echolocation. You know? Like a bat."

My lips curled further; we'd hit the mother lode. "Would you both be open to other opportunities? I'm a recruiter of sorts, and I think you two would be a great addition to our team."

I gave him a spiel, giving no details. I didn't want him knowing too much or scaring him off, and by the end of the conversation his sister had come over and was nodding enthusiastically. Especially when I told them it would fit in to the bar tending schedule if they needed it to.

We left with them when they shut down the bar, giving them the details of when to meet us at the end of the month for their auditions and to contact me at the palace in Thrimilci if they had second thoughts, but I knew they wouldn't. They were way too excited. I felt it. With Hopper's sister and Styg's pair of cousins, that made five recruits. I needed five more, minimum, for Brass to have a full team.

Brass walked alongside me to the portal. He'd been quiet most of the night. "I am not used to you speaking with other men. You have blossomed. Why Wildfire?" he asked.

"Because I don't want Scarlett Tio to be heard recruiting and draw unwanted attention."

No one knew Wildfire unless they were a Shadow Breaker. Everyone had heard of Scarlett Tio because of my engagement to Ash and being from a greater family.

We headed to the portal gate when a shadow detached from the darkness and crashed into me. The air rushed from my lungs and his weight prevented me from drawing another breath.

I held my hand up, stilling Brass from interfering. Slate's eyes flashed at the other man, daring him to come between us. We all knew I could blow Slate away with my calling in an instant.

"Does your plan include parading women through my home to tempt me while you spend nights with your boyfriend?" Slate growled.

"Air," I ground out, and he loosened his pressure on my ribs. "A husband and a boyfriend doomed not to have any children. I'm not sure who is getting the sugarfoot end of that stick. I don't know how I find the time."

Slate snarled and pushed again on my ribs. Brass took a step forward and Slate sneered at him.

"Stepping in already? That was not part of our agreement. Back off, Brass," Slate growled.

"She has made her stance clear. She told me to stop kissing her. I have yet to decide if I am going to abide," Brass smirked.

"Air," I ground out. Slate released me but held to my shoulders so I wouldn't slump to the ground.

"I am here with you. I have nothing left to give you. You have it all."

I knocked his arms away with my fists. Slate stepped forward to embrace me and I slapped him. His head shifted the slightest bit, and he shut his eyes.

"We were recruiting tonight. Goodnight, Slate. Scarlett." Brass gave

Slate a pat on the back and walked down the road alone in the moonlight.

"Slate is a rock and a color. When was your Ausa Vatni? You're a year older than you pretend to be. What else? What other secrets are there? You lie by omission. I'm far from perfect, but I strive to be as honest as I can be."

I would not cry again. Crying and fiddlesticking have been the only things I've done lately and getting old didn't quite cover it.

"I am a year older," Slate conceded, "It was to hide my identity. That is not what you are upset about though, is it, Torch?"

My insides heated and skirted past Slate to continue to the portal. Slate caught up to me with his long-legged strides and I kept my eyes on the big stone gate ahead.

"I did not fuck her," Slate rumbled, and I held my breath, hoping the constriction in my chest would release.

Slate must have bruised my ribs when he crashed into me. My body was in pain and tears desperately wanted to fall.

"Why not? You need an heir. Fiddlesticking other women is how you go about it unless I've misunderstood how the reproductive system works," I snapped.

"And what will you do while I am sleeping with other women? Wait patiently for me to come in every aspect?" Slate growled.

"Sure. Why not?"

Slate grabbed me roughly and crushed his lips over mine.

I pushed at his hard chest, but he drove me back into a narrow gangway between two buildings. His hand gripped my hair, spinning my body and his electricity thrummed through me, his heady scent of cloves and crisp fallen leaves intoxicated me. My palms scraped at the brick of the building in front of me. Slate didn't let up on my neck for a moment and I worked my jaw when he pushed my face against the wall, the grout of the brick ground against my cheek.

Slate's other hand pushed down on my leather pants, leaving my knife belt around my waist. He used his hand to turn my face so his mouth could devour mine. I sucked his tongue into my mouth and he moaned, making my insides coil. I heard the jiggle of his belt just before he ran his ridge along my slick folds. My skin prickled, spine curved as much as his hold would let it. I was Slate's own personal khoraz. However, whenever he wanted, and it was a two-way street.

He teased me, rubbing slowly between my legs until I moaned. "Tell me you need me," he purred, tugging my earlobe with his teeth, his words husky, sending my reservations about sex in a darkened street out the window.

"Ah. Don't tease me. I need you now," I said throatily, and he chuckled darkly. His breath tickled the fine hairs on the back of my neck.

Slate slid deep into me and swiveled his hips, letting me feel every rock-hard inch of him. I moaned, and he drove in deeper. His hand slid from my neck and under my shirt, pushing up the cups of my bra to run over the swell of my breasts. I braced my hand on my head to keep it from scratching against the brick and grabbed his powerful thigh with the other, feeling him flex with each thrust.

"Don't leave me," he breathed.

I closed my eyes, feeling my nose burn with unshed tears. "I'm here," I whispered.

Slate moved from behind me, leaving me feeling chilled and whirled me around. His hands fisted in my hair, and he kissed me deeply, "If you scamper, I will catch you, Rabbit."

Slate dropped to his knees and kissed along my stomach and still further south until he buried his face between my legs, yanking my pants even lower. My fingers intertwined in his wavy locks as my knees buckled. His tongue swirled and caressed.

"Do not make me beg. I only do one thing well on my knees," he breathed and flicked my bud with his tongue.

My body jolted, and I chuckled softly, "*Well* might be a gross understatement."

I pulled him up to his feet, and he bent down to kiss along my chest and up to my neck. He pushed my pants as far as my boots would allow and parted my legs with his knee and took my wrists in one of his big hands, stretching them high above my head. He kissed me with the back of my head against the brick wall and pushed into me.

Slate's movements were slow and full of all the passion I'd seen from him culminated in his lovemaking. It was a form of worship, what he did with his body to mine. The way he hit every chord, making me hit every high note. We'd made love so many times I'd lost count. When I left him, I'd be leaving this too.

I bit my lip hard to keep from crying and kissed Slate until my cries subsided.

"I love you," I whispered as I felt the pleasure roll over me in waves, igniting every cell in my body.

"Scarlett." He breathed against my lips as he shuddered into me.

I didn't want to be in Valla anymore. I wanted to be home, in our bed, in his arms. He pulled my pants up, and I buckled them as he tucked himself away and glanced back at me. I straightened my top before smoothing his hair, running my fingers through it, and rubbing the love rune carving.

"I want you in my bed," Slate rumbled, and I gave him a wry grin.

"Our bed," I corrected.

He took my left hand in his and kissed his mother's ring. "Say it again."

"Our bed."

He growled deep in his chest and embraced me, burying his face in the crook of my neck. "Come."

I'd never been in love before. Leaning against his chest with our arms wrapped around one another as we walked to the portal gate, it was these moments when I felt like I needed a good hard pinch. These moments that would be the hardest to put aside when everything went down.

FORTY-THREE

When I woke, Slate surprised me with breakfast in bed. I sent out two messengers once I was done. One to Hopper's shop, where Anthias lived in an apartment above his shop, and the second to where Brass told me I could find Styg so he could notify his cousins of their possible recruitment.

I walked up to the line and shot at the target far ahead. I was average at best at archery. Knives were my weapon of choice, but the provosts like to make us well rounded. Indigo and Tawny stood beside me, also doing target practice, and they were ridiculously good. They nocked arrows and shot in what looked like a single shift of their arms.

"You must be glad you are so good with those knives, Tio, since you are a mediocre archer," Crag barked.

The wide ebony skinned man's arms crossed as he marched behind us. My uncle's lover sure could make you feel like an idiot. He was the strictest of the three brothers.

After thoroughly embarrassing myself with some spectacularly terrible archery, I trudged over to the stone stadium seating that ringed the battle grounds like the Pantheon.

"For shame," Fox said with a wry smile, "Engaged life being good to you?"

There was a somber blanket that shrouded the university since word of Jonquil's death broke, so the teasing was very welcome. Fox was fishing. No one knew about Slate and me except for our family and Shadow Breakers. I gave Fox an impish grin and my eyes slid to Slate, who was sparring with long seaxes against Quick. Both men were dagger men, so it was a privilege to watch them work with the longer blades.

"Do you happen to have a particular fiancée in mind?" I asked coyly, and Fox's sky-blue eyes twinkled.

"Give him a blade. He will slice through anything." Fox nodded towards the two men sparring and laughing because Slate had sliced apart Quick's belt.

"He is not my fiancée, but he is looking for a good wife if you know any single ladies," I said absently as I watched Quick curse Slate.

Fox grunted, "You are joking. You two are two peas in a pod, word is you live in the same quarters. Neither even stay at the university anymore."

"Should I take that as a no, then?" I said, turning back and arching my bow.

Fox was silent for a moment, "Crimson — no one will court her after your trip to Mabon last year. There are many single young women these days, but only Crimson from a greater family in your age range."

"Greater families aren't important to him," I said, releasing my arrow.

"To whom?"

Slate's sudden presence makes my skin heat, and my stomach did a back flip. There he was, standing behind me and I hadn't even heard him approach. He towered over me from where I stood, his midnight waves damp from the exertion of sparring, his bronze skin beaded with sweat, dust marks marred his black dress code pants and shirt from rolling around the ground. Fox gave him a rakish grin.

I lifted my eyes to Slate's face. He'd shaven clean, the hard planes of his cheeks looked smooth over his chiseled features. His narrow grey eyes met mine over his high cheekbones and my mouth went dry.

"You," I said, without missing a beat.

"Ms. Tio tells me you are looking for a wife. Strange, since you both have been wearing rings since Alder's funereal," Fox said with a sly smile, folding his arms over his chest.

"I see. I have never turned down a woman," Slate's lips curled, "Whom did she have in mind?"

"It was my suggestion, Crimson." Fox nodded towards the pretty redhead who was doing hand to hand combat with one of the other female tyros. "There is also Sienna and Orchid..."

Insane jealousy smacked me upside the head. Crimson had been with Ash while I'd been with him, and her creamy porcelain body under Slate's... He made a noise of appreciation in his throat and my body heated with anger from my toes to the hundreds of hair follicles that lined my scalp.

My lips pinched together, and I clenched my teeth. Any doubts I had about leaving him faded into oblivion. There was no feasible way I could stay. It was a friendly reminder.

I didn't make any excuses when I returned my bow and quiver to its weapon rack. I started towards the prep room and was intercepted by Ash and Sage; I came to an abrupt stop.

"Where were you Sunday night?" Sage asked in his honeyed tone.

"In Ostara. Are you an interrogator now?" I asked, folding my arms.

Quick was an interrogator but, as far as I knew, neither Ash nor Sage had any special talents. Ash and Sage shared a look.

"What were you doing in Ostara?" Ash asked, narrowing his celadon eyes.

I tapped my index finger in mock contemplation. "Last time I checked, I wasn't engaged to you anymore." I gave him a sickly sweet smile, "Why do you care?"

"Jonquil was murdered in Elivagar. Her neck snapped while she was walking into town," Sage countered.

"I am sorry about that. I know you were close," I said, leveling my eyes at Ash.

"Problem here?" Jett asked, slinging his arm around my shoulders.

"Nope. Is there?" I cocked my head to the side with a smile as I looked at the two men.

"Jonquil was murdered. Your sister was out of the palace," Sage stabbed a finger in my direction.

Jett rubbed his arrogant jaw and I smirked, a habit I'd picked up from all the cocky men I hung out with. "*Our* sister?"

Sage's pouty lips twisted; it was Ash who stepped forward shaking his head with one of those cocky smiles. "What a team we would have made. Such a shame you slept your way through the Merfolk, rendering yourself barren. When I am Prime, and I will be Prime one day, we will readdress our relationship. All of you Sumar/Tios play by your own rules. There is a way to do things here, a right way and a wrong way. Everything you do is wrong," Ash's eyes quirked his brows at me.

"I think you make the mistake of thinking I give a flying fiddlestick what anyone thinks about me or that any of my family cares about what you or your cohorts think about us," I said in a low, measured tone. "Becoming barren was the best thing to ever happen to me because it got me out of my betrothal to you."

"Losing your baby was the best thing that ever happened to you? How does the father feel about that?" Sage pursed his pouty pink lips at me.

I must have looked like a deer caught in the headlights. Ash watched my look of betrayal and didn't appear to be relishing in it. He wanted me to hurt, but he didn't want to hurt me.

"No idea what you're talking about. You've got some bad information there. Right, Scarlett?" Jett's fingers tightened on my shoulder, shaking me out of it.

It was the only thing Ash hadn't broadcasted, and I thought it was one of those unspoken things that we would never reveal.

"Right," I agreed, feeling lightheaded.

"Bullocks." Sage's smile made me want to hide behind Jett. "I heard he buggered you up and made off with a blonde at the masquerade. I heard he fucked her in the very next stall to you."

My hand snapped out before I could stop it and Sage's nose gushed blood. Jett pushed me behind him and as Sage started for me, Ash held him back.

"You will pay for that, cunt," Sage growled; his dark blonde hair fell in front of his face.

"I'd be careful who you threaten," Jett said brusquely as he shoved me further back.

Sage's nose had already stopped bleeding, and he wiped it with the hem of his shirt. "You will be lucky if I do not have you thrown out for this."

"Tread carefully, Scarlett. You do not want to cross the Straumr family," Ash said, looking past us.

In that statement, I knew Ash wouldn't allow me to be thrown out. I never understood what he saw in me.

"Good luck with that, Ash. The Straumrs aren't always the family in power. We have several of the greater families on our side and you know it," Jett warned, and I felt the electricity that proceeded Slate crackle.

"Come on. Let Sage go clean his face." I made a face and tugged Jett away and ran smack into Slate.

"Did you do that?" Slate's grey eyes slid from me to Sage.

Jett chuckled softly, "She's got a mean right jab."

Slate hooked his arm around me and made a satisfied noise in his throat. "My Torch." I elbowed him irritated in the ribs and he grunted. "Jealous?" he whispered, and I elbowed him again. He only chuckled.

"You shouldn't have hit him. Now he's got your figurative balls in a vise. He can report you anytime he wants —"

I interrupted Jett and tried to shrug off Slate whose arm might be as heavy as my whole body. "And what? Have Moon kick me out?" I scoffed, and Jett's turquoise eyes narrowed.

"Ready to go home?" I asked Slate.

"Eager, are we?" he teased, and I rolled my eyes.

"You don't have to rub it in when you look at other women. I like it less than you do."

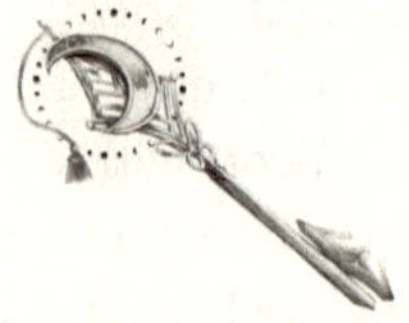

I'd filled Slate in on our altercation with Sage and Ash, including the ousting of our love child. Slate had wanted to go back to Valla U and tear Sage apart. It took a great deal of persuasion on my part to get him to stay home, but there we laid tangled in our white sheets watching the night breeze blow through the windows.

"Then do not discuss finding me a second wife. My first one is difficult enough," Slate rumbled as he braided the fetishes back in my hair.

I laid on his countless ridges of stomach muscles with my hands trailing up and down his trim sides. "Okay," I agreed and turned my head to kiss his silken skin.

"That was too easy," Slate said skeptically, and I folded my hands beneath my chin to gaze up his body to his eyes, soft and grey for the moment.

"I just don't want to fight with you. I'm meeting with Brass for more recruiting." Slate stomach rose and fell with a big sigh, and I smiled up at him. "Don't worry, I told him he's not allowed to kiss me or hit on me anymore. I think that's a fair agreement."

Slate cocked his brow, "What has he been promising you?"

"So you can fight with him? Nuh-uh. I'm not coming between you two. Besides, he means well."

"That he loves you? That if you plan to do something drastic to come to him first? Yes, he means well. Noble Brass always means well. Do not use him against me."

I pushed myself up, so I straddled one of his powerful thighs. When I tried to cover myself with the sheet he yanked it from my hands. He didn't look the least bit surprised when he spoke, and he wasn't being condescending.

"You knew?"

He blinked lazily at me and contemplated his answer. His eyes dropped to my bare chest and my skin prickled at his attention making his lips curl.

"I knew. I have always known." He pulled me back down, so I laid flush against him, and he tucked my hair behind my ears. "Brass cares very much about you. Has since..." He pursed his lips, "Since he met you, I suppose; perhaps before that when I had him watching you. You could do worse than Brass, but not while I am still alive."

"Well, that sounds like a ringing endorsement," I said dryly, and then rubbed my lips together summoning my courage. "Is there anything else you aren't telling me?"

"Yes, there is. Nothing that would hurt you, Scarlett. I swear it. A man must keep a few secrets."

I licked along his lower lip playfully and sucked it into my mouth. His silver eyes glittered with amusement and that bone deep lust that never ebbed. He could keep his secrets; I'd be long gone before they could hurt me.

My deadline was coming up fast. Too fast. I'd gone off the rousen, and it hadn't diminished our sex life in the slightest. My impending actions forced me to tear his clothes off whenever we had a moment alone and I was making time for those moments. Slate didn't act suspicious though I knew he was, just not complaining about our amorous trysts.

I kept my distance from Sage and Ash. Our family received engagement party invites to Ash and Quartz's formal gathering. Pearl, Hawk, and Sparrow were going; so were Tawny and Steel being the Vetr heir, she had to go. Slate's true patronage hadn't come out yet, so he wasn't obligated to go.

I'd found the rest of my recruits, with Brass's help, to total a whopping twelve and he was cherry picking his favorites for his own team; one benefit of escorting me around the five islands looking for good-looking, talented, single fighters. I had one week left to accomplish everything I needed to do and there was a substantial amount.

I was procrastinating on bringing anyone else in on my plans; it was just Brass so far and he had stopped trying to convince me to stay or attempting to kiss me. He was the only person I could completely confide in. I hated keeping things from Slate, but it was the only way to prevent an immense blow out and nonstop, pointless fighting until it all went down.

Lera, Chafer, and I were interviewing. Then, Brass was going to help me prep the new recruits and take them to Lera's box suite to watch a mock competition. Slate and Quick were helping us with the mock competition so I knew we weren't likely to run into them until we went to the prep room to give them a backstage view of things. I wasn't looking forward to seeing Anthias and Slate in the same room together. I kept telling myself, only two more weeks.

Sultry and dangerous was the look I was going for when I slipped into my red low cut, off the shoulder dress with long sleeves. It gave an impressive view of my cleavage even I had to admire. Lera sure could pick the hell out of a dress. I styled my fringe to the side and swept my long golden hair back into a low sophisticated bun, letting strands hang loose to draw the eye to my bare shoulders. I patted my necklaces and squeezed my silver torque. My wedding ring shone like a beacon on my *Happy Anniversary* white glitter polished finger.

My floor length dress hugged my shape snugly all the way to my knees, which made every step measured. I sauntered through the head-quarters feeling surprisingly good despite the end of my rapidly approaching time frame. Appearances made all the difference some-times, and I felt pretty darn good about mine, turning heads wherever I went.

I held my chin higher with my shoulders back as I sashayed to Cordillera's office and knocked on the door.

Chafer poked his head out, and his lips curled wickedly when he appraised me. "Embracing the dark side?"

"The dark side has better toys."

He chuckled at my answering smirk and opened the door wider so I could pass.

Cordillera's dark wavy chin length hair was swept to the side framing her narrow face. Her lips and nails were redder than ever and her dark eyes bright against her olive skin. "If today is successful, it will be the most Breakers signed on at once," she said raising a dark eyebrow.

"When," I corrected and poured myself onto the couch in front of her. A hint of a smile glinted in her eyes.

Oh yes, we were friends now.

"Who is collecting the recruits with Chafer?" I asked.

They'd need to be escorted blindfolded which would be hard to do in the daylight.

"Shale, Ama, and Brass since he was there to recruit them all with you. You two have been spending a great deal of time together."

"He's been a huge help."

Lera leaned back; she also had on a low-cut dress but hers was metallic gold, its sleeves capped her shoulders. "I bet he has, you two looked very cozy at the fight."

"Brass reads me better than anyone," I said with a dry smirk and Lera inclined her head. "He's been helping me with something." I leaned forward, "Lera, I need your help. I might do it with Brass alone, but for his sake... Slate can't know any of this. If you can't keep a secret from him, then stop me now because he does not know what I'm planning. If he did, I'd be caged in a dungeon somewhere with nix torques on every appendage."

Cordillera ran the back of her fingers along her jawline as she appraised me. "As long as it does not hurt him physically, I can keep it from him."

I turned to Chafer, and he quirked one of his slanted brows and rolled his eyes in irritation. "Yes, yes. I agree. Let us all lie to the pet."

"It won't hurt him physically and we're not lying. You can tell him everything once it's done. I plan on him finding out anyway, just not until after."

I stood, and Chafer walked me to the door. Chafer and Cordillera were in. They were lending all their support; it was a tremendous weight off my shoulders not having to worry about Brass taking on all the burden.

"You are tough shit. You belong here with the Shadow Breakers."

I blinked at Chafer trying to keep my face smooth at the unexpected compliment. "Despite having called me shit I believe you meant to compliment me," I said sarcastically.

Chafer smirked. "Try not to let it get to your head."

I smirked back at him and glided over to where the Breakers were eating their breakfasts. As promised, Brass ate with Shale and Ama. Their heads lifted when they saw me coming. I smiled and took the seat across from Shale, the other two next to me vacant.

"You're about to get your own team."

"I hope people do not think I slept my way to the top," he joked, but my cheeks heated anyway.

Brass's amber eyes glittered, and I knew mine did the same. We'd been spending a lot of time together at night in bars, eavesdropping in restaurants, trying to catch wind of any potential candidates. He'd even helped me come up with my plan, with all the details in place. Things were out of my hands.

Ama clapped her hands, "You deserve it. Have you picked your favorites yet?"

"I have. I am trying not to get my hopes up in case one of them turns out to be a dud," Brass answered.

Shale snorted leaning back on the legs of her chair. "You can read their minds; if one of them was going to fall short of expectations, you would not have recruited them."

"Ever astute, Shale. I wonder if they will recognize Scarlett since she has been introducing herself as Wildfire," Brass teased.

"Such a badass now," Ama giggled.

I pulled my tongue through my teeth with a smile and ignored their jests. "Are Slate and Quick getting ready?"

"They are. Try to keep your hands to yourself. Are you ready for our upcoming competition?" Shale quirked a delicate brow.

I laughed, "Are you ready?"

"Seeing as I spend my time training and I have not seen you in weeks. I doubt you will be much of a challenge. I almost did not recognize you off your back," Shale's teasing always bordered on the impossibly rude.

I jutted my jaw. "Since you're one of maybe ten women in Tidings who hasn't slept with Slate, I can only describe how... exerting it is."

Brass slapped his hand on the table. "That is my cue to leave." The three of us giggled at Brass's feigned modesty and he crooked his finger at Ama and Shale. "It is time to get the recruits."

CHAPTER
FORTY-FOUR

I'd made a profile on each of the candidates; figuring who would fit best where, what their talents were, if they had fighting experience, their weapons of choice, what island in Tidings they lived on, and general information. I memorized them, gone over them again and tried to come up with competitor names that would help Lera when it came to it.

I sat on Cordillera's blood red couch sorting through the files I'd created on the recruits. She pressed her fingers together under her chin as her foot dangled from her crossed legs. She'd gone over my work and let herself smile. Ever since she'd tried to seduce me and Slate told her we married she backed off. Cordillera was working with me instead of against me.

I felt awe and nervousness.

"They're here," I announced rising from my seat, "I felt them come in. So far so good."

"Let us go greet them," Lera said, elegantly flowing to the door.

I would have been excited. These recruits were all mine. One day I might've been the Grand Mistress, and these would've been the first people I hired on. All that had changed.

The twelve prospects stood clustered at the rumpus room doors directly across from us with Chafer, Brass, Ama, and Shale. We strode over, side by side, and their eyes scanned us with varying degrees of interest. I had met ten of the twelve. Styg's cousins were there, fair skinned with narrow noses just like his.

A haughty blonde, tall and lean muscled, measured me with her big blue eyes. She always did. The last time I'd seen her was when she exited the stall with Slate, and I'd almost killed her with my calling until Brass stopped me. She'd most likely be dead if it weren't for him.

Ama and Brass stood behind us, Shale moved to one side of the group and Chafer paced in front of them. "This is the Grand Mistress Cordillera and her delegate, Wildfire, whom most of you know."

A few looked bright eyed at me and I let my lips curl in greeting. Cocktails and his sister offered a quick wave, and I acknowledged them with a nod.

Chafer described what the day would detail, and what would happen should we offer them positions with our outfit and should they decide to accept. It was exhilarating, but I was glad I'd snuck in the back door without all the formalities. These people would eventually become like family to one another, like Slate's team was, but under Brass.

Chafer introduced Brass as the captain and I set the wheels in motion. We led them on a quick tour of the rumpus room, through the studio, the prep room, and out onto the Crash Course. The prospects oozed excitement.

For the first part of the screening process I sat on Lera's right-hand side, Brass sat on one of the blood red sofa chairs, and Chafer leaned against the wall after he let in the first prospect.

He was nervous, his broad smile crinkling the skin by his hazel eyes. It was a sweet look, disarming. The patrons would love him.

"This is much cooler than I imagined. My sister and I are ready to sign on the dotted line, when we pass your tests that is," Cocktails gave another nervous smile.

I returned his smile with a warm one of my own. "No need to be nervous. We need to see your talent in use. I've seen it, but if you wouldn't mind showing everyone else..."

He wiped his palms on his pant legs looking relieved. "Yeah, sure thing."

He spouted off something I hoped made sense to one of the other three people in the room, because it was nonsense to me. Cocktails ran a hand through his brown hair and gave another megawatt smile as his hazel eyes flitted to mine as if I was supposed to respond.

"I'm sorry. My uncle teaches languages at Valla U, and he says I'm hopeless. I didn't understand a word of what you said." I gave an apologetic smile.

I felt embarrassment, amusement, and frustration.

Chafer chuckled.

Brass's golden eyes met mine glittering, "He said your eyes are the most beautiful shade of green he has ever seen."

"Oh! Thank you."

I was blushing which was completely unprofessional when I started rambling on, "Brass would be your captain; you would answer to him when you come to headquarters. We shall arrange your missions, alert us of any inconvenient times as you know of them."

He shook hands with Brass and left the room. There were so many unique talents, I couldn't help but be intrigued as they performed each one. Cocktail's sister did her echolocation deal, one of them could make a force field, another could breathe underwater without calling. My favorite was the guy who could hang onto walls with his fingertips. Sure, he had to kick off his boots to climb to the ceiling, but it was serious superhero stuff.

Anthias was the last one, something told me she did it on purpose. She sauntered in, giving Brass an obvious once over and smirking at Chafer, whose wicked grin was the same one he'd used with me when we'd first met, not friendly in the least bit. Brass ignored her as she sat down across from Lera and me.

"How long did it take you to complete the Crash Course the first time?" Her tone was almost bubbly, as if she was joking, but there was nothing remotely funny about the look in her eyes.

"I trained her in three weeks. Shadow Breaker record. Work hard to beat it," Brass said in a business-like tone.

She smirked at me, and I tried not to raze her to a pile of ashes. "We need to see an example of your talent," I said tonelessly.

I didn't find her in-your-face demeanor very promising as a team member.

"No problem," she shrugged her toned shoulders and then I wasn't seeing her anymore. I was seeing me.

I sat where she just sat, my red off the shoulder dress exposing my cleavage, my deep berry lips pursed, long golden hair pulled back, wisps tickling the skin around her collarbone. My jaw clenched, and she mimicked me. I wrinkled my nose in disgust and so did she.

"You can replicate anyone?" Lera asked her dark eyes glinting in the soft incandescent lighting.

Anthias dropped the illusion, and her lips curled. "Yes, it is a projection into your mind. I still feel the same, but your mind tells you to see what I want you to see."

Anthias projected herself as Brass now and blew me a kiss. I flinched visibly; it was Brass's turn to gape.

Chafer laughed and reached for her head, "I can still feel her long hair, that is freaky."

"They call me Mirage. I know Hopper said you give nicknames. I would like to keep mine," Anthias said upon standing.

I felt approval.

"Yes, it suits you," I said in my most professional voice, "Is that how you wish to be introduced to the other Breakers?"

"Yes," she said and turned to Brass, "I am all yours now, Captain."

"Go sit with your teammates," he said brusquely, and she quirked an eyebrow before doing as he said.

He let out an exhale. "That one is going to start problems."

"If she projects me again, I will be the first one to give her those problems," I snapped.

Prospects changed into training gear, and we lined them up for their second part of the screening process. Like most people raised in Tidings, they didn't share my sense of modesty as they stripped.

We pitted Chafer against the men and Shale against the women; the prospects were accustomed to the training since most of them were already proven tried-and-true Guardians. I clasped my bare wrist where my golden torque would have been after the Ragnarök challenge next winter. One by one, Chafer and Shale annihilated the recruits.

Brass was looking at me from the corner of his eye, picking up what

I was thinking about no doubt. I tried to clear my mind and focus on the woman Shale was currently beating mercilessly. None of the recruits were spectacular fighters, but we would train them to be. What they were was eager and ambitious; two very important traits if we were going to whip them into shape.

The woman tapped out and Shale helped her to her feet.

"Run them through the Crash Course," Cordillera told Brass.

He gave her a curt nod and walked towards the prep room to retrieve Quick and Slate.

Brass came back a moment later with Slate and Quick in tow. They were in full competition wear; black leather briefs and greaves with black boots and vambraces for effect. My lips turned down at the lust rolling off the women gathered. Did Slate really have to move so every oiled muscle rippled? His brow quirked at me, and a mocking smile played on those beautiful full lips.

It was hard not to admire Quick; he was impressive with all his jagged black tattoos and, from the way the female recruits were looking at him, I wasn't the only one who thought so. Brass folded his arms next to me and we shared amused looks as the men stood a little taller, chins nocked higher. It wasn't good to be a smaller man with the likes of Slate and Quick displaying their assets. It wasn't just their look; it was their posture, their presence. Cocky, self-assured, and lethal.

That ought to ramp up the competition.

"That is not all it has amped." Brass noted, and nodded to the girls.

Quick didn't belong to Indigo, but I still didn't like to see him with other women. It was inevitable with the new women. Quick was far too sexual to ignore, except for me. I didn't notice at all. Brass snorted, and I nudged him with an elbow.

Slate caught us in our playful moment and his face went smooth. I shook my head once to prevent Slate from coming over and diminishing my role as an authority figure by making out with me or fondling me in front of them all.

I sauntered over to stand between Quick and Slate, Quick flashed me a dazzling smile and I thought I could hear the panties drop. "Slate is a captain like Brass, one or two of you he deems worthy will be assigned to his team —"

"I volunteer," Mirage raised her hand with her hip cocked out and I felt my heat rise.

"When I want your opinion, I will tell you what it is," I snapped and glared at her daring her to say another word. Cordillera and Chafer exchanged a glance, and I continued, "Next one to open their mouth and waste our valuable time will be sent on their way. Silver, Quick, to all of you, is his lieutenant of sorts. They have been kind enough to take time out of their day to show you how a competition would look should you be asked to join us."

I nodded to Brass, and he gestured to the stairs that led to the seats above the arena. "Watch and then we will have you run the course."

Brass led them to the seats with Cordillera and Chafer at the head. I hung back and Quick's dazzling smile turned its full force on me.

"Save it," I told him, fighting a smile that crept up to my lips and turned to Slate whose body was radiating heat for so many reasons. "Hopper asked me for a favor," I said simply, and his eyes raked over me.

"As long as this is not another attempt to find a wife for me. You think this dress is necessary? Those recruits do not know you are mine; I tire of watching them undress you with their eyes."

"If you thought I would try to set you up with Mirage, you don't know me at all. You don't like my dress? Men are allowed to look, as long as they don't touch. Have fun. Remember this is for show." I stood so close to Slate I could almost see the energy our bodies gave tangling around us.

Slate felt it too, his silver eyes filled with raw sexuality. When I caught his scent mingled with the oils, there was an undercurrent of bone deep unquenchable lust.

"Gods, you two could make a Valkyrie abandon her vows. Get out of here, Scarlett," Quick chastened, and I smiled, not breaking Slate's eyes contact before sauntering up to where the others sat.

Cordillera looked towards her suite and the lights dimmed like they did during competitions. The spotlights around the arena swirl around as Slate's glistening muscled body strolled from the prep room alongside Quick. Neither of them smiled as they reach the Guillotine. I saw Quick say a few words to Slate that make his muscles flex with a laugh. Slate's face turned towards the seats, his midnight waves plaited away from the hard planes of his face and his lips curled. I could see it from there when his mouth moved, his strong jaw flexed and there was a sharp tug from my heart. The bastard activated the bond, it was a little string that wrapped around the most traitorous organ in my body.

The *BOOM* sounded making me jump without fail and they were off. I watched awestruck at Quick and Slate made their way through the Crash Course. Slate was a freight train when he ran through the Guillotine. I thought the blades would shatter if they ever touched him. Quick climbed the tall trees like he was born to do it. They'd run the course so many times it was like a choreographed dance. I knew because my routine was the same way.

Slate caught and tossed boulders that fell near him as he plowed his way through the earthquake portion. Quick leapt with incredible agility from drifting slabs of rock over the hot lava. Slate was undefeated, so it wasn't a huge surprise when he leapt from raft to raft in the whirlpool to land on the dock a full two seconds before Quick. They were both sweaty and wet when they jogged back towards the combat circle.

We led the recruits back down as they chattered away and looked at Slate and Quick with new admiration. "Thank you for your demonstration," Brass said with a nod of his head.

Slate clearly did not like being dismissed by Brass, but Quick had turned without a second thought. Slate narrowed his eyes at me like it was my fault, and I supposed it was since it was my idea to promote Brass and walked back into the prep room.

Brass held himself taller, his hands clasped loosely behind his muscled back. I wasn't the only one appreciating his fine example of testosterone. Mirage, was practically licking her chops as her eyes followed him. The other two girls were as well; Cocktail's little sister and a girl with skin the color of creamy coffee followed Brass with a little more interest than strictly necessary with her honey-colored eyes.

"We ask everyone to try their best," Brass continued. "We do not expect anyone to succeed today. Amalgam will lead, then a prospect, followed by Chafer, and another prospect. Shale will tail the group; follow their examples. I will watch from the side and make sure none of you are seriously injured." Brass pointed to where he used to shout orders at me while I had trained not that long ago.

Lera and I walked with Brass to the oversee the first two prospects.

Brass leaned in close to me, "Care to explain why these men seem to be distracted by you?"

I arched my eyebrow at him with skepticism. "We approached complete strangers and make small talk while trying to convince them to meet me to be blindfolded and led to a hidden place. I used every asset I had to my ability. I may have flirted."

Brass's full lips push together, and I could tell he's holding back a laugh. "I was there, I saw what you did; Just short of manipulating them. They did not seem so enamored when we spoke with them initially."

"Results were worth it, they probably thought we were a couple. Looks like you're getting a few fans yourself." I told him with a nod to Mirage who volunteered to go first. The tall leggy blonde was already waiting for Ama to get further down the Guillotine to begin.

Brass's lips pursed to the side. "Stay clear of her. She has something to prove and plans to use you as an example." He scoffed. "She has no idea what you are capable of."

I internally rolled my eyes. "She can try. I'd gladly teach her a lesson. She should have learned the first time."

"Women in Tidings are like that sometimes — wanting to be the alpha."

He kept his eyes on the prospects running the course. Both had entered with the three Shadow Breakers and were getting to the tree obstacle that had been my hardest to conquer.

"I'm not an alpha female. I'm more like an Omega," I joked, "Lera would be alpha." I gave Lera a smirk and she arched one of her thick manicured eyebrows at me, the ends of her lips quirked.

Brass grunted, "Whatever you say, Delegate."

Girls had never gotten along with Tawny and I in high school. I never thought it had anything to do with me, I still didn't. Tawny was a huge flirt and indiscriminate to boot. Steel tamed that beast even though she kept her flirting to Quick, who didn't mind in the least and didn't have a girlfriend to piss off. There was the We Hate Scarlett Tio club that had grown smaller since Jonquil's untimely death, but that was because of Ash and Slate.

None of the prospects made it across the Crash Course, as we'd anticipated. Brass ordered them to shower, and I made some mental notes to add to my files once we went back upstairs. Cordillera gave me an approving smile before leaving Brass and me.

"Are you happy?" I asked, slipping my arm through his.

"The recruits are promising. Thanks again for recommending me for captain. I know Lera would have done it eventually, but you expedited it for me, especially with the recruiting. Lera has never actively recruited. She likes you. She hates that she likes you." Brass's amber eyes were full of mirth and leaned into him as we walked into the prep room.

The metal door behind us hadn't even shut when I noticed Mirage in her panties addressing Slate who was only wearing a towel around his waist. Her hand rested on the terry cloth fabric; the 'V' that led south prominently displayed on his flawless skin. The tip of her finger brushed the dark silky trail of hair that led beneath the towel.

I sucked in a sharp breath and Brass wrapped his arms around me, "Calm down, Scarlett."

"Brass, I love you, but if you don't let me go, you're going to get burned," I hissed.

The heat flared, the pin had been pulled, and I was fit to burst. Slate saw Brass manhandling me and slid his eyes back to Mirage. I raged and Brass let me go. I'd started to draw attention and Brass was on my heels as I stormed to where Slate and Mirage stood. She turned her head lazily towards me and looked haughtily down her nose at me. She was topless.

"Dress recruit. We have final interviews to conduct," I said, trying to maintain a modicum of my professionalism.

Mirage crossed her arms below her bared chest, that was significantly smaller than mine I might add, and leaned against the black metal lockers. "In a minute," she said coolly, and I took another step forward so we were nose to nose despite her being a good four inches taller than me.

"Now. Do not take my kindness for weakness. You're only here because I like your brother owing me favors. I don't have a need for favors that aren't worth the trouble," I gritted, fully aware of Slate to one side, Brass to the other, and the recruits filling in around us.

"You hide behind your calling. I admit, you are powerful. Otherwise, you are just a little girl with a big mouth who cannot hold on to a man," she said with a smirk.

"Anthias —" Slate started, and I turned on him.

"You are so disappointing," I spat holding his gaze before turning back to Mirage. "Get your gear on. You want to find out why I'm the delegate for a guild of mercenaries and assassins? You'll find out now."

My elemental fire eddied beneath my skin as I moved to my cubby and pulled out my boots and blades. I didn't even change. I kicked off my heels and tugged on my boots and walked out of the prep room bumping into Slate, who tried to speak to me on the way. I was buckling my wrist blades and fastening my belt around my waist when Brass came up next to me.

"Do not let her goad you," he said softly, and I raised my eyes.

... They both make me feel so stupid. It hurts, Brass. Seeing them together hurts. He should have known better. He did it on purpose to prove some ludicrous point. This is why I must leave...

Brass wanted to hold me, to tell me everything was going to be alright, but we both knew it wouldn't. "Keep it clean, not that Hopper will blame you. He knows what kind of woman his sister is. You were too nice to allow her here."

... Now you tell me...

I gave him a rueful smile and watched Mirage stride out of the prep room. The recruits came with her eager to see a fight; Ama, Shale, Quick, and Chafer were with them. Slate came out last fully dressed in head to toe black and moved to stand near Brass when I walked into the combat circle.

I should have paid attention to the knot of emotions in my head. Slate had been irritated before when I was standing near Brass, it grew to aggravation when we didn't enter the prep room, and finally it became anger. He had thought to teach me a lesson by allowing Mirage to speak so familiarly with him. If she was a different woman, I would have just been jealous. She wasn't though, she was the one who had helped to break my heart. I'd run back to Ash after seeing the two of them together and that next night my father and my unborn child were taken from me.

"Plan on fighting in that dress?" Mirage asked smugly, and I lowered my forehead in a challenging stance.

When I tapped into my elemental powers, my voice seemed to

reverberate in my body, sounding disembodied. Ama shivered visibly when I spoke.

"You have no idea what you've gotten yourself into."

I flexed my fingers springing my wrist blades and my body burst into flames. I heard a girl cry out as others gasped. Yes, it was frightening.

Slowly, I incinerated the dress from my body. My eyes lit to hot coals in their sockets. It was my body but made of a white-hot fire that constantly churned. My hair turned into flames and floated around my head licking at the air. Where my heartbeat was a constant pulse of white-hot heat.

Mirage took a staggering step back, but recovered and pulled her blades.

"No calling," she said, a hint of fear laced her tone, and I gave a wicked grin that made her wince.

"Not a problem," I said, and stamped out my fire in an instant.

I stood in the combat circle in the bright red corset I'd put on with my dress and matching lace boy shorts. I'd melted the pins that held my hair and it fell in loose waves down my back. My boots came to my knees, and I cocked an eyebrow at her.

She narrowed her eyes. Slate was furious the men were seeing me in my underwear, but it was a show. I had a point to prove. I cleaned up nice but I was deadly, and I would prove it. Mirage was a dagger specialist as well, all the better so when I beat her it will be because I was more skilled.

End of story.

Mirage was quick and lithe, her reach was further, but I lived and breathed training for the last year. It was all I did until the Merfolk had me.

She stabbed, I deflected when I thrust, she dodged. I was stronger than she was, I realized and started to throw more of my body into my moves.

I spun along her arm when she aimed for my midsection and hooked my arm around her throat, kneeing her in the spine. I slid my blade across her throat as she fell forward into a roll, and she dabbed her neck incredulously, gnashing her teeth at me.

"You drew blood, the fight is over," Brass shouted, but we both ignored him.

Mirage sheathed her blades, and I retracted my wrist blades as we circled one another. "I'd have ridden him all night, as I have done many times," Mirage said, her wide blue eyes fixed on me.

I wrangled in my elemental power as I charged at her holding back my scream of rage. I pulled up short and kicked down on her thigh. She gripped me by my corset and slammed me onto my back. I tucked my hand to my chest and drove my elbow into her nose. She staggered back and I jumped up to my feet and front kicked her in the stomach.

The air rushed from her lungs and her arms flew from her bleeding nose to her gut. The shallow slice at her throat blended in with the blood from her nose so her shirt bloomed red at the neckline. She wiped the blood from under her nose with her sleeve and spit out blood before she smirked a blood-stained smile.

"He came so hard I thought he was having a seizure. She laughed, moving closer to me but kept the loud tone of her voice steady so everyone could hear. You heard it, so you know."

The insides of my ears burned as if her words were searing pokers jammed into them. I shook with suppressed rage until I released it. I snapped; I admit it. I dimly heard several someone's shout, but it was too late. The thin line that had grown blurry between what was right and wrong since my life had gone so wrong evaporated into nothingness.

She lunged for me, and I swept her legs out from under her. Mirage fell back onto her backside catching herself in a seated position until I grabbed her head and knocked her in the face with a knee with a sickening crunch, I did it again. My hand fisted in her blonde hair, her teeth bit into the skin of my knee. Every spurt of blood brought a sick satisfaction, the crunch of her bones made me feel alive.

There was something very wrong with me.

A steel band clamped down around my arms pinning them to the sides and shook my arm until I released Mirage's hair. She dropped to the combat circle with her arms splayed, blood on her face the color of my corset. Dragging my feet as he pulled me away, I finally stopped struggling when I saw Shale and Ama run to Mirage's side and heal her.

Her blood was all over my hands, down my knee, it had sprayed me in the face. She had it coming. My chest heaved under the hard arm, and I watched her chest rise and fall. I hadn't kill her, thank the gods.

The recruits were staring open-mouthed at me and my eyes met Slate's. I shifted my head to see who was holding me, it was Brass. His nose was bleeding and my eyes widened with concern.

"Oh, gods! Brass, I'm so sorry." His hold on me loosened, and I turned around to heal him. "I'd give you something to wipe your nose, but I have appeared to of lost my clothes," I said ruefully and Brass gave me a stern look.

"You need to rise above petty words. You knew that she was lying, and you let her win," he scolded and I frowned.

Quick came alongside him and grimaced at me. "You look like you came straight out a horror movie. Here let me." He licked his thumb and started to rub along my cleavage. Brass backhanded him away and Quick chuckled impishly, "Fuck her. She was being a bitch."

I looked over my shoulder to find Slate, but he was gone. The recruits were still milling about, talking excitedly and Ama and Shale were helping Mirage groggily to her feet. Chafer's cruel mouth was working, and I could tell from his posture he was dressing her down.

Glad someone was on my side.

"I beat her," I said and hated how much it sounded like a question.

"Did you?" Brass asked, furrowing his forehead.

My cheeks heated under the layer of blood that coated them. Brass was one of the few people whose opinion really mattered to me and had a right to lecture. He held himself to a higher bar, and I felt about this big when he spoke down to me.

"She made up a bunch of lies. You knew they were lies. What did you have to prove? You are above her, them, all of this. You are the delegate, second only to Cordillera, and here you are rolling around on the floor with a recruit. Who won, Scarlett?" Brass asked, leveling his eyes at me.

I ducked my head and stared at his belt buckle. I was ashamed, he was right. Whatever excuse I had conjured in my head wasn't enough. Nothing was worth losing the respect of the people I'd just brought on. She'd won. Mirage had talked about Slate openly airing out our dirty laundry for all the Shadow Breakers.

Someone tapped me on the shoulder, and I turned around very

aware that I was in my underwear. It was Cocktail's sister, and she was looking at me all wide eyed and gaping.

"Will you train us to fight like that?" the little brunette asked.

"I shouldn't have done that. I don't normally spar with anyone who isn't fully trained," I admitted, and heard Brass grunt in ascension.

"Honeybee," she reminded me of her name. "Well, I want to learn. That was amazing. You moved like... I have never seen a woman move like that." Her eyes moved rapidly between mine and I knit my brows.

"Brass is your captain, he trained me. I don't think he approves of bloodying someone so badly, but he'll train you extremely well," I told her and went to put my hand on her shoulder, but fisted my hand and dropped it to my side. It was covered in blood.

Cocktails sister looked at Brass who nodded towards the prep room. "Finish getting ready. Tell the others. I will be in a moment and take you all to dinner in the rumpus room."

"Yes, Captain," she beamed and started off at a jog.

Quick smiled and groaned. "I want to be a captain. Did you see her face? Yes, Captain. She wants your cock. I bet she will call you captain when you —"

"Gods, Silver. Enough." Brass groaned looking up at the ceiling.

Quick only laughed and walked towards the prep room. I crossed my arms and looked up at Brass through my lashes.

"I hate disappointing you," I said softly, and Brass sighed.

"Slate should have stopped you. He is playing games and Mirage suffered for his game. Get cleaned up and join me for dinner, Scarlett. You are a mess. Do you have clothes to wear?"

I nodded, and he rubbed his knuckles against mine as he walked away. Such an innocuous little move, it felt very intimate now. Blood on my bond had activated it. The Crash Course emptied except for one other person. Slate was keeping his distance but had been watching me with a simmering anger the entire time. I closed my eyes and sank to the ground and brought my legs up to rest my forehead on my knees and I let myself cry.

Love made me a fool.

I felt Slate approach and he sank down behind me, placing a leg to either side of my body and waited for the okay to touch me. "Why?" I whispered.

"Because I am a jealous bastard. I am not a good man, Torch," he rumbled, and he moved forward.

His thighs pressed against my hips and his hand gingerly touched my back. Brass hadn't healed me, Slate did. The warmth filled me, and I sighed. I didn't realize how bad I was hurting or maybe my heart hurt much more than anything physically that I didn't notice.

"Scarlett, I need you. Let me make it better," he whispered.

I opened my eyes and rested my chin on my shoulder to look at him. "Do you know how easily you hurt me? I've never felt this way about anyone. I would do anything for you; your happiness means more to me than my own. My heart belongs to you. When you treat it, me, so carelessly it crushes me."

Tears streaked down my bloody cheeks and Slate leaned forward, pressing his lips to my salty tears. "What did I tell you about putting me before yourself? Do not ever do that. You are so very precious to me. I have broken all my rules to have you. I know I could never keep you but be mine for now until the end."

Slate's hands slid across my back and pulled my body into his lap. He used a finger to turn my face to his and slanted his mouth over mine.

"Stop. I'm covered in your lover's blood."

Slate's eyes were hooded, but they still flashed silver at me. "She is not my lover. I never made love to that woman. I make love to you and none other. Blood never bothered me," he growled deep in his chest and his hand gripped in my hair. It crunched with the drying blood that had splattered into it.

He crushed his mouth over mine and forced my jaw wide. I couldn't draw breath; he stole the air from my lungs, and I felt something inside him ignite. He twisted me around in his lap and pressed firmer to my lips. He bit deep on my lip and my mouth filled with the coppery taste of my own blood. I flinched, and he tugged harder making me wince. He'd never done it so hard before.

"Close your eyes," he rasped out.

"Wh —" I started to ask why, and he interrupted me.

"Do as I ask, Torch. For me. Do not ask questions." He ground out huskily, and I pulled back from him to search his eyes. "Now. Keep them shut."

I shut them.

Slate was all over me. I yelped when he tore the corset from my body in one brisk move. He groaned aloud and his tongue slid over my chest. He held my hands behind my back as he licked and sucked across my chest and throat. He took my hands next and slid my fingers into his mouth panting.

I could feel him. He was rock hard against me, aroused beyond anything rational. His scent was as primitive and feral as his emotions. I wasn't sure he was my Slate. I'd say it was another person entirely, calling what I felt a person would be a generous assessment. He was a carnal beast, depravity radiated from him that would normally have sent my red flags flying, but this was Slate. My Slate.

Two slices up my hips freed me from the rest of my undergarments and I gasped as he squeezed my backside hard, his face buried between my breasts. I was naked on the Crash Course in a building where fifty other people could walk in on us at any moment.

Slate cursed, but I was afraid to ask. His hips had been rocking against me and I had a good idea of what would come next.

"Now," he rasped.

My eyes would have widened if they were open, he barely sounded like himself. I didn't know what he meant, so I didn't move. I couldn't move much from the way he had my hands pinned behind my back. His free hand slid between my legs and dipped inside me. He moaned and I so desperately wanted to open my eyes.

What had gotten into him?

He released my wrist and picked me up by my waist and, turning me around, he shifted behind me and forced me onto my hands and knees on the Crash Course floor. Before I could drum up a protest, he drove into me. I gasped. He'd gone insane. We did not make love. He fiddle-sticked me so fast and hard I couldn't do a thing but try not to get whiplash. The slapping of his skin on my backside let out a loud smack multiple times a second I was sure the recruits could hear in the prep room. If not that, then the growling he was doing behind me that I could hear even over my heavy panting. I wasn't even doing any work and it was exhausting. I was going to need healing.

Slate fisted his hand in my hair, pulling me off my hands and he gripped my ribs tight as he slammed into me. He roared when he came and let my hair go so I fell forward. He shifted away from me, and I heard his heavy breathing.

"Open... your eyes," he panted. I pushed myself back onto my heels and turned to him.

It was Slate, just Slate. I knit my brows and he pulled his shirt over his head and handed it to me. I tugged it over my body as he lifted his hips and pulled his pants over himself. He laid his head back on the floor and just breathed.

I watched him with a knitted brow. "Is everything okay?" I asked.

Not that I was complaining, but Slate had never left me unfinished. He lifted his head and gave a wry grin before dropping his head again.

"Everything is good. I promise to take care of you at home. I do not want to spend a great deal of time out in the open in case someone walks in."

"That's not what I meant," I said dryly.

Slate lifted his body up into a sitting position and adjusted himself in his pants; he was still hard. Slate was barely contained soft. Hard — he looked like he'd stuffed his pants with tube socks.

"The urge came over me. I apologize for being so forceful," he said, wiping a hand across his forehead and freeing loose strands from his sweat slicked face.

"You're forgiven, even though these public trysts seem to be happening more frequently. I'm not a fan of being watched while we are together, especially when I'm in such a vulnerable position."

"Good point. I would not want a man to see you while we are together," he conceded, and got to his feet.

He held out his hands for mine and pulled me up to my booted feet, which was all that remained of my outfit. His shirt fell to my knees, and he slid his arm around my waist and guided me into the prep room.

"I mean, you licked blood off me, Slate. We've had... rough sex before," I blushed. Gods, I needed to get a grip. "This was different. You were different, like you were turned on because of the blood," I said and he started towards the showers.

He turned them on for me and knelt to pull off my boots. "Watching you fight, the way you lost yourself." Slate lifted his glittering silver eyes to mine. "By the Mother, my cock gets hard thinking about it. In the shower. I want to hear you sing your torch song," he purred.

I had to eat my dinner swiftly since my shower lasted longer than it should have. Slate had been off. He was still dealing with this... aggression. When we had finished, both of us that time, I hurried upstairs in my black Shadow Breaker shirt and pants hoping no one would comment.

Cordillera wanted me to help with the contracts. All twelve had passed our tests and wanted to join. We handed them a thin blade so they could sign their blood contracts binding them from speaking about the Shadow Breaker's inner workings and signing their lives over to Lera. Mirage didn't so much as comment as she pressed her bleeding thumb to the contract; she was wearing a borrowed shirt and glared at me when she thought I wasn't looking.

I stood with Brass, Quick, and Slate and the people I'd recruited for the Shadow Breakers in the rumpus room after everyone had finished their dinners and moved about to enjoy the rest of their night. I held my chin high and hoped my bearing reflected my position.

"Does anyone have questions? Now is the time to ask them."

"In the rooms with the patrons, what are we supposed to do?" asked a twinkling eyed boy.

Well, not a boy. He was Gypsum's age, the youngest I'd recruited. Malachite. I was only slightly embarrassed that I remembered his name because he had a puckish demeanor and was sinfully flirty. That was how we began speaking to begin with, he had tried hitting on me right in front of Brass. He was tall and leanly muscled, a long seax specialist was my best guess.

"Whatever you're comfortable with. What happens there, stays there. I call it Vegas," I said with a grin, "You're all adults; you decide whether you wish to have a conversation, or something more."

I left out the pressure to do more. It was significant, as I well knew.

"Have you ever fucked a patron?" Mirage asked, as haughty as ever.

"Yes," I answered coolly. I'd only had one, but it was Slate. Murmurs sprung up within the new Breakers. "Many do. Patrons can be very... persuasive if you don't have a firm resolve."

Quick chuckled to the other side of Brass.

"Really? I would not have thought you had it in you."

My blood boiled; I didn't like her personal questions.

"Any questions that are not personal?" I asked giving Mirage a withering look, she was unfazed. The woman was dense.

"Is he your husband? I see you have a ring on. Must be hard not to fool around with Brass while you work so closely together," Mirage said pointedly, crossing her arms in front of her chest.

Her words stung, but not me.

Slate was seething. "If you do not shut your mouth, Anthias, I will shut it. Permanently. Wildfire is mine, not Brass's or anyone else's."

I closed my eyes. I wished he hadn't done that. I hated gossip and now the recruits we had some crazy kind of love... square.

"Focus on crossing the Crash Course, Mirage. See if you can beat my record. Three weeks, recruits. Beat three weeks and I will do your victory massage myself," I promised and dropped my eyes.

Slate's head had whipped to me with a growl. None of the men had been insane enough to leer after Slate's proclamation of possession, but I could feel their lust. Brass was also pinching the bridge of his nose, which usually meant he was seeing a lot of explicit things.

"You'll love the competitions, that much I can promise you. It's my personal favorite; that, and the family you will become and love as you train. Look around, you will likely see one another more than anyone else in your lives," I said with fondness, and avoided Brass's eyes like a mad Red King.

I'd told him I loved him today. Not very smart given our current situation.

"Ama and Shale will lead you back to the portal. Now that you have signed your blood contracts you are permitted to know our location." I walked away as Brass went on and Slate followed.

Slate caught up to me and stopped in front of me, making me grind to a halt. "Say it," he growled, and I rolled my eyes.

I took his hand and placed it between my breasts. "Yours. Try not to trample it every single day."

He took my hand and placed it over his heart. Damn the man. Tender Slate got me every time.

"You didn't have to brand me. It's none of her business, anyway."

"I do not want you spending so much time with Brass anymore. There is no need." Slate crossed his arms expecting a fight.

Instead, I used his arms to balance me as I stood on my tip toes to kiss him chastely, "Whatever you say, love," I told him.

He narrowed his eyes at me and I kissed him again.

"I want to make love to you tonight. No rushing and not where we could get caught," I purred.

"Scarlett. Do not make me beg," he whispered, his eyes softening.

We laid naked, our limbs intertwined, staring at the ceiling after a rigorous session of lovemaking and Slate had finally healed me. I'd be lying if I said I didn't thoroughly enjoy it. I hoped other couples in Tidings were as passionate as we were.

Slate climbed up my back, so his hips rested against my backside, and reached over me to the bowl of fruit we'd brought upstairs. He peeled an orange with his big hands, the juices squirting on my skin. He offered me a slice over my shoulder, and I snatched it away with my teeth and was rewarded with a rumbling chuckle that pressed him deliciously against me.

"How do you feel about getting our portraits painted?" I asked him.

I hated that we had no pictures together, I wanted one. Needed one for later.

I felt him shrug against me. "As you wish."

An idea struck me. "Hold on."

I popped another piece of orange in my mouth left the bed. I rifled through the drawers in our closet until I found what I was looking for. I pulled it out and hid it behind my back until I got back into bed.

Slate arched an eyebrow over his grey eyes, and I swore he'd never looked sexier. His glossy hair in complete disarray, all the beads and fetishes in a bowl on the bathroom counter and his bronzed hard body glistened with sweat from our love making. I pulled up my old cell phone and quickly snapped a picture and giggled as I looked at it. Butterflies flapped in my stomach at my first photographic evidence of my breathtakingly handsome husband.

"Cell phone pictures?" he asked skeptically.

Then a smile spread over his face; one of his rare ones, his cheeks crease from his wide smile. I snapped another one, and he grabbed my arm as he popped the rest of the orange into his mouth. I giggled crazily as we struggled over control of the cell phone. He got it from me and started to snap away and I couldn't stop laughing.

I pulled the white sheet over me, and he lifted the edge of it and snapped another picture as he crawled over me. I snatched the cell phone away and snap, another picture, this time as he kissed me. The cell phone was temporarily forgotten as we roll over one another in our bed, blissfully happy.

I grabbed the pear out of the bowl and bit into it while I laid on my stomach. Slate bare chested, the white sheet pooled in his lap as he leaned against our headboard. Slate chuckled and I turned the camera on him.

"Say something to the video Savage Storm, your fans want to hear what your secret is to your undefeated standing," I asked him in my best reporter voice.

He laughed and its richness tingled me to my toes. "Be scary, very scary, and sex, lots of sex with the undefeated female champion. She keeps me on my toes," he growled and grabbed my ankle, yanking the phone away and turning it back on me.

I readjusted the sheet and smiled shyly even though I knew no one would see it, it was still awkward to be recorded. "You are recently married; how can your fans expect this to affect your performance?" He didn't do a funny voice, but he was still acting like he's interviewing me.

"Well, Mr. Reporter... you're pretty good looking. Don't tell my husband, but I think I'm going to have to call it off so I can get into your pants." I leaned forward and yanked back the sheet. "Whoops, not wearing any. Even better!" I jumped onto him and heard the phone clatter onto the floor, but I was too busy kissing my husband to care.

"I love you. Love, forever and always. Yours, mine, the world's, for all time," I told him and he flipped me around, so my back rested against the soft mattress, and he kissed me deeply, I swooned.

CHAPTER 45
JETT

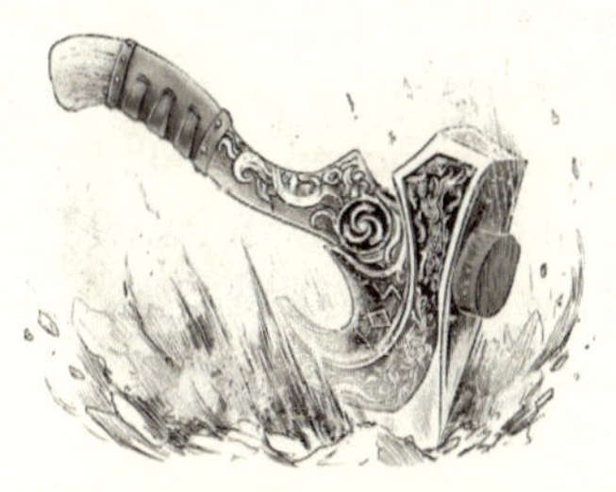

"There must be another way. I knew it. I fucking knew it." Jett paced and dry washed his face.

"Language, darling," Pearl said delicately and Jett gave her an apologetic look.

Scarlett held Indigo as the two girls cried. He, himself, was close to losing control too. He knew it, he shouldn't have been surprised. The way Scarlett was letting Slate get away with everything, the way they were caught in every gods be damned room in the palace going at it as if they didn't have an entire wing to themselves. Jett had walked in on them in the pool that morning. He'd turned right back around and back into the prep room to stop the others from having to scrub their eyes out as well.

Jett wished he had hair to pull. "Baby sis," he pleaded, and Scarlett lifted her tears-streaked face to his.

She hadn't come to her decision lightly, that was obvious. Her heart was breaking, and it hadn't even happened yet.

"He won't do the right thing, and if he did... I don't know what's worse. Staying here while he finds a wife, leaving me behind or leaving it all behind. I'll be okay. Mom did the same thing and she was fine. I've promised myself; I won't make the same mistakes. I'm not pregnant, no one is relying on me. I won't shut my heart from... others. I have a bachelor's degree that I have never used. It'll be an adventure."

Indigo sobbed harder and tears-streaked down Scarlett's face again, her body was trembling slightly, and Jett's anguished face turned to Pearl for wisdom. She was crying as well. What an awful mess this was.

"Fuck the Dagrs. You matter more than a gods be damned name," Jett cursed again and Pearl didn't scold him.

"I appreciate it, I really do, but I can't live with it. Everything happens for a reason. If I was meant to be with Slate, I would have had his baby." Scarlett's turquoise almond eyes were red rimmed and pouring forth tears.

Beyond her brave face, she still grieved deeply for their parents and her lost child. Jett squatted and held his head in his hands. This couldn't be happening. Things were supposed to be better when their mother and Scarlett came. They'd have a family; Jett had waited his whole life for them to return. He yelled in frustration and punched a wall. They were in Pearl's room. The highest turret of the palace with its whites and creams. It was where they'd been told Indigo was their sister and now, he was losing his other sister in the same spot.

"It's not fair," Jett mumbled.

"I'll still come back for Amethyst's baby shower, and when the baby is born. If things are good, maybe I can come back for the Midsummer festival. Who knows? Maybe I'll meet a nice man and he'll want to come live here with us, you never know. In the meantime, you guys can focus on babies and marriages. You won't even notice I'm gone," Scarlett said weakly and Jett snorted.

She was grasping at straws, trying to comfort them when she was the one who needed comfort. Her alone in Chicago, like their mother had been, broke his heart as well. He'd spent his whole life knowing he had a mother and a sister in the States. He was different from most other Guardians because he'd practically studied pop culture. When his sister and mother came to live with them he wanted to have things in common with them, with her. He wanted to be a Myopic as she had been raised. He tried to be the next best thing so she would feel at home.

Jett felt his face start to twitch, and Scarlett motioned him to join her and Indigo. Jett fell to his knees beside them and she kissed his cheeks, with lips so soft and swollen from crying.

"I love you both so much. I'll miss you every day. I promise to write all the time, you'll just have to frequent the technology room in Valla more often," Scarlett laughed through her tears.

Jett was always in the technology room, downloading music. When the university reopened, he'd gone to watch American movies on the internet and listened to the latest hits. He knew he'd done a good job when those around him started to talk as he had. Indigo was a fluke. She'd likely started speaking so informally.

Indigo laughed too. She lifted her face, puffy like Scar's from the crying.

"You won't be a Guardian," she said, realization dawning on her.

Scarlett dropped her eyes. Giving up becoming a Guardian had to be up there with leaving Slate. It was what their mother risked everything for and now she was giving it all up. Jett always knew Scarlett and Slate would end in heartbreak; he didn't count on his being one of the hearts to be broken.

"You shall want for nothing. I will have marks exchanged for American currency and put into an account for you first thing Monday," Pearl said, wiping her tears with an embroidered kerchief, a golden sunburst emblazoned the corner.

She looked older somehow to Jett, sitting there crying, saying goodbye to another one of her family members.

"I never thought I would have to do this again. When your mother and Hawk left I knew it was temporary, but this... You may never come back, darling." Pearl wiped the new stream of tears and Scarlett moved to sit next to their grandmother on the plush chaise.

"That's not so. I'll come back often, a few times a year at least. It won't be like Mom at all. I'll send pictures like she did, and you guys can come visit me. It'll be completely different. Only..." She licked her full lips and held Pearl's hands in her lap as she looked to Indigo and Jett. "Slate can't know. He's been weird lately, like he suspects, but can't figure out what my move is. I think he thinks I'll try to push him away. I thought about it, but I can't." She shook her head and her chin wobbled.

"What about Brass? Silver says he's crazy about you," Indigo pleaded with desperation.

Jett had thought the same thing, but he knew Scarlett's answer. "Brass and Slate are best friends. Cousins as it turns out. I couldn't do that. There's another reason I decided to leave instead of staying. Slate's prophecy. If I'm not here, it can't come true. He really believes it will and if I remove myself from the equation, it can't come into fruition. It's the least I can do," she sighed, and wiped her nose with the kerchief.

"So, you don't want anyone else knowing? Not even Tawny?" Indigo asked.

"No, she'll blame herself and I don't want Hawk trying to convince me not to go. It's best if it's a clean break. I'd tell Gypsum, but he and Slate have grown close. I don't want anyone else knowing that would have to lie to Slate. I don't want him feeling betrayed, but I couldn't do it and not say goodbye to you all first."

Pearl hugged Scarlett, fiercely stroking her hair, and Jett wrapped an arm around Indigo. "So, the night of your competition, you and Slate will be out of the palace. We'll pack your things for the States, check your flight, get you a rental car... what else?" Jett asked, blinking to dry the tears.

"That's all. Have it waiting in Rhode Island in case Slate gets back to the palace before me. I don't want a confrontation with him. It's important to me that it doesn't end ugly." She was shaking again, and Pearl gripped her and started to rock.

"I do not know of another alternative, Scarlett darling. Perhaps once you both move on, you can move back. We will make sure Slate moves to the Dagr palace so you will not have to see him. Does that sound good?" Pearl's voice broke and Jett swallowed hard.

He'd never seen Pearl so distraught unless someone had died. He guessed, to her, the grandchildren she'd fought so hard to protect leaving was a slow death of hope.

Hope was a dangerous thing. Jett had hoped for so long...

"That does. Don't go shoving him off just to get me back," she joked. "I'll be fine, really; everything with the Merfolk, Ash, mom, dad, and now Slate. I can't take anymore. I know when I've been beaten and I am. It's time for me to move on." Scarlett lifted her chin and pushed her caramel waves out of her face.

Jett wished he could dispute her, that he had one good thing to counter, but there was nothing. After everything, she'd come to filter herself through Slate. He gave her the love she craved that soothed all the wounds she'd suffered and now he was being taken away from her.

How fickle the Norns were, it wasn't fair.

CHAPTER

FORTY-SIX

It was the first Friday in February, my own personal doomsday. I didn't want to go to classes. Slate came home to our big white bed with me and we got very little sleep. Only when I passed out from Slate's talented tongue did I stop harassing him. Towards the end he kept laughing, trying to fend me off so he could recover.

"Give a man a minute, Torch." he said, breathless.

I kept holding my breath waiting for the wave of tears to subside. "I'll do the work, just lay back and relax."

Slate had laughed, rich and delicious.

I felt a simultaneous pull in my stomach and a knife in my heart. "I intend to, but even I need a minute or two to recover."

I had wanted to pass out from the multiple orgasms Slate bestowed upon me and not wake up in the morning. When the sunlight warmed my face shortly after dawn, it was usually my favorite time of day. Slate's face would be free of tension, all his hard planes smooth with his long thick lashes fanned across them. His lips would be sleep swollen

438

and he made the most adorable pout while he slept. This morning would be my last to wake up to such a sight.

Before he could see me cry, I'd climbed from our bed and showered. He joined me and I tried not to seem completely wretched while our bodies melded together.

"I am not complaining, but what has gotten into you, Torch?" he asked as we readied at the bathroom counter together.

I'd tried not to make a lot of eye contact. Slate was too good at reading me, even without our bond, but I couldn't look at myself either.

"Will you delve for me? It's been so long since it all happened, maybe some progress..."

I'd told myself if I got my period I would stay and hope for the best. It never came. I was a desolate wasteland. Slate dropped his head and reached out sideways. I brought my stomach to his outstretched palm and felt the warmth of his calling flood through me. I held onto it after the warmth faded. Slate didn't look at me and I sighed, my last hope in the dust. The floodgates were ripped asunder and I'd fallen to the floor crying. I hadn't cried since telling Pearl, Jett, and Indigo my plans. I needed Pearl's help, and I couldn't leave without saying goodbye. Abandoning them would be one of the hardest parts of this terrible plan.

"Scar."

Slate sank down beside me and pulled me to his chest. He never called me Scar. There had been another reason for my eager trysts I'd not cared to acknowledge even to myself.

Hope was a filthy khoraz. Sweet promises that could leave you feeling despondent and faithless.

"There has been little progress. It does not matter to me; you are my mate. You and no other. Forever and always. Yours, mine, the worlds. For all time."

He soothed me with my own words, and I turned to him and gave him a small smile. Slate wasn't the kind of man who told you he loved you, but this was close.

"I love you. Gods, you know that don't you? I certainly didn't want to, but it was a futile fight from the start. I wanted so badly to give you... to be able to..." I swallowed the wail that wanted to tear from my throat. "These past six weeks have been —" Slate stroked my hair. "I'd do anything for you. Sorry, I didn't mean to be so dramatic this morning." Slate used his thumb to wipe my tears away and kissed me.

"I have no one but myself to blame. I wanted all of you, seduced you for a year and this is all I get. Unconditional love." He gave me a slow sexy grin. "I suppose I will survive."

I chuckled nervously and he kissed me again. If we wouldn't have been late for classes, I would've forced myself on him again. Instead, I'd let him help me get to my feet. I finished getting ready.

Classes had gone painfully slow. And yet, too fast. I'd packed everything in my trunk in between classes so Tawny wouldn't find out. Jett was a terrible secret keeper, so Cherry and Amethyst knew about my departure. Cherry had taken me aside after following me to our shared room and said her goodbyes as she helped me pack.

It was really happening.

Jett kept staring at me with gleaming eyes so much like my own. I couldn't stop touching Slate. I didn't give a rat's fanny pack who saw me that day. I prayed that my plan followed through because I couldn't do this another month or two. Tawny and Quick looked at me with palpable skepticism when I told them there was nothing wrong.

Quick wasn't to be included in the plan. Slate would feel betrayed and he'd need someone to be on his side. I'd purposely left Quick out of it so he had a drinking buddy. I'd left Steel out of it because if anyone would be levelheaded, and Slate might listen to them and take Slate's sugarfoot, it was Steel. Lastly, there was Gypsum, wiser *way* beyond his years. He'd be there when Slate needed someone to sit with in silent contemplation.

Who knew? Maybe I'd be wrong. Maybe Slate would screw his way through the Valla University tyros and be over me in a week, a day. If that wasn't the case, I had saved as much as I could to help him. Jett would deposit the letters I'd written at their place settings in the morning to explain my absence. They'd be upset at first, but they'd get over it.

It wasn't until Battle Training that I broke down. I ran my thumb over the dark silver ring with its stone finish. I'd seen this ring on my father's hand every day since I first saw him in the alcove with my mother the first night we arrived in Tidings. Slate sat next to me as we listened to Crag drone on about strategy. It wasn't a boring class; I was distracted, and pain lanced through my heart at my every breath.

Unshed tears started to burn in my eyes and suddenly the battle grounds were so loud, too loud.

"Scarlett?" My limbs felt numb when Slate bent his head down to look at me.

My world was tilting again and I needed fresh air; my lungs burned, every breath full of pain. I squeezed my eyes shut and felt myself being scooped up into strong, sure arms. I melted against his chest and let myself be carried. What did I care what these people thought of me?

The freezing Valla air filled my senses. I felt the sunlight on my face in the winter chill, my closed eyes seeing red. I could smell the ocean that beat against the cliff face Valla U rested atop. I'd never been outside the university unless it was for the induction ceremony and I had gone directly into a big tent set up just outside that night, so I never had a real view of it.

"Are you thinking about this morning?" Slate smelled like a crisp autumn wind and sweat despite the cold winter air.

I wanted to say something bitter, something that would hurt him, but I couldn't summon the acrid persona I'd cultivated. As deep in my grief as I was, every breath was an effort. I missed my mother, my father. I missed Chicago and simpler times when the worst thing that happened all day was that I had left my homework assignment on the kitchen table.

In this world where I was orphaned and barren, I didn't know who I was anymore. I thought I had made myself feel better about my father's death by imagining him somewhere beautiful with my mother, that I was selfish to want him back, but I had only postponed my grief. Grief that had risen like a tidal wave pulling me under in an already vulnerable position. Every time I felt like I couldn't possibly feel worse, I did. I should stop tempting fate to prove me wrong.

"Open your eyes." Slate's voice was satin brushing silk.

"I just need some air," I croaked.

"Scarlett, if there is something you need to say, say it. Are you worried about tonight?" he whispered, his mouth inches away from my ear where he cradled me.

My breath caught until I realized he meant our time with the patrons. "Yes. I'm nervous about my first real patron." I wiped my eyes with the sleeve of my training uniform.

"Open your eyes." He coaxed again, and I shook my head. "You are strong. The patron should be afraid of what you might do if they try something. You have my word; I will be on my best behavior." I could hear the smile in his voice.

"You'd better be," I told him, attempting to lighten the mood. I sighed, "Tell me something about you I don't know. It doesn't have to be one of your secrets."

"When I was younger..." I felt him shift into a seated position and I curled against his chest, the weak little girl that I was.

Being this close to him made my skin tingle everywhere it met his, the pull I felt from him stronger than ever. I dried my eyes with my palms and felt him place me in his lap, the arm that cradled my legs wrapping over my lap. I wanted to nuzzle against his chest and stay in this safe place forever.

"I can't imagine you younger." I didn't mean to interrupt him; it just came out.

I finally opened my eyes and found myself leaning against his chest. He took his hand from my lap and leaned back on it while we sat in the grass, facing the edge of the cliff overlooking the ocean. I lifted my chin to look up at him, his grey eyes stared out into the water; he looked far away. His strong jaw perfectly symmetrical with his straight nose, the early evening sun highlighting his flawless bronzed skin, his black glossy waves spilled down to his chest threaded with silver beads and the carvings he always wore.

Creases appeared in his cheeks as he looked down at me, his full lips pulling back into a rare smile, that was no longer as rare as they once were. "You never asked me about my childhood before."

"Bet you were a hit with all the girls," I said, busy breathing him in.

His smile faltered. "No, I was troubled. Lera was the first relationship I had, if you could call it that after Larn'ra took me."

I didn't want to unearth bad memories. "What were you going to say?"

Slate looked down at me. Despite how close we're sitting, I was still far from his full lips. "I loved your mother. After my first memory of my birth mother, for nearly two years, there was only Wren. She changed me, fed me, and loved me. Her name for me for me was Stoic until my father chose my name. We all slept in their bed together; your mother, Jett, Steel, my father, and myself. It was the only time I knew what it felt like to have a real mother. I remember when you and Indigo were born. My father helped name you." He sighed and his expanding chest moved my entire body.

I try to process that tidbit without losing control, but I was finding it more than a little difficult. He knew I was a twin all along.

"I knew that. Not that it was your real father, but my father told me." I smiled. "Alder thought our parents would eventually fall in love." I dropped my head back to his chest.

"Perhaps. My second memory after my mother's death was of your mother holding me to her chest. Pearl was there when I was born. She gave me to Wren to take to the Tio palace. I remained there with the staff, with Wren and my father visiting as often as time allowed until she began to show with her pregnancy with Jett."

I'd never heard this story. It looked to caused him so much pain I wanted him to stop, but I also wanted to hear it told. I selfishly urged him to continue.

"My mother was poisoned. Pearl masked my death and hid me away. She told her last prophecy, about you, before she died." Slate's jaw brushed the top of my head and I wrapped my arms tightly around him.

"You don't have to continue. I'm so sorry, love." I felt his sorrow, it was deeper than my own.

"I have had a better life than I would have thanks to Pearl. If she had not saved me, I would have died long ago. If not poisoned by the same person who killed my mother, then in one of my fits of rage. That was why your mother could not take me. She would not split us boys up."

"Do you know who poisoned your mother?" I asked softly and felt his shake his head.

"Back then, they had a tight-knit group; lunching together, dinner parties every week. A few of the other wives were in the birthing room, but Pearl did not know which one of them gave her the poison in the commotion of my birth. It all started with my mother's prophecy. After that, Ridge Vetr was killed and your family saved Sparrow and Tawny, then the Red King Massacre. The Sumar and Tios have a lot of debt to collect."

After a protracted silence I ran one of his beads between my fingers.

"I, for one, am glad Pearl saved you. I am so sorry about your mother and father, Slate. My mother loved you dearly. Funny, I always felt like there was something she wasn't telling me about you. What are you smiling at?" I asked and started to push off him, but his big hands circled around my wrists. I wasn't even close to wanting to fight him off.

He spread his powerful legs, fitting my hips between them, and pulled me to his chest so I could lean against him. He rested his chin on the top of my head and we looked out to the glistening ocean. I was thankful my body didn't feel the cold. I didn't want to move.

"No reason. I am happier than I have a right to be. When we adopt children, Torch, you will be as good a mother as yours was." His smile was back.

My heart wrenched in my constricting chest and I squeezed my eyes shut tight, praying I didn't start shaking.

"One day." I slid my hands over his hard thighs. "Did anyone notice us leave?" I asked.

"Fuck them," he said with no inflection whatsoever, and it made the corners of my mouth curl.

Slate's life philosophy.

"We should go back in. We'll miss dinner."

I turned back in his arms and he was looking down at me, his grey eyes hooded. I shifted my body so I was on my knees in front of him, his eyes watched my every move. His full lips curled, but there was a dangerous animalistic gleam in his eyes. He wasn't a man; he was an animal caged in skin; full of carnal eroticism.

He smiled again and it was devilish.

Big golden birds flew in the distance catching my attention as they headed back towards the university. I felt like someone punched me in the gut, I could feel the color drain from my face as if someone had pulled a bath plug and my mouth felt open.

Before I could react, Slate grabbed me to his chest and rolled over my body, his wrist blades sprung as he looked in the direction I had been staring. After a moment, he looked down at me furrowing his forehead.

"What did you see?" he asked from on top of me.

"I've seen this place before." The words came out in an exhale.

Slate's body squeezing down on my lungs, pinning my arms to my sides so I couldn't struggle for space. He smiled and lifted himself onto his elbows, retracted his wrist blades. He didn't seem like he was going to roll off.

"Slate, move," my voice sounded panicked.

He frowned and got to his feet in one move pulling me up with him. I turned back around to face the university. I was chilled to the core.

How had I never noticed it?

Valla University for Guardian Mastery was an enormous yellow stoned castle. From where I stood on the edge of the cliff, I could see down the sloping landscape where the stained-glass dome of the green house and the recessed battleground arena were hidden up against the start of a forest. Behind me was the tree Valla U styled their sigil from, an enormous tree that grew from the water and held the cliff face in place. Part of the university was supported just by this tree's limbs that stretched far from the land itself.

I stared wide eyed and almost stumbled. "I've dreamed of this place my whole life, but there was a war, a battle, and monsters. Death is everywhere, the people are so angry."

I could feel their anger and wrath even now. I hugged myself and turned to Slate, distress written all over my face.

"Is it something I remembered in a book?"

Maybe my mom had some Tidings history book I'd found when I was little that gave me nightmares, but no...

Slate looked concerned, but also fearful. I pointed at him taking a step back.

"You're in that dream. What? I don't understand!" I shouted at him.

His hands were out, trying to reach me so he could comfort me. I was hyperventilating. I ran my hands through my hair and focused back on the university.

"This is your mother's prophecy. Isn't it? Why I'll be the death of you? What do I do that kills you, Slate? Tell me."

With my voice rising, my eyebrows climbed into my hairline. My stomach was in knots, and I had the feeling he was about to tell me something terrible.

He had sucked his lips into his mouth but released them. "It is what you do not do."

"What! I let you die?" I asked as some invisible force squeezed around my heart. I clutched my hand to my chest hoping to counteract the pain.

He nodded once and I let out a wail.

"I can't do this." I shook my head and ran back towards Valla U.

Slate would follow me and coax me into his arms again, those arms I turned to putty in. I knew running from him, my problems, the facts, wasn't ideal, but I panicked.

How could so much in the world be wrong? Didn't the bad things ever happen to the bad people? Why must they happen to the good? I didn't count myself in that number, but my mother, my father, and inevitably Slate. I couldn't watch another one of my loved ones die.

I was so out of there.

I sat in front of the mirror as Bronze did my hair and makeup. I was in my black leather get up that Cordillera commissioned for me. Slate was in the prep room with Brass, they were going against one another. I was competing against Shale, and she sat at the next mirror as Katydid got her ready while casting glances at Brass, who didn't necessarily ignore her but didn't give her the attention she craved either. I sympathized.

I wasn't the main event tonight since Brass was the former champion and Slate the current one — it was a big deal. The sides of my hair were braided back and the top teased and sprayed over and over; dramatic black cat like liner and pale glossy lips completed the look. Bronze dusted my skin with shimmering dust as I took off my ring and slid it onto my stone pendant necklace before returning it to my neck. I squeezed my torque and breathed.

"Beautiful as always," Bronze said, admiring her handiwork before slipping the thin black leather mask over my eyes.

"Thanks to you," I told her and stood up from my seat.

Slate and Brass were being oiled up by Cricket and they both smirked at me from where they stood. I must have looked jealous. I rolled my eyes and turned away from them. Shale sat down next to me on the bench as she tugged on her boots, which were exactly like mine.

"Ready for some real competition?" she asked.

Her dark tilted eyes twinkled. The shimmer on her skin made her cheekbones even more prominent. I recalled when I thought she and Slate were together and how insanely jealous I was, so much so that I had agreed to contemplate marrying Ash because of it. I could admit that to myself now.

"Are you talking about yourself, or do you have someone else in mind?" I asked, chidingly with a smirk on my face.

Shale's laugh is throaty and rich. "This is going to be fun."

I seriously doubted that.

Slate and Brass made their way to the benches as we all waited for the competitions to start. I was struck by how much more they looked alike when they were dressed the same in their little leather briefs, tanned bodies glistening with oils, dark hair styled away from their faces; Slate's was plaited and Brass's combed so that one rogue lock could graze his cheek bone.

"Stare any harder and our briefs will burn off," Slate said in a rough tone.

Brass gave me an amiable smile and I let out a long exhale. Things were tense. I felt a little tremor through my body as if butterflies had originally beat in my belly but had somehow hatched larvae that had made their way into my bloodstream and wriggled about under my skin. My nerves frayed, and I had a few scant hours left. Slate slipped his arm around me and I leaned into him.

"Are you going to behave yourself tonight?" he asked me.

I felt him stare at the top of my head. I looked up at him, my cheek against his arm.

"You want me to behave?" my voice was low and suggestive, and his lips curled.

"Normally, no, but make an exception tonight."

I sighed and nodded, "Yes, Captain." He pinched my hip, making me smile.

Brass's eyes slid to mine and tears burned at the back of my eyes. It was the last time Slate would hold me.

"Come with me," I said suddenly and got to my feet, pulling Slate up with me.

Slate gave me a questioning look, but I knew our time was limited. The announcer's booming voice started and the two other men in the room took their turns running out onto the course. The crowd went crazy for them. I almost forgot how loud they got.

I laced my fingers through Slate's as I guided him into the stall. "Where —"

I swallowed Slate's question and used my calling to lock the stall door behind him. "Take me now. I want you inside me," I breathed.

Slate pulled away, and his grey eyes questioned mine. I ran my fingers over his oiled abs and slid my hand beneath the fabric of his briefs. He sucked air in sharply as I gripped him in my hand. He was always ready for me.

"You despise bathroom sex," he groaned as I stroked him while popping the buttons on my shorts.

"I hate nothing I do with you," I countered, and he smiled.

It broke my heart, and I closed my eyes. Our oiled bodies slipped and slid over one another as he pushed my back against the side of the stall, while deep inside me.

"Fuck," Slate groaned; his corded neck strained as he spilled within me.

I muffled my own moans against his shoulder and tasted his slick skin. I wanted to remember every detail of our last time together.

Sight, scent, touch, taste, and his growl I loved so much.

We helped one another clean up and hurried back to the benches. Shale smirked when we sat back down. Brass's eyes were on the floor, and he looked unusually distressed. I knew the feeling.

Katydid brought in two dresses; both black, both silk halters, both backless. Shale looked at me and gave me a look that said, could be worse. Slate and Brass both stared daggers at the dresses, as if it was their fault. Slate pulled me closer to him and I slid my hand over his at my hip. I wished we could speak to each other like I could Brass in his mind.

"I love you," I whispered, and he kissed the top of my head.

Tonight was going to be rough for both of us.

The two men ran back into the room to fanfare. They both rushed through showers and dried themselves quickly. One man started pulling his clothes on right in front of us. My cheeks heated when I realized there was not a lot of time for modesty when you had to get out right away. The man smirked at Shale and I, which Shale returned, and he checked the ticker before stepping out. 230 - 1 flashed on the screen. He took a deep breath and readied a smile.

I took a shuddering breath. My body burned. It was a lot easier last time, thinking what happened with the patron wouldn't matter as much. Brass grunted and I knew he was reading my mind.

The announcer came back on, "For our second match, our first competitor stands at five foot two and weighs in at one hundred and ten pounds... THE WIDOW MAKER!"

Shale gave my hand a squeeze as she headed outside the doors to fanfare. I gulped as my heartbeat faster and faster.

"I do not want you to win," Slate said brusquely. It caught me off guard.

"I can't lose," I told him, pleading for him to understand with my eyes.

I kissed him deeply and choked off a cry.

"Our second competitor, and record-breaking bid winner, undefeated female champion, the ever alluring... WILDFIRE!"

I squeezed my eyes shut and kissed Slate one last time and strode off without looking back, swaying my hips like Wildfire would.

I was Wildfire.

The crowd was deafening as I came out. I let my lips curl as I made my way to the start of the Guillotine. I flipped my hair down as I trailed my fingers from my heel and up my leg, slowly letting the men in the crowd get their eyeful and felt Slate's eyes behind me. I swallowed hard and swung my head back up so my hair fell over my back dramatically.

"Slut," Shale said through her teeth, and I tried not to smile.

"Are the lovely ladies ready?" the announcer asked.

We both gave a curt nod and the BOOM sounded.

The swirling spotlights stopped, and we could see the course clearly as the fans screamed all the louder before we both broke into a run.

Shale couldn't use her turbo mode while we competed. That was her talent, like my empath abilities. It was a close call. It distracted me knowing Slate was watching and disapproving in the prep room, but I still completed several showy flips, including my finishing move of doing my handstand at the dock's edge before lowering my legs slowly, showing off my best asset. Shale was a second behind me. She hopped up right next to me and slid her arm around my waist as I smiled at the crowd.

"And the win goes to WILDFIRE!"

I manipulated the crowd on our walk back to the prep room, red roses fell from the stands instead of white, and I picked four up and broke the stems off two; sliding one into Shale's hair, one into mine, and kissed the petals of one before sending it into the crowd. The fans cheered as they dove for the falling flower.

We got to the prep room and I ran straight into the nearest shower, placing the fourth rose just outside it. Shale was in the next stall. I scrubbed my hair and turned around and saw Slate and Brass watching us.

I faced the wall and breathed deep; I hadn't expected that.

I dried off my body and wrapped the towel around me as I stepped out of the shower and dried my hair as I picked up the last rose. Slate and Brass continued to watch us in silence. I saw red numbers rising higher and higher on the ticker.

I could feel how irritated Slate was that Brass had seen me showering, but he knew it would happen if they were in the room when we changed. It was inevitable. I wasn't as modest as I thought I was.

I sat down in front of the mirror and Bronze and Cricket worked in a frenzy to fix my hair and make-up. Dark smoky eyes and glossy lips with soft wavy hair were the final product. They held up my dress as I stepped into it less than fifteen feet away from Slate and Brass. They continued to watch, not saying anything to me or one another, both their faces perfectly smooth.

Bronze brought me my shoes and I looked at the screen. It was still climbing. I picked the gloss up off the table and walked over to Slate. I kissed the bloom of the red rose and handed it to him. His full lips curled into a playful grin, and I averted my eyes before he saw how forlorn I really was.

His eyes flickered over my shoulder. 1600 - 2 flashed red on the screen.

"Your patron awaits you," he said coldly.

That was way too much. It had to be who I thought it was. I glanced at Brass, and he gave me a reluctant smile.

"Ah, Love, but a day, and the world has changed! The sun's away, and the bird estranged; The wind has dropped, and the sky's deranged; Summer has stopped. Ah, Love, but a day, and the world has changed! Look in my eyes! Wilt thou change too? Should I fear surprise? Shall I find aught new In the old and dear, In the good and true, With the changing year? Ah, Love, look in my eyes, Wilt thou change too?"

I sat on Slate's knee and wrapped my arms around his neck. "I love you. Forever and always. Yours, mine, the world's, for all time," I whispered into his ear and kissed his cheek before sliding off his lap.

He grabbed my hand as I walked away.

His eyes were soft, and a little crease formed between his brows. "I need you, Scarlett."

My lips curled as I applied gloss to them and tossed the tube to a gawking Shale.

"I want you."

My hips swayed as I sashayed out the doors. Besides my moment with Slate, I was in full Wildfire mode. I was astonished how easily I could swing between the two. Wildfire smirked at Slate, but Scarlett revealed her innermost love to her husband.

Black clad bodyguards pushed fans out of the aisles as I reached out so they could touch me.

It could really go to a girl's head.

We burst through the hall doors, and they laughed excitedly as they shut the doors behind us.

It was the same bright-eyed bodyguard from last time. "They really like you."

I smiled at him; he seemed sweet. "Thanks guys," I told them as I sauntered down the hall to room two.

My cheeks burned and my breathing was rapid right before I got to the door. I swallowed hard and mentally started a countdown. I picked the scab on my finger from the wound I'd made earlier and rubbed the blood on my new tattoo that hid beneath my emerald wedding ring. I opened the door, and a sweet mint smell assaulted me. I pushed back the deep purple curtain with silver tassels.

There was no mistaking the man for anything other than a patron.

I remembered him immediately as the man who lingered as he held my hand when Brass escorted me through Cordillera's suite when I went to my first competition.

The room was near identical to the third room, the only difference was that it was decorated in blue's and black instead of wine, but it had the same array of foods on the low table and plush velvety couch with the wall directly across from the door a two-way mirror.

He turned as he poured himself a drink in front of the bar. "Care for something?"

He wore a plain white matte half mask. His pants and boots were black leather, but his waistcoat was white leather, and his ascot was black; white shirtsleeves were rolled up to his elbows to reveal leanly muscled forearms.

"White wine would be nice," I said as I crossed the room to him.

He smiled and picked up a wine bottle. I moved closer so I could watch him pour. Rousen reminded to watch my drinks, so he dropped nothing into it. He turned and handed me the wine glass. His eyes were brown and so was his hair, it was combed away from his face purposely haphazardly. He looked to be in his late twenties or early thirties despite his trim beard. I knew he wouldn't be so old I couldn't find anything to talk about with him. I had to buy a little time.

"Care to watch the competition?" he asked, gesturing to the window.

"Yes, please." I walked closer, and he slid his arm around my back to rest his hand on my shoulder.

He led me to the window and the seats there and we sat next to one another. Slate and Brass are facing the crowd already and the *BOOM* sounded. I gulped my wine down as the men raced through the Guillotine.

"Another?" he asked amused, a smile playing on his lips.

I gave a small smile in return and nodded. "If you don't mind."

He rose gracefully and took my glass to refill it as I broke the spell

Brass and Slate cast over me to be sure he wasn't poisoning my drink. "That accent. You are not from here?"

Back story I could do.

"My family is from here, I was born here, but raised outside of it," I said, feeling more comfortable talking about something was familiar with.

"Chicago?" he asked, bringing back my glass and handing it to me.

"Thank you, near there. Have you been?" I asked politely, but I couldn't tear my eyes off Slate and Brass running the Crash Course.

They were both so incredibly powerful and fast. It was like watching two jaguars chase down their prey. Muscles beneath their skin moving in ways I never saw in daily life. It was mesmerizing.

He tucked a finger under my chin and shifted my face towards him. "I have, only stayed a short time. I may go again. I could use an expert tour guide."

I struggled with not wanting to be rude and wanting to watch them in their element.

Not being rude won out. "I am always looking for reasons to go back."

"Which one is yours?" His eyes gleamed under his mask.

I licked my lips; I didn't think he would take well to lying or playing stupid. "Both," I told him.

I didn't want to single out Slate, and Brass was mine. He was my friend, but that was just a detail.

The man looked like I'd just told him a secret. He sipped from his glass and his eyes shifted to the window. I looked eagerly; they were nearly through it. He watched me again, and I tried not to squirm under his gaze.

"What can I call you?" I asked him.

His long fingers pressed the velvet chair against the flow of the fabric, making it look like it'd been clawed. His legs were crossed so his ankle rested on his knee, and I could feel him weigh his answer.

"You may call me Mint." I wondered if he thought he was being clever since the room smelled like mint. I let it go. "I take it Wildfire works for you?"

"It does," I said, and finished my second glass. Before he could offer,

I got up and walked over to the bar to pour myself another. "Would you like one?" I asked him.

He passed me his glass, letting his fingers skim my hand, "Double bourbon neat."

I passed him back his glass just in time to see Slate and Brass jostling each other on a raft and Slate leapt onto the dock, Brass a half second behind him. My hand gripped tightly around the glass and the crowd went wild. Slate and Brass clasped forearms, but I saw the strain between them.

I bit my lip; it was over in a moment and then Heat and Savage Storm were trotting back to the prep room.

I wondered idly if it had ever been that close before, or if they usually make contact like that.

"Have I lost you again?" Mint asked, and I turned to him, smiling.

"I'm all yours. Do they always make contact like that? I have only been to two competitions before." His brown eyes assessed me, and I felt bared before him.

There was a constant sense of unease I was pushing through that had nothing to do with a stranger buying ninety minutes of my time.

"Come. Let us move back into the seating area."

I followed him obediently and cursed Cordillera for not keeping clocks in the rooms.

Mint sunk into the blue velvet couch and wrapped his arm around the back. I sat close enough so his arm was behind me, but not enough so we could touch. He smirked and moved closer to me. His hand at the back of the couch traced the skin on my naked shoulder.

"Sometimes it gets physical. Savage Storm and Heat tend to be very competitive. Most of the men do with Savage Storm, since he is a champion. It never comes to blows though, if that is what you are asking."

I monitored my wine drinking; I didn't want to be drunk with this man.

"You seem nervous. This is your second time with a patron, is it not?"

"It is," I explained and took a measured sip of my wine.

"Yes. I was there, bidding on you. I lost, unfortunately." He scowled as if he was genuinely upset he lost that first night.

"I am here now."

I smiled coquettishly and held out my wine glass for him. He tapped my glass lightly with his own, making it ring, and his brown eyes watched me over the rim.

I heard the fans as Slate made his way through the crowd and up to the room next to mine. My stomach twisted at the thought, and I hoped it didn't show on my face.

Judging by the permanent curl of his lips, he hadn't noticed.

We talked about my training with the Shadow Breakers and my favorite competitor, Quick, truth be told. He seemed to truly enjoy every aspect of the competitions, including the patrons. We didn't talk about him at all, not a single detail, and he never removed his mask. I expected that.

"I was sorry to hear about your engagement."

"I'm not," I said before I could stop myself.

He smiled at me. It was not a kind smile, and my mouth went dry. I was running out of time.

I stood quickly to get another glass of wine and to break eye contact with Mint — he was unsettling. My stomach twisted, and I felt fear bubble up. Actual fear, like I hadn't felt since my father and I were attacked.

He walked up behind me and placed his hands gently on my shoulders, rubbing his thumbs on the bare skin of my back. I felt callouses on his hands but his fingers were smooth.

The caterpillar larvae were back, wriggling under my skin, and my stomach turned. His bearded chin pushed the hair from my neck.

"You smell delicious," he purred, and I stiffened.

It was not the first time he'd told me that.

A knock at the door almost made me scream.

"I'll get it," I told him, fighting the urge to flee.

The curtain moved aside, and a tall brown-haired man walked in. He was the same height and build as Mint. He was also wearing a mask and dressed the same. The new man smiled at me; the two men are identical.

I could never mistake that smile for another's. It was a million-dollar smile. I knew it was coming and yet, it still shocked me.

I felt a sharp prick into my neck and my head pulled back roughly. First Mint laid me down on the floor as second Mint snapped a nix torque around my wrists, shackling them together and took out a cloak. My body felt heavy, and my head lolled as I tried to see what the two men were doing.

It happened so fast.

First Mint said something to second Mint, and they pulled me up to my feet to clasp the cloak around my throat. I felt like I did when Chafer mind blasted me. Every thought vanished before I could form it, and my eyes roamed, unable to land on anything for more than a second. My tongue was dead in my mouth, thick and useless.

First Mint gave Chafer a run for his money with the cruel grin that he flashed me. "Allow me to introduce my brother, Pepper. I could fuck you now and you would let me. Alas, there is a grander scheme in place. Be a good girl and do not make us hurt you before it is necessary."

Second Mint opened the door and looked down the hall before they took my arms and led me from headquarters.

They had set the plan in motion.

FORTY-SEVEN

I'd counted on them not wanting to risk taking to a portal gate in case a Guardian caught them leading what I assumed was an unconscious body off the island. I was conscious, horribly, terrifyingly conscious as they led me through the cobbled roads of Valla's town heart.

They'd taken off my heels and the first Mint, whose name was Spearmint, carried them under an arm as they dragged me along. They went by Spear and Pepper, the bearded Stygian Knights who had helped kill my father and delivered me to the Merfolk.

My feet skimmed the cold cobbles as they dragged me along towards the Urd gate and the darker side of Valla. I fought to keep awake. Whatever Spear had injected into me nearly paralyzed me and had a drowsing effect. A hood covered my head. If anyone passing us took the time to look into it, they would have seen my head slumping to my shoulder.

I knew where we were going when I saw the dead end ahead. The street was poorly lit, and the clouds covered what little moonlight there would have been. A sense of menace hung in the air around the riveted metal door to the left that a hand painted mark was over.

A red sickle blazed even in the darkness; I'd been there before.

Pepper glowered down at me. "Welcome back," he said scornfully, and swung open the door.

They dragged me deeper. A red light blinked on with a humming buzz in the low building. They climbed down the stone steps of a cavernous room that had a large pit with concrete walls and concrete stadium seating around it.

I'd fought the bies there.

My fear never surfaced; I had other people to worry about.

A trap door near the section that was normally roped off opened into darkness and Pepper climbed down. Spear pushed me down after him. Pepper caught me and righted me when Spear dropped next to us.

It was a long dim hallway, and I couldn't see anyway five feet past the incandescent light of the sconces that lit the hall and wide intervals.

"It is unfortunate that you denied us when last we spoke. Your life would have been much easier if you had agreed. Now, you will be forced to. You owe me thirty-one hundred daymarks, by the by. I plan on taking them once you have battled. An initiation of sorts." Spear's hand slid under my cloak to squeeze my backside, letting me know exactly how he planned to have me repay him.

I cringed internally. If Brass felt that through our bond, he'd show up before I gave the signal. As it was, I doubted he was far off. The timing had to be perfect. A door slid open, and the light spilled into the hall.

Four cloaked men stood against the far wall of a small room. Another man, taller than the rest, stood at the forefront. Clean shaven and young, something was nagging at the back of my mind.

The man smirked and his eyes glittered from beneath his black mask. "Get her dressed. Your fans will arrive soon."

The light was behind him, so I couldn't catch the details of his face or even the color of his eyes. I wished my tongue worked so I could have antagonized him into speaking more, so I could store away his voice.

No, I told myself. He lived on borrowed time.

He stepped forward. "It is simple really, you fight, or you die. You win or you die. Once you have won, you will be in the safe keeping of the Mints. I am sure they will find a good use for you until your training is through and then you may return to your family."

I doubted it was that simple. I worked my jaw and my tongue so I could find words. The men laughed at my effort.

"Slate?" I mumbled awkwardly with my numbed mouth.

A man stiffened against the wall, and I saw him sneer. The man at the forefront looked at him and back again.

A third man spoke from next to the one who sneered, "We suspect he will try to find you and when he does, we will take him. See, we are not all bad. We have no intention of killing him, yet. The mercenaries we sent were to retrieve him. They took it upon themselves to try to kill him. You will have company soon enough."

The man's smile was ridiculously warm for the words he'd uttered, and I blinked at him.

"Dress her and leave her until she passes the marawacian," the first man said, and he stopped at the door behind me. "I mean it, leave her. You will have her soon enough, Spear."

Marawacian must have been what they injected into me. The sneering man crossed the room and I heard them whisper behind me.

"He will dress her. The rest of you will leave with me now."

The first man left and the Mint twins set me on the floor, so I laid helplessly with the man who had sneered standing over me. He was even taller than the Mint twins, but shorter than the first man. He turned, and the light dimmed further, so only the vaguest shadows outlined his body.

The man walked to the corner of the room and picked something up before walking back to me. My heartbeat rapidly in my chest and my lips parted with my shallow breaths.

"Shh," he soothed and was astonishingly gentle when he undressed me.

When I laid nude before him, my skin prickled in the cool room and he stared down at me. Brass had activated his bond, and I felt his alarm at my panic. I tried to calm myself and calm him but then the man touched me. His fingertips went where his eyes strayed.

"Please," I slurred, still trying to get my feeling back, and he stilled his hands.

I didn't need my powers to catch his scent of desire, but it was tainted somehow.

He had unshackled the nix torques to have better access to me. He reconnected them in front of me now and shifted down to my bare feet. What he slipped up my legs I could only describe as red latex underwear, revealing underwear. He lifted a strip of latex that matched the bottoms that was about four inches wide and wrapped it around my breasts. I supposed it was better than topless as Spear had threatened the first time, and once I started sweating, it would stick to my skin.

Cordillera's leather bathing suits didn't seem so bad.

He slid two more pieces over each forearm and then pulled on a pair of matching boots that came to my knee with a hint of a heel. When he was done, he looked down at me again. I could move my hands and lift my head and he watched as I tried my limbs. He didn't say a word, and he didn't move to help me. He'd been gentler than I'd expected, I could even forgive his light groping. Spear would have done that and worse, much worse.

The man leaned down close to my ear and whispered, "I will try to stop Spear. He must be rewarded for your capture though, you see. You should be mine."

I closed my eyes and heard his boots scuff the ground as he left the room and the drop of a bar across it. Maybe he wasn't so nice. Not that a Stygian would have ever been nice.

Idly, I worked my limbs and wondered if the other combatants I'd seen had been in my position. I knew Chafer hadn't, but what about his opponent? Brass had said Chafer had done terrible things in the time he'd spent with the Stygians.

I lost track of time as my body returned to normal, and the murmur of a crowd grew. When I could move, I scooted to the far wall and hugged my legs, waiting for the men that would retrieve me.

Slate would still be with his patron; it couldn't have been more than an hour. Time was the enemy. I'd have to rush to beat Slate back to the palace... if I survived.

The bar lifted from the door and light shone on the room. They'd turned the sconces on brighter and it temporarily blinded me. I heard the men enter the room, and they grabbed me under my arms and lifted me to my feet.

"I'll fight. This is unnecessary. You don't have to manhandle me," I snapped and Pepper cocked back his hand to slap me.

Spear caught it and clicked his tongue at his brother. "I like her feisty. There is no challenge in fucking a corpse," he grinned lasciviously at me.

Pepper squeezed my arm harder, "Come along, girl. The sooner you win this match, the sooner my brother will quit boring me with his plans for you."

Spear chuckled wickedly, "I doubt she will find them boring. Quite lively, one can only hope."

"You're going to have to drug me again for that. I'd rather be dead than let you touch me," I cursed him and he chuckled.

"Clever girl. Why did I not think of that?" Spear reached behind him and pulled out a large vial of purple fluid and my heart lurched.

I struggled against them. I would never take rousen again. My body shook violently and Brass fed reassurance through the bond. He was close.

Be strong, the bond said.

Pepper forced a ring onto my middle finger and my face felt tingly, he had put a facial distorter on me. From the outside, my face was one big blur.

"Come along. It will not be all that bad. I heard you enjoyed your last time on rousen. No need for the show, girl."

Spear and Pepper took me through the hall holding on firmly under my arms no matter how much a struggled. They walked past the trap door and deeper into the hall.

"Where are we going?" I spat, and Pepper smiled.

If Pepper never smiled at me like that again, I'd die a happy woman. "To show you what happens if you should think of taking the easy way out."

Heavy wooden double doors with a thick board barred it closed. Pepper called, and the board lifted and fell to the side. Loud, deep growling sounded from within and I dug my heels in. The twins pushed me forward, and the doors swung back revealing a monstrous black wolf in a cage with bars as thick as my arm. It lunged at the bars and gnashed its teeth as long as my hand.

That wasn't the worst part. I could smell the blood and decay that suffocated me when they'd thrown open the doors. A carcass laid on the floor and a low wail tore from my throat.

It was a body. I no longer had to wonder what they did with the losers.

"Do not lose. We told her not to kill you." Spear gripped my face so I couldn't look away and banded his arm across my chest. "Lose, and Fenrir here will eat you alive."

He dragged me closer to the cage and the enormous wolf snapped at the bars. My boots slid on the stone floor as he pushed me closer. I whimpered, and the men laughed. Only then did Spear release me and, when I retreated, Pepper gripped my arm like a vise and pulled me from the room.

"Now, now, just relax. You will be superb," Pepper snickered in my ear, and took me to a short staircase.

"Kiss for luck?" Spear asked from further down the hall and I turned to look at the door.

The crowd was loudest where I was standing. I took a shuddering breath and looked behind me. The bearded Mint twins crossed their arms and Spear nodded towards the door.

"Go on. We will wait here until you are done," Pepper promised.

"Did you push my mother off the balcony at the Vetr castle?"

My voice was toneless as I looked at the door and waited for their response.

"Not us. Sorry to disappoint," one of them answered.

My stomach dropped. I'd been so certain they'd been behind it.

"The same one who nearly disemboweled you. He pushed your mother with a little nudge of air. He said she was just standing there facing the snow caps and had not even heard him approach. She was distracted. Too easy, I believe he called it."

Tears stung my eyes, and I pushed open the door.

The clean-shaven man. He was there.

Red, gritty dirt spanned the pit and my boots crunched against it. The rowdy crowd roared in delight; they rarely had women combatants and I was the first one out. I let their shouts wrap around me as I looked about. The roped-off section was there, and I spotted the clean-shaven man. He sat beside another whose face was deep within his hood. The clean-shaven man had killed my mother and father. I would not let him get far.

There was no announcer. I circled around to the doorless wall and waited for my opponent. Men shouted bawdy comments I ignored as doubts clouded my mind.

What if Brass was detained or Cordillera couldn't offer her support? Slate once told me that there were worse things than rape. I'd survived the Merfolk, but I didn't know if I would survive the Stygians. These men hid as Guardians, and I could be speaking to one and never know it.

While I contemplated letting myself die, despite Fenrir, my opponent entered the pit. Blood stained the red dirt just outside the door, I'd seen where the rest of the men who'd lost had been put.

I couldn't see her face; she wore a facial distorter like I did. She didn't have a weapon either and I wondered if she'd been invited to fight or forced.

The woman wasted no time. She was more sturdily built than I was, her tight, deeply tan body flexed as she charged at me. I felt Brass through the bond, stronger than ever. He was there. It distracted me and the woman saw me lift my chin to scan the crowd. She drop kicked me in the chest, and I went flying into the concrete wall. My head cracked hard and I fell onto my face.

I sucked hard at my saliva so my blood wouldn't activate my bond with Slate. That would ruin everything. The woman was already on her feet and I rolled away. When I tried to stand, my head swam, and she struck with her foot to my thigh dropping me to my knee.

She was by far the best female hand to hand combatant I'd faced and, for a moment, I thought I would fail.

I sucked in another breath and gritted my teeth as I threw my body at her legs. She didn't manage to dodge out of the way fast enough.

I gripped her red bottoms as she tried to kick me off her. She landed knees to my ribs, and I dropped an elbow onto her stomach. Air blew from her mouth with a grunt, and I climbed onto her hips and rained blows down on her.

When I felt her nose give, I stopped and backed away. The crowd got to their feet and started booing. She was still moving, and they wanted me to finish her. I couldn't give a sneer with the facial distorter, but I could flip them all off. I turned towards the roped-off section and gave them a double bird.

One of them laughed, but the two that sat at the forefront scowled.

Everything happened at once. Someone shouted a cry, and the room erupted. Four black-clad men and two women with blades drawn burst from the entryway hall and started cutting down the black cloaked men that lined the upper level.

The men that sat in the roped-off section shot to their feet and the room flared with the hundreds of people who had started calling. I ran and slid to the woman that was lying on the ground and yanked the distorter off her finger and winced. Her face was a bloody pulp, and she was gurgling blood. I couldn't take off her nix torques while wearing my own. I fed the bond my need and saw a cloaked man jump into the pit.

"Do not let her get away!" The man who had been sitting next to the clean shaven one shouted and pointed to me.

I stood at the ready until the man pushed back the cloak. I choked on my relief. I tore off the facial distorter and threw myself into Brass's arms.

"Thank me later," he said roughly and unclasped the nix torques, before bending over the broken woman.

While he healed the woman, I took off towards the door that led to the hall.

"Wait!" Brass shouted.

His cry fell on deaf ears. I needed to get to the trap door and kill the clean-shaven man.

I burst through the door and ducked as a fire ball blasted into the air where my head had just been. The Mint twins were still there, and I'd completely forgotten about them.

"Bitch!" Pepper ground out, and I ducked and rolled from the blades of air he sent slicing around me.

I cried out as one sliced through my shoulder and the blood spurted hot across my throat. I sent out my own calling. The air grew thick around them, and their movements slowed, but they kept calling. I divided my paths and sent boiling water in a constant stream towards Pepper.

Brass burst through the door open and the two men shot to him.

I screamed in warning and lost track of Spear who tackled me with a striking spear to my midsection. He landed on top of me and knocked the air from my lungs. His weight pinned me in place and his hands grabbed my wrists. I called a fire ball and his counter call cut through mine.

"After we kill your boyfriend, we are going to get your Slate and he will watch as I fuck you," Spear sneered.

My eyes went wide.

I saw Brass from the corner of my eye, and I used all my air to lift Spear up. He hadn't expected it and the blade Brass threw sunk deep into Spear's back. Spear's brown eyes went wide, and he turned fumbling for the knife wedged in between his shoulder blades.

I shoved him off me to run towards the trap door. Brass grabbed me as I passed him. Blood poured from slices on his arms and a wound at his scalp.

"Wait, Scarlett or so help me..." Brass cursed, and I looked down the hall but nodded.

I covered his back as he used the nix torques, he'd taken off me and the other woman and clasped them around an unconscious Pepper's wrists behind his back and a bleeding Spear's. Brass lifted his head to me and trotted to where I stood and healed me. I did the same to him and he slid his ring finger to touch mine deactivating our bond.

Bonds were until death. Ours were until love ended which would never happen. If Slate had found out, he would likely skin Brass's finger. He saw every other inch of my body; my emerald ring hid the tiwaz rune. Justice. Sacrifice. It was a little arrow with a stem pointed north on both of our fingers.

"The same man who killed my father, killed my mother. He's here now." I ran, and Brass followed until we reached the trap door.

Two cloaked men appeared and started calling. Brass squatted before me as I stood, both of us calling at the other men.

Funny thing about becoming so reliant on calling, you forgot that someone could walk right up and stab you. Chafer detached from a shadow and slit the throat of the man closest to him. Before his body dropped, Chafer sliced the head off the second man.

"We are not supposed to be murdering them if we can help it," Brass said, straightening.

Chafer smiled wickedly and wiped his blades on one of the men's cloaks. He unclasped the other and tossed it to me. I blinked and realized I had a tiny scrap covering my breasts.

"Thanks," I said, clasping it around my throat before starting up the ladder to the trap door.

"I am sure it was a minor oversight on Brass's part," Chafer teased. "Though he is getting a splendid view now."

Brass growled as he climbed up behind me and I emerged behind the roped-off section. Guardians in thick black cloaks and the three interlocked triangles were scattered around the stadium seats. They drew blades when I emerged, and I held up my hands in surrender.

"She is not one of them," Brass said, climbing up behind me.

He took me by the waist and lifted me out of the gaping hole so Chafer could follow. Guardians were leading out men in shackles everywhere I looked and there was no sign of the clean-shaven man.

"He's gone," I said in disbelief.

"They may have arrested him already. We can check through the carriage to be sure," Brass said smoothly, and I shook my head.

Chafer kicked the trap door shut and assessed the scene. "Lera pulled every string on this hunch of yours. I am surprised she believed the Stygians would try to capture you. Why do they want you?"

"He got away. There was another man with him. Older, I think. He is probably the ringleader..." Brass pulled me close, and I pushed away from him. "Gods, it was the only thing I needed to do before I left this cursed place. I had to find my parents' murderer. I failed them," I squeaked, and Brass gripped my shoulders firmly and leveled his amber eyes at me.

"Look around you. How many lives do you think you saved by exposing these murderers? The Shadow Breakers do not throw stones, but they have scruples. These men kill for the sake of killing. The men who took you are down there, now chained and ready to be arrested by the Guardians. One of them will know a name. We will catch them, Scarlett," Brass reassured me and I squeezed my eyes shut.

I wanted to see this through to the end and now I wouldn't. Chafer reopened the trap door and started down.

"I will make sure they do not get away. I promise I will not kill both." Chafer's wide mouth broke into another grin. "Scarlett, I would not be upset if I saw you again. Good luck with the myopics."

Brass pulled my hood up, "Come. You need to leave. We can check the carriages before we go. We should not be recognized."

I nodded and let him guide me out.

Guardians saw Brass and nodded; he must have been a liaison between the two groups. I didn't imagine Guardians often worked with mercenary guilds. Out of the corner of my eye I saw Cordillera and Moon Straumr speaking. My stomach dropped and her dark eyes met mine. She inclined her head, and I did the same. I had not expected to get along with Cordillera, but there we were. Perhaps not friends, but respected.

I clutched my cloak tight to prevent anyone from seeing what I wore, and Brass led me through the dozens of people arrested in the carriages. Fans and Stygians alike were being hauled to the jail until their trials. Many of these men would be sent to Karkinos for countless murders they'd committed.

The clean-shaven man wasn't with them, and Brass wrapped his arm around my shoulders and led me down the cobbled road. We walked in silence and my heart started to pound faster with every step.

"Why do you think they wanted you?" Brass asked as we finally reached a lit street.

"Bait. They said they wanted Slate, and I was there to lure him in. It would've worked too," I ran my hand over my forehead and held my breath.

"Do you still —"

"Yes. I have to," I strangled my words as they came out.

"Would it be okay if I helped you get ready?" Brass asked, and I nodded.

"Of course," I whispered, afraid if I tried to use more of my voice or I'd start bawling.

"My offer still stands. If you want to come to Ostara and hide out, you may stay with my family," Brass said smoothly and softly.

"And you."

"And me," Brass agreed.

I sighed, "That would hurt him. I could never do it. You two are so close, what kind of person would that make me?"

"That was not a no," Brass said, and I heard the smile in his voice.

"It wasn't, but it was not a yes. I love Slate. I always will. You deserve a woman who just loves you. Not whatever craziness I have going on in my mixed-up head." I swallowed against the lump, and he stayed silent.

"He will be away from the patron by now. We are running late. Why did you wait so long?" he asked.

"They drugged me with marawacian."

Brass grunted and picked up the pace.

I was glad he was there. If I'd been alone, they would have found me the next day slumped on the floor in some darkened street corner sobbing.

We walked up to the portal gate, the sculpted women whose arms turned into branches around the gate held a light dusting of snow.

"Ready?" Brass asked, and I nodded.

The bright white light engulfed us both.

Jett, Pearl, and Indigo stood under the blue starry lights of the Sumar palace portal room. Jett looked to Brass and nodded.

"You guys shouldn't be here. What if Slate comes home? He'll know something is up," I sounded panicked even to my own ears.

Jett's tall muscular form crossed the room and held me tight.

"Don't do this Jett, I'm not very strong. I'm trying to do the right thing, not what makes me happy."

"Hold fast to dreams. For if dreams die. Life is a broken-winged bird. That cannot fly. Hold fast to dreams. For when dreams go. Life is a barren field. Frozen with snow."

I wasn't sure I could handle one of Jett's untimely Langston Hughes quotes.

"We wanted to say goodbye. We'll leave now," Jett said, his voice thick as he stepped back.

Indigo had picked up a carrier from the floor and thrust it out at me. I took it in my hands, and she opened the little door and pulled out a white kitten with blue eyes.

"Skogkatts. Mine is Bee-Gold and yours is named Tree-Gold. Bee and Tree, sorry I named her for you. They grow to be very large, so I hope your apartment accepts small dogs," Indigo said, not meeting my eyes.

My throat swallowed convulsively, and I looked into the carrier; an identical white kitten peered out at me from inside, but with bright green eyes.

"Indigo, I love her." I choked and hooked an arm around my twin before drawing back.

Jett slung his arm around Indigo, and they walked off towards the hall. I turned to Pearl, who wrapped her arms around me. She had a floral musk that reminded me of the blue morning glories she'd grown in the informal dining room when I'd first met her.

"Darling, you shall be missed greatly," she whispered, and I hugged her back.

My eyes closed and I tried hard not to sob. She pulled away and wiped my tears.

"Once you get settled, send us a letter or email Jett. He says that will be much swifter." Pearl shook her head, not knowing what an email was. "Let me know if you change your mind about buying a house instead. Wherever you wish, I want you to be well taken care of."

I chuckled with a hysterical edge. "I will. I promise," I pleaded with my eyes for what I couldn't say out loud. "Thank you."

"We will try to help him. It is all for nothing if we cannot make him find a match. We will take good care of him," Pearl promised, and I nodded.

She pulled the stone pendant necklace from my cloak and rubbed it between her fingers.

"Keep this close, darling. I love you," she said and kissed my cheek.

Brass put his arm around my shoulder and urged me forward. "I do not want to rush you, but if Slate gets back before you leave. Things will get ugly."

I sighed. He was right.

My shower barely lasted two minutes, but I couldn't go on a plane with blood in my hair. Brass paced in the front room prepared to warn me if he felt Slate coming. I piled my wet hair on my head and tugged on my favorite Chicago Bears t-shirt. I wore jeans and a pair of my old beige UGG boots like a normal girl my age would have. With my old jacket on, I dove under the bed and grabbed my cell phone and stuck it in my back pocket.

"Ready? He will likely search the headquarters first with us both gone, but that does not buy us much time. Slate will hear about the attack if we are lucky and go there before coming here," Brass said with an edge of anxiety in his tone.

"One last thing," I told him and ran to the nursery.

I paused before the door and swung it open and kept my eyes focused on the one thing I wanted. I took the painting off the wall. It was the tree of life with deep curling roots, a blazing golden sun shone down on a cat and a deer dancing next to a pond a mermaid leaned from. My mother had painted it and Slate had gotten it for our child that would never be.

When I turned around Brass filed the doorway, his face etched with anguish. "The letter from your mother to your father, I hid it within the frame. Scarlett…"

I looked down to the white frame and nodded. "It's fine, Brass. The past. He'll find another woman to fill this room with his children and be happier for it. He thinks I don't see how badly he wants it, but I do. It's something primordial and innate that makes a man want to claim his woman and fill her with his seed, for it to take root and grow into their child. I… I am incapable of it. I'm done here," I said stiffly and he turned so I could pass him in the doorway.

I walked back to the bedroom and placed the letter I wrote him on the bed. "Should I leave his mother's ring?" I asked, twisting the emerald on my finger.

Brass was behind me, and he placed a hand on my shoulder. "You could. That may hurt him more. He has not given himself to a woman as he has with you, Scarlett. That may be more rejection than he can handle."

I needed that excuse. I didn't want Alder's ring back, and I didn't want to give up my ring. Slate would always be my husband even if no one knew it.

When Brass and I reached the blue lit portal room my body started to feel thick and heavy. "I —" I started to say and fisted my hands.

"Do not ask me to persuade you to leave," Brass whispered.

We stood before the huge double doors in the back of the room, mirrored with spokes radiating from a gold center circle, white ovals around each spoke. The same doors that brought us to Tidings over a year ago. A car waited for me on the other side with everything Jett and Indi had packed. I held Tree's carrier in my right hand and felt Brass's hand slide into my left.

"Walk out with me," I whispered, and Brass started forward.

FORTY-EIGHT

In the movies, Slate would have appeared. He would have found some magic potion that healed my womb, and we'd live happily ever after. It was not a movie; this was my incredibly sugarfoot life. Brass led me through the portal and the white light took us.

We appeared in a grass filled field. I looked over my shoulder and two trees that formed into an arch just big enough for a small truck to pass through stood behind us. It repelled anyone who lacked the ability to call. Out past the grass was an asphalt road with a single vehicle waiting.

My getaway car.

Bristol, Rhode Island was one of two portal gates Guardians had in the United States. The airport was in Providence and would take a half hour to get there. I stood in Colt State Park with Brass, stateside, and it felt surreal.

I still held Brass's hand when I turned to him. "Promise me you won't let him push you away. I know what kind of position I put you in by enlisting your help."

Brass's amber eyes said more than words could. He did not want me to go; he had fallen in love with me. The gods only knew why.

"I would do anything you asked of me," he whispered, and I squeezed my eyes shut and dropped my head.

I clutched at his hand like a lifeline, and he squeezed back. "This is harder than I'd anticipated, and I anticipated quite a lot."

Brass cupped my face and slid his hand to the two braids that held my beads and fetishes in my bun. He took his hands from me and brought them into his own hair. He took out two beads, one bronze and one ebony and stepped closer to thread them through my hair. He pulled down my wet hair and worked his fingers deftly through it.

"Something to remember me by," he whispered softly and my heart twisted.

"Thank you," was all I could manage before I threw myself forward and buried my face in his chest.

I didn't care that he had dried blood on him. He smelled of spring rain, cinnamon, and sweat. I inhaled him deeply and felt the tears spring to my eyes.

"I'll miss you. When I come back, can I visit you? Maybe you can visit me too?" my voice was muffled by his shirt while he stroked my head.

"I should hope so. I would be very disappointed if you did not see me when you came back."

I drew back and looked up at him as I dried my eyes. Brass bent his down, his mouth so close I'd need only to lift my chin a scant inch to meet it. His plump defined lips hovered there as we both breathed, and he pressed them to my cheek where he lingered.

"Don't do anything to stop a woman from flying; let fate take its course," he paused. "Take care, Wildfire," he said and moved past me and into the portal gate.

The white light cast my shadow across the field and Brass was gone. My breaths came ragged, and I woodenly walked to the car with Tree-Gold. I set her carrier down in the passenger seat and took the keys out of the glove box and started the rental car.

Sobbing so hard I had to pull over, I slowly made my way to the T. F. Green Airport. I took my luggage from the trunk with the painting and the cat carrier and started towards security. I checked two bags with all my belongings in the world within them and gave Tree-Gold over to their safekeeping. They let me keep the painting after a thorough check and I made my way to the terminal one for my nonstop flight back to Chicago.

The airport was deserted in the wee hours of the morning as I was catching the red eye back which suited me just fine. I collapsed into a faux leather seat against the wall and took off my emerald ring. Numbness descended, and I welcomed it.

I had to get a rental car when I got to O'Hare airport and had lined up five different apartments to check out within the next few days. Slate didn't question my time in the technology room in Valla and it had been simple to arrange.

My eyes slid shut when I rested my head on the back of my seat. I wouldn't feel better until my feet were back on Chicago soil.

I'm walking through carnage. I feel her, I hear her, my mother wears a white gown She tells me I can fix this. I try not to look at the bodies, the battleground alongside a castle. Not everyone is dead. Frozen angry faces stare up at angry faces on the castle, I can't even tell if the faces are human. They all look like monsters to me. The wind is whipping at me, I look up at the sky, even the sky is angry. Black clouds, lightening without rain. She's all around me, "You are night."

I stand in the middle of a circle, people around the edges. Slate lies in the circle in a pool of blood. Light and gushing wind blasts from my body, my hair, my hands, and shoot up. My mouth opens in a silent scream.

I gasped as I woke, and my eyes went wide as I tried to register my surroundings.

"I've never seen anyone cry in their sleep before."

I blinked several times before I realized I wasn't dreaming. Chris, my prom date, and the man who I thought was my first lover, was sitting down next to me. He was tall and broad; college football had done him good. Chris held out a tan hand with a tissue and I plucked it from his fingers. His baby blues looked me over and he sank back in his seat next to me, running a hand through his trendy chestnut brown hair. He was dressed like a frat boy with his navy polo collar popped and a white shirt underneath with distressed jeans on.

I dabbed at my eyes and blew my nose in a most unladylike manner. Chris and I used to be friends in high school. I played soccer and volley-ball, and he was captain of the football team. When he'd asked me out to prom, I'd never been so flattered in my young life.

"Sorry, I didn't mean to surprise you," Chris said, running his hands over his thighs.

I knit my brows. Chris was cocky, we had a right to be. He was stun-ning by anyone's standards; the modesty act was totally out of character.

"What? No sugar lips?" I asked pertly, and Chris ran a hand over the back of his neck.

I hated that pet name.

Chris angled himself towards me and his dreamy baby blues scanned me. He used to make my heartbeat faster and slower with a twist of his beautiful mouth, now I was wary.

"I've had a crash course in humility. I am sorry, Scar. About every-thing." I narrowed my eyes at him, and he chuckled nervously, "By everything, I mean, the sugar lips bit, Chuck's party, not calling you after prom; most especially prom. I was a huge douche. I don't expect you to forgive me, but I have been trying to get ahold of you to apologize for a while now. I left voicemails and texts. I never expected to find you crying in the airport."

I slapped my hands to my body until I found the emerald ring I dropped. I sighed with relief and slid it onto my stone pendant chain.

"You're right. I'll probably never forgive you, but I appreciate the apology, Chris. That means something. Not sure what, but something," I said, folding my arms over my chest.

The flight attendant announced boarding, and we both stood. "Going back to Chicago for a visit?" Chris asked, rising.

He had really filled out, he had to be six foot four now and his upper body strained against his shirt. Chris turned and put his weight on a cane. My mouth dropped open as I stared.

He chuckled nervously again. "My cane. Yeah, it sucks."

"What happened?" I asked as he pulled a backpack over his shoulder and walked with his cane.

He gave me an apologetic smile. "Your boyfriend kicked my ass that day at the theater. He broke my hip. I lost my football scholarship. That's why I'm here, I tried to stay and finish my classes but it's too much. I hate being here. Football was everything."

I cursed Slate internally; he said he'd not broken anything permanently. I'd say that was pretty permanent. Slate had ruined Chris's life.

"And you apologized to *me*? Chris, I had no idea he did this. I am going back to Chicago. It's not for a visit, I'm moving back. Gods, I mean, Christ. I'm so sorry, Chris." I picked up my mother's painting, and we lined up to board.

He waved his hand dismissively, "I was an asshole. I drank all the time and was a dick to women. After I had my surgeries, I found out who my real friends were and how bad I'd been. I've stopped partying and focused on rehab. I'm thinking I could be a P.E. teacher when I finish college. I'll take some courses at NEIU when I get back. It's not that bad, Scar. Your boyfriend may be a bigger dick than I was, but I needed an eye opener."

"Not my boyfriend anymore," I corrected and Chris gazed down at me.

"No? I didn't want to say, but you look like you've been through shit ton and back again. Did things end badly or something?"

"Very badly, that's why I had to leave."

Chris and I boarded the plane, said our goodbyes, and took our separate seats.

The flight was practically empty. I glanced back and caught Chris looking at me. His tan cheeks reddened with a small smile, and I sighed. I might be able to heal him. If he fell asleep on the flight, I could mend his bones.

I got up and asked the flight attendant if it was okay if I sat next to him and she approved with a smile.

Chris's brows shot up when I sat down next to him.

"Hi. I'm Scarlett Tio. I'm twenty, single, with no job, and no place to live. I just got out of a serious relationship and am on my own for the first time in my life. Pleased to meet you," I said, shaking his hand and he chuckled.

"Pleased to meet you, Scarlett. I'm Chris Moore, twenty-two, single, no job. I live with my parents and have recently dropped out of college because a girl I screwed over's boyfriend beat me down and I lost my scholarship."

"I am sure that girl could forgive you if you apologized seeing as you are now also a victim of a douchebag," I teased and Chris smiled.

"All joking aside, Scar. What happened the limo that night... you should have kicked my ass. I know we were both wasted, but that was no excuse. I thought..." He licked his pink lips and dropped his eyes. "That was my first time, Scar. I barely remember it. I was so into you and I took advantage of you. You weren't sober enough to be into it." His face winced as if he saw is sloppy kisses and my holding my breath to keep from puking on the floor of the limo in front of him. "Even if you forgive me, I'll never forgive myself. You deserved, *deserve,* so much better."

I placed my hand over his. "I've thought about that night a lot. I didn't date anyone after that until last year. That night is very blurry for me too, but technically, we didn't have the sex we thought we did."

Chris knit his brow, but still wouldn't meet my eyes. I tried to explain with as little detail as possible and he grew more uncomfortable with every word.

"Jesus, it was way worse than I thought. No wonder your boyfriend tried to kill me." Chris breathed with his face looking strained.

I shrugged. "Why are you flying so late or early?"

"It's cheaper. I'm broke," he said honestly, and I smiled. He visibly relaxed, but still seemed hesitant. "Not too broke that I can't buy you breakfast when we land. It might be from the dollar menu, but I think I owe you that much."

I ran my teeth along my lower lip. The new humbler Chris had thrown me for a loop. I planned on getting a motel room, crying myself to sleep, eating a continental breakfast with the other bleary-eyed hotel guests, and looking for apartments alone and miserable.

Was someone up there finally making a case for me? I decided that the Norns couldn't possibly be that cruel. It wouldn't just be kicking me while I'm down. It'd be Longinus's spear.

"That'd be nice," I said with a small smile.

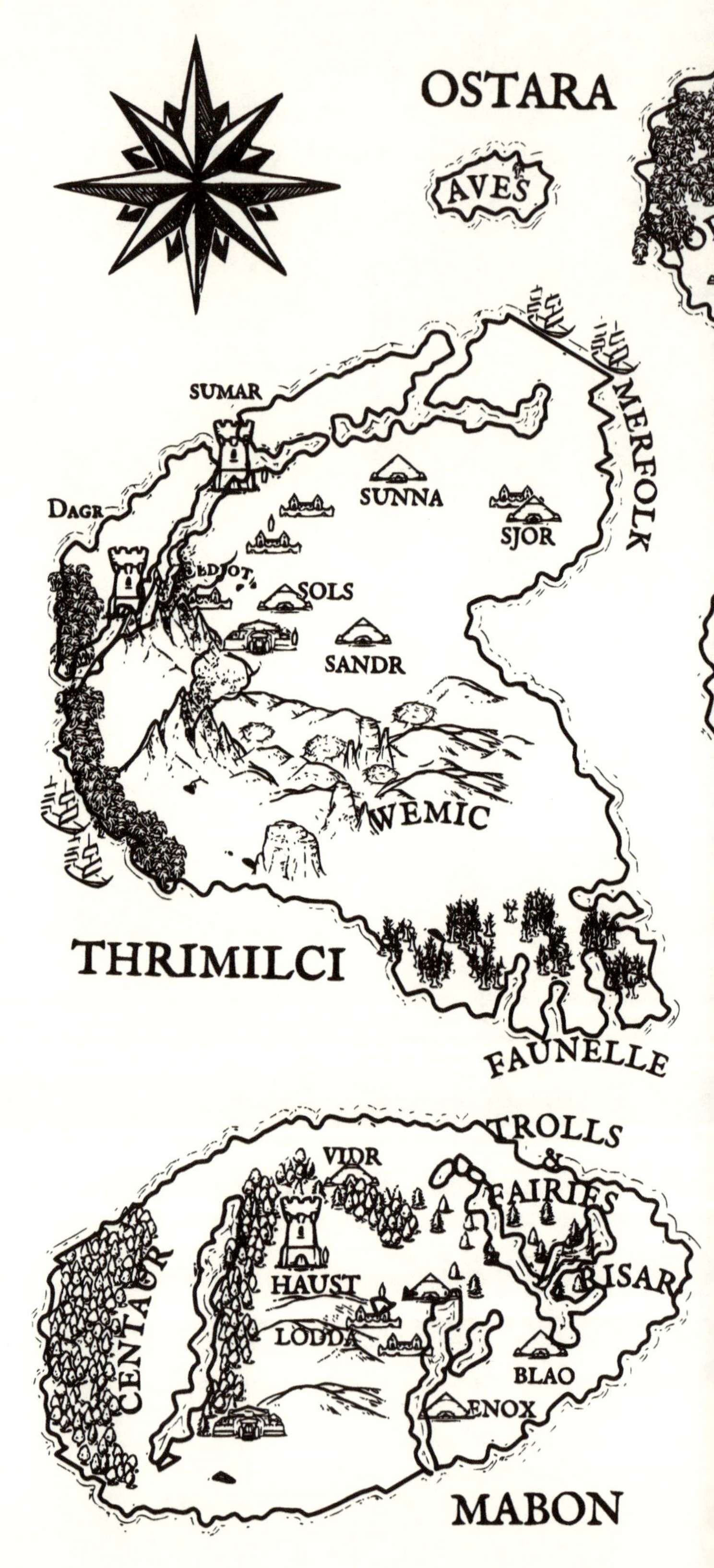

OSTARA
AVES
SUMAR
DAGR
SUNNA
SJOR
SOLS
SANDR
WEMIC
MERFOLK
THRIMILCI
FAUNELLE
TROLLS
&
FAIRIES
VIDR
HAUST
LODDA
CENTAUR
RISAR
BLAO
ENOX
MABON

TIDINGS
ELIVAGAR
ANGUELFAN
LITR
REGN
ROT
VAR
LYCANS
NATT
BJORN
GRAULODE
VETR
SVELL
MINTAUR
KALLA
SNJAR
KALDR
JOTNAR
DRAGONS
STRAUMR
MOSSUR
TOWN CENTER
STOKER
HVALL
VALKYRIES
JARN
LLA

AFTERWORD

For more Tidings facts and fun, including an interactive family tree, quizzes, and world building fun, check out www.charlirahe.com.

BIBLIOGRAPHY

"My Star" by Robert Browning
"How Do I Love Thee?" (Sonnet 43) by Elizabeth Browning
"Whoever You Are Holding Me Now In Hand" by Walt Whitman
"The Torch" by Walt Whitman
"Ah, Love, But a Day" by Robert Browning
"Dreams" by Langston Hughes